Rosie Nixon lives in London with her husband and their two young sons and is Editor-in-Chief of *HELLO!* magazine. She previously held senior positions at glossy women's magazines, including *Grazia*, *Glamour* and *Red*. Rosie has a love of all things celebrity, Royal and fashion-related and has been lucky enough to attend a multitude of glamorous showbiz events all around the world. Ever discreet and protective of the big stars she has worked with, Rosie's experience has enabled her to write her debut novel *The Stylist* and its sequel, *Amber Green Takes Manhattan*.

Also by Rosie Nixon

The Stylist

AMBER GREEN

takes Manhattan

ROSIE NIXON

ONE PLACE. MANY STORIES

HarperCollins
PUBLISHERS
Since 1817

This novel is entirely a work of fiction. The names, characters and incidents portrayed in it are the work of the author's imagination. Any resemblance to actual persons, living or dead, events or localities is entirely coincidental.

HQ
An imprint of HarperCollinsPublishers Ltd.
1 London Bridge Street
London SE1 9GF

This paperback edition 2017

1

First published in Great Britain by
HQ, an imprint of HarperCollinsPublishers Ltd. 2017

Copyright © Rosie Nixon 2017

Rosie Nixon asserts the moral right to be
identified as the author of this work.
A catalogue record for this book is
available from the British Library.

ISBN: 978-1-84845-508-5

Printed and bound by
CPI Group, Croydon CR0 4YY

CHAPTER ONE

I nuzzled in and breathed deeply. I could sniff the vulnerable patch of bare skin just under his collarbone all day long. It was light outside now and I couldn't get back to sleep. My mind was spinning. I traced the edge of Rob's tattoo lightly with my finger. An intricate feather design on his upper arm, it was quite a work of art and had taken me by surprise the first time I saw it in full, after our first date. He had teased me with glimpses of it poking out of T-shirt sleeves for a long while before that. It had taken three sittings to create, by the steady hand of a Muswell Hill tattoo artist. The feather, he said, was to symbolise the freedom of flight; to remind him that he too was free to fly, if he ever needed reminding. *Deep and meaningful!* I teased him at the time, but the sentiment had played on my mind a bit ever since. Tonight it was resonating strongly to me. *Does he want to just take off and fly away from me? Leave me broken hearted, like his last girlfriend?*

It all started yesterday evening.

Rob came to the door in tracksuit bottoms and a baggy hoodie. I loved him in his comfy house clothes. He was holding Pinky under one arm.

Pinky: the cute pet micro-pig partly responsible for getting us together. Rob had adopted the little piggy and relocated him from Los Angeles after Pinky was abandoned by one of my former ditzy Hollywood clients. *Yes, really*! It all happened last year, during my temporary job as stylist to the stars Mona Armstrong's assistant. Rob doted on the creature – literally worshipped the sawdust Pinky walked on. He was more than a pet; he was his child.

Of late, I'd noticed that the novelty of having an alternative to a house cat was starting to wear off for Rob's flatmate. Ben was, understandably, getting fed up with the lingering smell of pig pee in the hallway, trotter prints on the sofa, and the wet snout he regularly found snuffling in his clean laundry. But when you looked into Pinky's dark little eyes you could forgive anything. Well, Rob could. In the same way that I became pretty pathetic whenever I looked into his.

The little creature squealed in what I'm sure was piggy happiness when he saw me on the doorstep.

'Ben's here,' Rob warned, meaning no proper kissing until we reached his bedroom.

I smiled, pulling on his tracksuit cord. 'I can control myself.'

Rob hovered by the door. He looked anxious.

'Everything okay?'

He paused for a bit too long. 'Sort of. I'll explain later.'

I followed him into the living room. Ben was in his usual position, lying full length across one of the sofas, bare feet and lanky legs dangling off the end, a litre bottle of Coke by his side. He was sweaty, like he'd not long been home from the gym.

Theirs was such a boy flat. It was sparse and functional, yet still managed to look untidy. The front room consisted of a large flat-screen TV, two sofas, a coffee table and an Ikea rug that should never have been bought in cream because it had rarely seen a vacuum cleaner in the two years they had lived here. Shelves crammed with DVDs and books in no particular order and curtains that didn't quite stretch across the width of the whole window. No surprises, then, that they affectionately referred to their home as 'the pigsty'.

'So have you heard the big news?' Ben said when he finally took his eyes off the TV and registered my presence.

'No,' I looked at Rob, confused.

'Pinky's gay,' Ben blurted out, shifting himself sideways to get a proper view of both of our faces.

Rob smirked: 'Don't flatter yourself.'

'Oh, it's nothing to do with me – though if he fancies me, who can blame him? Pinky always goes for the guys. C'mon, bet you've noticed too, haven't you Amber?' He winked at me.

'Enlighten me, Ben,' I said cynically. I could tell he was desperate to get on with his story.

'Nina's bulldog, Freddie: Male. Can't stop sniffing around his rear every time he comes over. The cat from next door: It's a Tom, and Pinky's entire face lights up every time he jumps over the fence. His trotters could barely move fast enough when he tried to chase him the other morning, I saw it with my own eyes. And I'm not joking, he takes an unhealthy shine to your and my boxers in the laundry basket, Rob, mate. You might not have noticed, but I certainly have.'

I chuckled and dug Rob in the ribs. 'Got competition, have I?'

'What is it they say?' Rob asked, stooping to gently place Pinky on the floor and ushering him towards Ben. 'Takes one to know one?'

'Oh, I've got nothing against gays, you know that, Rob. Two of my best mates are gay *and* I went to a gay wedding last year – granted most of the guests fancied me, but that's another story. No, I'm wondering if there's a marketing opportunity here – "Meet Britain's First Gay Miniature Pig" – I can see him being a hit in Soho. Don't you think, Amber?'

I tried not to laugh.

Rob scowled in mock irritation. 'Pinky and I are going to make dinner, and if you're on our side you're invited to join us, Amber. Get yourself a takeaway Ben.'

'Flouncing off in a strop – *so camp*!' Ben uttered, turning back around and taking the TV off pause.

I followed Rob into the kitchen and watched him lovingly top up Pinky's bowl of slop. The fact he was an animal lover was one of the things I adored about Rob. He couldn't walk past a cat in the street without stopping to give it a stroke.

'So, tell me more about your day,' I said, opening the fridge on the hunt for white wine. Rob failed to hear me; he seemed lost in thought.

'You okay?'

'Hey?' He almost jumped. 'Sorry, just sorting Pinky out then I'll get dinner on. We're having fish. Okay with you?'

'Sounds great. Do you have any wine in here?'

'There's a bottle in my bag in the hallway, should still be slightly cold.' He seemed nervous and it wasn't like him not to open a bottle straight after a stressful day at work.

He was making me feel jittery too. I found the wine and returned to find Rob scrolling through emails on his phone. He was lost in thought as I unscrewed the top and poured us each a glass.

'Shall I get the oven on then?' I asked.

Finally, after dinner on our laps in front of some terrible sci-fi film Ben refused to turn off, Rob opened up. We were in his bedroom and I was reading an email from my boss, Joseph, who wanted a load of changes to the clothes I'd chosen for our latest window display at Selfridges.

'How was I supposed to know he wanted muted candy colours rather than brights?' I moaned. 'He could have mentioned the fact two weeks ago when I started pulling it all together. It's so frustrating.' Rob was miles away. '*And* he's asked me to come into work naked tomorrow.'

'Eh?' He'd spent the last ten minutes fiddling with the iPod dock, but there was still no sound coming out.

'He's asked me to… nothing. Perhaps you can tell me what happened at work? You're clearly not listening to me.'

He turned and sat on the bed next to me. Then he looked at me earnestly. 'Louise, the series producer, had a chat with me about a pitch the company's just won for a shoot in New York,' he began.

'New York, wow,' I uttered, though I felt my stomach knot as I sensed what was coming.

'It's to make a fly-on-the-wall series about Angel Wear.'

'As in, Angel Wear, the underwear company?' I asked.

'Right,' he said, avoiding eye contact. The knot in my stomach was pulled tighter. 'She's asked if I want to produce it – there'll be directing involved too.'

'In New York?' I repeated, just to check I'd heard correctly. A mental image of the Angel Wear lingerie models popped into my head, all tanned, long-limbed perfection.

'Yes, it would mean moving out there – for at least three months, maybe longer.'

I took a moment to process this. 'Do you want to do it?'

'I don't know.' He looked truly pained.

'Well, when do you have to let her know?'

'As soon as possible, they're keen to get visas in place and a team out there in the next few weeks.'

I knew I must look as if I was desperately trying not to cry, every muscle in my face straining to retain its composure. I ached for him to pull me into a big bear hug and kiss my forehead reassuringly. But he didn't. I'm not even sure he noticed my strange facial expression because he just lay back on the bed and sighed.

'Listen Amber, I'm not sure about all the details yet, maybe I won't take it, I thought I wanted to move away from this kind of telly. But it's an opportunity to direct. I'm going to talk to Lou properly in the morning. I just wanted you to be in the loop.'

I managed to utter the words, 'Yes, great, just got something in my eye,' and escaped to the bathroom where I locked the door behind me. I sat on the side of the bath and held my head in my hands as I tried to imagine what this meant for us. *Finally, I find someone I really like – someone I think I love; someone I can imagine building a life with – and now he's going to move to New York. Maybe I'm destined to be single forever, after all.*

When I finally emerged from the bathroom, Rob was already in bed looking at his phone again. Self-consciously I undressed, pulling on one of his T-shirts and awkwardly undoing my bra and wriggling out of it without showing any flesh. Instead of finding my usual sleep position: legs entwined with his, face buried in his chest, I stayed on my side. My feet were freezing.

And now, here I was, lying in bed awake at five in the morning, thinking too much, sniffing him and stalking his tattoo.

The events of last spring were still raw in my mind, nine months later. A fateful trip to Hawaii had changed the course of my life: I had finally realised Rob *did* have feelings for me; my then boss, Mona, completely lost the plot; and my best friend Vicky ended up shagging Trey Jones, *the* Trey Jones, the famous film director and man who we were meant to be watching get married. You couldn't have made it up.

Vicky moved in with Trey in LA almost immediately, but it had taken Rob and me a whole four months after that to finally get together, when he tracked me down at work in London. I've been starring in my own rom-com ever since – Vicky providing the 'com', even from the other side of the globe.

Rob had said he needed to be out of the house extra early in the morning, which wasn't unusual, but this morning I was happy to pretend to be still asleep while he tip-toed around the room, gathering his clothes before going off to shower. I stirred as he gently kissed my cheek goodbye but waited for the front door to slam before I got out of bed and dragged myself to the bathroom.

I'd gone to sleep trying to convince myself that things are never so bad in the cold light of day, but why did I still have the same feeling of impending doom? I tried to tell myself that three months was nothing – it would be over in a flash. *But when you've only been dating for five months, it feels like forever.* As a waterfall of hot water cascaded onto my head, I was lurched out of my despondency by the even more horrific realisation that there was no shampoo or conditioner in this shower. And soon after that, I realised there was none anywhere in the bathroom, so I went to work with hair washed in Lynx Deep Space shower gel. The day could only get better.

I called Vicky as I walked to work from Oxford Circus tube. 'He's going to be filming underwear models.' Saying it aloud made it sting even more.

'Man, that's tough,' said Vicky, confirming what I already knew.

'Underwear models!' I exclaimed again, thinking that

making them sound faintly ridiculous might make them less threatening.

'I heard you. The Icons all have legs up to their armpits, washboard stomachs, perfect racks, peachy—'

'Yes, yes, okay, I think I know what an underwear model looks like, Vicky. I feel crap as it is, no need to rub it in.'

She paused, before replying, measuredly, 'What I was going to say was peachy bottoms – *and air for brains*. Amber, stop doing the paranoid girlfriend thing and rise above this. It's *you* who Rob's going out with, and that's not going to change. Well, unless you start acting all insecure and paranoid about the underwear models and their peachy bottoms that he will be *filming*. Not dating or having sex with – just *filming*. Okay?'

'Okay.' She didn't have to spell it out quite so bluntly. Although she had hit the nail on the head.

'Anyway, when are you coming out to see me?' She changed the subject. 'Not being funny but it's been nearly a year, and you still haven't got on a plane. We've got tons of space. I'm even naming a suite after you – the Green Suite. Come on Am, book it! Bring Rob too if you want. I'm going nuts out here in this huge mansion. And I need some English humour, desperately. I also need digestive biscuits dunked in Earl Grey tea. But most of all, I need *us*!'

She was right. I needed 'us' too. I missed Vicky so much – her wry sense of humour and the hilarious escapades we'd got up to when we shared a home.

'Anyway, how's things with you?' I asked

'Not great, to be honest. Why do you think I'm still awake

at two in the morning and not at a party? I'll tell you, because I'm lying in bed – alone – trying to work out what I'm doing with my life.'

'Oh, honey, sorry to hear this, and I've been banging on about me. What's going on?'

'Nothing really. And that's half the problem. I'm so bored here, Amber. Trey's out at the crack of dawn each day and back late, if he comes back at all. He's working on a big feature film and although it's filming in LA, I hardly see him. I know more about our pool cleaner's life than my own boyfriend's right now. I even made lunch for the hedge trimmer yesterday, I was so bored of cooking for myself. He was pretty hot, as it goes, I was starting to find his strimmer sexy. Honestly, if Trey hadn't come back that evening... Amber, I don't know what I'm doing out here.'

'You found his strimmer sexy? That's desperate. Have you told Trey how you're feeling?'

'If I had a chance I probably would, but, like I said, he's barely here and I don't want to do the whiney girlfriend on the phone thing. I never wanted to be that girlfriend, but I'm getting close to having no option. Be careful what you wish for, Amber, maybe there's more spark living apart.'

'But not living in separate continents. God, it's never straightforward is it? What are we going to do?'

'I wish we could go to the Chamberlayne and get drunk.'

'Me too. I could murder a girlie drinking session with you.'

'I miss you so much, honey. I keep thinking of my room in the flat. At this rate, I could be back before you know it.'

'Listen, let's keep each other posted, okay, and if it all goes wrong, of course you can just move back. We've still got the flat, your room is exactly as you left it, and we'll just carry on like before. Our lives weren't so bad, were they? Sainsbury's must be suffering from a loss in revenue from hummus and Popchips since you've been away, I'm sure they'll welcome you back with open arms too.'

Finally, she laughed. 'You're right. It will be fine. This film is meant to end in a couple of weeks and then Trey's mentioned a holiday in Mexico, so I'm sure we'll be back on track. And Rob does love you, Amber, I know it. He might not take the job anyway.'

'I s'pose. Let me know if you speak to Trey. Love you, bestie.'

'Love you more. Night night from here.'

I had our Kensal Rise flat pretty much to myself these days. Trey, being loaded, was paying Vicky's half of the rent so they had a London bolt-hole, but they were yet to use it; the one time they popped back for a premiere, he checked them into a suite at the Soho Hotel. Even so, she was definitely still there, haunting the place. Some of her belongings were still strewn around her room and many of her pictures still hung on the walls: the black-and-white framed print of Brigitte Bardot in the living room, cigarette casually hanging from her lips, wind-swept hair, black scarf tied loosely around her neck, to remind us how to be cool, like Brigitte; the collection of Instagram photos from various holidays, printed out and carefully framed, to remind us of our best moments, if ever we needed reminding – usually on the Saturday nights when

we were in our PJs, having a living room picnic in front of
Ant and Dec. It was all so carefree, silly – and single.

And now here we were, coupled up in our late twenties.
Much as I loved the days of being in a platonic relationship
with Vicky, I was so happy about that fact I didn't have to
face the prospect of being a thirty-year-old spinster. While
Vicky always had some guy on the go, whether it was 'Sunday
Simon' or 'Sexy Jim from the art desk', I was a bona fide 'car
crash' when it came to relationships; another traffic-based
pun on my full name, Amber Green. Yes, after ten years in
the single wilderness, it felt *so* good to have someone who
would go to the twenty-four-hour garage for a family bag
of Maltesers or run me a bath after a shitty day at work;
someone who embraced the role of human hot water bottle,
taking pleasure in warming my block-of-ice feet when I got
into bed. Life was great. But now the thought of Rob taking
off for New York was following me around like a shadow.

The walk along Oxford Street from Marble Arch was very
different in January compared with before Christmas. The
strings of bright lights across the road were gone and, bar
a few sad, forgotten decorations in some shops, the festive
period had been packed away. The London sky was heavy
with big, grey clouds.

Christmas came and went in a bit of a blur, to be honest.
Rob went to his mum's big house in Holland Park and I went
to the family pile (read: suburban semi) in deepest North
London. As per usual, everything revolved around my sister's
six-year-old daughter, Nora: 'Nora prepared the Brussels

sprouts!'; 'Nora nearly recited that song from *Matilda* by heart!' The 'Nora Show' was in full effect. And it was every bit as grating as a pantomime – for three days solid. *Urgh, listen to me. My New Year's resolution is to be nicer to Nora.*

After polishing off a couple of morning glasses of dry sherry, moving on to prosecco and red wine with lunch, then on to port, by way of a Baileys, I was feeling very fluffy around the edges by nine o'clock. Instead of watching *Big* for the trillionth time with my sister and Nora, who was being allowed to stay up as long as she wanted, much to my horror, or allowing my dad to beat me at Trivial Pursuit circa 1990, again, I called it a night. Apart from booze, the only thing keeping me going through the day was texting Rob and later sexting with him until I fell into a port-induced coma in the tiny spare bedroom, because my old bedroom had been commandeered by – you guessed it – Nora. Rob seemed to be having a much more civilised day, his mother having decided to take him and his older brother, Dan, plus Dan's fiancée, Florence, out for a champagne Christmas lunch in a trendy Notting Hill restaurant, then home for charades and posh liqueur chocolates. *Maybe next year I'll be there too. Please Father Christmas, I promise I'll be good all year.*

There wasn't even time for a Boxing Day lie-in for me. The only downside to working at Selfridges – although based on my Christmas, it could be classified as a bonus – was that I had to be at work at five in the morning on Boxing Day. Alongside our regular team we had twenty contractors and, behind huge vinyl stickers, we carefully stripped the fairy-tale festive display from the windows, and then the glass was covered with shouty red paper advertising the January sales. As Big Ben chimed nine in the morning, a stampede of hungry customers from all around the world charged through the doors and set to work dismantling the entire store, snapping up the designer bargains of the year. It was the shopping equivalent of the bull-run through Pamplona. As fervent fashionistas turned the shop into a glorified jumble sale, our windows team sloped back to bed. This time I headed to my own bed in Kensal Rise. Work was a distant memory by evening, because Rob came over in a Christmas jumper with a mountain of leftover cheese and we roasted chestnuts and scoffed Quality Street cuddled up on the sofa watching *Elf*. All I needed was him. We were lost in each other and I had never felt happier.

But now, the heady glow of Christmas had disappeared, along with the shine on my relationship, it seemed.

As I entered my super-cool work place through the staff entrance round the back of Oxford Street at nine thirty, I felt a sense of pride. I'd been working as a window designer at Selfridges for six months now and it was my dream job. Finally, that irritating voice in my head telling me to 'get a proper career' could shut up because I finally *had* a proper career. Instead of dreading the point in conversation with friends of my parents or mates of mates down the pub, that would eventually crawl around to the inevitable, 'So, what do you do, Amber?' I could embrace the question, invite it even, because I had a decent response.

'Oooh, what are you working on now?' they often asked.

'It's all a bit hush-hush,' I'd tease, though it was actually the truth – pulling back the vinyl to unveil the new Selfridges window display was a big, closely guarded event.

'Jesus, what happened, babe?' my boss, Joseph, exclaimed as I entered the studio.

'Happy Tuesday to you, too,' I sneered.

'Sorry, babe, but if you're sick, perhaps you should go home. Pale and interesting is *not* this season.'

'I'm not ill, just tired,' I muttered, marvelling at how stupid I was not to get a muffin as well as a coffee from Starbucks on the way in. Thankfully, our studio office was at the very top of the shop, and when we weren't tucked away up here, we were downstairs tweaking the windows. I was rarely required for face time with senior management.

Joseph, the creative director for visual merchandising at Selfridges, never looked sloppy, just like his name was *never* abbreviated to Joe. Tall, handsome and confident, he was fancied by literally the entire female workforce – despite the fact he was gay. He wasn't particularly camp, which made a certain portion of his admirers cling on to the fantasy that he could be 'turned'. And of course all the gay guys – which was most of the male staff – had a deep yearning for him, too. Joseph blatantly knew he was God's gift, and strutted around the store like Mr Selfridge himself. His hair was wavy and shoulder length and he wore it tightly tucked behind his ears, like ram's horns. If you didn't know better, to look at him you'd think he was French – arty, Gauloises-smoking, air of superiority – but when he spoke his dialect was pure Joey Essex. Everyone was a 'babe' and life was 'sweet'.

After working with him for half a year, I was getting
to know the real Joseph and, although he genuinely lived
the life of a moisturising modern man who adhered to the
five:two diet and had been known to get hooked up to a
reviving vitamin-packed IV drip during his lunch break, at
the end of the day he was a first-class creative director and I
loved having him as my boss. As well as my solid experience
styling the windows at Smiths boutique, I think he was
wowed by my time spent assisting Mona – in our world, it
would be hard not to be – as he gave me the job without
a second interview. When I started, he took me under his
wing as a protégée of sorts and it was a great position to
be in. It gave me some protection from the less friendly,
uber fashiony senior managers who swanned around our
floor in their top-to-toe designer threads, trying to catch a
glimpse of Joseph.

Then there was Shauna: white fingernails with gold tips,
big gold hoops and curly afro hair, channelling a modern day
Diana Ross. Her iPhone clicked in my face and then traced
my body. A deeply unflattering video of my stunned mug
and greasy-looking hair was now playing live on Snapchat.
Shauna loved to share. She worshipped at the altars of
Instagram and Snapchat and was dedicated to the daily
documentation of selfies, shoefies, Instafood, Instacocktails,
Instacats – and fairly often me, with #nofilter.

'You're so 'grammable today, babe,' she said, crouching
down to snap my Starbucks cup as I placed it on my desk.
Until that moment, I had failed to noticed that the barista
had scrawled the word 'Antler' on it, instead of my real name.

Shauna found it hilarious and shared the image with her 1.4 thousand followers. 'Big night, deer? Get it – Antler, deer?'

I frowned. 'So I look like something the cat dragged in, can we all just get over it, please?'

Shauna sucked in her cheeks and waggled her finger at me, intimating that I was not one to talk about anything this morning.

Joseph broke us up. 'Now, now ladies, there's no time for bickering today, Jeff wants the final designs for the summer windows by EOP, so I need you to finish the edit. And that's before we get cracking on phase two of the "Chelsea" display.'

The great thing about my job, especially on days like today, was that time passed quickly. I loved putting the mood boards together and then sourcing clothes from the collections about to hit the shop floor to bring it all to life. We were always working on two themes at any one time, currently we were completing the spring windows, inspired by the famous Chelsea Flower Show, and also planning our big summer production, a homage to the 'Traditional British Seaside', which would come into play soon after. I was transported from grey January to sunny July and a world of ninety-nines, beach huts, rubber rings, candy-coloured Kate Spade bags, Linda Farrow sunglasses, Matthew Williamson bikinis, palm-print dresses and everything in between. *Heaven.*

Although Shauna and I didn't always see eye to eye outside work, we were a great team in the studio, her eye for props perfectly complementing my choice of fashion from the designer look books. The time flew as I busied myself finalising clothes for the Chelsea windows and lining them up on rails ahead of Joseph's inspection – a cacophony of vibrant pink, lemon, lilac, peach and turquoise, the sartorial equivalent of a fragrant bouquet. Bright clothes were amazing for lifting my mood. But they couldn't stop me from checking my phone every five seconds. Nothing from Rob.

CHAPTER TWO

Two days had passed since Rob told me the news that he was thinking of moving to New York. In that time I had cried in the loos at work once, eaten MacDonald's for dinner twice, bought a Marc Jacobs top I couldn't afford, despite my staff discount, and looked at the Angel Wear website five thousand times as a conservative estimate. Krystal, Jessica, Roxy, Leonie, and Astrid were the names of the main Angel Wear 'Icons'. I could tell you their vital stats by heart. And I hated their perfect thirty-four–twenty-four–thirty-four guts. It was now Thursday and today Rob had been unnervingly attentive, texting me more than usual just to see how my day was going and wanting to arrange to meet up. *He's taking the job and he's feeling guilty, I know it.* In my head, we were already on opposite sides of the Atlantic. But I hadn't worked out how to handle things the next time I saw him, so I hadn't yet replied. The reality was that we'd only been dating for five months. I couldn't stop thinking about his feather tattoo. *This could be Rob's perfect opportunity to just catch the wind and fly.*

Work continued to be a good distraction, but Joseph and Shauna didn't do compassion. I'd come clean about Rob to

Shauna in the loos the first morning, when she caught me redoing my mascara and, of course, she had blurted it out to Joseph.

'Hate to say it, babe, but it sounds like a case of "He's just not that into you",' Joseph said, causing my eyes to prickle all over again. I carried on tweaking a mocked-up candyfloss stand.

This morning, we were waiting for Jeff to come and cast his critical eye over our final plans for summer, when my phone rang: Rob.

'Let me speak to him.' Shauna tried to grab my iPhone from my hands, but failed, sending a fake nail onto the floor.

I spoke to Rob from the hallway outside the studio. *It's impossible to get any privacy around here.*

'I thought you were going to avoid me forever. I've been getting paranoid.' He sounded nervous.

'I've not been avoiding you,' I lied, 'just been busy. Anyway, what's happening with you?'

'I wanted to see if you're free tonight. I could meet you from work and we could grab some dinner, chat, you know – what boyfriends and girlfriends do?'

He's still using the b-word, that's surely a good sign. I paused. 'Are you there, Amber?' he continued. 'Are you pissed off with me?'

I swallowed hard. 'New York, what's happening with that? Are you going to move?'

'That's what I want to talk to you about,' he said.

'Are you sure you want me to be your girlfriend, Rob?'

Silence on his end. *This is it. It's over. Joseph is right, he's just not into me.*

'Amber—'

'Don't tell me, this opportunity, you can't turn it down, blah, blah, blah. It's fine, I can handle it, tell me I make a great friend but it's you, you're not in the right place for a relationship.' A hot sensation was working its way up into my cheeks.

'Listen, I didn't want to have this conversation on the phone, I wanted to meet up with you and talk about it properly, but—'

'I get it, you're just not that into me...'

'Amber! Shut up for a second.' His tone took me aback, Rob rarely raised his voice. 'Yes, I've done some thinking and I do want to go to New York, I think it will be an incredible experience – but not just for me, for both of us. I wanted to ask if you would consider coming with me?' He paused. 'Wouldn't it be fun to flat hunt together in Williamsburg or Queens?'

I was so shocked I could barely find the words to respond.

'Really?' I uttered at last, leaning back against the wall, finally allowing every muscle in my body to relax.

'Really.' He was smiling into the phone; I could picture it.

And that was it, suddenly everything was rose tinted again. *New York or bust?* It was a no-brainer.

Rob met me from Selfridges that night, even skipping Pinky's slop time, so I knew he meant business, and we spent the evening plotting the weeks ahead. I would speak to Joseph about a three-month sabbatical; we would give up my Kensal Rise flat and move everything into Rob's room while we were away. I felt sure Vicky would understand – she'd probably be overjoyed that I was going to be a mere five-hour internal flight away. Besides, she was probably making it up with Trey this very moment.

The following morning I broke the news to my parents.

'Isn't this a bit crazy, Amber?' Mum said after doing me the courtesy of listening quietly as I excitedly babbled away for five minutes. Bearing in mind Mum's idea of adventure is a day out in April without bringing her umbrella and Dad thinks anyone who eats hummus is on the road to ruin – how could I expect them to understand?

'It's what people my age do *all* the time, Mum,' I told her, bristling. 'Anyway, it's only for three months, initially – it's hardly a long time in the scheme of things. You and Dad could even come and visit if you want.' I crossed my fingers behind my back.

'*Initially*, darling? You're thinking of staying longer? This is a whole different scenario. How are you going to do that legally, you know you need a visa to work in America? You're going to do it all by the book, I hope? They'll lock you up if you don't.' I could picture her shaking her head disparagingly. 'You won't have the same rights in America.'

My mum hadn't got her position as a top barrister without thinking through the legal implications for every situation.

'I know, Mum. And of course we're going to do it properly. I can stay for three months as a tourist anyway, and we'll take it from there. Rob's company are sorting out the visa for him. He's getting an O visa.'

Suddenly my dad's voice came on the phone. I hated it when my parents put me on a three-way conversation, especially without telling me. Surely it was a violation of my privacy.

'O visa? How old did you say he is?'

'It's an O-1 visa, not OAP, Dad. It means he's got an extraOrdinary ability.'

'Don't tell me he's a psychic?'

'No, he's a TV producer, as you know – not just anyone can make a top TV show, he's got tons of experience.'

'What's this TV show about, then?'

I squirmed; the last thing I wanted was for them to pick up on any insecurities about going to New York on my part, and 'a show about an underwear company' didn't exactly sound like something that would impress one's parents. I casually wandered out of the kitchen and into the sitting room so Rob couldn't overhear the half-truth I was about to tell.

'It's about a top company out there, it's kind of an American institution. Rob will be telling the inside story on how it works.'

'Anyway, Amber,' Dad interrupted me, 'we wondered if you'd like to bring Rob to dinner at home next Sunday? Especially now that you're practically eloping, we'd like to meet him properly.' I almost choked on my tea.

'If you're disappearing off to the other side of the world with this fellow, we'd better get to know him,' Mum added.

'My parents have invited you over next Sunday, if you can bear it.' I broke the news as I re-entered the kitchen, to find Rob serving up scrambled egg.

'You're not exactly selling the opportunity,' he said, smiling. 'But your folks seemed lovely when I met them the other week.'

'You met them for precisely fifteen seconds,' I reminded him. They'd dropped me off at Rob's one evening on a detour after we'd been to visit my sister. He'd politely come out to shake my dad's hand. Dad didn't bother getting out of the car and shook it through the window. Bit rude, I thought at the time.

'I don't remember him having a hook for an arm,' he said, teasing me. 'But,' a hesitation, 'my mum has invited me over next Sunday too, along with Dan and Florence, and, well, I was going to see if you fancied joining us?'

I took a large swig of tea from the mug in my hand, wishing it contained something stronger. 'If I'm not mistaken, Robert Walker, are you asking me to meet your family? Not only your mother but your brother and his scary-sounding fiancée, too?'

'I am, Miss Green, now will you please accept because I want to eat my breakfast before it goes cold?'

I leaned over and ran my fingers through his unkempt bed hair. I smiled into his lips before kissing them.

'I'd be honoured.' And I texted Mum the bad news before flying out of the door to work.

'A sabbatical?' Joseph repeated the words back to me, then he sat back and pushed his curls behind his ears with both hands. 'No one's asked for a sabbatical before.'

'Just three months – it will fly by,' I pleaded, desperation no doubt showing in my face. 'I absolutely promise I'll come back.'

'But what if everyone wants a sabbatical?' he asked, looking around us to check no one was eavesdropping. We were sitting at a table in the Selfridges food hall. 'It won't be easy to find cover for that amount of time. What if Shauna wants one too – what then? I'll have to speak to Jeff, find out what the company policy is.'

'But it's not a no?'

'Not yet,' he smiled. 'Listen, babe, I'll see what I can do, because I'd like to keep you, but you'd better come back, and don't tell anyone, for now.'

'I will, I promise. Let me buy you a Krispy Kreme Deluxe Donut as a thank you – in advance.'

And I got up before he could change his mind.

I was looking forward to spending time with Rob's mum, but for some reason I was even more excited about meeting Dan's fiancée, the infamous Florence. On Boxing Day evening, Rob had moaned about how his mother, Marian, was like a lap dog around Florence – she thought she was the best thing not just to happen to Dan, but to their entire family.

'She hasn't met *you* yet, though,' he qualified, though he had polished off a number of glasses of mulled wine.

From what I could glean, without turning into an A grade stalker, Florence was a high-flying PR executive for a boutique agency in London with a roster of clients across the luxury world – from London's hottest restaurants and spas, to art galleries and high-end fashion and beauty launches; Rob gave the impression she knew everyone worth knowing in the whole of London. Unfortunately, her Instagram account was locked, so I couldn't carry out the full extent of my desired snooping, but hopefully, after we'd met, we'd be tagging each other in photos from fashion parties and I'd be on her VIP guest list. In my role as a window designer for Selfridges, I hoped she would see me as someone worth knowing in London too.

Rob had decided we should break the news about New York to his mum together, the thought of which was making me feel sick with nerves as the day drew closer.

'Are you sure this won't make me come across as the girlfriend who's stealing her precious son?' I quizzed Rob on the phone on Sunday morning. 'I'll be like, "Hi, I'm Rob's new girlfriend – by the way, we're off to America, so you won't be seeing him for a while. Thanks for dinner!"'

'Course not. I think our delivery will be a bit more tactful than that. Anyway, it's no biggie – besides, Mum loves to travel, we'll invite her to visit – she'll be thrilled.'

'Have you told Dan yet?'

'No, we'll tell them together and it will be fine. Dan will support us, and I bet Florence will think it's the coolest thing. Mum will go along with whatever Florence thinks anyway. Relax.'

Relax, I tried. I ironed a silky blue Zara dress bought especially for the occasion, had a long soak in the bath and then, in a move I hoped would make me feel empowered for this family meeting of meetings, I decided to try out a new method of curling my hair. It involved heated rollers borrowed from Vicky's room and an upside down blow-drying technique I'd seen on a YouTube video. What could go wrong?

Plenty. The resulting hairstyle – Scary Spice, electrocuted, times ten – was so terrifying my eyes nearly burst when I caught sight of myself in the mirror. There was no way of relaxing it so I had to take another shower. Consequently, I was running late for dinner and there were sweat patches on the silky dress.

I jumped off the bus and headed down Westbourne Grove, half walking, half running, feeling far too hot. Plus, a strap broke on my bag and I was clutching it in an ungainly fashion under my arm, trying not to let the contents fall out. I was carrying all my overnight stuff for staying at Rob's and didn't particularly want my best knickers to end up in a puddle. As I dashed past the shops – Heidi Klein, Tom's Deli, Joseph – I thought how much I loved this part of London, just walking the streets felt like being in a Richard Curtis film. *Perhaps Rob and I might get a place around here one day.*

I turned left off the main road and reached Rob's mum's house. Glancing at my phone I realised I was a whole forty-five minutes late. Rob had texted: You ok? x. I needed to turn on a full charm offensive this evening.

It was a tall, impressive, white-fronted family house, complete with black metal railings and well-tended geraniums on the steps. The epitome of Notting Hill chic. Walking back a couple of paces to be out of sight, I swapped my flats for some new black, shiny Kurt Geiger heels, panic bought in the store on Friday to wear with my dress. My staff discount was burning a hole in my pocket recently and the shoes were blatantly for Florence's benefit more than anyone else's. My toes were crushed after walking up the steps. Rob opened the door and gave me a big hug.

'You look gorgeous,' he said, making me light up inside and out. There was classical music playing, candles flickering on a side table, and a delicious smell of home-cooking.

'Sorry I'm late.' I lifted my head for a kiss.

He took my face in his hands and kissed me softly.

When we parted, I paused to take in my surroundings: everything was cream, white, and glossy – it was a well looked after, tasteful home. 'Nice pad. I can't wait to see all the embarrassing photos of you growing up.' I scoured the hall table.

'Quick update,' he whispered, looking over his shoulder. 'Dan's here, but Florence isn't. Not quite sure why, but I don't think things are going well right now. He doesn't want to talk about it – not around Mum, anyway. If she starts to dig, we'll change the subject. She used to be a therapist, remember. Mum *loves* relationship problems – if there is a problem, I'm not even sure. Anyway, families, hey? Go with the flow, like you always do... Do you mind taking off your shoes? Mum's got a thing about shoes indoors.'

It was great to see Dan again, he was such a friendly, easy-going guy who instantly made me feel at ease, and the brothers were sweet and attentive to their mum. They loved her to bits, it was clear to see, and Marian was the kind of woman who relished the attention from her 'two beautiful boys'.

It was heart-warming to witness such stability compared with the uneven keel I felt between my sister and me, in my parents' eyes. She being the perfect one and I being the one who worked in fashion and was, therefore, certifiably 'bonkers'. Marian was well groomed, with blow-dried brown hair, good make-up, and what looked like a very real Chanel twinset. I felt glad I'd made an effort with my appearance, though she wasn't the kind to compliment me on it.

Maybe it was because Marian had never had a daughter, or perhaps it was just the way she was, but it quickly became clear that she found it hard to relax around her son's girl-friends – this one in particular. She eyed me with the kind of cynicism of a *Gogglebox* family watching TV.

'So, tell me about your work, Amber – it might not be worthy, but it sounds terribly thrilling, from what I've heard. You style celebrities, right?'

I was taken aback by the 'not worthy' dig. *Would she prefer me to work for Christian Aid?*

Rob gave me a look that said, 'let it go'.

'Well, I *did* work with famous people,' I replied. 'But these days I style dummies for the shop windows at Selfridges and, to be honest, the fact they can't answer back suits me better.' Her crestfallen face indicated that I should have gone along with the celebrity line.

'Right. But you must have met some huge names when you were out in LA – you know, when you and Rob were working on the show together?' She glanced at her son. He'd obviously filled her in on our backstory.

'Oh, you mean with Mona Armstrong?' I looked to Rob

for help. 'That was certainly an interesting time in my career – we worked a lot with Jennifer Astley.' Her eyes widened. *Everyone loves a celebrity encounter, evidently even those who might claim to be 'worthy'.* From then on I caved in and gave her what she wanted – an embellished list of the famous names I'd been in fairly close proximity to at the BAFTAs and the Oscars, giving her plenty to regale her friends with, and – hopefully – pass on to Florence.

My career done, she then moved on to family. 'So, what do your parents do, love?' she asked, oblivious to the fact I was dying to get the subject off myself.

I dunked a hefty piece of ciabatta in olive oil and chewed it for a few seconds, giving myself a moment to think.

'Mum was a hot-shot lawyer, she worked for years at a firm in the city handling litigation cases mainly, and now she's semi-retired she still works freelance for them but can take or leave cases as she likes. And Dad was a stay-at-home dad, he did all the school runs while Mum was working and did some work as a handy man. There's nothing dad can't fix.'

She gave me a stare that felt like she was trying to read my soul.

'Keep the hubby at home, clever woman,' she remarked finally, a wry smile across her face. 'How delightful.'

When my five minutes of grilling from Marian was finally over, she proceeded to spend ten minutes telling us about Florence's latest work projects – including a campaign for a new London art gallery filled with paintings created by children with behavioural problems, and a charity project sending make-up products to women in remote African villages.

'All fantastically worthy,' Marian gushed. She had a wicked glint in her eye.

Noticing my puffed-out chest and reddening cheeks, Rob placed a firm hand on my knee.

'Let's take out the plates.' he said. Dan looked as though he wanted to slide under the table. Marian looked at her watch. I was clearly dull as ditch water compared to Florence.

'Mum adores you, it's obvious,' Rob said in the kitchen as I placed two empty plates on the side. He had wound his arms around my waist and was peppering my neck with little kisses.

'Have we just been in the same room?' I asked. 'I feel like I've been in front of a firing squad. She's infinitely more excited about how Florence is saving the world than anything I have to say.' I rolled my eyes.

'Please, Amber, don't take it personally. Mum's just testing you, she likes a woman who can stick up for herself, it was the same when Florence first came round. I know when Mum likes someone and she likes you. You passed.'

'I passed?' *It's a weird kind of test.* 'Anyway, when are we going to—' I stopped abruptly as Marian joined us and leaned against the work top.

'To what?' she asked, and we both averted her eyes. 'I'm worried about Dan,' she continued, looking earnest. 'He's not himself at all this evening and he's stepped out to make yet another call – to Florence, I'm sure – but he won't let on if anything's wrong. He barely said a thing over dinner, and he didn't even finish his lamb. That's a first. Has he said anything to you, Robert darling? I just want to be sure he's all right.'

Sensing a mother-and-son private moment, I excused myself for the loo.

I locked myself in the downstairs toilet and sat down, breathing a huge sigh. My eyes wandered around the tiny room; there was a super-cute photo of Rob and Dan in a paddling pool on the wall – I imagined it was taken in the garden of this very house. I guessed they were aged about four and six, with grubby hands, freckled faces and huge smiles. Rob looked a cheeky blond scallywag and Dan more serious and dark haired. It must have been captured not long before their father left. Rob had told me a little about what happened, but not much detail.

'It was the biggest cliché in the book,' he had said. 'Dad went off with his young PA and broke Mum's heart. I don't think she's ever got over it. After going to some counselling sessions she decided to train as a relationship therapist herself. What is it they say about therapists? They're the most messed-up people out there.' I knew that Rob now had a fractured relationship with his father, who went on to have three more children with the PA. They saw each other maybe once a year. It was sad, really. Knowing this made me feel a little more sympathetic about the dig Marian had made about my dad's job over dinner and perhaps helped explained why she hadn't exactly been warm to me so far. She clearly had a deep mistrust of other women around her men. *Unless they're Florence.*

And then my gaze fixed on another photo; this one looked very recent. It showed Dan on a white sandy beach holding an attractive, bikini-clad blonde woman in his arms; she was flaunting what appeared to be a big diamond engagement ring. It had to be Florence; all big bouncy platinum curls and an innocent smile.

'Quick loo break, that's better.' I smiled, joining them all in the kitchen.

Rob smiled quizzically. 'Thanks for the update, Amber.'

'Dessert will be another five minutes, let's go back through.' Marian ushered us, rapidly putting an end to whatever they had been discussing. She placed a hand on my arm to guide me through first, an indication that I wasn't completely repulsive to her.

Rob poured us all another large glass of white wine and I gulped down half of mine immediately. *Thank God for wine, I mean, seriously, what would I do without wine?* Judging by the speed with which Rob finished his glass and then refilled us both, I knew the moment had arrived.

'So, Mum, Dan, there is something Amber and I wanted to talk to you about tonight.'

Marian clutched Dan's arm. 'Jesus, don't tell me you're getting married,' she squealed, horrified.

I shuffled to the back of my chair. *She really knows how to make me feel welcome.*

'No, Mum, it's more of a short-term plan. We, er, Amber and I are going to be moving to New York for a few months.

I've been offered a filming job out there and we thought it would be a great adventure if we both went together.'

He paused to take in their expressions. Marian looked like she'd been turned to stone.

'Mum? You've always said I should seize opportunities – isn't it great?'

'Sounds bloody exciting. Congrats, man,' Dan piped up, filling the silence from Marian. He held his hand out across the table to Rob and then he shook my hand. 'Got space in your suitcase for me?'

'Always got a sofa for you, come and visit. You too, Mum, it's only for an initial three months, so you'd better take advantage of the cheap accommodation.'

Marian forced her mouth into a kind of tight smile. 'Super, darling, I suppose it sounds great fun,' she said, before looking me right between the eyes. 'You must be pleased.' I wouldn't have been surprised if she'd then hissed. *You'd think I'd just told her I was taking him to Helmand Province.*

'Yes, I'm excited, too,' I offered, 'and it's not for long, you know, we'll be back.'

'Lovely. When do you go?' she asked, arms folded across her chest defensively.

'In a few weeks. We're just looking into our tickets and visa and we have to sort out living arrangements and then we'll be off.'

'A few weeks? Just like that,' she said.

'Just like that,' Dan repeated, impersonating Tommy Cooper. Rob and I both sniggered.

***

We were wrenched out of some awkward small talk about journey times to New York by a strange smell emanating from the kitchen. Rob noticed it first.

'That's smoke,' he got to his feet. 'Mum, I think something's burning.'

We all lifted our noses to the air.

'God, yes, and your smoke alarm's not working,' said Dan, sounding animated for the first time all evening as he leapt up to join Rob on his way to the kitchen.

Marian jumped to her feet, too, calling after them. 'Oh Lord, it's the sticky pudding, I forgot all about the bloody pudding. It'll be ruined.' She looked stricken.

I pushed my chair away from the table and joined them.

In the kitchen, the three of them were staring at a smoking layer of melted plastic mixed with a toasted toffee pudding. Marian's eyes had gone glassy and I was afraid she might cry.

'Left the damn plastic film on it, didn't I.' She swallowed, her voice trembling. 'Some lids you pierce, others you don't, it's so bloody confusing.'

'Bang goes pretending it was home-made,' Rob remarked, trying to lighten the atmosphere. He put an arm around her shoulders and she leaned into him.

'Well, perfect end to a pretty disastrous evening wouldn't you say?' Marian remarked finally, once the backdoor had been opened and the pudding placed out of sight on the patio. I didn't know where to look. 'Both of my boys are having early mid-life crises and then I nearly set the house on fire.'

'Come on, Mum, it's not that bad.' Dan put a hand on her arm. I noticed he didn't try to deny the crisis part. She covered her face with her hands and began sobbing into them. Half of me wanted to put my arms around her too and join the group hug, as I'd do if she was my mum, but I had no idea how that might go down. Instead I watched as Rob and Dan enveloped her and the three stood there for a few seconds, hugging. I wondered whether to grab my coat and disappear, but I'd promised Rob I'd stay at his tonight; besides, I was wearing new underwear. Instead I comforted myself with a realisation: *Maybe my own family is not so dysfunctional after all.*

CHAPTER THREE

'How bad would you say it was on a scale of one to ten?'
I asked Rob, when we finally made it into bed at his place
that evening. We were cuddled up in our usual position, legs
entwined, my face pressed into his chest.

'I'd give it a seven,' he said eventually.

'*Seven?*' I gasped, lifting my head to look at his. 'What the
hell would a two evening be like?'

'There's been worse,' he whispered nonchalantly, not even
opening his eyes. 'Mum means well, and she does like you,
I promise. Now can we go to sleep?'

I lay there for a few minutes, my head too full for sleep.
Finally, I rolled over and lifted my phone from the bedside
table. I texted Vicky:

Met Rob's mum – she hates me.

In the morning there was a response from Vicky:

How could anyone hate you? Anyway, is he going to New
York?

By that evening, I had filled her in on the whole situation.
To say she was excited about the move was an understate-
ment. She did a lap of her garden, singing, 'Rule Britannia!',
at the top of her voice, while I was still on the phone. She

didn't even seem to mind that I would have to move her stuff out of our flat. The fact we were to be a mere six-hour plane ride away from one another made up for everything. It was just the enthusiasm I needed to make the whole thing feel real. We spent the next thirty minutes discussing all the things we could do together when she came to visit, which included a weekend in the Hamptons, jogging in Central Park, and munching our way through stacks of blueberry pancakes.

I was worried about work, though. Joseph had been strangely elusive almost all day on Monday, holed up in meetings with Jeff, and I was getting increasingly paranoid they were talking about my future at Selfridges.

Eventually, at five o'clock, he returned with a face like thunder saying we needed to 'up our game' and that the summer window theme hadn't exactly 'set the big wigs on fire'.

'Not original enough,' he said. 'Apparently, we "must try harder".' He drew more quote marks in the air with his fingers. 'What do they want? Windows that chat you up as you walk past?'

'Actually, there could be an idea in that,' I muttered, unhelpfully.

As I was leaving work that evening, he pulled me aside. 'As you can tell it was a heavy day, wasn't the right time to ask about your sabbatical. I'll try later in the week, when, *hopefully*, we're flavour of the month again. Okay, babe?'

'Okay, thank you, I really appreciate it.'

'What are you two gossiping about?' Shauna asked, bounding over to stick her nosy beak in.

'Shop windows, what do you think?' I shot back.

'Come with ideas tomorrow,' Joseph added, before giving me a wink.

'So I think the wink was an indication that it's basically going to be fine,' I reported to Rob when he arrived at mine later that evening. We were staying over with each other almost every night at the moment and it was great. *I'm having regular sex! I'm eating something other than hummus and pitta bread for dinner most nights! I'm watching the news with someone to explain the repercussions of Brexit!*

'But what will you do if it's not?' he asked, confronting the big question that so far I'd been refusing to acknowledge. And he had a point; it could very well go out of my favour if Jeff remained in a foul mood all week.

'I guess I'll quit,' I replied after a beat.

Rob sucked his cheeks in and sighed heavily. 'Blimey, that's pressure,' he said.

'Yes, it is, but I'm sure I'd get another job when we got back.'

'That's a lot of pressure on *me*, I mean – I make you lose your job just to come with me to New York for three months.'

'Yes, but I'm not your sheep, Rob, I've made the decision too. It's me that's taking the risk. Or are you trying to say something else? Are you *sure* you want me to come to New York with you?'

The words hung in the air between us for a second too long.

'Rob?'

'Of course I do, we've been through this before – I'd love nothing more. I just want you to be certain too.'

'I am! I'd give up my job tomorrow if I had to – opportunities like this don't come along often and I know I'll regret it for the rest of my life if I don't come with you. I want to spend as much time with you as I can. Why, are you having second thoughts?'

He took my head into his hands and looked at me, telling me with his eyes that I should shut up.

'I love you Amber,' he said finally, 'risk taker, adventurer and woman I can't wait to get to know even more in New York.'

My heart leapt.

Oh. My. God. He said it. He said he loves me. And the way he said it made me feel like I was the only person in the world.

'I'm pretty sure I love you too,' I whispered.

The corners of his mouth turned up and the movement continued until there was a huge grin spread right across his face, lighting up his whole being.

'*Pretty* sure?' he said, 'Have I still got some convincing to do?'

I blushed.

'Well, I'm pretty sure I know how to start,' he continued.

We melted into one another, lips on lips, hands all over one another, his strong body guiding me to the bedroom. Just a few short words, a few seconds in time, and we were on the next level. *We are a couple in love.*

This time when we made love it felt different, it was more

intense than ever before. I couldn't help it but afterwards, tears streamed down my cheeks. I don't think he noticed in the darkness, because he rolled over and was soon lightly snoring, one warm arm flopped over my body. I cried because in that instant it was like I was letting go of all those years as a singleton, all the times I weathered whatever life threw at me on my own, getting on with things, relying on no one but myself. Don't get me wrong, I was fine with it during that time – but it wasn't always easy, doing everything alone. Now I had a reason to give myself completely to somebody else, to this gorgeous man, because he loved me and wanted us to be a team.

I must have been radiating something the next morning, because the man in Pret à Manger gave me a free latte and no sooner had I arrived at work than Joseph pulled me aside to say he'd been in early to chat with Jeff, and Jeff had approved my sabbatical.

'Told him if we didn't let you go, we'd lose you anyway. You're lucky, Amber. And with some of that luck I hope you'll befriend Tom Ford while you're out there and set him up with me,' he said, smiling. 'Just promise you'll come back, or that will be the end of sabbaticals, forever. I'm not joking.'

I looked him in the eye. 'I promise Joseph, thank you *so* much. I cannot tell you how much this means to me. And I swear I will carry around your photo so I'm prepared when I meet Tom. And I will.'

'Thanks, babe.' He winked his trademark wink. 'Let me

handle Shauna and the rest of the team. When are you planning to go?'

'We want to fly in a couple of weeks.' I took a deep breath. Saying it out loud was exhilarating, but also terrifying. 'We're looking into flights. I'll let you know the second we book.'

'You lucky cow.' He beamed. 'I love New York. Now, what are your ideas for the windows, now I've told Jeff how irreplaceable you are?'

'Well…' I pulled him aside.

In between packing up the flat, sorting out travel arrangements and discussing what Rob was going to do with Pinky, I spent the rest of the week putting in extra hours at work and doing all the things I wouldn't be able to do in New York, like buying Greggs' 'three for five pounds' milk-chocolate cookies and eating them all in one go and getting on a Routemaster bus using the back door and watching Oxford Street whizz past the window on my way home from work. London suddenly had a romantic quality that I was going to miss so much.

Things were moving apace for Rob and on Wednesday evening, over a Thai takeaway at his, he gave me the good news that his work were going to cover the rent for a studio apartment in New York.

'Now I've just got to work on Ben looking after Pinky,' he said.

'Good luck with that,' I said, giggling. 'Gay Pinky and bachelor Ben? Can't see it happening, somehow. What about your mum?' He gave me a look. 'Of course, stupid idea.'

'Your parents?' he suggested, lifting a brow.

'No way. They hate pets.'

'It's either Ben or a pig sanctuary then,' he sighed.

And then I had a brainwave. 'Nora! Why didn't I think of her before? She loves farm animals – her first word was "oink!" Her eyes almost popped out of her head the first time she saw a photo of Pinky – it was love at first sight. I'll work on Nora to persuade my sister to look after Pinky. They've got a shed in their garden and plenty of space. Pinky will be the toast of suburbia – and we'll be able to FaceTime him whenever we want. It's perfect!'

'That is quite possibly the best brainwave ever,' Rob enthused. 'When can we see Nora?'

'I'll see if she can come for a sleepover this Friday.' 'Project Pinky' had begun.

'But you've never offered to have Nora for a whole night before,' my sister remarked, suspiciously, on the phone. 'You and Rob don't have any *news* you want to share, do you? You seem very keen to get some kiddie practice all of a sudden.'

'No, Luce, nothing like that, I just thought it would be nice for you and Rory to have a date night, that's all. And it would be lovely to spend some time with my beautiful, clever niece before I go.'

'Well, we haven't had a night out together in ages – there are cobwebs in my make-up bag, not to mention other places – so it would be lovely, if you *really* don't mind?' I could hear the excitement in her voice, she was already mentally planning her outfit. 'We could drop her off at yours and then get the tube into town. Christ, I haven't been into town for about three years! Do you still need an Oyster card, or is it all done by electronic implants these days?'

'Perfect! I'll get out of work a bit early. Come any time after five. Oh, and what's Nora's favourite dinner? I want to make everything perfect for her.'

'Fish fingers and chips and she'll love you forever,' she replied. 'Not too many chips though, no sweets and limit screen time.'

'Sounds like great fun. But don't worry, I've got something planned.' I smiled into the phone. 'See you Friday.'

Back at work, Joseph had taken our new concept for the windows to Jeff and it had gone down a storm with the boardroom bosses, so we were working long days to get the revised plans off the ground. They were to feature a 'world first' interactive treat for the senses with scratch-and-sniff panels smelling of ice lollies, sun cream and coconut – all the scents of high summer against a backdrop of beach huts and candy-coloured fashion. In another major window, digital touch screens featuring summer rope-soled platforms and seventies sunglasses which could be viewed from any angle and followed you down the street; and another featuring slick city styles for polished power dressers, with voices calling out to passers-by, transporting you to the trading floor on a blistering hot afternoon. The whole thing was a meeting of high-tech and high street and we were bursting with excitement about it all – I was even a little peeved I wouldn't be around to see it all come to fruition.

As Friday rolled around, I worked through my lunch to ensure an early exit so I could get Nora's dinner under the grill before she arrived, thus winning me brownie points from Lucy before Project Pinky came into play. Also, there was no way I'd get Nora to sit still and eat dinner once Rob had come round with the evening's miniature entertainment. I'd instructed him to ensure Pinky was groomed to perfection: 'Think Crufts for pigs,' I said, 'make sure Pinky's had a bath and smells nice. Lucy's got a nose like a blood hound. There's no way she'll take him if he's smelly.'

I was just making my way to the front of the store to go home, when I noticed something going on. There were crowds of shoppers being held back by security guards. *Oh God, not a fire drill or worse, a terror alert. I've not got time for this.*

'Stay back everyone, won't be long now,' the head of security was telling the excited faces all around him. Locking the doors to one of London's premiere stores on a Friday afternoon was a very rare occurrence. I scanned the area for a member of staff I recognised, finally spotting one of the girls on the Mac counter who I'd befriended once when I was hungover and in desperate need of an in-store makeover. I elbowed my way through the crowd, flashing my staff pass to reach her.

'Hey Sam, what's going on?'

She was craning her neck and barely took her eyes away from the direction of the boxed-off Hermès area as she spoke: 'Celebrity in the store.'

Although this was a relatively common occurrence in

Selfridges, it was still exciting. My eyes widened. 'Ooh – who?'

'We're not meant to say, but seeing as she's currently trending on Twitter.' She leaned towards me and whispered: 'It's Amanda Sykes. Word got out and suddenly tons of fans have turned up, trying to get a selfie with her. It was so crazy they had to close the doors. She's currently buying up the entire Hermès concession. Literally all of it, according to Lisa in fragrance.'

Amanda Sykes. 'Wow,' I gasped. Amanda Sykes was the biggest thing to hit the internet since Kim Kardashian's bottom. Even Amanda Sykes's right foot had its own Instagram and Snapchat accounts, with millions of followers. And those accounts had thousands more spoof accounts.

I looked in the direction of Hermès too.

'Have you seen her?'

Samantha ushered me close. 'Seen her? You can't miss her. Let's just say, her waistline is now a *coast*line, if you get my drift.'

I giggled. 'I need to see this.'

I was just about to ask her if it would be okay if I stood on one of the make-up-counter stools to try to get a better view, when a frenzy of flashes went off outside the store. They lit up a whole window. Word spread that Amanda was holding up a necklace to the light.

Six security guards struggled to hold back more fans, who were trying to storm through the doors from the street.

I spotted Mike, one of the security guards I had got to know when working through the night on the windows, and pushed my way through a gaggle of Japanese tourists to reach him – they all had their iPhones and cameras lifted in the hope of snapping the top of Amanda's head.

'The doors – are they really locked, Mike? I need to get out.'

'Afraid so,' he replied. 'You'll have to use the staff exit. But we shouldn't be more than five minutes now. There's barely anything left in the concession, according to one of Ms Sykes's body guards.'

I pulled out my phone to check the time: 4.45 p.m. There was a text from Lucy:

5 minutes away from yours. Lxx

Shit! I was really late for Nora's arrival.

'I don't have five minutes,' I pleaded. 'I've got to get home for my five-year-old niece.'

'It's intense out there right now, you'll have to wait until she's gone,' Mike explained.

I looked through the doors; the crowd around the window closest to where Amanda was believed to be shopping was ten people deep.

'Honestly, I can't, I beg you, Mike, it'll take me two seconds to get out. I *really* need to.' My mind was racing to come up with a reason why I couldn't wait. 'I really need to go to Superdrug because I think I might be getting my period,' I pleaded. His face reddened. Before I had to elaborate, he surreptitiously opened the door a few inches, indicating I should squeeze through. Behind me, the perfume counters were seeing an unexpected rush, as fans masquerading as shoppers gathered to witness Amanda leave the store and get into her waiting car.

Squeezing out, I found myself in the middle of the throng, still clutching my Selfridges staff pass.

'Hey, do you work at Selfridges?' one girl shouted in my direction. I shoved the pass into my pocket quickly. 'This girl works at Selfridges!' she continued, 'I saw her pass. Can you get us in? We want to see Amanda.'

'Sorry, but the store's closed,' I replied, feeling a little intimidated. Fans this close to their idol were a force to behold. In seconds the crowd around me had doubled. Chants of 'Aman-da! Aman-da!' filled the air. In every direction were pointing fingers, phones and excited conjecture about when Amanda might be coming out and where she might be going next. I had to admit, I felt buzzed by it too.

I made my way through the tightly packed group, towards the kerb, where a large, blacked-out people carrier was parked. I'd found myself a good vantage position now, and there was a kerfuffle going on around one of the shop doors, so I imagined Amanda might be on her way out. Seeing as everyone else was doing it, I stopped, just a quick look at Amanda in the flesh would make an interesting story for Lucy and Nora this evening; I might even get a photo good enough for Instagram.

Suddenly the window on Amanda's people carrier lowered and a shrill American voice called out, taking me by surprise: 'Hey, Amber! Amber Green, is that you?'

I turned around. *No, it can't be.* A section of the crowd turned too, camera phones held upwards all clicking, flashing and recording at once. *It is, it's that actress, Poppy Dunn.* I'd come across her in LA last year during awards season and now she was sitting in Amanda Sykes's car, presumably waiting for Amanda to come out and join her.

'Hey, stranger!' she said, pointing at me, causing the people with camera phones to turn en masse to capture my shell-shocked face. 'You're Mona Armstrong's assistant, we met in LA last year. No way!'

She used the word 'met' loosely; it was more that Poppy had given me evil eyes a few times over canapés and baggage carousels on the awards-season circuit, when she was hanging out with Mona's nemesis, her assistant before me, Tamara. And now she seemed pleased to see me. Maybe she was enjoying the juxtaposition of seeing me stand in a London gutter, while she was in a megastar's luxury car. From nowhere, a paparazzo turned up and started snapping Poppy through the window. She immediately produced some expensive-looking sunglasses, swished up her hair and wound the window down lower, beaming madly.

'Poppy,' I raised my hand in acknowledgement, moving a little closer to the vehicle and lowering my voice: 'I don't work with Mona any more, like Tamara, I saw the light in the end.'

'Don't blame you!' she squealed. 'She's a lunatic! So why are you waiting for Amanda?'

'Oh, I'm not,' I said, feeling embarrassed to have been spotted ogling, like a teenager. I was now just the other side of the car door to her. 'I work as a window designer for Selfridges. Somehow, I got caught up in this on my way home. I've got my five-year-old niece staying over tonight and now I'm really late to meet her.'

'Cool job,' Poppy said. 'Did you do the Christmas windows? Man, I loved them.' A frenzy of close-up flashing blinded me momentarily. Poppy had nailed posing through a car window. Chin lifted, she beamed, flashing her whiter-than-white teeth for the photographer. It was quite a skill. When the flashes had subsided, she pushed her glasses down lower on her nose and looked over the top. 'Would you like a lift?'

My eyes darted round – still no sign of Amanda, but this was her car, surely she wouldn't be happy to find a random Selfridges employee in it, when she did eventually return, laden with shopping bags.

'What about Amanda?' I asked.

'She'll be cool,' Poppy said. 'She might seem like a diva on TV, but she's actually the sweetest.' She leaned forward and the window smoothly rose up. Through the glass, I could just about make out that she was leaning forward, talking to someone. Seconds later, a man I hadn't even noticed sitting in the front passenger seat jumped out and opened the door next to Poppy. He was wearing a head set and looked really stern, like some of the personal bodyguards I had come into contact with last year.

'Quick! Get in,' Poppy instructed.

And then I was sitting on the back seat of Amanda Sykes's giant car. It was a thrilling place to be. The car had a sleek matt-black interior and an enticing smell of brand new leather upholstery.

'How do you know her?' I asked Poppy, once my breathing had steadied.

'We share an agent in LA,' she revealed. 'There's talk of me appearing on her show, it's going to be rad.'

Suddenly an almighty cheer ripped through the crowd. A video camera had appeared and a second opportunistic paparazzo had joined the first, waiting by the car ready to capture Amanda getting into it, ideally displaying a glimpse of her gusset. The guy from the front seat received something through his headset and hurtled out of the vehicle, clearing a route towards the shop as he went.

'Must be on her way,' Poppy remarked, craning her neck to look out.

'I think I'll split,' I said, seizing the moment to exit the car while everyone's attention was turned. 'I don't think Amanda will especially want me here.'

'Give me your number,' Poppy asked, 'I'm going to be in London for a while working. I'd love to keep in touch, I might need some styling.' She pulled out her phone and, as I hurriedly told her my digits, she punched them in.

'Thanks for the offer of the lift!' I yelled, a bit gutted that I didn't have time to tell her about my move to New York. I quickly stepped out of the car and slammed the door.

And then a tunnel opened up in front of me and Amanda came into view at the end of it, flanked by security guards laden with Selfridges bags. Samantha was right, she was wider than I imagined, her ample curves flaunted in a figure-hugging black dress. Her famous feet were encased in heeled black sandals with at least ten buckles going halfway up her calf. More flashes erupted and yells of 'Mandy! Mandy!' rang out from every direction.

If I wasn't mistaken we locked eyes for a second or two – maybe she saw me jump out of her car and wondered who on earth I was – but her lips seemed to turn up and she flashed me a smile.

I darted across Oxford Street, heading in the direction of Bond Street tube, thankfully narrowly missing being run over by a double decker – even the bus driver was distracted by the fuss. Once across the road, I turned back briefly but Amanda had disappeared behind the blacked-out glass of the car. I continued dodging people and shopping bags as I became lost in the hordes of shoppers who constantly packed Oxford Street's pavements and didn't stop rushing until I was through the barriers and safely on a tube train.

CHAPTER FOUR

I slowed my pace as I turned the corner to my street in Kensal Rise. The terraced houses on either side of the road were not unattractive, they were 'characterful', an estate agent might say, when they meant 'tired'. Now that New York was in my sights, everything seemed to look more shabby. But it wasn't so much my street that made me slow down, it was the fact that I could see my sister, Rory and Nora sitting in their car. Lucy had a face like thunder.

'Ever heard of ringing if you're going to be late?' she stormed, opening the door and pushing her hair out of her face. 'Five-year-olds don't enjoy being cooped up in a car, especially when it's approaching the witching hour.'

I peered into the car, Nora was wriggling around on the back seat with a variety of dolls laughing hysterically, her hair ruffled and cheeks flushed. She looked perfectly happy to me, not remotely like a witch. Then I pulled out my phone, it was nearly six and there were four missed calls from Lucy on the screen.

'I was on the tube, it didn't ring. I'm sorry,' I muttered, once again feeling like the naughty little sister who can't do anything right. 'The store had to be closed for a bit and I got caught up in it.'

'Another drama in fashion land.' Lucy tutted. 'Anyway, this one's now high on Ribena and Calpol and needs her dinner. And I need a glass of wine – shall we go in?'

Judging by the amount of luggage they had, it looked like Nora was moving in. There was a giant holdall, a duvet, plus another big bag apparently full of the toys, books and three night lights required to recreate Nora's home environment for *one night*. As Rory dragged the endless bags up the communal stairs and into my flat, I placated Lucy with a glass of sauvignon blanc and then spun a yarn about how I planned to take Nora to the local fish and chip shop instead of cooking, as a special treat. Lucy's face dropped, but thankfully, before she could veto dinner, the little girl's eyes lit up and she grabbed my hand tightly.

'Chips! Can we go now pleeeease?' she squealed.

'Oh, it's only a one-off, Luce, it's an auntie's prerogative. Now, you two had better get off – go on, shoo,' I commanded, 'and don't worry about coming back early in the morning. Nora and I are going to be just fine, aren't we?' I looked at Nora nervously.

'Fine, Auntie Nana,' she replied. The fact she had referred to me as 'Nana' from the age of one did nothing for my image as a fun young auntie. 'Can we get the chips now?'

After two greasy dinners and a bag of pick-and-mix, we arrived home to find Rob had just turned up with Pinky. The little pig was excitedly scurrying around the living room, pausing now and again to hoover up stray crumbs from under the coffee table.

'Hey, Nora! Look who I've brought to see you. Rob's little piggy, Pinky. He wants to be your friend too. Would you like to come and play with him?'

Pinky's wiry tail lifted when he caught sight of a new potential playmate.

'Me no like Pinky!' she uttered, as Pinky darted between my legs to reach her. She clung onto my trousers as though her life depended upon it.

'So, this is going well,' Rob muttered, after umpteen attempts to get Nora and Pinky to interact, always ending in Nora running off to hide, whilst shrieking, 'I want to go home!' at the top of her voice.

We then spent an hour constantly retrieving Pinky from behind the TV table, where he was particularly interested in gnawing through cables, before I decided it was time for bed. All four of us were becoming overtired and angsty.

'Oh, by the way, nearly forgot to tell you,' Rob said. 'I spoke to Dan earlier, the wedding is on hold.'

'Oh no,' I said, sighing, 'poor thing. Did he say what happened?'

'Nope, he's not good with opening up and doesn't seem to want to say more – despite mum pestering him endlessly.'

The doorbell buzzed loudly just as we were coaxing Nora into her bedroom with a trail of popcorn. Pinky was darting around our feet, trying to scoff the popcorn before Nora and thinking it was all a huge game as she became increasingly wound up.

'I want Mummy! Is Mummy at the door?' Nora whined.

'Ignore it, I can't handle seeing anyone right now,' I commanded Rob over the racket. 'Mummy will be here to pick you up first thing tomorrow morning, I promise,' I told Nora. 'Now, let's go find your toys and I'll read your favourite story.'

The doorbell buzzed again just as I closed her door.

Thirty minutes later – four readings of *The Gruffalo*, one protracted pretend tea party, the full-length version of 'Let It Go', sung badly, and two failed attempts at putting to bed – and Nora was showing no signs of tiredness, so I decided to admit defeat and brought her back into the living room. As I crossed the hallway, at first I thought Rob was on the phone, but then I heard a familiar female American voice talking back to him. I peered through a gap in the door: *Poppy Dunn*. Looking very at home on my sofa – with Pinky curled up in her lap, like some bald, chubby kitten – while she chatted away to Rob like an old friend. Her discarded Chanel flats lay on the floor.

She leapt up when she saw me, causing Pinky to jump off the sofa.

'Hey, Amber, babe, hope you don't mind me popping over, but it was so great to reconnect with you today. I want to hear more about what you're up to. Rob picked up your phone when I called. He says you guys are moving to Manhattan together. I'm so excited for you. New York is the coolest city. Probably my favourite in the world, after London, and Tokyo, oh, and probably Miami.'

'Not at all.' I grinned falsely, slowly turning my expression into a grimace as I slyly sideways-glanced at Rob wondering why he had given her my address.

Then she spotted Nora. 'Hey, there, little princess, aren't you the cutest? If I'm not mistaken, that is a *Frozen* nightie you're wearing, isn't it?' Nora nodded, and came out from behind me to get a better look at the glamorous woman who looked as though she'd stepped out of a Disney film herself. With her poker-straight honey-blonde hair, pale blue skintight jeans and cream jumper, she would certainly have turned heads on her way to Kensal Rise. 'Do you know that I'm friends with Elsa in real life?' she continued, as Nora's eyes widened. 'I can tell you all about her, if you like, while you show me your dolls and we talk about *Frozen*.'

She gave me a wink and, miraculously, Nora was only too happy to take Poppy's hand and be led straight back to her bedroom.

'She's got the magic touch,' Rob commented, as the two quietly disappeared back across the landing, making me feel like a failure.

'Good luck to her,' I replied, which unfortunately came out sounding slightly sarcastic. 'So I don't think Nora's going to be begging her parents to adopt Pinky any time soon,' I added.

'Agreed, I think we can safely say she hates micro-pigs.' Rob laughed, pouring me a glass from the bottle of red he and Poppy had already drunk half of.

'But, every cloud,' he said, grinning, 'because Poppy might just be our saviour. She's taken a real shine to Pinky and the feeling seems to be mutual.'

Just then, Poppy bounded back into the room, carefully shutting the door behind her.

'Sound asleep,' she declared, proudly. 'Still haven't lost my nannying touch.'

'You used to be a nanny?' I asked.

'Yes, for four years, while I was at drama school. I looked after two girls for a wealthy family in Chelsea. I know every bedtime trick there is.'

'I wish I'd known that earlier,' I said, smiling, warming to our unexpected guest now we had some peace. 'I would have invited you for the whole evening.'

'I guess you haven't seen the *Evening Standard* yet today, then?' She pulled a rolled-up copy of the newspaper out of the dreamy cream Chloé bag I'd clocked by the side of the sofa. 'Tada!' she thrust it into my hands. 'We made the paper, girlfriend!'

I straightened out the newspaper and took in the full horror of a page-five-splash which featured a large photo of Amanda coming out of Selfridges and a smaller photo of Poppy and me sitting in the car – her looking gorgeous, smiling broadly, and my startled face, one leg in the car, getting in, in an ungainly fashion, unaware I was being photographed. Both Amanda and Poppy looked like models with their perfectly coiffed hair and made-up faces, whereas I looked like a flustered frump. The headline accompanying it read: AMANDA SYKES SHOPPING SPREE CAUSES CHAOS AT SELFRIDGES. I wondered what the big bosses would make of this; whether they would spot who the person was inelegantly getting into Amanda's car. *Perhaps my sabbatical will be recalled now. Perhaps they won't want me back.*

'Rob came and leaned over my shoulder. 'Classic! You didn't tell me about this, Am. Look at your face! Come on, you've got to admit, it's a little bit hilarious?'

'I look like a homeless person.' I sulked.

'Anyway, Amanda is thrilled,' Poppy revealed. 'She only went to the store at the busiest time of day to try to score a photo in a paper. You can't buy PR like this.'

'Won't she wonder who the random person in her car is, though?' I asked.

'Don't worry, she's cool,' Poppy assured me.

Out of the corner of my eye, I noticed my iPhone, muted but blinking on the coffee table. I picked it up and began scrolling through the messages and missed calls, there was even a thread on Facebook, thanks to Shauna posting the image of me. Vicky had seen it, and texted:

I hear you're BFFs with Amanda Sykes. WTF happened babe?!? xxx

Mum had texted with her lawyer hat on:

So you're famous? If you're being hounded, say No Comment and walk off. First rule to remember, darling. Hope Nora's been cheering you up. Mx

One of the texts was from Lucy:

Saw the Standard – so that's why you were late. Hope Nora is asleep? Don't forget you can give her milk if she wakes and if she can't sleep, try reading the Frozen book, she might want to sleep with it next to her. She'll probably wake up at 6ish, if you're lucky. xx

I only replied to Luce:

All quiet, hope you're enjoying your evening. Switch off! x

The others would have to wait. I noted that Joseph hadn't said anything which either meant he hadn't seen it, or was waiting to grill me tomorrow morning.

Pinky was snuffling around Poppy's toes, angling to be picked up.

'Hey, little fella,' she purred, scooping him into her arms. 'Did we forget about you? Tut tut. Come and give your adopted mummy a kissy.'

'Adopted mummy, hey?' Rob's ears pricked up. At last, attention was being taken away from the newspaper I'd placed face down on the table.

'I've been thinking… if you need to re-home him and it's only going to be for three months, I'd love to be your new pig-sitter.' Poppy smiled. 'I talked to Nora about it earlier, and she agrees. I could use a new flatmate and Pinky won't nick all my toiletries. Do you think I'm up to the job?'

Both she and Pinky looked at us, her big blue eyes and his little dark peepers shining.

'I think Pinky's already made the decision,' Rob said, looking lovingly at them both. For a moment, he looked bereft, as though he was giving away his own child.

'Well, that's perfect,' I seconded. 'Let's toast Pinky's new home!' and I refilled us from the second bottle.

'I'm so excited!' Poppy gushed. 'I'll clear out some space this week and get him next weekend – if that suits you, Rob? Oh, and Amber, don't let me forget: I want to hook you up with Dana LeRoy. She runs a stylists' agency in New York.

And she'll love you, I know it. I'll hook you up over email – she'll get you some jobs in no time.'

She'll love me. The words played on my mind. They insinuated that I, Amber Green, from suburban London, could wow people, just by being me. I was going to need to do a lot of wowing in New York, if I didn't want to be stuck in our apartment all day out there. *But what if people don't love me? What if I'm not cool enough?*

As the wine flowed, so did the conversation, and I began warming to Poppy, big time. Despite the unfortunate photo opportunity, she genuinely seemed to want to be friends and help me out with some contacts in New York.

It was nearly two in the morning when Poppy finally left; Rob and I were now in the bathroom together, brushing our teeth and talking in whispers, fearful of waking Nora before we'd even got into bed.

'So, it's all falling into place then,' he enthused. 'What a sweet girl Poppy is, too.'

'Yes, amazing how first impressions can be so off,' I admitted. 'Thanks to Mona, I had her all wrong.'

'Well, there weren't exactly many people Mona managed to keep on side, let's face it,' Rob remarked. 'Maybe Poppy can help you build up some clients while we're in New York – Dana sounds worth looking up, for starters.'

'Yeah,' I said, sighing, 'if she thinks I'm worth getting back to.'

'You what?' said Rob, taking my electric toothbrush from me and placing it on the side, before pulling both of my hands into his. 'I won't hear any of this "if I'm worth it" stuff. You may not have any idea how talented and beautiful you are, but I certainly do. And the Danas of New York should be bloody glad to meet you, not the other way around. Okay?'

I smiled, trying to look seductive, though I wasn't convinced I'd got all the red-wine stains from the rim of my lips. 'Okay.' I made a silent promise to take a leaf of self-confidence out of Poppy's book and take Manhattan by storm.

'Anyway,' he continued, 'we need to get into bed before a hyper five-year-old or a hungry pig wakes us up in, precisely, urgh, four hours, you said…?'

Nora must have been exhausted by Pinky's taunting because by some miracle, I woke up before her, at seven the next morning, my mouth dryer than the Sahara and head gently aching. Rob muttered something about 'too many tannins in that red wine' and rolled over. I noticed Pinky had made himself at home in a pile of laundry in the corner of my room and was snoring gently. The image of them both made me smile. *Our little family*. I was going to miss Pinky while we were away.

I forced myself to drink a pint of water and, by the time Nora woke up twenty minutes later, my lounge floor was strewn with items resembling the sad, unwanted items on a Portobello market stall at the end of a Saturday afternoon. Packing up the flat was going to be hard work and more emotionally draining than I imagined. There was a lifetime's worth of belongings to sort through and, no matter how ruthless I tried to be, there were some items that it was hard to bring myself to part with. The furniture would be easy to shift via adverts in Gumtree, but it was the items currently gathered in the middle of the room that would feel like throwing away a bit of my soul if they were to go. Take the wooden footstool in the shape of an owl bought with Vicky from Camden market when we first moved in; or the poster-sized framed astrological chart which had remained propped up against a wall for the past four years as I never got round to having it hung; and then there were the two pretty, albeit battered, crochet cushions brought back from a holiday in the south of France when I was a student. The flat was full of things I had once loved, important purchases for one reason or another – but, I told myself, it was time to strike out the old to make space for the new.

Vicky proved tougher on the chucking-out front, instructing me over the phone to take any of her clothes that I wouldn't wear myself to the charity shop. Unfortunately, my fashion taste was infinitely more conservative than hers, so I had two big sack loads to unleash on the nearest Oxfam.

'To be frank, babe, I can't even remember any of this crap,' she had said, when I paraded a few items in front of her, *Generation Game*-style, over Skype one evening. 'Anyway, it's liberating starting afresh – think of all the shopping opportunities because you *need* a new bag or jacket.' It was a valuable point.

This morning, I might have known Nora would be the harshest when it came to identifying the chintz I should chuck. There was something distinctly Simon Cowell about her verdict.

The owl footstool: 'Horrible!'

The astrology chart: 'No, no! Chuck!'

The two faded crochet cushions: 'Nasty!'

She made her commands with glee, pointing and giggling at each treasured belonging I held up. A five-year-old was giving me a complex.

'This is like *Britain's Got Talent*, only more *Amber's Got Rubbish*!' Rob finally joined Nora on the sofa as they both burst into laughter, then pretended to press a buzzer, making a farting sound each time they disapproved of an item I was debating whether to keep or chuck; they seemed to think I should get rid of the lot.

Later, after Lucy had returned for Nora, we loaded all my junk into a minicab and deposited it at the charity shop. On balance, Vicky was right – lightening the load felt good.

I might have no fixed abode, minimal belongings and no job after next week, but I had a hot boyfriend and a one-way ticket to New York. *OMFG!*

CHAPTER FIVE

Dad insisted on driving us to the airport, and for the whole journey I was consumed with teenage angst. I wanted to begin this adventure with Rob like an adult – I was an adult! – on the Heathrow Express, or in an Uber, not being chaperoned by my dad, who ran through a checklist of all the things he hoped I'd remembered to pack. It was making me nervous, as well as stroppy.

'...Yes, Dad, I definitely have my driving licence, even though everyone gets cabs or the subway in New York...'

'... Yes, I have two plug adaptors...'

'... No, I didn't get DVT socks, but they'll have some at Boots in the airport. I'm not exactly in the high-risk category, anyway...'

'...You already asked if I have my passport.'

He even asked Rob if he had his passport.

My eyes were rolling around my sockets; I thought they might never straighten up.

Rob kept playfully nudging my leg, aware of how increasingly wound up I was becoming. The only saving grace was that we were on the nine-forty flight, so we beat rush hour and our journey to Heathrow Terminal 5 was fast. Still, I couldn't get out of the car quick enough.

'You're so funny sometimes,' Rob said as we loaded my extensive luggage onto a trolley and Dad hooted as he drove off. 'Now, are you absolutely certain you've got your passport?'

'Yes, I frickin' have… don't you start!' I squealed, in mock annoyance. 'Does Dad really think I'm that much of an idiot?'

'He just loves you,' he said, looking amused. 'I thought it was kind of sweet that he was concerned for me, too.'

'I know he does and I know I'm lucky to have him.' I softened. References like that reminded me that Rob didn't have the luxury of a father figure. 'But I'm quite looking forward to breaking away from all that. Anyway, is it too early for a drink?'

Once through security, we treated ourselves to a big breakfast and Buck's Fizz. I breathed a sigh as we chinked glasses.

'Wow! I can't really believe we're actually here, doing this, can you?' Rob said, reading my mind.

'Nope! It feels like a mad dream. But do you realise that, at this moment, we are technically homeless?'

He laughed anxiously. 'It's a scary thought. But we're not going to be on the street, we're just going to be tourists for a few days until we find an apartment.'

'An apartment,' I repeated. It sounded so dreamy.

With an hour to kill before boarding, we wandered around Duty Free and spent ten minutes trying on sunglasses. Then I fell in love with the most beautiful pair of Pradas, so I bought them on a whim. I'd rarely spent so much money on one item – an item I didn't even know I wanted eleven minutes before – but they had cute little flicked-up corners. *They called to me, in that voice only amazing sunglasses have.*

'I need to look the part if I have a hope of getting some freelance styling work,' I said, justifying the expense to Rob, as one eye wandered over to the Jo Malone counter. Designer sunglasses weren't exactly factored into our tight budget for the next few months. 'I'll see them as an early treat to myself, bought with an advance from my first pay packet.'

'Whatever you say...' Rob was already heading in the direction of Dixons.

Milling around the shopping concourse, we bumped into Amy, a colleague of Rob's from the production company, 20Twenty, who was also relocating for the show. Wearing skinny white jeans, a white T-shirt and long white cardigan, she looked like an advert for the White Company, immediately identifiable as one of those girls who doesn't have to try too hard to look stylish.

'*Rob!*' she shouted, genuinely pleased to have spotted us.

'Hey, Amy, this is my girlfriend, Amber. Amber, Amy. Amy's my AP on the show. She works twice as hard as anyone.'

'Well, I'm not sure about that,' Amy replied, looking down at her ballet pumps.

I looked at my sandals and freshly pedicured toes. I'd been worrying about my choice of footwear all the way to the airport and had almost convinced myself I needed to stop by Kurt Geiger for a new pair of shoes. *Money spent in the airport doesn't really come out of your bank account, right?*

'I didn't realise you were moving out as well,' she said, turning her attention to me. This time I noticed how pretty she was; she had the kind of skin that tans easily, freckles dotted across her face even though it was mid-winter, and beachy waves in her chestnut hair. I wondered what an AP actually did. 'Do you work in TV, too?'

'No, no… I'm hoping to get some freelance styling work when we're out there. I work in fashion.'

'Cool!' She scanned my outfit, clocking my Longchamp bag and Cos jersey dress with renewed interest now she knew my line of work.

'I'm hoping the weather stays warm when we arrive, too,' she said, her examination of my clothes coming to rest on my gladiators and red toenails.

True, I do look more like I'm going on holiday to Marbella than moving to New York, but she'll soon see when we step off the plane in bright sunshine and I put on my new designer sunnies.

After lunch on the flight, Rob nodded off next to me. I lifted the plastic shutter on the aircraft window and stared out at the expansive stretch of bright blue nothingness above the clouds. The sun was burning brightly; it looked so serene and beautiful, but also kind of blank, transitional. Like the Etch-A-Sketch drawing of my life was being wiped clean. In just a few hours, we would be landing somewhere else, in an alien city, full of people I didn't know and places I was yet to discover. I would have to find a purpose there; I didn't want to be Rob's hanger-on. *I hope I can do it.* I felt a wave of anxiety rush through me and I shivered. The thin aeroplane blanket was doing nothing for my icy-cold legs and feet. *I knew I should have worn jeans.* I looked across at my sleeping boyfriend. My love, Robert Walker, so handsome, kind and strong. *How did I, Amber Green, manage to bag such a gorgeous, loving, successful bloke? But what if New York changes him in some way? Or changes me? What if living together doesn't work out, or he meets someone else?* We were embarking on so many firsts together. My heart was beating fast. My old flat, my family, friends, old job, they already seemed so far away, but they were more than just far away – right now, they were gone for the foreseeable future. I was taking a huge leap of faith, jumping into a new life for the sake of this man.

I looked upwards to the grey plastic ceiling and the space from where the oxygen masks that you pray you'll never have to see would pop down in an emergency. I closed my eyes and said a little silent prayer. After all, I was probably physically closer to God than I'd ever be in this life; it was worth a punt. *Please let this trip work out, please, dear God. Please make it amazing and life affirming and everything I want it to be. Please.*

The thought of it not working out and me having to come home alone was too awful to contemplate.

An air hostess came by, handing out water, breaking me away from my morbid thoughts. I resisted the temptation to ask her for a double vodka. In need of clearing my head and warming up a bit, I decided to go for a little wander down the plane. I bumped into Amy in a queue by the loo.

Unlike me, she had changed into her flight clothes, and was now a vision in dove grey, with soft leggings, a matching sweatshirt and cosy cable-knit socks. *One day I'll be as organised as that.*

'How's it going?' she asked.

'Good flight so far,' I replied, 'though I'm crap at sleeping on planes. Rob dropped off straight away, but I can never do that. Can you?'

'I normally take a pill,' she responded. 'But with a daytime flight it's hardly worth it. I'd rather get a good night the other end.'

'Have you got your accommodation sorted?' I asked.

'Yeah, I'm staying with my friend Kate for the first couple of weeks and then we're moving into a place together – she's got some leads. I'm hoping that this job will lead to something full-time out there and then I want to apply for a Green Card.'

'Sounds like you've got it all worked out.'

'It's always been my dream to live in New York, let alone be an AP for a cool TV show out there. I'm so excited it's finally happening. What about you?'

'Yes, similar,' I said, trying to sound as though I wasn't plagued with anxiety. 'So will you be busy as Rob's PA?' I asked. 'I mean, I know it's a crazy hectic job…'

She chuckled. 'I'm not his PA, Amber, I'm his Assistant Producer. Yeah, it's going to be manic, but we'll basically be inseparable – we'll get through it.' She smiled, showing perfectly straight, white teeth. Her presence made even the toilet area of a Boeing 747 look attractive.

'Right.' I said, my body turning rigid as I processed what this pretty girl might be doing with my boyfriend five days a week for the next three months.

'Anyway, catch you on the other side.' She pushed open the toilet door.

Rather than let insecurities take over, I decided to take a leaf out of Amy's book and change my mental attitude before it became a self-fulfilling prophecy. *I'm moving to New York. With my hot boyfriend. It's a dream come true and it will be brilliant, in every way. It has to be.*

Rob stirred as I returned to my seat, not very deftly stepping over his legs.

'Okay?' he muttered sleepily.

'All fine,' I replied, before settling back down and letting my head flop onto his shoulder. His familiar scent consumed me for a moment.

We'll be fine. I love you so much.

Within two minutes of exiting Arrivals, I had my first reality check: the weather in New York does not do what the forecast says. BBC Weather said it was unseasonably warm and sunny when I was packing and now it was cold and raining; in fact, sleet was falling in diagonal sheets from the sky. The cute blue jersey dress worn with bare legs and sandals I had spent weeks planning for this very moment were wildly inappropriate. I wished I'd shoved a pair of leggings in my bag. Fat lot of use my new Pradas were, too – there was no sign of sunshine. Rob pulled a sweater out of his rucksack and was putting it on over his white T-shirt. Amy looked cosy in her skinny white jeans and grey cashmere jumper as she was met by her friend. I noticed Rob watch her disappear and scowled at him for not passing on the weather memo to me. *Why didn't he tell me he was packing a sweater? Isn't that what couples are supposed to do?*

He must have read my mind, or the scowl was very obvious, because he began reversing out of his sweater and offered it to me. I wasn't too proud to accept.

The fact that my legs were turning blue was soon forgotten when I finally took note of our surroundings outside the terminal – a glorious line of iconic New York taxis stood in view. *My shiny, yellow-brick road to a new beginning.* We gave our driver the hotel address and were soon speeding up the freeway towards Manhattan. Real-life New Yorkers were at the wheels of their cars all around us, probably swearing and cursing the traffic like Robert De Niro in *Taxi Driver*, salt-beef bagels, half eaten on their laps. I was buzzing, and so was Rob. I kept straining to see through the big plastic divider between the driver and us for my first glimpse of the famous New York skyline.

Finally, as we tipped over a hill, there it was: the shape of Manhattan, a vista so familiar yet thrillingly new to me. Giant grey buildings reached into the sky – tall, proud, imposing – it was a film set come to life.

'There's the Empire State,' Rob pointed out as the skyscrapers drew closer. And then we were among them, a jungle of brownstone, red-stone, bricks and concrete. Signs to Downtown, Crosstown, Uptown hung across the road.

'Which town are we, then?' I nudged Rob, who was equally engrossed in the passing scenery.

'I guess Downtown to start with,' he responded, not taking his eyes off the streets whizzing past, 'but, after that, who knows? We'll have to see where we fancy.'

We passed corner taverns, diners, indoor markets; we sped across wide main roads and down little cross streets. We saw the fronts of brownstone houses with black metal railings and steps leading up to the porches; it was all so intoxicating. I wondered if any of these places flashing past the taxi window would soon become our regular haunts. If one of these neighbourhoods would be *our* 'hood.

The rain had stopped now and the sun was coming through. I fumbled around in my bag for my new shades and put them on, feeling like a movie star. *I love this city already.*

The taxi continued past Park Avenue, Madison Avenue, Madison Square Garden – *I recognise the names!* Crowded pavements in every direction packed with people in trainers, high heels, sandals, walking with purpose. I spied a giant Coach store and made a mental note to remember its exact location, then an even bigger Urban Outfitters, Victoria's Secret, Sephora – and there was Bloomingdales! So many cool shops I couldn't wait to discover for myself. *I'm really going to need to find a job fast if I'm going to survive the shopping potential in this city.*

Finally, we pulled up outside the Best Western, our home for the next five nights at least. It wasn't exactly the flashy W Hotel, where I'd spent so much time kitting out celebrities with Mona in LA, but it was the most the production budget could stretch to, until we found a more affordable apartment. But the location was perfect, in the Bowery, a stone's throw from Downtown's most fashionable neighbourhoods.

Within twenty-four hours of landing and three appointments with real-estate agents, it became blindingly obvious that Rob and I would not find our dream apartment in this salubrious part of Manhattan, where it cost approximately ten times our monthly budget for a space more suitable to house Pinky. Instead, we were packed off with some numbers for realtors in Bushwick, on the other side of the Brooklyn Bridge.

That afternoon, we decided to take a break from apartment hunting and be tourists for the day. We wandered through SoHo, with its upscale boutiques and chain stores, big imposing buildings with cast-iron façades and tall windows, and into Greenwich Village with its more bohemian feel, trees on streets, and cafés with tables spilling onto the pavement. Then we headed west, on a mission to visit the Whitney Art Museum. The queue was already at least a block down the street when we got there, but we decided to join it anyway. *At the very least, Mum and Dad will be impressed I've taken in some culture during my first days here.* The wind blowing off the Hudson made me shiver, but this time I was more prepared and took a scarf out of my bag and wrapped it around my neck. It was a vintage Cavalli, something I had picked up in a vintage store in LA on one of my scouting trips with Mona. Rob went to fetch us a coffee while we waited.

An older man standing in front of me in the queue turned around.

'New in town?' he said. He had a soft French accent with an American lilt.

'Is it that obvious?' I smiled, shuffling on the spot and burying my hands into my biker-jacket pockets to keep warm.

'Your footwear gave it away, even before I heard your English accent,' he replied. He had heavy lines around his eyes; it almost looked like he was wearing eyeliner. I placed him in his late fifties. I looked down at my trusty gladiators. I was determined the March sun was going to come out again today, as it had yesterday.

'Yes, optimistic, I guess. Anyway, the forecast says it will get warmer.'

'First rule about New York – never trust the forecast,' he said, smiling, confirming the lesson I should have learned yesterday. 'First time at the Whitney?'

'Yes. You?'

He chuckled. '*Mais, non*, I've been coming almost once a week since it opened. It inspires me. Not just the artwork inside, the building itself is a work of art, designed by Renzo Piano – are you familiar with him?' I shook my head. '*Pas de problème*. The views are spectacular, and I love the sense of space on each floor. It gives me a chance to think creatively.' He stopped, a wistful look across his face, as if momentarily lost in thought.

'Surely you should be able to jump this queue by now then?' I remarked.

'I don't want to – this line is all part of my experience,' he replied. 'I use the time to people watch.'

'Watch people in inappropriate shoes, like me?' I asked, aware that my toes were cold.

He laughed. 'Funny you say that. You have nice feet.' I smiled awkwardly. 'I love shoes, but also coats, dresses, jewellery – all forms of adornment. Clothes are never boring to me. They say so much about a personality – much more than the wearer realises.' He was eyeing my feet again, and then his eyes slowly worked up my skinny jeans to my jacket and scarf, finally resting when they met mine. It made me feel uncomfortable. *Oh great, he's a foot pervert. I've read about people like him. He'll be fantasising about sucking my big toe as we speak. Where are you Rob?* I looked over my shoulder; the queue had grown some three times in the twenty minutes we'd been standing here. I shuffled on the spot, uncomfortable and self-conscious. The wind from the river was really whipping against us now and I pulled my scarf further around my chin, checking to ensure I wasn't showing the slightest patch of bare skin between it and my cleavage. You couldn't be too careful, even in the queue for a museum.

Thankfully, the man had turned around again. I noticed his slightly greying dark hair was tied in a small knot at the back. My eyes fell to the floor to check out his shoes, as I idly wondered what kind of footwear a shoe pervert wears himself. His were black, Cuban-style pixie boots, with a thin silver edging around a lifted heel, giving the impression he was at least an inch and a half taller than he really was. They were quite a style statement for a man of his age.

At last, Rob returned, clutching two coffees.

'Sorry, got caught up chatting to the man at the coffee stall. Everyone's so friendly in New York,' he gushed, his face flushed with enthusiasm. 'There's a great food market near here, apparently – we should eat there afterwards.'

The foot-fetish man turned around again when Rob spoke.

'Chelsea Food Market, just down the road,' he informed us. 'They do a fantastic burrito in Takumi Taco – check it out – Japanese-style; sounds kind of odd, but it works.'

'Oh, cheers, mate.' Rob smiled, always so open and happy to talk to complete strangers. I gave him a nudge, and tried to tell him telepathically that we shouldn't engage with the foot nut. He was probably having strange thoughts about what lay beneath Rob's pair of Adidas.

Thankfully, the queue began to move. As we exited the revolving doors inside the museum, the man pressed a card into my hand.

'Nice talking to you, lady. If you need a guided tour of the city any time, call me. I know all the best shoe stores in New York. *Au revoir.*' He winked and he was gone, swept into a giant lift and whisked up to the top of the impressive building.

'Let's start on ground,' I said to Rob, stuffing the card into my pocket, glad the man was off my case.

The sun was beginning its descent as we finished at the Whitney, and it cast a stunning orange glow across the buildings. Luckily, the place was big enough for us not to bump into the foot perv again, though Rob just laughed when I told him my suspicions.

'New York is not like London, you know,' he said.

'Everyone talks to everyone here. It doesn't mean a man is a pervert, just because he gives you a compliment to pass some time in a queue. Besides, you do have nice feet.'

'But the way he was staring at them, I felt his eyes dissect me,' I protested.

Buoyed by the exhibits we had seen, not to mention the additional cups of coffee which helped fight the jet lag, we weren't ready to return to the hotel yet. We walked two blocks north and found the Chelsea Food Market straight away, soon becoming lost in a delicious rabbit warren of food stalls. We found the Japanese taco stall and then shared a chocolate crêpe, before stopping for a beer at a local tavern. It was getting on for nine o'clock and we were ready for bed as we began wandering back towards the Bowery. On a SoHo street corner, a saxophonist was playing soft jazz to a backing track. We stopped to join the circle of appreciation forming around him. Rob wound an arm around my waist.

'I'm so glad we're here together,' he whispered into my ear. I turned to look at him, I mean really look at him. His eyes were twinkling in the street light. 'Thank you for coming with me.'

'I'm so happy I did,' I replied firmly, lifting my lips towards his, a huge beam across my face.

'Come on, let's treat ourselves to a cab.'

CHAPTER SIX

The next morning, Monday, Rob headed uptown for his first production meeting at the Angel Wear offices, and I tried to make an appointment to see Dana LeRoy. True to her word, Poppy had given me her contact details and she obviously held some influence as Dana went from stand-offish to super-friendly the second I mentioned her name. I was over the moon when she said she could see me the same day. Apartment hunting would have to wait.

I turned the corner of Fourteenth Street and there I was, standing on the famous cobbles in the heart of the cool Meatpacking District. I gazed up at the red-brick Gothic building in front of me. All the buildings were so tall in Manhattan, even the ones that weren't supposed to be sky-scrapers. I scanned a panel of gun-metal-grey nameplates to confirm I was in the right place. They bore the names of about fifteen companies inside the building. Eventually, I located the one I was looking for – just one word: SHOOT.

Instead of taking the name at its word and bolting straight back to the hotel, I took a deep breath, gripped my iPad tightly and pressed the entry buzzer.

'Yeah?' said a brash American voice.

'Hi, it's Amber Green. I've got a meeting with Dana?'

'Come up, lift's broken,' the voice replied. *I'm glad my portfolio is online.*

Inside, the building was plain and cold. Another metal board on the right-hand side repeated the names of all the small businesses, this time with floor numbers next to them. SHOOT was on the eighth and top floor. *Lucky I'm not wearing heels.* It wasn't the kind of establishment I could imagine an A-list star like Jennifer Astley swanning into for a pre-premiere meeting with her stylist, but I supposed that was what plush hotel suites were for.

The gum-chewing girl on Reception looked like a model herself: her lank, dirty-blonde hair hung around her face, partly obscuring it, but I could tell that, with some good make-up and the right clothes, she'd come alive in front of a camera.

'Amber?'

'Yes, I have a meeting with Dana at eleven o'clock.'

'I know, we slotted you in. Take a seat, she'll be out.'

I sat on the red sofa opposite the reception desk and took a moment to look around me. The walls were crammed with framed photos of fashion shoots, and images of highly polished celebrities on the covers of magazines, including *American Vogue, Elle, Women's Health* and *Vanity Fair.* In less obvious spots, there were advertisements for cleaning products, vitamin drinks and diaper brands, starring white-toothed all-American models and blonde-haired babies.

Five minutes later, Dana appeared. She was a short, plump woman with lots of brown curly hair, a small smile, yet kind eyes.

'Amber, welcome.' She held out her hand and a chunky gold bracelet jangled on her wrist. 'We'll go to my office. How have you been settling in?' I followed her down a corridor with more photography either side of it. It certainly gave the impression of a busy, high-profile agency.

'Great, thanks. We did some sightseeing yesterday.'

'Where are you living?'

'Not sure yet, still looking – maybe Bushwick.'

She shuddered. 'Right. Watch out for the fat-cat landlords. You're best off getting somewhere through word of mouth or a small ad. There are notice boards in most coffee shops – you should check them out.'

'Thanks, we will.'

'How do you know Poppy?'

'I met her last year, when I was assisting Mona Armstrong in LA.' The look on her face turned into a grimace. The mention of Mona's name always seemed to have this effect on people in the industry. No surprises why. 'And then I bumped into her in London recently. I'm on a sabbatical out here.'

'Love that girl. Man, we've had some nights out.' She drifted off for a second.

'Are these all styled by your clients?' I was desperate to stop and look properly at the images decorating the walls.

'Of course,' she responded, as we reached a large office at the end. There was a desk in the middle, another red sofa and a coffee table in the corner. The vista beyond the floor-to-ceiling windows almost took my breath away – a patchwork of rooftops all around. Manhattan was so photogenic, I was dying to pull out my phone.

'It never grows old, even to me, a native New Yorker,' she said, acknowledging my goldfish impression. *Shauna would be so jealous if she saw this*.

Dana then sat on one side of the desk and gestured for me to sit, too. 'We could stare at it all day, but – your portfolio?'

'Of course,' I lifted my iPad on to the table and began talking her through my jobs. I felt a flush of pride as she moved through the images – when you looked at it all together, it was pretty impressive, even I had to admit. I was glad Rob had talked me into including my press cuttings from *Vogue* and national newspapers, which showed my work for Mona and the plaudits Jennifer Astley and Beau Belle had won for their gowns last year; plus, my photos of the windows at Smiths and Selfridges showed I was familiar with putting together looks from all the major designer brands.

'You may have some great A-list names on your résumé, but a stylist is only as good as her last job,' she commented finally. 'And you've been out of the game a while. Dressing dummies in a shop window? I'm afraid it isn't the same, sugar.' She shook her head resolutely. After a pause, she continued: 'Do you have a visa?' She held my gaze as my face flushed, revealing the answer.

'Just an ESTA at the moment. I was hoping…'

'You are aware that a stylist without a visa can't work in this city?' I shifted the weight on my seat. I knew this, but I was hoping there might be a way around it. 'I've got an idea for you, though,' she added.

I smiled. 'I'm willing to do whatever it takes.'

'You need to get out there – build relationships again, up your online presence. Do you have an Instagram or Snapchat account?' I nodded, sagely. 'Being successful in fashion is as much about who knows *you* – as who *you* know. Luckily, you've timed things well: as you know, New York Fashion Week is next week, and I'll be able to get you into a couple of shows. Maybe not seated, of course, but you'll get the atmosphere and have a chance to mingle. But from there, you're on your own. Network, network, network! Make friends, post, blog, pin… anything to demand attention – this city doesn't work for shy little British mice; you need to be the lion, Amber. You need to make yourself heard.'

Be the lion. Jesus, I've never had to be a lion before. I smiled nervously, faintly relieved that she didn't actually ask me to roar.

'So, um, I guess, no paid work until the visa comes through?' I wanted to clarify the situation.

'No, sugar. But once we're good with the visa, you're looking at five hundred to one thousand dollars a day. On a good day. That's as the lead stylist. Plus, a few expenses for calling in and returns: bikes, taxis and stuff.' I felt my shoulders relax again. *I'll be rolling in it! The Prada sunglasses will be paid off in just one day of work.*

'Fine, that's great,' I said, cheerily.

She wagged her finger at me. 'Hold up, sweet cheeks! Of course, *you* won't be on that level; you're more likely to get assisting jobs, and for that you're looking at one hundred dollars a day, maximum. No expenses.' I mentally did the sums. *That's little more than £50 a day. A work-experience rate.* She paused to take in my crestfallen face, but I wasn't going to give it to her.

'Great! When will we know about the shows?'

And that was it: just one meeting and my O-1 visa application was on the way to being processed and, all going well, I was to be a stylist – okay, assistant stylist, on a minimum wage – but for SHOOT agency, NYC, US of A. *Yee-hah!*

Dana was confident she'd have me paid jobs before long and, meanwhile, I could keep myself busy with any unpaid work she could put my way. 'And then there is always tons of catalogue work,' she said, rolling her eyes. I didn't care, it was perfect and meant I wouldn't be dependent on Rob the whole time I was out here – not just in terms of money, but time. I resisted the urge to high five the moody model on Reception, as I skipped out of the SHOOT offices and back to the subway, calling Rob on my way.

Back at the hotel, I opened my Instagram page. Thirty posts, fifty-three followers. Dismal. Plus, the last time I'd posted anything was over two months ago: a photo of Mum's Christmas cake. Delicious though it was, it wasn't going to set the fashion world alight. Fashion people don't eat cake; most of them think you get fat just by looking at it. I decided to spend the afternoon re-branding my online profile. First job: start a new Instagram account. Potential bios:

Amber Green – @NewYorkStylist (*not strictly true – yet*)

Amber Green – @BritGirlInNewYork (*not fashiony enough*)

Amber Green – @IHeartClothes (*cheesy*)

After a desperate call to Instagram queen, Shauna, I finally settled on:

Amber Green – @BritStylistTakingManhattan

I added a cute Union Jack emoticon at one end, the Stars and Stripes at the other.

'So did you get anywhere with the realtors?' Rob asked when he arrived back at our room after work that evening.

'Not exactly,' I said, from my position hunched over my iPad, propped up by five pillows on the bed. 'But I have had a great day work wise.'

He seemed buzzing, too: 'Tell me about it in a minute, because, I'm actually glad you didn't do any house-hunting…' He dangled a bunch of keys in front of my face.

'Whose keys are those?' I asked, confused.

'They're *our* door keys!' he said, beaming. 'Talk about piece of luck. After the first production meeting this morning, one of the Americans on the show happened to ask if anyone was looking to rent, because his mate had a short-term sublet he needed to get rid of quickly, in – *wait for it* – not Bushwick, or anywhere on the wrong side of Brooklyn, but right in the middle of everything in Willamsburg! I went to look at it quickly on my way home, and it's perfect. I mean, it's small – it's pretty much a sardine tin – and it needs a bit of a clean, but the rent is capped, so it's a steal and it's got character. I think you'll like it.'

'My clever boyfriend!' I leapt off the bed and threw my arms around his neck, planting a big kiss on his lips. 'When can we move in?'

'The current tenant is moving out on Saturday and then it's ours. He gave me his spare keys so I can take you over to size it up tomorrow. It'll be barely furnished, so we'll need to get a few things, but that shouldn't be hard to do cheaply.'

And there was my first Instagram upload – a photo of our new door keys; Lark filter; caption: 'Unlocking the door to my new life #Fashion #NYC #London #Williamsburg #Movingin'

We capped off our Monday with a Thai meal in a local BYO restaurant as we filled each other in on the rest of our respective pretty perfect first day as New Yorkers, rather than just tourists.

The next morning, we got off the subway at Bedford Avenue. Williamsburg felt like a whole new world compared with the area our hotel was in on the other side of the Hudson. The buildings were smaller here, less intimidating; many were painted sandy colours with wooden slatted façades. As we headed down Bedford Avenue, we passed vintage furniture shops with chairs, lamps, mirrors and colourful oil paintings stacked up outside, eyebrow and nail bars, liquor stores and a couple of tattoo parlours. Many of the people we passed on the street looked like hipsters with well-groomed ironic moustaches, or bohemian musicians who had just rolled out of bed, or girls dressed in parkas with satchels slung across them and spectacles that surely didn't require a prescription. As we turned the corner onto Sixth Street, I felt pleasantly optimistic about what we were going to find.

Rob and I had barely spoken as we took in our new neighbourhood, trying not to gawp like the obvious new kids on the block as we followed his iPhone on the ten-minute stroll from the subway, sucking it all up to discuss later on. A few houses up the street, he began to slow the pace.

'Now, I don't want you to have too high hopes for the apartment,' he said, touching my arm, as he almost reached a standstill.

I nodded, but the truth was it was too late. I hadn't slept well last night, my mind racing with thoughts of our new love nest. In my head it was a cross between Carrie Bradshaw's compact Manhattan apartment and Monica's kitchen in *Friends* – bijoux but cute, the perfect place for rustling up bacon-and-maple-syrup breakfasts for cosy weekend brunches with new friends.

At last we stopped outside 215N Sixth Street. The pink wooden façade looked a little tired in places, but it was quaint. Rob stepped up to the front door.

'Most of the numbers have been rubbed off,' he said, turning over his shoulder.

'Following years of takeaway deliveries…' I replied, looking at the almost overflowing garbage bins on the pavement just outside. 'Someone obviously likes pizza.'

Within five seconds of walking through the door, my dreams were shattered.

Even Rob's 'sardine tin' description was generous. The place consisted of a small kitchen-diner with a stove with only two gas rings on it, and then a doorway led into a bedroom with just enough space to move around the double bed, and an unloved chest of drawers stood lopsided in a little alcove that I guessed was probably damp. Off the bedroom was a tiny bathroom with a shower attachment over a grubby bath and toilet that I knew I wouldn't be sitting on until it had been disinfected at least three times.

'It's compact, for sure,' Rob said, turning on the hot tap in the kitchen. We both held our breath as it spluttered a little, but then water began to come out and, after a few seconds, it got hot. 'That's something.'

'All mod cons,' I said, sighing, unconvinced that much else was working properly in this place.

Taking in my deflated expression, Rob put an arm around me. 'It's not so bad.' *For a person who was used to living in a pigsty, it probably wasn't.*

I snorted. 'If you walk around with your eyes closed. I'll dip into my own savings to pay for some proper cleaners before we move in. No arguments.'

'Fair enough, but then I think we can work some magic on it. I mean, what more do we need, really? We're going to be at work or out most of the time.'

'Well, I guess a *little* more space would have been nice, maybe an oven so we could cook something other than soup, just occasionally, and— *urgh!*' I instantly regretted opening the microwave. 'But, I know we'll save money living here.' My voice faltered: 'Have… have you actually paid the deposit?' I was on the verge of tears as Rob explained how he'd already put down our non-returnable deposit, because some others had shown an interest in it too, this being one of the coolest addresses in Brooklyn, and he didn't want us to miss out.

'It's just not the kind of place I'd imagined us making our first home together, you know?' I said.

He squeezed me tightly. 'I know, me neither, but what is it Kirstie and Phil say – "location, location, location"? Seriously, this couldn't be a better address and, with your sense of style, we'll make the best of it. Did you see all those vintage furniture shops we passed on the way from the subway? We'll check them out tomorrow and we'll hit the flea market on Saturday. It'll be fun.'

'After the cleaners have been?'

'After the cleaners.' He was doing the head-holding thing again, always picking the right moment to take my face in his hands, look at me straight on and tell me with his eyes that whatever it was, was going to be okay.

'At least we haven't seen a cockroach yet.' I half smiled, my eyes wandering around the tiny living area and spotting an ominous brown patch on one of the walls.

'Well, that's something.'

Vowing to turn our sardine tin into a tiny palace by way of some bleach and elbow grease, we got the subway back to Manhattan.

As the doors closed and the train left the station, the sound of some heavy rap blared out of a portable ghetto blaster. I gripped my purse in my pocket; I'd heard about muggings on downtown trains.

'Ladies and gentlemen, sit back, relax, it's show time!' boomed a voice in the centre of the carriage. I slunk back in my seat and averted my eyes, but Rob did the opposite; he leaned forwards to get a better look as a breakdancer began skilfully swan-diving down the centre of the carriage floor in front of us. Then he jumped up and swung between the ceiling rails, spinning 360 degrees through his arms. Some of the passengers on the train burst into applause, and others barely looked up from their reading material. Then another dancer jumped forwards, clinging onto a vertical railing and twisting his body around it as he hugged his way down, before leaping onto the next railing – like a flying monkey – and doing the same, until he had worked his way down the carriage from pillar to pillar. A few people got to their feet around the edges, clapping them on. Forget *Britain's Got Talent*, I'd never seen anything so cool and I was starting to shed my inner Londoner – who would ordinarily be timidly peeping over a copy of *Metro*, looking for an exit route – and clapped along too.

'How wicked is this?' Rob nudged me, not taking his eyes off a third dancer who was walking through the carriage on his hands, legs bouncing in time to the beat, and then finished off his routine by flipping off his friends with a flourish of perfectly choreographed backward somersaults. *Without breaking anyone's toes! I wonder if my insurance would cover that, Dad.* Finally, as we sensed we must be nearing the next stop, all three began spinning on their heads, gliding with ease through at least fifteen rotations, before jumping back onto their feet and holding their headscarves in their hands for a quick whip-round from their audience. Some of our carriage mates coughed up a few coins, while others just sat there coolly, hands in pockets, as if this happened every time they took the L train to work.

'Only in Brooklyn,' a guy next to me commented, as he

seemingly reluctantly tossed a five-dollar bill into a sweaty headscarf. I tipped all the change I had in my purse into the dancer's hands and swiped a card from a fan poking out of his top pocket.

Seconds later the train came to a halt, and one of them picked up the ghetto blaster and they were gone, probably darting into the next carriage to entertain all over again.

Rob and I were buzzing.

'So we might be moving into a shoebox—'

'Make that a children's shoebox,' I interjected.

'Okay, a shoebox for a millipede – whatever you want to call it – but I really don't care, because I'll be living there with you and I couldn't love you – or this city any more right now,' he said, sighing. 'You'd never get that in London.'

I had to agree. 'And we'll make our little millipede box the cosiest home ever. It's going to be great. And you're clever for sorting it out. I love you too.'

The next day, after cleaners had made the place smell of lemon disinfectant, rather than someone else's toilet, and a year's worth of burnt cheese had been scrapped off the microwave, we took a taxi across town with our suitcases of belongings and moved in.

On our first night in the flat, we were woken up listening to our next-door neighbours having very loud sex. She was a screamer, he a shouter. We might not have known their names before, but we certainly did now: *Max and Tina*. In between the thumps on the wall and the shouts, any chance we had of sleeping was put to an end by the fact we had so far failed to notice that we lived opposite a fire station. A whirring siren sound went off a couple of times just in the hour that we were trying to get to sleep.

On the second night, Max and Tina held a dinner party with some equally shouty friends. We opened another bottle of beer each and pretended it wasn't as loud as it was, already feeling like an old married couple in our late twenties. Then we turned up our own music and tried to have sex on the sofa, but the noise from next door was too distracting. So we went out and got drunk on tequila and more beer at our new local, passing out back home, some time after the dinner party had finished.

On the third night, we wore earplugs and managed to sleep reasonably well, save for the strobing orange light from the streetlamp positioned directly outside our bedroom window and the occasional siren from the fire station.

'Blackout blinds,' Rob muttered woozily.

But, to be honest, when the light buzzed on for long enough for me to admire my boyfriend's matinée idol profile on the pillow next to me, I didn't really mind. And I knew I'd get used to the sirens.

There was something kind of pretty about the way the light hit our bed and bounced off the 1970s I HEART NEW YORK print we found in a thrift store earlier that day and which now hung on our bedroom wall, covering the brown marks. The only picture to grace our walls so far.

In the next blast of orange, I captured the image and uploaded it to Instagram; Rise filter; caption: 'Goodnight Williamsburg #NYC #stylist #newhome'

CHAPTER SEVEN

Dana was true to her word and the following afternoon my new American cell phone rang with an unpaid rush job putting together a suitcase of cool looks for a 'hot, young, model-stroke-actress' desperate to make her fashion mark at the boho lover's festival of music festivals, Coachella.

'None of my girls has a free day this week, so I'm offering this opportunity to you, sugar,' she drawled into the phone. 'This will help get you back in the game while we're waiting for your visa.'

'Sounds great!' I enthused. Thankfully, an inordinate amount of time spent scrolling through the Instagram feeds of the likes of Kendall Jenner and Poppy Delevingne had given me an insight into Coachella festival chic – and it was a million miles away from the mud-soaked Hunter-welly, waterproof-poncho practicalities of Glastonbury.

Coachella was the annual fash-pack pilgrimage to the Californian desert. It involved rock music, hot boys, even hotter weather and lashings of suede fringing, frayed denim, cropped tops, crochet, gladiators and flower garlands. The biggest decision for the rich kids in attendance was whether to go kaftan or cut-offs.

'Who's the celebrity?'

'Liv Ramone – you might remember her name. She was a big shot in the late noughties, but lost her way a bit. Well, now she's coming back with a bang. If you get this right, you could have a regular client,' Dana said while briefing me. 'I'll bet most of her wardrobe is funded by the Bank of Mum and Dad – her flip-flops have a price tag of three hundred dollars – but she doesn't have a clue how to put it all together. Liv's manager says she's really into accessories at the moment, so be sure to pull plenty of fun jewellery too. Good luck!'

Liv's arrival was promising. She bounded over to me like an excitable puppy. She had incredible long, red, wavy hair, lithe limbs, big grey eyes and a sparkling smile – all qualities a stylist falls in love with at first sight. Plus, she had an immediately endearing demeanour, which was unusual for a former child star, who – so Dana had warned – were usually the worst divas of all. When she came closer she smelt of strong musky perfume, hairspray, and one too many cigarettes. When she opened her mouth, you could see the gum. She arrived at Milk Studios, where Dana had given me a corner to work from, piggybacking another photo-shoot due to start later that day. Her manager was a large, puff-chested man called Mickey, who had whiter-than-white teeth and obviously dyed-black hair.

'I'm *so* glad to meet you, Amber!' She launched at me, arms open, embracing me with a hug so big you'd think we were long-lost relatives. 'Dana told me you used to assist

Mona Armstrong.' I smiled in acknowledgement. 'I mean, *wow!*'

'Even a guy like me has heard of Mona,' Mickey added, 'Liv's brought you a gift.' He gestured to the neat little pink bag she was holding and she handed it over, presenting it alongside another hug; this time the hug went on a little longer than was strictly necessary. The gift made me instantly suspicious.

'That's so sweet of you!' I gushed, mustering up all the American enthusiasm I could. Inside the bag was a white square box, heavy with the weight of its contents. I looked at the sleeve – it was a luxury candle; the scent matched the heady perfume Liv was wearing and was described on the packaging as 'Sensual Sunset'. On it was a black-and-white photographic image of Liv lying seductively – *Oh God, she's naked* – on a shag-pile rug in front of a fake-looking sunset. Because of her model-perfect proportions and attention-grabbing hair, it was a gnat's whisker on the passable side of soft porn.

'The candle line comes out next month,' Mickey informed me. 'I took care of the production and styling, in case you were wondering.' He winked, sleazily. 'It's the first step in launching Liv's new lifestyle range. The candles are calming as well as deeply erotic; they help with anxiety too. Liv has ten burning away at one time in her house. The calming effect is better than any drug. Let's light it while we work, yeah?' Just the thought of ten candles releasing that overpowering scent was enough to give me a migraine. *And, ah yes, the drugs.* Following some online research, I had discovered that, unfortunately, Liv did a little too much Liv-ing during her late teen years when she shot to fame with the lead role in a hit film about an off-the-rails teenager on the run from her parents. It was a case of reality mimicking fiction, because Liv too left her nice, wealthy, suburban roots and moved in with a bunch of new friends in a hip enclave of LA. For a few years she ran with a fast-paced, heavy partying crowd, who thought nothing of staying up for three days in a row, cleaning out hotel minibars, setting up a pharmaceutical counter as good as any private hospital, getting naked on balconies and waking up in bed with strangers – all on what they considered a 'little bender'.

Throw in a drink-driving rap, an ill-fated twenty-one-day marriage to a guy she met and married within twenty-four hours in Las Vegas, and numerous community-service appointments, and you could see how she earned a rep for being a wild child. Three stints at top rehab centres and, five years later, at the age of twenty-four, she was a cleaned-up act, ready to unleash the new Liv on the American public.

Mickey took a lighter from his pocket and lit the candle.

'Get your nose into that,' he said, holding it in front of my face as though it contained a stash of cocaine. A strong, heady, musky scent much stronger than Liv's perfume wafted out.

'Oh, yeah, got it – that's… *unmistakable*,' I uttered, before sneezing uncontrollably for a few seconds.

'I'm so happy you love it!' Liv screeched, lunging at me for the third time in a matter of minutes. She then turned to high five Mickey and back to high five me. I raised a limp hand to hers, before sneezing again.

Candle lit, lights dimmed (by Mickey, not me – I could barely make out the clothes) and, sneezing subsided, I showed her to a rail of seventies flared jeans. Thankfully, Dana had introduced me to a friend of hers – Patti Rose, owner of Rose's Fashion Emporium, the biggest fashion rental house in New York – and she'd kindly put me on the books of 'trusted lenders' as a favour to Dana, in advance of my getting any paid work. It was already becoming obvious that Dana had a lot of industry influence.

'Anyone who D recommends, I look after,' Patti had said. 'She's evidently got high hopes for you, girl.' *There was pressure.* But it meant I was able to pick some New Season designer wear for Liv as well as vintage pieces from the extensive collection in Patti's warehouse.

'The seventies is a huge trend this season,' I began to explain to Liv, grateful I knew the entire summer collections of Chloé, Moschino and Coach by heart, thanks to our forward planning for the windows at Selfridges. 'Hudson, Acne and Seven all have great choices too. You could go super pale, or dark denim – either works. Team with a clog, if you want a lift, and a suede-fringed waistcoat, and you'll rule the social media coverage, I promise.'

Liv ran her finger down the rail of clothes, as if she was lightly strumming a guitar. Every now and again, she seemed to sort of drift off somewhere else and I wondered what she was thinking.

I moved on to the vintage rail – perhaps some one-off pieces would get her more excited. So far her expression gave nothing away. 'An original seventies jumpsuit, this would

look great, and this Biba crochet top is divine. I fell in love
with this bubble-chain belt – it would make a really cool look
on you,' I raved. 'Or if you want to go more ethereal, how
about this stunning embroidered kaftan? It was once worn by
Joni Mitchell for a *Vogue* shoot. And I brought you a whole
selection of lace-up ghillie sandals – they're the cutest things.'

Still little reaction from Liv, who was swaying gently to
the folk music Mickey had put on.

'So, do you want to try anything?' I pressed her, aware
that we only had another hour or so in this studio before the
shoot would begin and we had to be gone.

'What about the accessories? Liv's more of an accessories
girl,' Mickey suggested, his eyes scanning the area in which I
had laid out my offerings in neat rows, like a backyard sale.

'Of course, I've got tons – all over here,' I led them past
the rails of clothes to a carefully assembled table of gleaming
costume jewellery.

'This is more like it!' he exclaimed, guiding Liv forwards.

At last, her eyes lit up, showing more animation than I'd
seen for any of the clothes.

'Love the daisy chains!' she enthused, picking up one
of the delicate original hippy-era creations and placing it
around her neck.

'And these bangles are cool.' She pushed a pile of twenty
or so thin gold bracelets over her slim wrist and jangled them
to illustrate the point.

Then, in a move that took me aback, but didn't seem to
make Mickey even blink an eye, she kicked of her cowboy
boots and began peeling off the black minidress and low-slung

belt she had been wearing, until all she had on were some sheer knickers plus the daisies and bracelets.

I wasn't sure where to look as she slinked off towards the full-length mirrors in the dressing area, her breasts fully exposed.

'Oh, yeah, that is be-you-ti-ful!' exclaimed Mickey, as she twirled for our appreciation in front of the mirrors, her bottom and breasts enviably pert. 'What do you think, Amber, she's rocking, yeah?'

'Yeah, I guess, it's minimal, but if you feel comfortable, Liv?' I asked, desperate to get some eye contact with her to ascertain whether she really was okay, or whether she had been cajoled into this slightly shocking display of nudity by Mickey.

'Oh, Amber,' she mewed, turning to look at me full frontal, her barely there knickers leaving nothing to the imagination, 'I *love* this look! I feel so free, so connected to nature – so *me*. And it's *so* Coachella too, don't you think?'

And before I could say 'No! You're practically stark naked, woman, you were styled this way on the day you were born!', she had flung her arms around my stiff body once more and it felt as though she might never let go.

When she finally did, she couldn't stop thanking me. And because I was in a rush to leave the studio before the shoot began, I didn't have time to argue.

It turned out that Liv's idea of Coachella cool was basically being naked in a field, running around barefoot, adorned with nothing but an eccentric accessory and a seductive smile. When our styling session was drawing to a close, after she had picked out a few more pieces of jewellery – including a feathered headpiece which I had partly brought along as a joke – Liv put her clothes back on. As she did so, Mickey took me aside to explain that she was currently on a path of intense physical and spiritual growth and, as part of this, was feeling a little anxious about the encumbering nature of clothes.

'Your job, ahead of Coachella,' he commanded, 'would be best spent sourcing her some flesh-coloured G-strings from Macy's and perhaps some funky nipple tassels.'

Funky nipple tassels? All I could do was nod and try to look understanding.

When they had left the studio, in the blacked-out limo they arrived in, I hurriedly packed away the beautiful gypsy-inspired tops, cool kaftans and denim flares I needn't have spent so much time carefully picking out, and reflected on the missed opportunity of turning Liv into the American equivalent of Alexa Chung, instead of a hippified Playboy bunny. Mickey had seemed more of a pimp than her manager. At one point, he had goaded her into trying on the fringed waistcoat with nothing else, and taking a few snaps, 'for research', on his phone. He seemed to have some kind of unspoken hold over her and Liv was willingly submissive towards any request he made. The whole thing turned my stomach, making me feel more like a professional fluffer than a fashion stylist. I wouldn't have been surprised if they'd asked me to source a merkin so she could prance around the festival with nothing on at all.

'I mean, why bother going to the length of engaging a stylist if you don't want to be styled?' I said to Rob when he got home that evening, after I'd spent the rest of the day returning all the unworn clothes to Rose's and shelled out for a load of nude knickers and body stockings in Macy's, out of my own pocket.

'Sounds like she thinks she's going to Burning Man rather than Coachella,' he remarked. 'Anyway, not your problem. How Liv wants to express herself is up to her – you're there to make that dream come true. It's all part of the weird world of celebrity styling.'

'I hope she doesn't go around praising her stylist while she's there, though,' I said. 'It's hardly going to do me any favours. She was a sweet girl, if a little needy.'

'Anyway, we've been invited to our first New York party next weekend,' Rob said, grabbing two beers from the fridge. 'It's at Amy's place and it's fancy dress,' he added with a strained laugh.

My facial expression dropped. 'Oh God, I can't go.'

It was the reaction he knew he would receive. We didn't need to go through it again. I'd bored Rob with the sorry stories already: the one where I nearly blinded a guy I fancied at university by getting false eyelash glue in his eye while helping him get into his *Clockwork Orange* costume; the one where I split up with an ex-boyfriend while dressed as a crab because he was coming on to Jessica Rabbit right in front of me; and the one when I got so drunk on sake while portraying a piece of sushi, I couldn't eat sushi for over a year – and still hate sake. In short, me and fancy dress do *not* mix. *It's just* not *my idea of fun.*

'Oh, come on, this could be the party that breaks the mould,' Rob pleaded. 'Besides, it's not so much about the costumes, as the people – the main reason for going is to mingle, make some friends, you know? It's not as if everyone will be paying a huge amount of attention to what us two are wearing, anyway.'

'What's Amy wearing?' I asked tentatively, knowing full well that it didn't really matter because Amy would look amazing in a J-cloth.

Rob tapped into his phone, replying a few seconds later: 'She hasn't decided yet – maybe Westwood.'

'Hmm, Vivienne Westwood, great idea,' I murmured. The key was to find an identity that made you look cool and reasonably attractive at the same time. *I've learned that lesson the hard way.*

'Why don't we go as something really British, too?' he suggested. 'There will be loads of New Yorkers at the party, so we should be typical Brits. It'll be an ice-breaker.'

'What, like Kate and Prince William?' I pondered, think-ing at least I could look reasonably stylish and pretty in a royal-blue Issa dress with matching ring. 'We could have a little Princess Charlotte doll with us?'

'I like your thinking. But a bit boring,' he replied. 'What about the Queen and Prince Philip? We could get a toy corgi.'

It was a brilliant idea. My mind began racing with the plaid-skirt suits, pearls, sensible court shoes and black handbags I could pull from Rose's. This was flexing my fashion muscle already.

'I'll get started on our outfits tomorrow. I need to go back to Rose's anyway, to see about some actual clothes for Liv,' I added, accepting that me and fancy dress were going to have to make amends.

'Oh, and while you're out, can you get a second set of keys cut?' Rob put our door keys into my palm.

The costume hunting would have to wait because, shortly after Rob left for work, Dana came through with an invite to my first New York fashion show for the following morning. It was Michael Kors, which filled me with serious excitement, having been a fan of his clothes for, like, forever. I spent the rest of the evening primping and preening myself as best I could, bearing in mind the lighting level was so low in our bathroom I could barely see myself in the mirror. I tried on eight different outfits before settling on what to wear. *I bet Corine Roitfeld doesn't have this problem.*

Early the next morning, my yellow taxi pulled up outside a huge warehouse building at Chelsea Piers. There was no way I was going to risk the subway today, not wearing the one pair of amazing heels I'd brought to New York with me – fortunately, as it turned out, a pair of sky-high Michael Kors black platform sandals – a leftover from my days working at Smith's boutique where we'd sometimes get to snaffle a really hot sales bargain ahead of the customers. With these shoes on, I could wear jeans and a T-shirt and it would work. Except jeans and a T-shirt would definitely not work today.

It was just gone eight o'clock and the street was awash with glamorous women, dressed to the nines, carefully stepping out of blacked-out SUVs, limos and taxis, preening and posing as if on a catwalk themselves. Occasional splashes of colour could be seen among the generally black-clad fashion posse streaming into the building for the show. I pulled my dress down and slung my Michael Kors bag over my shoulder, glad that at least I blended in – wearing pieces by the designer we were all here to see is an absolute must for a fashion show. I had finished my look with a plain black smock dress that *could* have been from H&M or Michael Kors; only a very well-trained eye would know the truth.

There was a buzz in the air and it was impossible not to get swept along by it, yet, as I neared the entrance, where two going on six foot, black-clad model types stood with iPads, checking off names, my heart rate quickened. *I really hope Dana has remembered to put me down. I can't bear to be humiliated and have to turn against the tide. Especially in these shoes.* Suddenly a frenzy of flashbulbs erupted and we were all shunted to one side to make way for supermodel Gigi Hadid and her entourage. I watched in awe as the newly blonde star slunk her way towards the front row, way taller than I imagined, and so thin, wearing a skintight shimmering silver gown from the new Michael Kors collection. I recognised it immediately from my research last night. The diversion caused a panic among the door staff just as the lights began flashing and a Tannoy announced twenty seconds to show time and kicked off the countdown, the lights chiming in sync. Now it was a free for all, as a surge of desperate fashionistas from behind me began stampeding to the front. Someone's stiletto trod on my toe, making me shriek out loud. My bag was nearly dragged off in the opposite direction to my body and I had to use all my strength to yank it back. There was nothing glamorous about this, yet all around me bouncy blow-dries, petite bosoms and thin limbs elbowed their way past, desperate to get in before the lights went down and the big doors slammed shut. The first show of the day simply has to run on time.

The door police had given up by now and I scrambled past one of their iPads to find a spot on the nearest bench seat – miraculously, on the third row. *This almost makes me a somebody!* I caught my breath as the countdown reached its conclusion – 'Three... two... one...' – and then the room fell pitch-black and a loud beat pounded from speakers in every direction, making my throat pulsate.

In the darkness there was a kerfuffle in the gangway as someone entered – a small, sparrow-like woman with a peroxide bob and an entourage of three deeply tanned, good-looking guys. A few disgruntled women sitting in the second row on spaces marked PRESS were hurriedly turfed off the bench to make way for the group, right in front of me. As the lights shot up, bathing us all in bright daylight, I recognised her immediately as Lola Jones, one of the biggest stylists in New York, famed for her arty, off-beat shoots in the cool underground fashion mags like *System* and *Intermission*.

I studied her mannerisms in detail, from my perfect bird's-eye view, as entranced by her and the inaudible whispers she shared with her handsome companions as by the parade of clothes being churned out, one after another, on the runway. I snapped away on my iPhone, like everyone else around me, capturing both Lola and the catwalk collection before me and uploading photos to Instagram as fast as my fingers would let me. A stream of perfectly preened models wearing opulent fur coats, camel grandpa cardigans and belted tweed suits marched down the catwalk in perfect time to the heavy beats. Knitwear, cashmere and tweed was complemented by lavish bias-cut evening gowns studded with twinkling crystals or sparkling chokers; a pyjama suit in gun-metal grey made an appearance, too – a sure message that the women of New York could step out in pretty much anything they liked this Autumn/Winter. I moved on to video, creating short Instagrammable clips of the fashion parade and uploading them immediately. There wasn't any time for clever captions; today I was all about being first.

It was only after the show, when the lights were turned back to a normal level and some background music played, that I had a moment to gauge the reaction to my postings on social media. To my astonishment, my Instagram likes were in the hundreds and a stream of new followers decorated my feed with beautiful + signs. One particular image of Lola seemed to be generating a lot of attention. I opened the shot and began scrolling through the comments underneath. They ranged from emoticons insinuating shock and laughter to actual comments, such as:

'OMG Lola Jones is going bald!'
and
'Lola's hair loss #cringe'

I scrutinised the photo as a rising level of panic began burning its way through my body. *How could I not have noticed before?* I'd been so enthralled by everything going on around me. But now it had been pointed out – and after I'd spent some time zooming in on my own image – it was painfully obvious that Lola had a rather large patch of wispy hair barely covering her scalp, right in the middle of her crown.

To my horror, very quickly it had snowballed; my photo of the renowned super-cool stylist was being reposted and re-grammed right across the internet, crediting my account and – worst of all – tagging Lola Jones herself almost every time, and there was nothing I could do about it. Even if I removed the post, the damage was done – it was already out there, multiplying faster than a fungus in a chemist's lab. And unless you lived on Planet D'oh, you'd know that this meant I had offended one of the city's biggest names in fashion. Shit. *Shit. Shit*! #Mortified didn't cover it.

The saving grace to this monumental mess was that Lola and her three escorts had already been whisked out of the warehouse – presumably for the next show, Victoria Beckham, across town – and would not have seen that a little-known stylist from London seated directly behind them had outed her hair loss for the whole world to see. Not only was this an off-the-scale mistake, but I also felt deeply disturbed that if Lola *did* have a genuine alopecia problem that she had been hiding from the world, then I was the back-stabbing bitch who had mocked her misfortune.

Outside the show, I felt painfully conspicuous as my photo continued to gain momentum in the social media universe.

All the fashion people around me looked glued to their phones and tablets. Were they all gawping in shock at the same image, currently gaining speed as it ricocheted around cyber space? I bowed my head and weaved my way towards a queue for taxis. While everyone else had a fashion breakfast or a ticket to Victoria Beckham, I bought myself a family bag of Reese's Pieces and quietly retreated back to Williamsburg to hate myself and assess the damage from the privacy of our shoebox.

Dana called when I was in the cab. She cackled down the phone: 'You've certainly entered the fashion world with a bang this morning, Amber Green. What a way to kick off New York Fashion Week! You're damn lucky I don't rep Lola Jones, too – I bet she can't wait to bump into you on the scene.' The mess I had created for myself seemed to tickle her. 'But, anyway, this is *fantastic* for your online presence. It takes some people years to get up to two thousand followers and you've done it in two days! Bravo, Amber. You sure are taking Manhattan by storm.'

Two thousand followers. Christ. It was something I would practically have killed for a few days ago, and now I wasn't sure I wanted the notoriety that came with it. *What if Lola and her three guys come looking for me? What if she gets me barred from every fashion show from now on? Worst still – what if she's so upset, she attempts something stupid?*

Panicked, I phoned Vicky. 'Jesus babe, what's with the six o'clock wake-up call?' came the half-asleep voice at the other end.

'Sorry, hun, forgot you're still three hours behind. Can you talk? I'm in a bit of a shit storm and I need your advice.'

A rustling of bedding followed by a few coughs ensued, then: 'Of course. I'm awake now. Trey didn't come home last night. Again. I don't know what the hell is going on. Amber, he's driving me mad. It's all work, work, work and literally no play. Never mind play, I'd take just setting eyes on him. I barely see my so-called boyfriend. I mean, he could at least call. I bet he's seeing someone else; I've just got this feeling. And the star of his latest film is that minx Joni Tozer, which isn't exactly helping my paranoia.'

'Oh, honey, I'm sorry,' I said, sensing she would much rather talk about this than listen to my current drama. 'Doesn't he ever call to let you know he's not coming home?'

'Call? You must be having a laugh. He *never* answers his cell phone. Leaves it here most of the time because he needs to be "free of communication" to concentrate on directing. Honestly, I've never felt more bottom of the pile. I've just about had it. Anyway, what's the shit storm?'

'I'm wishing I'd left my phone at home, too.' I sighed. 'I've got the opposite problem.'

'What, Rob's ringing you *too much*?'

'No, I've posted something on Instagram and it's spiralling out of control.' As I told her the story I watched my iPad in horror as another five hundred strangers 'liked' my photo and another two hundred followed me.

Vicky paused. 'To delete or not to delete, that is the question.'

'You think I should delete it?' I asked hopefully; perhaps

this course of action would somehow erase the whole thing, like rubbing out a pencil drawing.

'No, there's no point,' she finally conceded, confirming what I'd thought earlier. 'You're already tagged in every post and Lola will have seen it by now. The only thing you can do is embrace your new-found popularity. Try to see it another way, Amber: you've not done anything malicious on purpose – thank God, you didn't caption the photo or point out Lola's alopecia problem – all you did was show the truth, from your viewpoint. No one can hang you for that. Not even Lola herself. Anyway, maybe she's relieved the truth is out there.'

'Hmm, I doubt it, somehow,' I muttered.

'Yeah, me too,' she confessed. 'But, hey, you're starting to build a following and that's what you want at the end of the day. What's that phrase? "All publicity is good publicity." I still can't get to three hundred followers. For some reason, even photos of our hot new gardener aren't setting the social networks alight: whereas, you've cruised into four figures with just a few photos of your new apartment and one fashion show. Just pretend you haven't realised the fuss you've caused, but give your new followers the *real* you, I say.'

The feeling of nausea in the pit of my stomach was ebbing slightly with every word. Good old Vicky, she always had a way of cheering me up. And I suppose she was right – I *did* want to make a name for myself and at least more fashion followers now knew I existed. It wasn't exactly the way I intended that to happen but, as she said, I didn't set out to do anything mean; I hadn't pointed out Lola's bald patch intentionally. *I would never do anything so mean.* So, yes, now I had to let people get to know the real me.

Instead of lolling about in a state of panic, I decided to dust myself down, move away from the Reese's Pieces, and get right back on Instagram, posting a photo of myself in a rocking #ootd – ripped Topshop skinny jeans, Whistles T-shirt, prized vintage biker jacket, Ray-Bans – going about my business, like I hadn't noticed the drama my previous post had caused. Valencia filter; caption: 'Hitting the stores to style a big star for Coachella #shopping #stylist #NYC #Coachella #festivalfashion #letsgo'

And I hit Rose's again, to see if I could find any cool pieces of barely there clothing – a see-through negligée or a silk dressing gown, perhaps – to tempt Liv to put some actual fashion into her Coachella suitcase.

CHAPTER EIGHT

There was something deeply pleasing about stepping into Rose's Fashion Emporium. The huge, three-storey showroom on the Upper East Side was more a fashion library than a store. Filled with rail after rail of designer gowns, day dresses, trousers, tops, jackets – you name it – plus racks containing at least eight thousand pairs of exquisite shoes, and cabinets filled with handbags and glittering accessories, there was something for every taste and every occasion. It was a stylist's mecca and, thanks to Dana, I was part of the 'club'.

Although Rose's held most of the current collections from the main design houses – from Agent Provocateur to Zuhair Murad – I found myself gravitating to the vintage section, where every item had a past life and a story to tell. Sometimes you could smell it on the clothes – leather jackets, with an ingrained smoky scent of parties gone by and hangovers weathered; delicate silk gowns that might have once waltzed with a President or led an A-list star to the bedroom. It was enough to send my imagination into overdrive. I was drawn to the glitzy gowns – some dated right back to the early nineteenth century – and there was a fantastic section of *Dynasty*-style eighties dresses that would still set a party alight today. I wondered if Rob and I should change our outfit plan for the fancy-dress party – that was until I spied the most amazing apricot crepe dress and coat that had 'Her Majesty' written all over it. I was sizing up the outfit in front of one of the full-length mirrors, when I felt I was being watched.

'*Très bon*, looks like a Hardy Amies original, if I'm not mistaken,' a man said, almost making me jump, as his body appeared around a rail of similar suits. 'You just need a matching hat and you'll pass for Her Majesty Queen Elizabeth of England.'

'Funny that,' I replied, 'that's exactly the look I'm going for. Hi, again.'

It was the shoe perv who had spoken to me in the Whitney queue last week. I wondered what he was doing here. The man just smiled.

'Do you really think it's an Amies?' I continued, finding the silence awkward.

'I'd recognise his style of tailoring anywhere,' he said at last, stepping further into the light, allowing me to be sure it was him. 'Check the label.'

I swivelled the skirt around on my hips and peered down. 'You're right. It's dated 1959. Do you think the Queen actually wore it?' I was overcome by the prospect and admired my reflection.

'I doubt that,' he said, chuckling. 'Her pieces are probably still under lock and key at Buckingham Palace. But his ready-to-wear line was a hit Stateside as well as in the UK. Anyway—' He stopped abruptly and stared at my feet. 'You need to get those sandals off – Her Majesty wouldn't be seen dead in gladiators. There's an amazing range of patent-leather court shoes over here.'

I shuffled uneasily. His slightly greying hair was still tied in a knot at the nape of his neck, and he was wearing the same Cuban heels. Although I'd said 'Hi, again' just now, perhaps he hadn't recognised me.

'We've met before,' I announced. 'At the Whitney Museum, a couple of weeks ago.' At first he looked puzzled. 'You remarked on my sandals then, too. It was cold and I was wearing the wrong shoes. Obvious tourist.'

'Ah, and your scarf, you were wearing a beautiful vintage Cavalli scarf?' His eyes sparkled.

I smiled; he seemed to know a lot about fashion for a foot perv. 'Well remembered.' He had to be something to do with the fashion world, just to be standing within these sacred walls. *What was it Dana had said? Network, network, network – make new friends.* 'Do you work here?' I continued.

He laughed. '*Mon dieu, non.* But I am a regular at Rose's.'

'Are you in fashion then?' I probed; he didn't seem to want to give much away.

'I was,' he revealed, a tinge of sadness in his voice. 'Anyway, let me show you the shoe section.' And he led me down a narrow corridor of separates that turned into racks of vintage footwear, Manolo Blahnik, Christian Louboutin, and more famous labels jumping out at me as we passed them. We stopped in front of a row of rather sensible-looking court shoes in black, white and brown.

'Shoes fit for the Queen,' he said, pulling out a particularly

shiny pair of patent heels with a single gold buckle across
the front. 'These will do the job.'

'And they're even in my size,' I replied, looking at the
reverse and then stooping to undo the zips on my sandals
to try them on. 'Sold – for one night only. I'm going to a
fancy-dress party as Queen Elizabeth, you see. I'm not just
a mad British Royalist, honestly. But, anyway, I'm also here
to pick out a few pieces for a star I'm styling for Coachella.'

'You're a stylist?' he asked, his eyes giving away a glimmer
of surprise.

'Yes, well, I'm trying to make my name as a stylist out
here,' I said, defensively. 'I used to assist the stylist Mona
Armstrong – you might have heard of her? – and now I'm
trying to build up my own clients.'

He nodded in acknowledgement when I mentioned Mona's
name. 'Good for you.'

I sensed he was getting ready to go.

'Hey, would you mind if I took a quick snap for my
Instagram account please?' I asked. 'It's just, I'm trying to
build up a following, you know – my agent says it's essential.'

He hesitated. 'Well, okay. But, if you don't mind, I'd like a
little disguise.' He pulled a bowler hat down from a nearby
shelf and put it on, tipping it to a jaunty angle, partially covering his face. Then he whipped down a partly netted black
tippet and placed it onto my head. We pouted for a selfie.

'Catch you again some time,' he said, smiling, and he was
gone down a musty corridor of clothing, lost in a labyrinth
of fashionable dreams. I stopped for a moment to watch him

disappear. He was a curious-looking man, but so polite and easy to talk to.

Damn, I completely forgot to ask his name.

I tagged Rose's in the photo and uploaded it immediately: X-Pro II filter; caption: 'Hunting down treasures at Rose's with a new friend #fashion #stylist #NYC #friendship'

Rob called just as I was finally making my way to the lingerie section on the hunt for 'funky nipple tassels' for Liv.

'Honey, where are you? I've been ringing for the last fifteen minutes. I'm outside the flat but I'm locked out. I thought you'd be home this afternoon?'

'Oh, sorry, I've been in Rose's, choosing clothes for the fancy- dress party. My phone must have been on silent, and I lost track of time. I'll leave now and get a cab back, it shouldn't take more than fifteen minutes.'

'Did you get me a dashing Duke of Edinburgh outfit?'

'Didn't get that far, but I'll come back later in the week, there are thousands of options. See you soon. Love you.'

'I love you too, Your Majesty.'

When I got back to Williamsburg, Rob was sitting on the steps of our apartment block, among the seemingly never-ending pile of pizza boxes. A mangy looking dog was sniffing around the bins. I delved into my Michael Kors for my keys. A minute later, I had tipped the contents of my bag into Rob's lap and, although I found a lost hairclip, half a packet of chewing gum and the receipt for a top I wanted to return to Urban Outfitters, there was no sign of any door keys.

I sighed. 'We've been here less than a week and already we're going to have to pay for a locksmith.'

Rob was already on his phone, calling up Amy – who seemed to be the oracle for *everything* – to get a number.

'No reply,' he mouthed, then left a message.

Just then, someone came out so we made it into the communal hallway. But now, we both just stood staring at our locked front door.

'What now? Kick it in?' Rob asked, pounding the door with his shoulder, just to check it wasn't as flimsy as most of the furnishings inside.

'And have to get a new door as well as a locksmith?' I held him back. 'I wish this was a dream. We're idiots.'

'Hang on, weren't you the one tasked with getting a second set cut today, as you seem to have conveniently forgotten?'

'Hmm,' I muttered, sheepishly. Cutting keys had been the last thing on my mind after the Instagram emergency. 'It's not like I haven't been busy. It was very nearly the day from hell.' And I regaled him with the sorry story of the balding stylist and my social media meltdown, while we sat on the floor outside our apartment waiting for Amy to ring back.

Rob found it amusing. He smirked. 'Why didn't you check the photos properly before you sent them out?'

'I would have done normally,' I insisted, 'but it all happened so quickly – I wanted to get my pics from the show up straight away. In fashion, it's all about being first.'

'At whatever cost?' He gave me a knowing look.

His mobile starting ringing: Amy.

'We've gone and got ourselves locked out of the apartment,'

he told her. '... I know, yes we've only been here a week... I was wondering if your mate Kate happens to know any good locksmiths in the area... Thanks, you're a star.'

You're a star. Amy strikes gold again. I hated myself for feeling narked.

And then it came to me. 'Wait a minute, we might not need a locksmith – why didn't we think of it before, we live opposite a bloody fire station! I'll go over and see if someone there can help.'

Rob rose to his feet too. 'I give you full permission to flirt with all the guys in uniform,' he said, winking. 'But only because this is an emergency, okay?'

I smiled. 'Whatever you say.'

Station 40, Brooklyn Fire Department, were taking an afternoon break when I wandered up the drive and inside the garage doors. Save for two gleaming fire engines parked up side by side the place looked deserted. *Seemingly they only get busy at the exact time I have a genuine emergency or want to go to sleep.*

'Can I help you m'am?' A serious, deep, male voice coming from somewhere within the garage startled me. I turned around, suddenly feeling like an intruder, unable to see the person who had obviously seen me.

'M'am, this is federal property, not a tourist attraction. What are you doing in here?'

I scanned the area, still failing to locate the person demanding answers.

'The screen – look at the CCTV screen in the corner

behind your right shoulder,' the voice continued. 'No, that's your left, honey, look over your *right*.'

Now I felt like a complete idiot. I turned again and there was the face of a burly fireman filling a small screen attached to the wall, another guy visible over his shoulder with a faintly entertained expression on his face.

'I need some help,' I said firmly in my best Queen's English. 'I live across the street.'

'Is there a fire?' The man said, getting to his feet now.

'Not exactly, but it is an emergency, of sorts.'

He muttered something inaudible, and then said, 'I'm coming down.'

Instead of a dramatic Fireman Sam-style flourish down a pole, he soon appeared at the foot of some stars inside the garage just a few feet away from me.

'Now what's going on, lady? Are you from Eng-ger-land?'

'Yes.' I smiled, thinking how encouraging it is to see a six-foot-something, half-uniformed fireman standing in front of you. 'Like I said, I live over the road –' I pointed behind me, '– and, well, it's not a fire, but I've sort of got myself locked out and was wondering, if you're not busy, whether someone could give me a hand getting in?'

'I'm Bart,' he said, before bellowing up the stairs: 'Corey! Jacob! We got an English with a domestic.'

Five minutes later, three ruggedly gorgeous firemen were following me across the street. Rob smiled with approval as we approached.

'It's that one up there,' I said, pointing to the first-floor window. 'I'm pretty sure it doesn't have a lock.'

'You wait inside on the landing,' Bart ordered and I obediently joined Rob in the corridor, ready for our knights in shining armour to open the door and let us in.

Rob and I shuddered as a sound of breaking glass could be heard on the other side of the door.

'I guess the window was locked then – typically the one thing that actually works in this place,' he said quietly. 'We're going to have to tell the landlord.'

'Well, rather that than kicking in the front door,' I replied, and we waited as the sound of more breaking glass and then heavy footsteps could be heard heading towards the door on the other side of the wall.

And then Bart appeared from behind the door. The only problem was, it wasn't *our* front door. It was the one immediately to the left of it. There was silence for a few seconds while Rob and I took in the situation and the fireman read the alarmed expression on our faces.

'Um, that's not our front door,' I said, finally, just as the other two men appeared registered that we were not thanking them for their help.

'This is Max and Tina's apartment,' Rob uttered.

'Who are Max and Tina?' Bart asked. 'You claimed this was your home. What are you trying to tell me?'

Grimly, I replied, 'Max and Tina live next door to us, in the apartment you have just broken into. *This* is our front door.' I pointed to the adjacent wooden door.

'Lady, you showed us your window outside.' He looked angry. 'God damn, it's always a mistake to do people a favour.'

'I thought I did point to our window,' I whispered, knowing that to cause an argument was futile. 'It's not a biggie, I'm sure they'll understand,' I continued brightly, batting my eyelids, praying that a bit of English feminine charm might help. 'But perhaps you could, er, do the same, with the next-door window first, though, so that we can get into our own apartment?'

Thankfully, Bart was in an obliging mood. As it turned out, there was no lock on our window so it didn't even need to be broken.

And that was how we ended up meeting – and laying on an expensive meal for – the shaggers next door.

It turned out that Max and Tina, as well as being probably the loudest people I had ever met, were also – *thank God* – two of the most understanding.

'You gotta laugh,' Max had said, once we pressed a cold beer into his hand no less than two seconds after he'd returned home from work that evening, before he saw some wood nailed into position by the fire brigade where the glass in his sitting-room window should be.

'Tell me you got a cell number for the firemen?' Tina teased when she joined us in our apartment later on.

They were probably in their late thirties, Brooklyn natives, who had been together for knocking on fifteen years and living in their apartment, which was the same size as ours, for almost as long. It turned out that Max also worked in TV, as a cameraman for a local station, so he and Rob hit it off immediately. Late into the evening, when Max goaded Rob downstairs for a cigarette, Tina dragged me off to tell me about their fertility problems and how they were considering a course of IVF. Suddenly the sound of them going at it like rabbits most nights took on a new meaning. Her eyes moistened as she recounted their long, difficult wait to become parents.

'Are you two thinking about children?' she asked pointedly when she'd finished.

'We haven't talked about it yet,' I replied, 'we've not been dating that long. But, yes, I guess I've always imagined I'd be a mum one day.'

'How old are you?'

'Twenty-seven.'

'Start trying early,' she advised, a concerned look across her slightly Hispanic features. 'Unless you have your fertility checked regularly, or you've been pregnant before, you never know. I mean, has Rob ever got anyone pregnant that you know of?'

'God, I don't know,' I said, knocking back a large glug of wine and feeling slightly awkward about such a personal line of questioning from someone I barely knew.

'You'd be wise to find out,' she said, 'before it's too late.'

When Rob came back, I steered him into the kitchen area and put my arms around his waist. His breath smelt of smoke and beer. He looked really sexy this evening.

'The fag was a bad idea, it's gone straight to my head,' he admitted, kissing my hair.

'Did you ever get a girl pregnant?' I asked. Tina had made me feel I needed to know the answer this very second.

'Blimey,' he said, pulling back for a moment and looking

at me square on. 'Not that I know of... it was only a scare with my ex, I told you all about that. Why are you asking, all of a sudden?' He looked over his shoulder, but Tina and Max's tongues were locked on our sofa. 'Oh God, don't say they're swingers,' Rob whispered, turning away quickly.

'It was just something Tina mentioned,' I whispered ominously.

'She said I got another girl pregnant?' Rob's face turned white. 'She barely knows me!'

'No! Just something to do with them and fertility issues. I'll tell you later.'

'There don't seem to be many issues from what I can see,' he said, stealing another look just as the two pulled apart.

'Whiskey nightcap, anyone?' Max called, holding up a bottle of Jack Daniel's he must have picked up from his apartment when they went for a cigarette.

'Now you're talking, mate.' Rob joined them again.

'I'm off to bed, in that case,' Tina said, seemingly not impressed.

'I think I'll do the same.' I went to give her a hug. I had so much to work on tomorrow, managing my social media and finishing the job with Liv, I didn't want to wake up with a pounding head.

'Great talking to you tonight,' she said. 'Let's do it again some time.'

'Definitely,' I replied, 'and – good luck.'

'Thanks.' She looked across at the two guys, now sitting on our sofa, already enjoying a large measure each of JD over some ice.

'Don't worry,' I said cheerily, 'I'll make sure they're not too long.'

'So what was the impregnation question all about then?' Rob asked, his voice slightly slurred, a little later, after Max had left.

'Tina was telling me they're having problems getting pregnant,' I explained.

'And Lord knows they've been trying,' Rob said, chuckling.

'It's not funny, she's really upset about it. I hardly know her and she told me the whole story. I think it's something to do with him. Anyway, they're going to try IVF.'

'Well, good luck to them, I hope it works, but what has this got to do with me?'

I sat up in bed, pulling the covers up around me; it was really cold in here tonight.

'I guess it just made me think about whether we might want a family one day, and if, you know, everything was working.'

'So you can decide whether to dump me now, if I'm firing blanks?' We stared at each other awkwardly. 'Jesus, Amber, this is a bit full-on, isn't it? Give me a break.'

'I just wondered, that's all. It's not like I'm even wanting to have children right now – God, we haven't even had that conversation yet. Oh, forget it.' I clicked the light off and shuffled down under the duvet. *Terrible timing, Amber.*

'No, sorry,' he said, clicking the light on again. 'Let's not forget it. In answer to your questions, no, I haven't got anyone pregnant before – that I'm aware of anyway – because

I generally practise safe sex, as you should know by now. And, yes, I do imagine having children some time in the future. But, as I'm only just thirty, I'm not really thinking about the family thing just yet. And, finally, for the record…'

I held my breath.

'… I–I think you'd make a fantastic mum.' He paused.

'Really?' I asked quietly, a smile spreading across my face. I hadn't expected such an amazing compliment. He folded me into his arms and held me close, telling me the answer in one big bear hug.

'Though your timing regarding big conversations leaves a lot to be desired,' he added. 'Oh, and you'll have to improve your baking skills. Those were home-baked pretzels Tina brought round, you know.'

'You cheeky, sexist—' He cut me off with a big, long kiss.

'Now, is the third degree over and can I get some sleep, before this hangover really kicks in?' he asked when we came up for air.

'Yes, my gorgeous man, you can,' I said, my heart swelling. 'And I think you'll make a great dad some day, too.' I blushed.

He clicked the light off again.

The first thing I did when I woke up the following morning was check my Instagram account. Expecting to see a few more regrams of the fateful Lola Jones photo, I was surprised to see I had somehow attracted another two and a half thousand followers. *Either the Lola Jones photo has really gone global, or someone is fiddling my numbers?* But this time it wasn't Lola Jones that was causing all the fuss. To my surprise, the photo of the foot-fetish man and me in Rose's was generating a lot of interest. There were hundreds of likes and reposts, plus a whole stream of comments underneath it. Feverishly, I began reading through them all, a feeling of panic growing as I did. Most centred around one topic:

'Is that who I think it is??'

'OMG back from the dead!'

Further down the thread a name began to emerge, until it was being repeated over and over again by everyone leaving a comment:

'It's Maurice Chan! #legend'

'THE Maurice Chan'

'No way, Maurice Chan, back again!'

Maurice Chan. The name sounded familiar to me. But, not far beneath this, some, more negative, comments made their entrance:

'He's got a nerve showing his face around town #fashionoutcast'

'About time he faced the music #MauriceChan'

'Nazi #MauriceChan'

Soon the Maurice Chan hashtag, along with a Nazi hashtag, was flying around Instagram, sparking its own stream of photos and discussion.

Rob stirred as I shifted the pillows behind my back and googled Maurice Chan. As I did so, the penny dropped for me, too. I remembered my old boss at Smiths boutique in London once going through some of his clothes that had been withdrawn from the shop floor some years before. There were a million stories about him online, many telling of a 'Fallen designer forced to retire from fashion following Nazi allegations'.

I barely noticed Rob place gentle kisses up my arm as I continued to read article after article about the disgraced designer, once the creative director of a huge brand, who had also run his own eponymous label, and his dramatic fall from grace after a misguided decision to put 'Hitler-style moustaches' on male models for his Paris runway show five years ago. It didn't help that the venue for the show – a former World War Two air-raid shelter beneath the Paris Metro – was taken over by the Germans during the Nazi Occupation. I felt sick to my stomach as the gravity of what I had done continued to incessantly blink away on my handset.

Stories told of a 'strained' French designer, forced to make a public apology, but the moustache debacle had already ended his career. In his one and only interview with a big American news channel shortly after the furore, he spoke of his 'struggle to cope with the pressures of fame' as his label went from strength to strength, and how he had 'sought refuge in drink and drugs to escape the pressure', which he believed had somehow led to making the 'gross misjudgement' – that the moustaches were a tribute to Charlie Chaplin, rather than Adolf Hitler. 'I was foolish, I followed some bad advice, and it is a decision I will regret for the rest of my life,' he had said.

When I had finished reading, I shuddered and sat back against the pillows, ignoring the gentle prods that could quite easily lead to morning sex from my woozy boyfriend.

'So what's going on?' he muttered sleepily, conceding that

he was getting nowhere with me right now. He lifted himself into an upright position.

'It's Maurice Chan,' I muttered. 'Who'd have thought it. That guy I met at the Whitney on our first day. The shoe perv, remember?'

'Yes, the one you couldn't wait to get away from.' He wiped the sleep from his eyes and peered over my shoulder at the screen.

'Well, he's *the* Maurice Chan – the famous, or rather *once* famous, fashion designer.'

'Maurice who?' Though he tried, the limit of Rob's fashion knowledge right now was of footage of scantily clad Angel Wear models.

I returned to Instagram to read more of the comments now that I understood Maurice's back story. The mixture of emotions felt towards him was shocking – some thought he had paid his dues and should be forgiven, while others branded him an 'anti-Semite' who should never show his face again. I didn't know what to believe.

I began to feel guilty; whatever the truth, it wasn't as if Maurice had staged this comeback himself – rather he was mistakenly outed by an Instagram rookie. Just like Lola Jones. *Jesus, what have I done?* I looked at my fingers accusingly.

Back on Instagram, photos of the former fashion designer, including his collections and catwalk shows, began circulating in threads of their own. I noticed one blogger had mentioned a small retrospective of his work being shown at a back-room gallery in Chelsea the following week, marking the fifth anniversary of his retirement from the fashion scene. Hurriedly, I looked up the details online, wondering whether he would be planning to attend. One thing was for sure, he could hardly do it incognito now.

'I need to find Maurice again,' I said aloud. 'Seriously, I can't believe how stupid I was not to ask his name or even get his number yesterday. I'm such an idiot – trying to make contacts without actually getting their contact details? I bet he's livid with me for putting him back in the spotlight like this. No wonder he wanted a disguise.' I sunk back down into the duvet.

'You didn't out him on purpose, baby,' Rob sympathised. 'I just think you need to maybe watch those little digits of yours, because they're getting a bit trigger happy. And it's a dangerous game to play.' He laced his fingers with mine.

'I know,' I said, squirming out of his grip. 'I'm a prize klutz for doing this twice in a matter of days. But how am I going to find him? I need to get to Maurice as quickly as possible, and then hopefully, I can explain before he disappears all over again.'

'You also need to discover whether the guy you *think* is Maurice, is actually him,' Rob advised me. 'Social media is not the oracle, you know. Some eager fashionistas could have got it all wrong – that's how rumours spread.'

I stopped to ponder this. But really, in my mind, there was no doubt. I was itching to track him down, to find out the truth and apologise. I began furiously googling, to see whether I could find anything that might lead me to Maurice. But all I drew was stories about his collections and his fall from grace.

'Wait a minute,' Rob said, more awake now. 'Didn't this,' he began, then, adopting an OTT French accent for his name, 'Maurice Chan give you his card, when we were at the Whitney? Though whether you kept it is another thing – seeing as you were quick to dismiss him as a dirty old perv…'

'Yes! You're right!' I exclaimed, now returning his advances with a peck on the lips. 'I knew there was a reason I decided to go out with you.'

I flew out of bed, narrowly missing tripping over my Michael Kors heels, still strewn on floor, and dived into the rickety wardrobe to try to locate the jacket I had been wearing that first day.

When Rob had cajoled me back to bed, keen to take advantage of my elated mood, after retrieving the business card from my jacket pocket, I slipped it under my pillow. For a while, Maurice Chan was forgotten as Rob smiled the smile that made my tummy somersault and pinned my hands above my head. Suddenly, his soft skin was melded with mine and I lost myself in his long, searching kisses. *He's so good in bed. My delectable boyfriend.*

When we were finished, Rob rolled over and began softly snoring, but my mind was still racing. I retrieved my iPad from the floor and noticed a number of direct messages waiting to be read.

One of them was from the editor of *Vogue* online: 'Hey @ BritStylistTakingManhattan we'd love to speak to you about Maurice Chan. What number can I reach you on? Vanessa'

Another was from the *Daily Mail*: '@BritStylist-TakingManhattan Love to talk to you about Maurice Chan,

can you call Maria on this number please? 212 937 6547.
Thank you.'

The story had hit the mainstream press.

I pulled the business card from under my pillow and read
the wording again. All it said, in an italicised scroll font was:
'MC. New York', and then there was a cell number and an
email address. It was enough for me. Without thinking too
hard, I jumped out of bed, went into the living room and
dialled.

CHAPTER NINE

'Rob! Rob!' I shouted towards the bathroom; this apartment was so small it was impossible to get any privacy, even when on the loo. 'I've just spoken to Maurice Chan!'

I pushed open the door; the room was full of steam.

'Last night you were on about making babies, and now we're at the stage where it's acceptable to storm in on your boyfriend taking a naked, post-shower dump, is it?' he asked.

'I just had a great chat with *the* Maurice Chan.'

'Okay, I heard you.' He pushed the door to with his foot.

I sat on the edge of our bed and talked to the door. 'From what I can make out, it turns out Maurice had to go into hiding after the Hitler moustaches scandal at Paris fashion week. But, according to *Vogue*, he's been quietly planning a comeback – hence, he was in Rose's yesterday doing research. He said there's much more to his story than was ever reported and he's ready to reconnect with the fashion world. Apparently – strictly off the record – Anna Wintour is a personal friend. Babe, don't you know what this means?' I pushed the door open again. Rob had stood up and was brushing his teeth now. He looked at me blankly. 'This means I should try to work with him. And quickly. If anyone's going to grab attention and get me noticed in this city, it's Maurice Chan!'

'Whoa, whoa! Calm down, honey, just take a breath for a minute.' Rob peeled my iPhone from my tight grip and laid it down on the side of the sink, before clamping my arms to my side so I couldn't escape. 'This all sounds terribly exciting, but just think for a moment about what you could be getting yourself involved with. Becoming cosy with a Nazi sympathiser who you hardly know doesn't sound like something you should rush into. Surely your agent would agree. Have you run any of this past Dana? I think maybe you should, that's what agents are for, after all. After two social media explosions within twenty-four hours, you might want to tread a little carefully.' He acknowledged my crestfallen face and cupped my head with his hands. 'Baby, I'm not trying to be downbeat, I'm just saying be cautious – okay?'

I stared him out, feeling like a sugar-high kid being reprimanded by their dad.

'I hear you,' I mumbled, 'but he sounded really nice on the phone, even a little relieved that his identity had been revealed. Anyway, he's not a Nazi sympathiser – all Maurice wants to do is set the record straight and he thinks the time is now. He wants to meet up for a coffee, to explain. Doesn't everyone deserve a second chance? Or at least a fair hearing? He really seems to want to talk to me.'

'It depends,' Rob said, letting my head go and taking my hand to lead me back into the bedroom so he could get dressed. 'Listen, you know I'll always support you, but call Dana before you meet him. For me?'

I nodded my head solemnly.

'But now I have to get to work. We're going to be filming late tonight, the girls are doing a photo-call at an opening event for the new store in the Meatpacking District and then I think there's some kind of after-party we'll want footage of, too. I love you.'

As Rob left, his words were still ringing in my ears: *Call Dana, call Dana.* Although my natural instinct was to call Vicky instead, I knew he was right.

'Honey, you sure know how to make an impact!' Dana guffawed down the phone. 'I was glued to your Instagram all evening. First, Lola, now, Maurice – is there anyone in New York City who's safe from Amber Green?' She laughed throatily.

'Well, you did tell me to up my online presence,' I quietly replied. 'Though even *I* didn't expect it to happen so fast. What's your take on Maurice, anyway?'

'He was a tour de force for many years,' she said, sighing, 'the toast of Paris, New York, you name it. His clothes were exquisite. But such a fall. No one would go near him after the Nazi episode. I'm mean, it was shocking. It's no excuse but, by all accounts, he was in a terrible state when it happened. Rumours were flying about in-fighting at his label. His cocaine dealer must have been set up for life, judging by the amount he was reportedly shovelling up his nose during those dark days. Sad, so sad. Anyway, how did you come to be playing dress up with him in Rose's in the first place?'

I paused, as I briefly considered whether to pretend I was

aware of who I'd been mixing with in Rose's. *But lying has never been my forte.*

'Honestly? I had no idea it was him, Dana. I actually met the guy in the queue for the Whitney Museum on our first day in town, completely by chance. And then I bumped into him again at Rose's as I was sourcing clothes for Liv. It was my followers who recognised him.'

'Oh, doll face, you and your new-found followers. But the big question is, what are you going to do about it?'

'That's why I'm calling. Maurice has asked me for a coffee – he says there's more to the Nazi story than people know and he's ready to face the world again. Do you think I should meet him?'

'Hell, yes! Honey, this could set your career sky rocketing! Keep me posted.'

And she rang off.

Set my career sky rocketing. Surely the words that anyone trying to build their profile in a competitive industry, in a new country, wants to hear? Good old Dana had said exactly what I wanted to hear. I called Maurice back and arranged to meet him at a low key joint in Williamsburg the following morning.

For the rest of the day, my mission was to get more keys cut – including a spare set to leave with Max and Tina; after yesterday, I didn't fancy having to call upon Bart again – and to find some more pieces for Liv. Nipple tassels? I mean, was Mickey serious? *How the hell are nipple tassels going to get her onto the Coachella Best Dressed lists? She'll be a laughing stock and, as her stylist, so will I.*

*

When I made it home at last, later that afternoon, my feet were throbbing from pounding the entire length of Broadway, familiarising myself with American fashion stores and picking up underwear. I spent an hour inside the flagship Angel Wear shop in uptown Manhattan, choosing thongs and doing a bit of research on exactly who my boyfriend was currently filming all day long. I soon wished I hadn't. Emblazoned on the walls were five full-length photographs of the Angel Wear 'Icons' – Krystal, Jessica, Roxy, Leonie and Astrid – all statuesque models with out-of-this-world bodies, supremely talented at showing them off in provocative poses. Surely it wasn't natural to be born that way. I found myself staring at Leonie's unbelievably pert bottom – barely covered by a rhinestone G-string – for so long that a security guard came over and asked if I was feeling okay. Although I nodded and shuffled off, I definitely was not feeling okay.

I moved on to the endless units full of lacy briefs and racy bras, running my fingers through the multicoloured soft fabrics; I spent a while spraying myself with eau de parfums called things like 'Tender is the Night' and 'You Inside Me', trying to decide which scent was the favourite of each Icon, and then whether Rob had a favourite Icon. I left the shop feeling a little subdued and slightly sick. In other words, suffering from a condition more commonly known as jealousy.

How come Rob had barely mentioned these goddesses to me? Did he favour one of them? Did he fancy them all? I mean, show me a man who'd be fussy. I tortured myself by gazing up at their bottoms again.

I'd been so wrapped up in trying to forge a career for myself that I had barely paid any attention to the long days and late nights Rob had been putting in at work – with *them*.

My head was still buzzing as I made my way to SoHo, figuring some of the more upscale sex boutiques would probably be the best place to look for extra bits for Liv. Once I had decided that, despite singling out some tasteful lingerie by Stella McCartney and Agent Provocateur, it was basically impossible to find anything that wouldn't make her look like a stripper crossed with a hooker, I felt a lot better about things. But a hooker at a cool music festival? The whole thing was sitting very badly with me.

I called Mickey to deliver the news that I needed to delay the final fitting.

He sounded out of breath as he answered the phone and two seconds later Liv was on the end of the line, sounding equally flustered.

'So when are you coming over Amber?' she cooed. 'How about tomorrow afternoon? I go to Coachella in four days' time, so it doesn't give me much time to pack.'

Not that it will take very long to pack a few daisy chains and some thongs.

'Give me another day. I just need to go to a few more stores,' I said, floundering. 'Message me your address and I'll come to you.'

*

After his comments about my gladiators, on two occasions, I took a lot more care over my appearance as I got ready to meet Maurice on Wednesday morning. Teaming a pair of plain black trusty Topshop loafers with cropped back trousers and a white shirt, I decided that 'sharp and classic' was the safest bet for meeting someone with fashion credentials as off the scale as him.

He asked to meet at the Black Cat coffee house in Williamsburg, which was fortunately in walking distance from our apartment so I wasn't in danger of getting lost and being late. Nevertheless, I meticulously plotted my route the night before.

When I arrived, Maurice was sitting at a corner table, tucked away at the side of the window away from the door. He was wearing a battered black fedora pulled down low so half of his face was in shadow. His hair was tied back in his trademark bun underneath. If you didn't know better, you might mistake him for an ageing hipster or someone who'd fallen on hard times. I supposed both were actually true.

Maurice was already nursing a cup of coffee, an intense look on his face as he stirred it slowly and steadily as if searching for something in the liquid within. He didn't look up as I approached, he was so deep in thought. I had loudly pulled out my chair, coughed, and was beginning to question if this was actually him, when he finally acknowledged my presence:

'Amber, *chérie*, excuse me, I was lost in thought. Please, sit down.'

As I sat a waitress approached and he ordered us both flat whites.

'You don't strike me as a decaf type,' he said, and smiled. 'The flat white here is the best in Brooklyn.'

'Great, and, yes, I'm more of your full-roast double-shot type,' I replied.

'You must think this is very unusual,' he commented, sinking back into his seat and tilting the hat slightly so a little more of one eye was visible. He really had the most striking, sparkling green eyes, like marbles. 'I mean, it's not what I imagined either but, well, suddenly people are asking questions again. And I'm not quite sure how to handle it.'

'I feel responsible,' I said, hanging my head. 'But, honestly, I want you to know I had no idea who you were at the time. I mean, of course I do now, Mr Chan, and I'm so honoured to be sitting here with you. Seriously, I'm pinching myself, but I want you to know I didn't mean to thrust you back into the limelight like that. Especially if it's not somewhere you want to be. I really need to watch what I post – this isn't the first mistake I've made on Instagram recently – and I should have got your name when we were in Rose's. I'm so—' I stopped, realising that I now had verbal diarrhoea and Maurice was looking into his coffee again.

'I'll shut up. Can we start again?'

'Let's start at the beginning,' he uttered calmly. 'You're a good person, Amber, I could see that from the moment we met. Do you have anywhere to rush off to?'

'Not until later this afternoon,' I replied, my heart sinking as I thought of trudging the streets, looking for nipple tassels.

And so it came to be that fabled fashion designer Maurice Chan lifted the lid on the truth about his rise to the top and then his catastrophic fall, in a Williamsburg coffee shop, to little old me. Once he got into his stride, he didn't stop talking – it was as if a dam had been busted and years of pent-up frustration and sadness came tumbling out. He told his story with great passion and eloquence, stopping at opportune moments to dab a tear from his eye or signal another coffee from the waitress. It transpired that Maurice had been the victim of an overly ambitious assistant, a man who had once been his lover, until Maurice 'wasn't a good fit' for his career, who had completely stitched him up by plotting the Hitler moustache debacle behind his back. And when it all blew up for Maurice, the assistant distanced himself from his former boyfriend and mentor, even stealing copies of original sketches for his upcoming collection, and landed himself a top position in a rival design house within a matter of weeks.

Two hours passed in a heartbeat and, when he had finally finished telling the story, Maurice slumped back into his seat, drained and emotional.

'But why did you take the fall for him?' I asked. 'It wasn't your fault.'

He hung his head. 'I was his boss, not to mention his ex-lover, the label was in my name and I should have had tighter control over my business, so in that sense it was completely my fault – and I paid the ultimate price. I lost everything.' His French accent became even more pronounced as he talked. He paused, as his eyes became moist with emotion and he struggled to keep his black eyeliner in place with his index finger. Instinctively, I leaned across and placed my hand gently on his forearm.

'So where did you go?' I probed, sensing there was more to come.

'The damage was done immediately. I'm no Nazi sympathiser – I swear to you.' He gripped my hands tightly with both of his and looked me dead in the eye. 'It brought shame not only on me, but my family, too. And that was hard to take. The press were camping outside my mother's house in Bordeaux. It almost finished her off – she has a weak heart as it is. I fell into a deep depression, barely leaving my apartment in Paris for six months. And then I was invited to move to New York by an elderly great-aunt. I decided that I could make myself useful looking after her and start over again, in a city where I was less likely to be recognised every time I left the house.'

'Do you still live with your aunt?' I asked.

'Sadly she passed away last year.' He looked out of the window, wistfully.

'I'm so sorry,' I whispered.

'It was a tough time. But she left the apartment and all her belongings to me.' He smiled. 'Marianne was her name. She was a real fashionista in her day – a known face around town at all the most glamorous parties. She had made her name as a burlesque dancer in the top clubs in Paris – the

Moulin Rouge, Les Folies Bergère, she performed at them all – before she moved to New York to chase her dream to become an actress. A few risqué stage roles followed, but it was on the social scene that she really sparkled. She never married, but she had a few long-term relationships and incredibly exciting liaisons with a handful of famous actors and millionaires – her photograph collection is to die for. And her clothes, well, they are something else. I haven't done a thing to her wardrobe, it's exactly as she left it, down to the very last outfit she wore – a genuine 1920s silk kimono, hanging over one of the doors. She was glamour personified, right until the end.' He stopped to sip his coffee. 'So the truth is, fashion is in my blood. Maybe it sounds bizarre, but I see life in clothes. I remember exactly what I was wearing when I was backstage at that fateful show, I remember the outfit I wore when I told my mother I was gay, and when I felt the flushes of true love for the first time. I notice the clothes on every person I pass on the street. Nothing excites me more than fashion and the choices people make when they get dressed in the morning. It is all I think about.' For a moment he seemed to drift off somewhere. I looked down at my white shirt, trousers and loafers wondering what he made of my clothes today, but stayed mute, giving him the space to continue.

'That's why I spoke to you that morning at the Whitney,' he continued. 'I could tell you cared too – just by looking at your shoes and your vintage Cavalli scarf. I could tell you were cold, but you still decided to wear those things because they looked and made you feel good.'

'You spotted the Cavalli?' I had to admit I was chuffed.

'Of course. We are like-minded, Amber. Do you think these boots are the most comfortable footwear I could choose?' He lifted a Cuban heel off the floor and we both peered at it. 'Of course they're not. But they make me feel invincible. They are my armour. Oh, *chérie*, I feel so inspired right now. I've designed my new collection ten times over in my head.' He stopped again, averting his eyes from mine as tears sprung into them once more. I felt mine prickle too. It seemed so unfair that this man, clearly such a talent and so passionate about his art, was now washed up. The waitress stopped by, offering us more coffee and as we both accepted – by this point we were flying on caffeine – an idea began to form in my mind.

'I think I can help you,' I said earnestly when our refills had arrived. He looked up and held my gaze, and for the first time all morning a hint of possibility shone in his eyes. 'I'm working with Liv Ramone at the moment. You might remember her, she was a fairly successful actress a few years ago and then it all went pear-shaped when she fell in with the wrong crowd and went off the rails. She's now a self-styled 'cleaned-up Hollywood wild child' wanting to relaunch her career.'

'I know how she feels,' he muttered.

'But there's a problem,' I continued. 'Quite a big problem. The thing is, she prefers to be nude rather than clothed, but it's doing nothing for building her image – let alone mine as her stylist. She's going to Coachella in four days' time and, so far, I've got a few negligées, a daisy chain and some nipple tassels for her to take with her to wear. It's a disaster and I'm struggling to know what to do about it. What if you could design some cool lingerie pieces for her, to smooth the transition back into clothing? You could do it anonymously if you like. It would really help me out. I'm finding it impossible to source anything that doesn't look tacky. What do you say? Could you do it in time?'

He sucked in his cheeks. '*Ooh, la la*. I wasn't expecting to receive a commission today. Four days, though… that is nothing, Amber, darling. I would like to help you, I would be honoured; in fact, I would love nothing more – but *four days*?' He shook his head. 'I'm afraid, *ma chérie*, it is impossible.'

Now it was my turn to feel deflated. I looked at my phone; it was nearly three o'clock, we had completely missed lunch and I needed to get back to my reconnaissance mission for Liv's non-existent festival wardrobe.

'Don't worry, it was silly of me to ask,' I said. 'Really, it's fine.' I stirred a lump of sugar into my umpteenth coffee. I was starting to feel a little agitated; it wouldn't be long before Mickey would be back on my case wanting to arrange her next fitting and I had nothing else to show. Suddenly, Maurice gripped my arm.

'Wait!' he exclaimed, taking me aback at first. I looked over my shoulder, wondering for a second if someone had spotted him. 'I've just had a brainwave! Why didn't I think of it before? *Quatre* days you say?' I nodded sagely. 'Four days is plenty, for I already have a whole wardrobe of incredible vintage pieces fit for the fieriest burlesque star in Paris.

Marianne's wardrobe! You know, my aunt. Her wardrobe is full of the most exquisite corsets, stockings, negligees and boas – I'm talking classy, not trashy, the real deal – proper Parisian burlesque. Darling M never put a fashion foot wrong. And I'm sure she will be high-kicking in heaven right now, to think her beloved clothes could be brought back to life on an *ingénue* of the moment'

'More *enfant terrible* than *ingénue*,' I mumbled, 'but if you really are sure, this could be the answer to my prayers.'

He looked me straight in the eye. 'I would be honoured, my darling – as would Marianne. It's as if you are my guardian angel, sent over from London to help me. This was written in the stars. Come on, let me show you the wardrobe.'

We grinned gleefully at each other and asked for the bill.

CHAPTER TEN

Maurice and I jumped into a taxi and reached his apartment on the Upper East Side twenty minutes later. I had to pinch myself several times as we criss-crossed through lanes of traffic, Maurice staring out of the window. Though my index finger hovered over the miniature camera, the little blue bird and the tempting blue 'F' icon on my phone, I resisted the urge to post anything on social media. I was too scared about the storm that might follow. *Rob will be pleased.*

When we exited the cab, I looked up at the tall, elegant, brownstone building in front of us, right in the heart of expensive, old-money Manhattan. It was a home from a film set: black metal railings, cute metal post box affixed to the gate.

'We're on the top floor,' Maurice informed me as we climbed the steps to his shiny black front door. Inside, we went through a second wooden door and entered a beautiful hallway with a wooden staircase to the right, the steps covered in a bottle green runner, and there were smart black and white tiles on the hallway floor to the left. The smell of furniture polish and hoovered carpet hung in the air – there was something old-fashioned but deliciously chic about it all.

Maurice smiled, indicating the staircase. 'I've only walked up once the whole time I've been here.' I gazed upwards to see it spiral majestically across several floors above us. The ceiling was so high it made his voice echo. We took the lift to the fifth floor, me feeling as though I was in *Pretty Woman*, only Maurice wasn't exactly my Richard Gere. He was barely taller than my five foot six, even in heels. His little grey bun bobbed down the hallway ahead of me.

When we reached the top floor, he turned his key in the lock and it was as though we had entered a Parisian apartment from a time gone by. If I wasn't mistaken there was birdsong playing. I half expected Edith Piaf to appear from behind a door and start singing to us. The walls in the hallway were painted deep red and crammed full of framed photos. Most were black and white, depicting curvy women, their bodies strapped into corsets or posing for the camera wearing jewelled bra tops, feathered wings and boas covering their modesty, with jaunty miniature top hats and feathered headpieces finishing off the look. There were a few framed posters and flyers for burlesque and cabaret clubs – including the Moulin Rouge and Le Crazy Horse Saloon – a number of them featuring the name 'Marianne'. *Just one word, like Madonna. So cool. She must have been a huge star in her day.* One face appeared in nearly all the images, so it had to be her. She had striking black curly hair sitting just above her shoulders, painted lips, big eyes and an hourglass figure. One image stood out in particular: her hot-pants-clad body on display, her breasts covered by an exquisite, intricate bra made of jewels cut into the shape of petals. She wasn't looking into the lens seductively this time, she was staring off into the middle distance and she looked a little sad.

'Are these all images of your great-aunt?' I asked, lagging behind Maurice, desperate to take them all in.

'Mostly,' he replied over his shoulder. 'She was photographed by all the top names of her day.'

'She was beautiful,' I declared. 'Especially in this one.'

Maurice had got bored of waiting for me further down the corridor.

'Ah, I love that one, too.' He smiled, joining me. 'She was broken hearted that day, her latest millionaire boyfriend had given her that bra. It was an incredible piece, made from the finest rubies, but when the photo was taken he had just called off their relationship. She thought she might die of a broken heart, she told me once – she really thought he could be The One. You can see the pain all over her face, yet it is so beautiful at the same time. She returned the bra to him that very evening. He was called Clark Claybourne. She told me never to forget his name – he must be well into his nineties by now, as she would be. God rest her delicate soul.'

We both stared at it for a moment longer, engulfed by her sorrow.

The spell was broken by my mobile ringing loudly. I looked at the name flashing before me: Mickey.

'Drat, it's Liv's manager. He's going to hassle me about her next fitting,' I thought out loud, before cutting him off.

'Her bedroom is this way.' Maurice beckoned me. We

stopped outside the third door on the left-hand side. As I moved down the hallway, I gazed right, where a giant archway opened up into a large sitting room, with a highly polished wooden floor covered in antique pieces of furniture; the same dark-red colouring was on the walls and black picture rails and skirting boards gave it a formal air. In the far corner of the room by the window stood a large ornate birdcage with four little canaries inside. *So that's where the chirping is coming from.*

Maurice was waiting for me.

'You've spotted my girls,' he proclaimed as I gawped at the room before me. 'Meet Brigitte, Catherine, Ines and Edith – the most faithful friends a guy could have. They know all my darkest secrets.' He winked. He seemed so much more relaxed safely at home, away from the outside world.

'They're beautiful. It's *all* beautiful,' I uttered, transfixed by the place.

'Come, let's get styling.' He chivvied me back down the hallway behind him.

Instantly, I knew that Maurice was not exaggerating: the room was indeed a shrine to his beloved departed great-aunt. Her make-up was still laid out on the dressing table and her four-poster bed was still made. Adjacent to it stood a huge walnut wardrobe, taking up most of one wall; one door was closed, the other flung open with a sky blue silk kimono with a gold dragon on the back draped over it, just as he had described.

I sighed, itching to rummage through the wardrobe. 'It's a stunning room.'

Maurice had stopped by my side; I hoped he wasn't having second thoughts.

'So how should we do this?' I asked cautiously.

Nearly two hours later, we had unlocked a treasure trove of incredible vintage burlesque costumes: glittery sequins and seductive fringing over skintight dancer's leotards, a fabulous long gold fringe belt with rhinestone detailing to show off feminine curves but still leave something to the imagination, a couple of stunning satin form-fitting corsets in pale feminine colours with layers of cheeky feathers around the bottom and then, the *pièce de résistance*, a pair of sky-blue theatrical ostrich feather fans, just asking to be teased apart by their saucy wearer. At last I had found what I'd been searching for – a bit of theatre and glamour to add to Liv's 'barely there' approach to festival fashion. There was nothing tacky about it – Marianne's burlesque wardrobe oozed sex appeal from a time gone by. With a few of this season's designer accessories, it would make an original look, worthy of the pages of *Vogue*. I couldn't wait to see Liv try it all on. When Mickey called again soon after, I could truthfully tell him his star's Coachella wardrobe was 'sorted'.

Maurice seemed exhausted when we had finished. It had clearly been an emotional process for him – as much about laying his great-aunt's life to rest and moving on as helping me with a styling job. I glanced at a pretty carriage clock on Marianne's bedside table – it was gone six o'clock, and Rob would be home from work soon and wondering where I was.

*

When I got through the door, I could instantly tell something was wrong. The door wasn't double-locked, which meant Rob was home, but there were no lights on. I gently put down my bag in our poor excuse for a hallway (it lasted approximately two steps before you were into the living-cum-dining-cum-kitchen area) and padded around the corner. Rob was sitting on the sofa, an open bottle of red wine on the coffee table in front of him, and a nearly empty glass in his hand. A packet of cigarettes lay on the sofa. He barely registered I was there.

'Bad day?' I stated the obvious.

'Just slightly,' he muttered. 'Did try calling you several times to see if you could meet me.'

I pulled my phone from my pocket. I'd been so fixated on wondering when Mickey would next ring back, I had barely registered the three missed calls from Rob earlier in the afternoon.

'Sorry, I was with Maurice, going through his aunt's wardrobe, would you believe. It was hard to speak.' He refilled his glass. 'Anyway, talk to me – what's happened?'

I grabbed a wine glass and sat down next to him, putting my arm around his neck and coercing him into turning to face me. I'd never seen Rob look this depressed before.

'It's Dan,' he finally said, swigging another half glass of wine, before filling us both up from the nearly empty bottle.

'Oh God, your brother – don't tell me something terrible has happened?' Now it was my turn to freeze up.

'He's okay. I mean he's not had an accident or anything, but it's all off with Florence. He was in bits, Amber.' He turned to face me. 'He called me earlier at work and I've never heard him so done in. You won't believe what happened today – he had to pop back home for something and caught her in bed with another guy, in *their* bed! In *his* bed, rather. He's the one who paid for everything in that Notting Hill show apartment. It's such a cliché.'

'Oh Jesus.' I took a large swig of wine. 'That's awful. Poor Dan. What did he do?'

'He slammed the door and walked out, of course,' Rob said. 'That's when he phoned me. I think he was still in shock. He's furious. She's made a fool out of him.'

I shook my head. 'Does he know the guy?'

'Dan thinks he's the boss of the PR agency she works for. To make things even worse, he's married with three children. So she's not only ruined her own engagement, she's a marriage wrecker, too. God knows how long it's been going on for.'

'Oh man, I'm so sorry.' I cradled him in a big bear hug. 'Poor, poor Dan.'

'And *then*, as if my day wasn't shit enough,' Rob continued, 'then the bloody main stylist for the Angel Wear show we're supposed to be filming had an almighty hissy-fit, culminating in a stand-up shouting match with the owner, Ron, in front of everyone at the studio. A difference in opinion over "artistic direction", apparently. I mean how many ways can you wear a bra and some knickers? Anyway, now Ron says the show is off. He can't see how we could pull it together credibly in the time left. I mean, he's fuming with this stroppy stylist.'

'So what does this mean for you – and the filming?' I asked.

'It means the whole thing is in jeopardy.' He sighed. 'If there's no big show, there's no TV programme to be made about it. We've all been given tomorrow off and there's going to be a crisis meeting on Monday, once everyone's calmed down, to find out what's going to happen.'

I breathed out deeply. 'That's a tough day.' Then I finished the remaining wine in my glass. 'No wonder you needed a drink.'

It also dawned on me that this had big implications for me, too – no TV show meant no New York for Rob, which in turn meant the end of the Big Apple dream for me – just when things were starting to kick off. My mind was racing. 'Do you think I could help, with the styling, maybe?' It just came out before I'd had time to think it through.

He looked grimly at the empty bottle and then a little of the familiar Rob sparkle came back in to his features.

'That's not a bad idea,' he said, after a beat. 'You could be just what we need. I'll text Ron now.'

And before I could say, 'Hold your horses, John Wayne! I'm not sure I'm up to this!', he had sent a text to his boss.

Seconds later, his phone beeped.

'"Bring her in"' Rob read straight from the screen.

'So what do we do now?' I muttered, unsure if I felt excited or petrified.

'We get drunk?'

'Great!' I replied.

He reached out and turned my face towards his. 'I love you, Amber Green. But let's not get too drunk, because you're coming to meet Ron, tomorrow. You also need to tell me about this Maurice what's-his-name? and how you've single-handedly instigated his return to the scene.'

'Well, it's quite a story…' And we left the apartment for our local dive bar.

The next morning, we both woke feeling as though we had swallowed the entire contents of a liquor store. My head was banging. Rob was already out of bed and lying in the bath, presumably hoping that the hot steam might tease out the remains of the alcohol we'd consumed last night. But judging by his blotchy red skin and sweaty forehead, it was having the opposite effect.

'Not working,' he grimaced, as I slowly made my way towards him and perched unsteadily on the side of the bath. I had a feeling of foreboding that I should not be in this state ahead of a meeting with a new potential employer.

'I'll bet Dan's doing the same thing right about now,' I replied. 'So, although we're not there with him, at least we are feeling his pain.'

'I spoke to him while you were still sleeping,' Rob said. 'He's at Mum's and has told Florence to get out of the flat by the end of the weekend. And if she's not, I wouldn't bet on Mum not heading over there to drag her out by her blow-dry.'

'I bet he doesn't know what to do with himself,' I said,

trailing my hand in the warm water, as I contemplated whether joining Rob in the bath was a good idea or not.

'Well, he was wondering about getting on a plane and coming out here,' Rob said, looking at me expectantly. His eyelashes were stuck together with water. He looked gorgeous even in spite of his bloodshot eyes and blotchy skin. 'How would you feel if Dan crashed over here for a few nights, just to get his head straight?'

'Of course I wouldn't mind at all,' I assured him. 'He's your brother, baby. God knows, I'd feel the same if this happened to Lucy.'

For a few moments, I thought of my sister, of Rory, and little Nora back home. My own family had barely crossed my mind in the few weeks I'd been out here, I'd been so consumed by social media and Maurice Chan. Thinking of home also made me think of our other little family member currently on the other side of the Atlantic.

'I wonder how Pinky's doing,' I said, a soppy warm feeling washing over me as I visualised his dark little eyes and rounded pink belly.

'Aah, Pinky, I miss him,' Rob said quietly. 'But judging by Poppy's Instagram account, he's having a fantastic time. Have you not seen the pics? He was having lunch at the Ivy Chelsea Garden a couple of days ago, and getting his trotters cleaned at some pet spa in Knightsbridge the day before that. He's a real 'man about town'. He might not want us back.'

'Anyway, I guess I'd better start downing coffee and ironing a dress. What time is Ron expecting us?'

'Oh, sorry!' he replied. 'Forgot to tell you, he's asked to rearrange. I'll get on to him first thing, so keep your phone on.'

I breathed a hefty sigh, thinking, *Thank God for that*, and headed back into the bedroom to retrieve my phone for a scroll. As if telepathically, there was a missed call from Mum.

Once I'd assured my mother that I was working hard to earn my keep out here, and my headache had finally begun abating, I called Mickey to arrange the final fitting for Liv before she headed off to Coachella the following day. He asked me to meet them at a suite at the Soho Grand hotel in Manhattan.

Fortunately, given my deathly pallor, the hotel was trendily dimly lit, the spring sunshine locked outside, when I arrived shortly after midday. Mickey met me in the lobby. I felt like a shifty sex industry sales person carrying my suitcase filled with burlesque pieces from Marianne's wardrobe.

'At last!' he said, taking the case from my hand and heading straight for the lifts. 'Liv's been getting her knickers in a twist about this styling business.' *I know he means it literally.* 'It's going to be scorching in the desert so she's been in the gym all hours honing that cute little ass.' *God, he makes my skin crawl.* 'We absolutely *have* to make a mark these next few days, her career depends on it.'

I resisted the urge to mention the fact that, at present, Liv didn't exactly have a career to speak of.

When we reached the private sixteenth floor, we took a left and followed the corridor to the end, where Liv was

holed up in one of the luxury suites. At least she was supposed to be, but inside she was nowhere to be seen. Mickey
set the suitcase down on the California king-size bed and
unzipped it. He didn't seem concerned that his client had
clearly done a runner. The windows revealed stunning views
of Manhattan.

'Amber's here, babe,' he called, finally, towards a closed
door off the bedroom.

When there came no response, he gently pushed it open.
A fug of steam whooshed out. 'Jesus H— you'll be a prune
by now! C'mon honey-pie, Amber's got some rad gear for
you to try on.' *Rad?*

'I'm so cosy in here, I don't want to get out yet,' a
voice trilled in response. 'Come in, I can talk to Amber
from here.'

Following a nod from Mickey, unconfidently, I made my
way towards the bathroom.

Liv was stretched out in the ample bath tub, her wet hair
held in a top knot by a scrunchie, her cheeks rosy from the
heat of the water, and her face free of make-up. She had
beautifully clear, alabaster skin. Fortunately, the bath was
full of foam, and it covered the essential areas, hiding my
modesty as well as hers.

'Great to see you, Amber, come in.' Liv gestured with a
shiny wet arm. 'Sorry to be a slob but, this bath – man, it's
the greatest bath I've ever lain in. Want to join me?'

Mickey sniggered.

'Um, I'm okay, thanks,' I mumbled, wondering what I'd
entered into. *Surely she's not a swinger as well as a nudist?*

Nothing would have surprised me at this moment. 'I brought your Coachella looks,' I pressed on. 'I was thinking you'd want to try some of them on and then I can help you put your wardrobe together, if you like?' Hopefully, I looked over to Mickey for some support, but he seemed more interested in ogling Liv in the bath.

She lifted one foot out of the water, nimbly wrapping the chain around her big toe and giving it a gentle yank to release plug. There was a gurgling noise as the water began emptying out.

'Of course. So tell me, what did you bring?' she asked. 'You know I don't want to look like every other rich Beverly Hills hipster at a festival. And the *last* person I want to emulate is that Kendall Jenner. Ugh, such a stereotype.'

Less water meant fewer bubbles, which very quickly meant more Liv and within seconds she was fully naked before us. I didn't dare look at Mickey. As she held on to the side of the bath and lifted herself up, I averted my eyes and began backing out of the room.

'Don't be shy, Amber, I've only got what you've got. Anyway – the LA clone girls, I can't bear that look. That's why I'm going for the less is more approach.'

She put her hands on her hips and jiggled her bits, to emphasise the point.

Thankfully, Mickey chose that moment to bring her a towel.

Now rubbing herself dry, Liv continued. 'I just feel that stripping off is a way of expressing purity of emotion,' she said, authoritatively, and completely unaware at how awkward I was feeling right now, as I couldn't help my eyes from wandering to the most perfectly trimmed muff I'd ever seen in the flesh. 'And I want to be memorable,' she declared. 'Everyone's waiting to see what I do next and I want it to be shocking. I want to get people talking. I mean, why not?' It was a perfectly reasonable question for a person addicted to fame. *But why naked?* I wanted to ask. But at this precise juncture, more shocking than seeing Liv totally in the buff was the unsettling feeling I had witnessing this display of crude nudity alongside Mickey. Somehow it made me more uneasy that he wasn't even pretending to look away – *and* he was still wearing his un-ironic eighties-style leather jacket – it made this clean and pure young woman look so vulnerable; it felt horribly voyeuristic. As she finished drying herself and flung the towel on the bathroom floor, instinctively I pulled a fluffy white bathrobe from the back of the door and threw it over the side of the bath next to her.

'I hear you,' I said, deciding to act professionally, despite the fact that the heat in here had made my hangover return with a vengeance. This was the second steaming-hot bath I'd witnessed so far this day and I hadn't even had time for a soak myself. 'I just think that with a few choice items, you can have people remember you for a whole host of cool reasons, and not just your body,' I told her as assertively as I could. 'Anyway, I've totally gone for the "less is more" approach – I think you'll like what I've got planned.'

Liv seemed to take the hint and pulled the robe around her slender body as she followed me out of the bathroom, leaving a trail of damp footprints on the cream carpet behind her. Mickey had gone ahead and already opened the suitcase. He was posing, holding a feathered wing over his crotch area, in what was supposed to be a joke, but made me wince. I brushed him aside and the stylist in me sprang into action.

As I unveiled piece after piece of rare vintage burlesque wear, straight from the wardrobe of one of Paris's most famous muses, Liv's eyes grew wider and wider. As she tried the items on, I kept one eye on my phone, in case Rob had left a message about another time for me to meet Ron. The idea of styling the Angel Wear show was starting to have big appeal – especially if the alternative was to force clothes on a reluctant client.

It had to be said Liv looked incredible in the bustiers, and the long fringed belt made her slim legs look sensational; a seriously sexy black negligée cut so low it showed her belly button at the front, teamed with some studded Saint Laurent leather biker boots, created a truly original, cool festival look for the evening that she managed to pull off perfectly. As well as a killer body, Liv had bucket-loads of confidence.

I could see it all hanging together beautifully as a cool festival ensemble – one that would stand out from the cardboard cut-out Coachella crowd. After over an hour of trying on and picking her favourite pieces, both Liv and Mickey seemed thrilled with the results.

'Now, all I ask,' I commanded – as she was jumping around the room nymph-like, flapping the ostrich-feather fans, screaming '*J'adore! J'adore!*' – 'is that you take great care of all of these items I'm lending you. They've come straight from the wardrobe of someone very special – she was one of the original dancers for the Crazy Horse in Paris.' Liv 'Ooooh'-ed in response. 'These items are the real deal and their present owner will have me strung if they don't all return in the same condition.'

Pausing, she looked at me earnestly. 'I'm so grateful to you, Amber. Don't panic! I promise I'll have it all back to you in mint condition. Isn't that what you Brits say?'

CHAPTER ELEVEN

With still no word from Ron, Saturday rolled around and I gave myself the day off work to get ready for the fancy-dress party. Rob and I felt we had earned ourselves some fun in this city and tonight was the night.

Looking at ourselves in the bathroom mirror, we had to concede we looked fantastic as Britain's most famous couple – HM Queen Elizabeth II and her dashing husband, HRH the Duke of Edinburgh. Tina and Max swung by the apartment for a drink and a laugh at our outfits before we left.

'Honestly, those are the best outfits I have *ever* seen!' Tina gushed when I opened the door and invited them in with a royal wave. 'You don't even look like yourselves. I frickin' love it!'

'The dress is a 1950s original by the dressmaker to the Queen himself, don't you know,' I proudly informed her, a tiny bit miffed that I pulled off ninety-plus with such ease.

'Honey, you are *so* styling me next time we get invited to a costume party. Now, let me take your picture.'

I uploaded the image of Rob and I, arm in arm, corgi tucked between us, as the regal couple, just before we set off

in a taxi to the party: Juno filter; caption: By Royal appointment – dressed up and ready to rock as The Queen and
Duke of Edinburgh #Royal #RuleBritannia #NYC #Fashion
#HardyAmies #Corgi #Party #OOTN

The party was in Amy's loft apartment in a trendy area of
Brooklyn. You could tell just by looking at the building that
it was going to be at least five times the size of our sardine
tin. We'd spent so much time drinking wine with Tina and
Max, the party was in full swing when we arrived.

'Hey, guys!' Amy said, opening the door, her face swiftly
turning to a look of shocked amusement as she clocked
our outfits. 'Loving the costumes, um, to what do we owe
this honour, er, Your Highnesses?' She bowed her head and
curtsied, before putting a hand across her mouth to stifle
a full-blown laugh. 'It's not Halloween is it? Come in, the
others have got to see this!'

'When, erm, are you going to be putting on your costume?'
I asked her, my voice small and weak. It had to be said, she
looked stunning in a slinky red Vivienne Westwood cocktail
dress. She didn't even have to open the door very wide for
us to immediately realise, to my horror, that no one else was
in fancy dress.

Here I was, painted on wrinkles, powdery white bouffant,
demure apricot-coloured dress and coat, pearl necklace,
glittering crown, white gloves, sensible black shoes, matching
handbag and a cuddly corgi – that cost a bomb to be sent
by Air Mail from Hamley's in London – nestled in my arms.
At my first hip Brooklyn roof party.

Amy's flatmate, Kate, had joined her in the hallway, to take in the full spectacle of the unpaid entertainment.

'Oh, wow!' she exclaimed 'You look ah-mazing!' I didn't flinch, I couldn't bear to, this outfit was so scratchy.

'I'm so sorry, guys,' Amy said, trying desperately hard to look sincere, despite every muscle in her face wanting to crack up. 'When we said, "fancy dress", we meant "dress, fancy". I thought everyone knew a fancy-dress party is called a costume party in America?'

'Evidently not,' I muttered, feeling more ridiculous by the second. I looked to Rob for help. He only had to take off his top hat and tails, wipe off some of the wrinkles I had painted onto his face and he looked perfectly 'fancy' in his white shirt and dress trousers. There was no hope for me. The girls sensed we needed a minute alone to work out our position, that and to neck a strong drink.

'I thought you checked what Amy was wearing?' I said, snapping at Rob. I needed to blame someone for this humiliation and he was by far the best candidate.

'I did! I asked what she was wearing and she said Westwood – I told you that. We both jumped to the wrong conclusion.'

'But wasn't everyone talking about their costumes at work?' I said, pursuing the topic. 'You must have noticed they weren't?'

'It's rather stressful at work right now, as you might have noticed,' he retorted. 'Besides, you were having such a great time sourcing everything – you said yourself you wanted to surprise everyone – so I didn't feel the need to go into it at work, too. Come on, Amber, it was a genuine mistake. Anyway, we're here now, and the way I see it, we have two options.' He pulled me further into a corner, downing one of the miscellaneous very strong cocktails put into our hands by Kate. 'We can either have a complete sense-of-humour failure and leave. Or embrace the situation and get drunk. *Very* drunk. What's it going to be?'

I tried to ignore the prickly feeling building up behind my eyes.

'You know how much I hate fancy-dress parties – I knew it would be a disaster,' I protested, feeling angry now, as well as humiliated. A few party-goers moved past us in the corridor, commenting on my 'royal great-grandma' outfit, not even trying to hide their sniggers. Let's face it, the only place I would have blended in would have been the actual Buckingham Palace balcony. I looked away from them and back at Rob, taking a deep breath and a large swig of the cocktail, which was basically neat vodka. *I absolutely must not cry or I'll look even more ridiculous. I must rise above this. I must do what the Queen would do.*

The terrace was already full by the time we made our way upstairs. Some hot guy with a tattoo sleeve put a mojito in my hand, and someone else led everyone into a sing-song of the British National Anthem as I found myself being cajoled towards the centre of the terrace. I lifted my gloved hand and began twirling it regally, as a cheer went up around me. People stood up, offering me their seats, drinks and cigarettes were thrust towards me from every direction – along with flashing camera-phones. Despite how horribly conspicuous

I felt at first, the drinks helped take off the edge, and I soon saw the funny side, getting into character and embracing my role as Her Majesty Queen Amber of England.

As the hours passed, I had to admit I was having fun. I chatted to so many people – everyone was super friendly and nice. I had such a scream with a gay couple, Pierre and Peter, who, it turned out, lived just around the corner from us in Williamsburg, and we were soon plotting to get together again – they even invited Rob and me to their holiday home in Long Island. Rob gave me his undivided attention all evening, stealing me off for tipsy snogs and whispering, 'I'm so proud of you, baby,' and, 'You're the sexiest queen I've ever seen. Just wait 'til I get you back to the palace,' whenever we were pressed together, which was often. The corgi became the second most popular person at the party, being passed around and used for a never-ending stream of selfies.

I posted a photo of myself, crown at a jaunty angle, surrounded by all my new mates – my courtiers, as I was calling them by the end of the evening – on Instagram later that night: Lark filter; caption: Rule Britannia in Brooklyn! #stylist #NYC #GodSaveTheQueen

I wasn't sure what time we made it to bed that night, but by the state of the regal paraphernalia dotted around the apartment the next morning, we were feeling very amorous. I'd even gone so far as sourcing myself an ironic 'Crown Jewels' diamond-studded G-string (spotted in a SoHo sex shop as I hunted down nipple tassels for Liv) as a surprise for Rob, and this morning it was slung over the lamp by the TV.

As I lay in bed with a dry mouth and a sore head, the memories of the evening before slowly began to return. I grabbed my phone to scroll back through the photos, chuckling as they appeared on the screen. Rob was still asleep, mouth open, lying naked and mostly uncovered next to me. I'd taken close to thirty photos throughout the evening and they were so funny, my hangover was almost forgotten. And then I opened Instagram.

'Oh, my God!' I exclaimed. 'Oh. My. God.' I repeated the words, even louder.

'What?' muttered Rob, waking with a start. 'What's happened?'

He hoisted himself over, wiping the sleep away from his eyes.

'The Queen photos got over a thousand hits between them! My followers have gone above six thousand overnight!'

Rob lifted himself up onto his elbows, running a finger through his messed-up, slightly crusty, 'Prince Philip' hair.

'Queen Elizabeth of England, tell me, what *were* we drinking last night? My head feels like a blender with the top off.'

I was sitting bolt upright now, scrolling in disbelief through some of the comments under the image of me in full Queen regalia. Under the images, people had said things like:

'You rule!'

'Fashion Royalty'

'Where did you find the suit?'

'I want a corgi like that!' under the images.

Everything was positive and fun; not a troll in sight. Hundreds of hearts, crowns, fist pumps and Union Jack emoticons littered the page. Rob had snuggled up to my side now, for a look at the screen, his body still hot and clammy from sleep.

'It looks like Liv saw the photo and reposted it on her page – tagging me as her stylist! And then Hailey Baldwin picked it up from her, and now it's pretty much gone viral!' I exclaimed, as another thirty likes appeared just in the time I was looking at the screen.

'Are you an internet sensation, baby?' Rob asked, sarcastically, kissing my bare shoulder.

'Well, I'm certainly upping my online presence. If this is what Dana wants, she's got it.'

'Glad we didn't leave in a sulk last night then?' he asked, prodding me in the side. 'Oh, hater of fancy-dress parties.'

'Maybe. And, *d'oh*! They're called costume parties in America,' I said, smiling, before throwing the handset onto the floor and pulling the duvet over us both as we disappeared under it and enjoyed a long, sexy, snogging session.

Almost as good as being the star of a party was the lack of a major comedown, so buoyed was I by the steady stream of likes, comments and views of my page throughout the day. Likewise, my phone buzzed with texts and WhatsApp messages from my new friends. I barely remembered giving my number out to so many new people.

Later that day, Dana sent me a message, too. 'Hey, sugar, just seen your Insta – go girl! – loving the Queen get-up!'

It was funny how not even working had done more for my career than I ever imagined.

Late morning, I got a text from Pierre and Peter, inviting us to brunch at a nearby coffee house. We put on comfy clothes and joined them for a Full American – pancakes with berries, crispy bacon, avocado, eggs – basically as many sides as the menu would allow – drenched in puddles of maple syrup.

'Now *this* is living in New York City,' Rob remarked, squeezing me close as we devoured it all, alongside a never-ending stream of coffee.

All I managed was a contented nod.

'And then it's back to bed to sleep it all off,' Pierre instructed. 'That's my Sunday recipe for success.'

Thankfully, any trace of a hangover – food- *or* alcohol-related – had finally passed by Monday morning, and things were looking up by eleven o'clock, when Rob called to tell me the news that Ron had decided to keep the Angel Wear TV production going. I breathed a sigh of relief. Over the weekend, I had managed to bury the nagging worry that our New York dream could be cut short, as it was completely out of our hands.

'So we're stuck with the sardine tin for the next few months after all,' he said. I sensed a 'but' was coming. 'There is something else, though,' he continued, his tone more sub-dued, confirming my fear. 'Instead of canning the TV show, we're going to make his search for a new stylist part of the filming.'

'Great…' I breathed heavily. 'So – does he want to see me?'

He took my hand. 'I'm really sorry, but he's asked to pass. I really tried, Amber, but he and Dimitri, the lead designer on the show, didn't want to waste your time.'

I hung my head. Whilst I wasn't entirely surprised – it was such a huge job for someone just starting out over here – the rejection still stung.

'Do you have any leads on who the new stylist will be?' I asked, trying to sound upbeat.

'Well, I hate to say it, but Mona Armstrong's name got mooted in the meeting,' he revealed, making me bristle. I still hadn't come to terms with some truly hideous memories of carrying the can while she was either drunk, hungover, or in police custody when I was her awards season assistant.

'You're not *serious*?'

'Don't panic, I told everyone what a nightmare she is,' he explained. 'They won't choose her. And then your mate Lola Jones came up.'

'Ah, baldy.' I sighed.

'They want a big name to draw in the column inches,' he said. 'If you have any ideas, let me know. There are a couple of others coming to an audition tomorrow, as we need to get them in place by the end of the week. A few months isn't very long to pull together a world-class stage show. Ron's got the jitters about it already. Anyway, I've got to go, I just wanted to let you know, and to tell you that we don't need to re-pack our suitcases after all.'

What with the Maurice mayhem and then the fancy-dress frenzy, I had barely allowed myself to dare to imagine I might be in with a chance of the Angel Wear job, but now that it was out of my grasp, I felt completely flat. It would have been such a coup; something worth calling home about and enough to cause a genuine stir among my social media followers.

I hadn't been able to look at Lola Jones's Instagram account since the fateful 'alopecia incident', for fear that she had mounted a campaign to have me hunted down and publicly humiliated, but an hour later, I was still glued to social media. Just this morning, Lola had posted an image of herself, head shaved in a defiant skinhead, rocking scarlet lips and an ear full of studs, on the cover of *New York* magazine. BEYOND THE WIG: LOLA COMES CLEAN ran the headline. As I read the accompanying interview, she actually thanked 'British fashion blogger and stylist Amber Green' for finally giving her a platform to tell the truth about her debilitating alopecia – brought on by the stress of her job, combined with a secret eating disorder – in the hope that it gave hope to others suffering too.

'Fashion blogger and stylist!' I raved to Rob when he returned home that evening. 'Not only does Lola Jones know my name, but she's made me a bona fide stylist and my name is printed in *New York* magazine!'

Rob leaned across and planted a kiss on my shoulder.

He smiled. 'That's great, baby.'

'It's going to make me!' I exclaimed, a little perturbed that he didn't seem more genuinely excited about this pivotal moment in my career. It was a situation like this that could literally launch me on to the world stage.

'Seriously, I'm chuffed for you,' he said. 'Now, isn't it your turn to make dinner, or are we going out again?'

'In a minute.' I barely heard him. 'Oh, and my followers

have gone up by another few hundred today – and I haven't even posted anything. I'm nearly over seven K!'

'Seven K. Fantastic.' I detected a note of sarcasm in his voice. 'Now, isn't it time you showed *me* some affection, rather than being all misty-eyed about seven thousand strangers?'

The following morning, no sooner had I wriggled out of bed at seven o'clock to check social media – I always got an influx overnight, the UK being ahead of us – and then wiggled my way back in again to tell Rob of the hundreds more followers I'd picked up, than I was sliding out again, to see who was buzzing at our front door.

'Jesus, you're like a jack-in-the-box this morning. Leave it,' he mumbled, reaching for my wrist but missing.

'But what if it's Maurice?' I said, already throwing the duvet back.

'Why would Maurice be knocking for you this early on a Tuesday?' he mumbled. 'And, anyway, how does Maurice know where you live? It's probably just the postman.'

'He could have asked Patti Rose and she could have asked Dana – I'm sure there are a million ways someone can find someone's address in this city if they really want to,' I replied, pulling down my oversized T-shirt on the way to the intercom.

'And how do you know *he really wants to*…?' Rob shouted after me. But I was already pressing the button.

'Hello?'

'Amber?' said a small female voice at the other end. The accent was immediately detectable as English, so at first I assumed it was Amy, come to pick up Rob on the way to work perhaps.

'Is that you, Amy?'

'No, it's, um—' The voice stopped, as if it was having second thoughts. *I know that voice.* 'It's Vicky.'

'Vicky?' I caught my breath. *There is only one Vicky.* 'My Vicky?' I said, already knowing that it was her. 'What the…?'

'Yes, babe, it's me. Let me in, it's f-ing freezing out here.'

I buzzed her in and ran back to the bedroom to grab a sweater and my big fluffy slipper socks, before screaming, '*It's Vicky! On our doorstep!*' to a bemused Rob, and flying out of the front door.

I took the stairs two at a time, although I needn't have been in such a rush, because someone had let her in through the communal door.

'*Vicky!*'

CHAPTER TWELVE

'Sorry, I pressed a few wrong buzzers before I found you,' Vicky said softly. When she looked up her eyes were puffy and red-rimmed.

'Honey, what's happened?'

She set the suitcase down and launched at me for a big bear hug. I pulled her in close, feeling suddenly maternal towards my oldest friend in the world.

'It's okay, you're safe,' I whispered into her ear as she began sobbing on my shoulder. 'Whatever it is, we can sort it together, just like we always do. It's going to be okay.'

When we pulled away I took in the extent of her red-stained eyes and slipped make-up. Her normally groomed, glossy hair looked unkempt and she wasn't wearing her usual layer of immaculately applied flicky eyeliner. This wasn't the Vicky I knew.

'I'm sorry,' she whimpered. 'I thought I'd got it together in the cab, but it was seeing you. I couldn't help it.'

'Come on, you never need to put on a front for me. Let me give you a hand with that case.' And we hauled it up the stairs together.

Rob met us halfway and took over suitcase duties. He

and I exchanged a puzzled look as he took in Vicky's blotchy face. When we reached the top, he considerately disappeared into the shower to give us some space. And when I had put steaming big mugs of tea into our hands and we sat down on the sofa, Vicky began to explain what the hell was going on.

'I've told Trey we need to consciously uncouple for a while,' she said, her breathing a little less erratic now. 'I mean, I hope we'll re-couple, when I get back, I'm sure we will, but I just need a bit of time to remember who I am again.'

I looked at her blankly. 'But tell me you're not actually using that phrase in real life?' She shrugged in response. 'Consciously uncouple? I don't think the world's big enough for two Gwyneth Paltrows.' I tried to lighten the atmosphere before conceding that she wasn't in the mood. 'So what actually happened with Trey?' I probed gently.

Vicky remained mute for a while. Every now and again, she looked as though she was going to speak, but it was as though she was forming sentences in her mind, and then couldn't let them out. Eventually, on her third cup of tea, she visibly seemed to relax. 'Sorry, I sounded like a dick just then. It's great to be here with my bestie. Believe me, all I want right now is to have my old life back.'

I pulled her in for another hug, like the old friends we were. Over the next two hours, save for breaking briefly to wave Rob off to work, we were locked in conversation about how the honeymoon with Trey had basically ended a couple of months ago.

'He literally works every hour known to man,' she complained. 'And there are only so many Pilates and yoga classes

I could make myself go to, plus solo trips to coffee shops. Honestly, I have more chat with the servers in Starbucks on Sunset Boulevard during the week than with my actual so-called boyfriend. LA can be a lonely place when you don't have any real friends,' she lamented. 'I was honestly starting to feel like an alien out there. Trey's doing nothing for my self-confidence.'

As Vicky recounted examples of how her successful movie-director boyfriend had neglected her time and again, the tears fell hard and fast. It seemed that the idyllic, showbiz lifestyle she appeared to be living when you viewed it on Facebook couldn't be further from the truth. I told her everything she needed to hear – and I was telling the truth – that she deserved better, that he was a fool, that there were plenty more guys out there and that she didn't have to turn herself over to a life of misery and loneliness if it wasn't making her happy.

When she had finished venting, the conversation turned to practicalities. Her eyes at last began to properly take in our surroundings; we had made the apartment as cute and cosy as we could, with limited time and resources, but there was no getting around the fact that it was a shoebox. I tried to shake off a feeling of inadequacy – that this humble home was all Rob and I could afford in this city.

'So, well, I was wondering whether you might have a little corner of a sofa that I could crash on, just for a few days, until I get my shit together and formulate a plan?' she asked.

I didn't need to think twice.

'Of course. Honey, you're my best friend, there's no way I'll let you sleep anywhere else.' We hugged again, and then

I looked her in the eye and waggled my finger mischievously. 'So you can dust yourself down – there's no chance of you forgetting who you are around here, I promise you that. It's not like we have servants to sprinkle chia seeds on your almond-milk bircher muesli every morning, or a gardener to prune your roses. LA is a long way away now, girlfriend. This is more like your old Kensal Rise life, just in Brooklyn, in a much smaller flat. Welcome back!'

She launched at me for the umpteenth bear hug that morning.

At some point in the late afternoon, I realised I'd better run the 'Vicky crashing over' situation past Rob. I had left her in a changing room, racking up a shopping bill on Trey's credit card – *turns out he does have some uses* – while I called him.

'But, baby, what about Dan?' he asked. 'I told you he wanted to come over for bit to get his head together over Florence fuck-for-brains.'

'Oh, damn, I totally forgot – you hadn't mentioned it again. When's Dan meant to be coming?'

'I'm just waiting for him to let me know his flight details, but he could be arriving as soon as tomorrow. There's no space for the two of them in our sardine tin. And Dan is my brother at the end of the day – plus, he staked his claim first.'

'But what am I going to tell—' I faked a smile and nodded approvingly as Vicky came to the shop door and gave me a twirl in a gorgeous little red Prada number. A dress I could only dream of being able to afford brand new.

'Tell her you made a mistake. Surely her rich Hollywood-director-boyfriend can afford to sub her a hotel for a few nights, can't he?'

'I suppose. But not tonight, she's shattered. I'll deal with it tomorrow.' I sighed, looking at Vicky through the shop window, as she gleefully pulled more clothes off the rails in Williamsburg's most upmarket boutique and threw them over her arm. *She is currently displaying the kind of boundless energy I know her for. She'll be fine.*

Late afternoon, back on the sofa in the apartment, bottle of white wine and bowl of crisps in front of us, Vicky was showing me her iPhone snaps. There was Trey's house – make that mansion – with its electric gates and palatial exterior; the sumptuous living room, all white sofas, modern light installations and contemporary art; a close-up of just one vase, holding more roses than I had probably ever been given in my entire life; a view of the tropical garden taken from their bedroom; a hot guy cleaning the pool; Trey's bulldog; Vicky's pedicured feet on a lounger; her bikini briefs showing a bit of tan line; her tits. *Her tits?*

'Wait a minute, what was that?' I asked, as the photo was quickly swiped off the screen and replaced by an image of an orchid.

'Oh, the orchid? The gardener put a new rare breed in the beds a couple of weeks ago,' she muttered quickly.

'No, the one before it.'

'My new bikini, I wanted to see how it looked.'

'No, the one after that – it looked like some tits.'

She paused.

'Vicky?'

I grabbed her phone and swiped to find the image again.

'These tits – see,' I said, smiling.

She took a large glug of wine.

'They're tits, okay? My tits, as you probably guessed.'

'Why did you take a photo of your tits? I mean, I know they're great tits, but do you need to refer to them that often on your phone? Don't tell me you had a boob job?'

'No! No boob job, I swear it. Listen, I meant to delete them.' She sat back in the sofa, acting all coy.

I waited for her to carry on.

'Okay, so I took a photo of them to send to someone,' she said, after a beat.

'And why do I get the impression that the lucky someone isn't Trey?' I asked

She hung her head.

'I'm not proud of it, okay.'

I flung my hand over my mouth, aghast. 'I knew it!'

'You're so prudish sometimes, Am. Lighten up, you've got a pair too, you know.'

Yes, I am generally more prudish than Vicky. And, yes, she does have an exceptionally good rack. But, text them to someone – really?

'So, if not Trey, who did you send them to?'

She unfurled her legs from underneath herself. 'I'm not sure I can tell you.'

'Sending pics of your tits to someone other than your boyfriend – isn't that what glamour models do to footballers?'

She looked away. 'Oh God, don't tell me you sent them to a footballer…'

'It's called *soccer* in America.'

'Touché. Anyway, don't change the subject.'

I could tell by her face that she was now starting to enjoy watching me squirm. In fact, if I wasn't mistaken, she was trying not to laugh.

'What, you sent them to a random person then?' I asked, not letting it lie. 'Or did you put them on the internet? That's porn. That's disgusting.'

She started openly laughing now. 'Oh, Amber. It's not porn and it's not disgusting. You sound like a bloody matron. It was an old flame, okay.'

'Sunday Simon? I thought you hated his guts.'

'No, someone else.'

'Are you having an affair, Vicky? I'm not sure if I can condone—'

She held up her hand before letting out a sigh and looking away, across the kitchenette towards the window.

'So that's what all this is about is it?' I was feeling a bit annoyed.

She turns up here, in tears at the door of my new home, all devastated over Trey, then ridicules me for being prudish and thinks it's a huge joke that she's got some other guy on the go. 'You've met someone else and that's why you've uncoupled, or whatever you're calling it, with Trey?'

Finally, she looked me in the eye.

'No, I'm not having any affair, Amber, I swear it. Okay, so I sent my tits to Jim from the art desk at my old job in

London. I was feeling shit about Trey and I was bored. We had been texting that week and it was a spur of the moment thing. It was nothing. And I'm really, *really* sorry you had to see them too. So that's it.'

We both slouched back into our seats, unsure what to say next. The silence was awkward. Vicky had been here for less than twenty-four hours and now we'd had a kind of argument.

'I'll get some bedding ready,' I said finally, standing up and making my way to the bedroom. 'Rob will be back soon.' Vicky followed me.

'Look, I hate arguing with you, Amber, let's start again. Can we? I'm sorry if you think I'm being a dick. I'll sort myself out, okay. Now how about we pop out for a proper drink? We've haven't properly toasted being back together yet and you must have some great neighbourhood bars around here. Come on, I'm dying to explore some more. I've only been to New York once and never to Williamsburg.'

I smiled at my friend. 'As long as you don't get your tits out.'

'Promise,' she said, giggling.

No matter how contrary or infuriating Vicky could be, she was still my best friend. I knew every freckle on that face, every crease when she laughed, and she was a comforting sight to see out here.

'There is a particularly good dive just around the corner, as it happens,' I said. 'Let's do it, before Rob gets back.'

She was already putting on her new Marc by Marc Jacobs coat, also bought on Trey's card this afternoon.

CHAPTER THIRTEEN

After a few drinks in Williamsburg, we decided to get a cab and hit Manhattan proper. Being a New York nightlife novice, I decided to call Amy for advice on where we should go.

'No way! Kate and I are in the Meatpacking District right now. Come join us – let's have an impromptu girls' night out!'

I looked towards Vicky and shrugged. 'Impromptu girls' night out in the Meatpacking?'

'As long as we're not going to be actually butchering anything, sounds good to me,' she said.

Amy, of course, picked one of the coolest nightclubs in Manhattan, for the time being at least. It was Le Bain, a rooftop club affiliated to the achingly hip Standard High Line hotel, and for which you had to be on a guest list – or look like Rosie Huntington-Whiteley – to gain entry, where you then mingled with other beautiful people and paid an extortionate amount for cocktails while taking in incredible views. The other thing was that we couldn't actually go in until past eleven o'clock, which meant I was feeling the effects of I forget how many vodka and tonics in a nearby bar before we even got to the main part of the evening. The door was manned by a bald-headed, deeply tanned, barrel-chested man dressed in a black overcoat and trousers and wearing an ear piece. He looked more like a celebrity bodyguard than a bouncer.

He beckoned her over with the bearing of a good-natured bruiser as we approached the queue. 'Kate, baby – looking hot tonight.' Our party of three fell into line behind her as Kate batted her thickly made-up eyelashes and turned to check we had noted the bouncer speaking to her with such familiarity. A vein bulged on his neck suggesting a seriously muscular physique beneath his coat. Within seconds we were being swept through a heavy curtain and into a lift up to the penthouse level of the hotel. Inside, the club was heaving with bodies, the music was loud, the baseline thudding. I felt a rush of excitement. We headed towards the crowded bar area. On our way we were intercepted by three extraordinarily tall women wearing skintight dresses with plunging necklines leaving little to the imagination. I recognised one of them instantly as an Angel Wear Icon, and the other two had to be models.

'Hey, Amy!' one of them called. It was Astrid; I'd rec-ognise that perfectly tousled long platinum-blonde hair, washboard stomach and legs up to her armpits anywhere. She really was incredible to look at – almost other worldly, her limbs so slim and skin so golden and flawless, it was as if she had been airbrushed all over. I tried hard to find just one flaw on her perfectly made-up face, but it was impossible. I glanced at Vicky, who was staring fixedly at her too, her eyes slowly wandering up and down that heavenly body. As I looked around me I noticed most of the club patrons were doing the same. *I wonder how much she has her assets insured for.*

Amy was thrilled to have been singled out by the resident celebrity and was chatting animatedly to Astrid and her friends, who turned out to be secondary Angel Wear Icons, sitting on a kind of subs bench, ready to step in if an actual Icon was taken ill or had to pull out of an Angel Wear engagement at short notice. I could only think they didn't quite make the grade because, if you really scrutinised them for imperfections, one was at least an inch smaller than Astrid, with lips on the thin side, and the other had a marginally wonky nose. In the great scheme of Angel Wear models, they were the misshapen biscuits that didn't make the deluxe variety pack.

Amy gestured towards me. 'Have you met Amber yet?' she asked.

Astrid's vivid-green cat-like eyes took in my outfit (a not particularly sexy pair of grey jeggings and black batwing top combo, as I hadn't realised at the start of the evening – as with so many evenings out with Vicky – that things would take an unexpected turn. *Thank God, I thought to fling on some heels.*) 'Amber is Rob's girlfriend,' Amy continued.

Astrid looked puzzled. 'As in Rob, the director?'

Finally, a flash of recognition on Astrid's stunning face. *She's dim! I knew there'd be something – she's got cotton wool for brains! Hooray!*

'Of course, how cute,' she purred, showing me as much warmth as a person with very little body fat is able to emanate. She held out a dainty hand and I shook it. Her handshake was flimsy and, despite the searing heat in this club, her skin felt cool. However, the fact that Astrid didn't instantly know who Rob was actually offered me some comfort. I'd been desperately trying to block out feelings of jealousy around the glamazons my boyfriend was spending time with every day, and she had pretty much proven in a few seconds that the only people the models were really interested in was themselves.

'Have you checked out the pool yet?' Astrid asked.

'Pool?' I shrugged.

'Over there, it's fun – let's go,' she pointed towards a dimly lit area in one corner of the club, where floor-to-ceiling windows framed an incredible view of Manhattan twinkling beneath us. A huge glitter ball twirled above a plunge pool where the party was just getting started. Four bikini-clad babes sat on one side, their legs dangling into the water. And a group of bare-chested guys sat ogling them from a seating area in front of the windows. As Astrid led the way, her two friends fell into line behind her and as they wound their way through the crowds to the pool area, heads turned and voyeurs whispered behind hands that we were in the presence of an actual Angel Wear Icon. As the evening went on, I soon realised that being one degree of separation from a real-life Icon was a passport into another world. Groups of men found her magnetic and, by association, neither Vicky nor I had to dip into our own purses for drinks for most of the evening.

We based ourselves in a little cordoned off area by the side of the pool – presumably pre-arranged for Astrid so that she didn't have to constantly pose with the 'normal' people asking for selfies. I entertained myself by imagining what would happen if she were to 'accidentally' trip on her heels and belly flop into the water. At one point she kicked off a heel and trailed her toes in the pool, teasing the assembled male admirers with the thought that they might be treated to seeing her strip off and actually get in.

'It's toasty...' She smiled as all the men in the room willed her to slowly peel off her skintight silver dress and dive in. 'Dare you, Amy!' she goaded.

'Are you joking? Babe, it took me a whole hour to get my bangs this straight this evening. No way am I fucking that up for a quick dip. I double dare you.'

Astrid knocked back a shot of tequila, one of which had somehow found its way into each of our hands from another random admirer of hers.

'Only if you'll do it too,' she cajoled her friends, Brandy and Sophia, who looked as though they probably wouldn't need much goading.

Suddenly, from nowhere, a guy jumped up high and hurled himself into the pool with such vigour we all got splashed.

'It's hot in here – come and join me!' he shouted at the models as he resurfaced.

'Fuck it!' Astrid screamed, kicking off her heels and jumping in after him.

'Fuck, fuck, fuck!' yelled Brandy with the wonky nose and joined her, causing a cheer to go up from the assembled clubbers as more people shed items of clothing, gripped their knees, and bombed into the pool sending waves over the edge.

'Triple dare you, Amber!' Vicky squealed, giving me a nudge. I recoiled, moving to a safe position further away from the water's edge.

'Over my dead body – don't you—'

'Amber!' a shrill American voice called out. I looked over my shoulder, at first assuming someone else by my name must be drinking nearby. But then a small, soft hand reached for mine, saving me from a near-certain soaking.

It was Poppy, looking red-hot in a white broderie mini-dress and next season's Most Swooned Over shoes – the new studded Chloé black ankle boot. I'd been trying to work out how I could afford them ever since they appeared on Net-a-Porter. She held her arms open to hug me.

'Wow, you look sensational!' she stole the words right out of my mouth, except I didn't look half as sensational as she did and she had to know it. The girl-next-door-actress with a penchant for micro-pigs who was sitting on my sofa in London just a few weeks ago was gone, and in her place was a fashionista movie star no doubt racking up another appearance on a 'Get the Look' page of a fashion magazine with her outfit this evening. But, most importantly – why was she in New York and not at home looking after Pinky?

The guy minding the entrance to our roped-off pen evidently recognised her too and she was ushered through to join us, no questions asked.

'How come you're here?' I shouted above the music, which had suddenly got very loud and very Kanye.

She pulled me close and whispered in my ear. 'I'm here for the bag drop. Same as you, I guess?'

'The *what*?' I wasn't sure if I'd heard her correctly above the booming music. *What the hell is a 'bag drop'? Something to do with lost luggage?* But Poppy just touched her nose and winked knowingly. Not wanting to look clueless, I smiled and winked back.

'How are you getting on with Astrid?' she bellowed. We both turned to look at her in the water. By now there were at least ten practically naked guys buzzing around her like she was their queen bee. *How her make-up stays put and her hair still looks glamorous despite being dripping wet, I don't know.*

'Rob's getting on okay with them during filming,' I told her.

She rolled her eyes. 'Spending every day with those girls? Tough job, poor lamb. Is Rob here?'

'Not tonight!' I yelled back, thinking how much I wished Rob was here and not only because my head was starting to spin – I was concerned that should I end up in the water, I might not actually resurface. I had a realisation that school swimming lessons and the seemingly pointless exercise of making floats out of pyjamas were clearly designed for situations like this in which you might unexpectedly need to create a life raft from your clothing. *Shame my head is too scrambled to remember how to do it.*

'Phew!' she exclaimed, wrapping an arm around my shoulder and pulling me tightly into her slender body. 'You won't tell Rob about this, will you? I'd *hate* him to think I was neglecting his pig. Pinky is perfectly safe round at my friend Charlie's house. Charlie's the biggest vegan you'll meet. And I'll be back in London next Friday.'

The fact that this Charlie was unlikely to chop Pinky up into pieces and eat him for dinner didn't offer me much comfort.

'Next Friday? That's a whole ten days away, you know how much Rob adores that pig. Are you *sure* Pinky's okay?'

'Amber, chill out. Pinky is fine. It's not exactly hard to keep a pig alive. Come to the toilets with me?' I noticed her eyes looked wider than normal, her pupils dilated. Her aggressive tone startled me. 'Sorry, didn't mean to shout, it's just I'm not up for heavy chats – I'm celebrating tonight,' she continued.

'I wasn't trying to be heavy,' I muttered. 'Anyway, what are you celebrating?' I shifted myself around awkwardly within her tight grip, wondering where Vicky had got to. I scanned the pool but couldn't see her frolicking in it. Poppy was chatting away so fast I was finding it hard to keep up.

'Somehow I've managed to get a part in the new Channing Tatum movie. The casting director offered it to me on the spot, today. It was a last-minute audition after Amanda Sykes had to pull out. As we've got the same agent, he put me forward immediately. Channing "top-off" Tatum, can you believe it? I can't! Anyway, about the bag drop, I want to ask you something – in private. Let's go to the loos.'

The 'bag drop' sounded dodgy as hell and, judging by Poppy's mannerisms tonight, I could only think it was something to do with drugs. I certainly didn't want to get involved but, at the same time, Poppy's presence was making me look fantastic in front of Amy and Kate, who were quietly gawping at me chatting to another celebrity in our growing VIP area. I took Poppy's hand and we weaved our way through the crowded dance floor to the Ladies'. En route, we bumped into Vicky returning from the bar with four tequila shots in test tubes.

'Oh! I only got four,' she said dismissively, clocking Poppy, whose arm was threaded tightly with mine like *she* was my BFF and not Vicky.

'No matter, I can't do more than two at a time anyway!' Poppy replied animatedly, stealing two and downing them in a flash, one after another. We both looked at her aghast. 'Oops,' she hiccuped. 'My round next. We'll be back in a sec.' And she whisked me off leaving Vicky bemused in our wake.

'Don't mind me then!' Vicky called after her. I turned back in an effort to tell her with my eyes that this wasn't my idea – it was Poppy's – and caught her swigging back the remaining two shots. I got the sense these two were going to clash.

The toilets were small and busy. An attendant stood by the door tutting as each woman left without crossing her tips bowl with a dollar bill. When we reached the front of the queue, she moodily passed us a folded up tissue each and gestured towards a collection of perfumes, deodorants and hairsprays. Signs on each of the cubicle doors read: ONE PERSON PER CUBICLE.

'Don't mind if I do,' squawked Poppy, lifting a can of deodorant and spraying so much under her armpits it turned the room into a foggy cloud of powder and made me sneeze.

When the attendant turned to do the same, Poppy yanked me into a cubicle with her.

'But we're not—' She silenced me with her finger, closed the toilet lid and sat down on it, lifting her feet off the ground like a pro.

'Why the need for all this secrecy?' I asked, while she fished around in her oversized clutch bag for something. She pulled out a crumpled brown envelope.

'It's about the bag drop. I couldn't ask you out there, because I don't want anyone to overhear us,' she whispered. 'The guy will be around in less than an hour and – as you're clearly here for the same reason – I was wondering if you could take this – it's more cash than you'll need.'

I stared suspiciously into her very big and round eyes. I was expecting her to start racking up lines of cocaine on the toilet seat at any moment. *How naive does she think I am?*

'Listen, Poppy,' I began, 'each to their own, but drugs aren't my thing – I'll leave the bag drop, if you don't mind.'

She laughed in my face. 'What are you on about, silly? I'm after the three-point-one Phillip Lim Pashli satchel in black. You know the one. I've been thinking about it non-stop. What are you getting?'

Now she's talking to me about It bags. What kind of substance is she on, something far more sinister than cocaine!

'I'm sorry, Poppy,' I whispered, 'but I don't have a clue what you're on about. If it's drugs you're after, I'm afraid they're not my thing – you'll have to sort yourself out, or ask someone else.'

'Drugs? What do you mean?' she hissed. 'Do you really

think I'd risk losing my visa for the sake of a bag of coke? Cocaine is *so* five years ago. *Everyone's* talking about the three point one – if you don't have one, you can't say you're in fashion. I'm going on set next week and I *need* this bag to carry my scripts in.'

'Well, why don't you just go and buy one?' I snapped, feeling ridiculous to be having such a pointless, bizarre conversation in a toilet cubicle – especially when my oldest friend was outside, upset and doing tequila shots on her own.

'That's what I'm trying to do, you moron! Of course I can't afford the real thing, who can? This is the next best thing. There's four hundred dollars in the envelope – it shouldn't cost more than three hundred. But don't let him peddle you anything else, I need the change.' She winked. 'For tequila.'

Finally, it twigged. 'So this "bag drop" – you're talking about some guy selling knock-off designer handbags?'

'Durr!' she exclaimed. 'Don't tell me you really didn't know? The "third Tuesday bag drop" is legendary. The Bag Man comes to this part of town on the third Tuesday night of every month. That's why you'll find the fash pack filling out the clubs in the area – it's no coincidence that half the hottest models in New York are in this club tonight – they all placed their orders days ago. Those girls you see swishing around fashion shows and industry parties with Hermès and Chanels on their arms? Eighty per cent of them are fake, and no one will ever know because the Bag Man's knock-offs are *that* good.'

'But they work in fashion or they're famous, surely they're falling over designer freebies?' I asked, unconvinced that this wasn't a front for some kind of drug-mule operation, with kilos of Columbia's finest hidden inside the latest leatherwear.

'Not any more!' Poppy explained. 'The fashion houses don't give out freebies like they used to. And have you seen the price tags for the real things? You have to be a genuine millionaire to live in that world and believe me, most people who work in fashion are *not* millionaires. *You* should know. Anyway, there's no time for this. When it's your turn, you'll get a text from the Bag Man – go meet him in the allotted place for the handover. I've taken the liberty of texting him your cell number.'

'You *what*?'

'Seriously, Amber, you don't think *I* can be seen loitering on a street corner with a brown-paper envelope at this time of night, do you? The paps will have a field day. The gossip mags will be claiming I'm a woman of the night before you can say, "Belle du Jour."'

'So you thought *I'd* enjoy loitering on a street corner in the freezing cold, instead?' I uttered, feeling incredulous that she'd got me involved in a dodgy deal without my consent; one that could quite possibly end my career if I got caught. There's nothing the fashion houses hate more than rip-offs of their signature accessories. *I'm sure there's even a law against selling counterfeit goods. I could probably end up in prison. Rob's going to hit the roof.*

'Look, if you want Pinky to stay safe and sound while

I'm over here, you'll do this for me Amber.' She was staring pleadingly at me.

'Are you trying to blackmail me, Poppy?' I looked her dead in the eye and saw her wince.

We were cut off by a loud knocking at the cubicle door and the voice of the angry attendant. 'Has somebody died in there? Hurry up, lady, there's a line out here!'

'Looks like there's no time to argue about it,' Poppy whispered, flushing the chain, and yelling, '*Coming!* Dodgy stomach!', before ushering me out. 'You distract her with a tip, while I follow.'

I pulled my mobile out of my bag as we left the loos and, sure enough, there was a text message from an unknown number:

Meet me behind the Gansevoort Hotel in 20 mins. When you get there don't text, call me

It had to be the Bag Man.

I showed the text to Poppy who nodded sagely, and told me to reply:

OK, see you then

Immediately, a response:

No talking about me in public. No number passing without my clearance. If you fuck up – you get cut off. OK lovely? Big kiss x

It was the most passive aggressive text I'd ever read. A chill ran down my spine. *Who and what am I getting involved with?* I still didn't completely believe that Poppy wasn't setting me up with the local drug dealer.

Back in the main club room, I spotted Vicky instantly;

she was with Amy and Kate in the VIP area, standing on the seating and throwing shapes at a group of nearby blokes. They all had huge grins on their faces and were laughing hysterically as their 'dance off' broke into some vigorous twerking to some heavy hip hop. I wished I was up there with them having fun rather than getting involved with whatever it was with Poppy. My head was swimming, my heart pounding, and not in a fun way any more.

'I'll get the tequilas in!' Poppy shouted, disappearing off towards the bar.

I rejoined Vicky.

'This is hilarious!' she gasped, breathless and dizzy from all the twerking, 'Don't point, but the guy in the white T-shirt at two o'clock, we've been eyeing each other up all evening. How fit is he?'

I tried to zone in on who she might mean.

'Hey, hands off, he's been shaking his booty at me!' Amy chimed in. 'I'll fight you for him if I have to.'

'Ooh, there'll be murder on the dance floor if I don't get there first!' squealed Kate as the three of them dissolved into giggles once more and the white-T-shirt man began blowing kisses at all three, clearly revelling in the attention from a trio of gorgeous single-ish girls – the 'ish' being Vicky.

'Anyway, where were you? I thought you'd got flushed down the loo,' Vicky said.

'I need to speak to you,' I whispered. 'Bloody Poppy, she's got me involved in something and I need your help.' I grabbed her hand and reluctantly Vicky climbed down from the banquette and followed me. Making our way through the jungle of bodies crushed together, I had no idea where I was leading her, but it didn't really matter, we just needed to be far away from the bar, so we wouldn't risk bumping into Poppy. We squeezed past the white-T-shirt man and I'm sure Vicky would have stopped and tried to snog him had I not yanked her past. I could tell she was finding it hard to walk in a straight line. *What is everyone on in here?*

CHAPTER FOURTEEN

'We shouldn't do this. We could end up in really deep shit, Amber,' Vicky cautioned, leaning into me as we turned the corner, finding ourselves on a dark and empty narrow street behind the Gansevoort Hotel, not more than five minutes from the nightclub. We had walked most of the way in silence, each considering what on earth we were doing. 'It's so bloody obvious, Am. The Bag Man? Jesus! Poppy is blatantly talking about bags of cocaine, not knock-off Chanels – it's some kind of code. I wish I'd been there when she was feeding you this Grade A bullshit, Amber. You saw how wired she was. Granted, I've not met Poppy before, but her eyes…? She was blatantly on something. How gullible could we be?' This was Vicky being kind – she clearly meant how gullible could *I* be.

'But Pinky…' I said in a whimper. 'I'm doing this for Pinky – Rob will go insane if anything happens to his precious pig. I can't believe Poppy's blackmailing me.'

But Vicky wasn't listening because it was too late – a suspicious-looking black sports car complete with blacked-out windows was slowly approaching our bit of the pavement, its engine gently purring like a predatory lion. It looked every inch like your archetypal drug dealer's car.

I stared at Vicky then turned towards the vehicle. 'Well, whatever he is, he's here now.' She sounded as worried as I felt.

'It's fine.' I tried to reassure her, though my face, I'm sure, told a different story. 'I grew up in North London. I can handle it and I'm going to see this thing through. We haven't done anything wrong – remember?' My words belied a panicky feeling starting to sweep over me, sending a chill through my body, sobering me up.

'You grew up in Zone Five London suburbia, Amber. This is New York,' Vicky pointed out, before snapping: 'It's completely different!'

We'd stopped under a street light – I wanted to be able to see who I was about to get into a strange car with. I lifted the collars on my biker jacket, to try to make my appearance look tougher. Vicky reached out and gave me a firm pat on the back, for good luck. 'Take down the number plate, will you,' I whispered quickly, as the car finally came to a halt. 'If I'm not back in ten minutes, you can call Rob and call the police at the same time. Call whoever you like – just not my mum.'

I was shocked to see that Vicky had a look on her face that suggested she was about to burst out laughing.

'Oh, God, I'm sorry, babe... you know I always want to laugh when I'm nervous.' She was properly giggling to herself as she took out her phone and began punching in the car's number plate. 'I can't believe we're doing this.' *She wouldn't find it so funny if it was her about to get into a car with someone who could well be Manhattan's biggest drug's baron.*

There was no point delaying the inevitable, so I began

tentatively walking the few steps towards the other car, willing the windows to wind down and a friendly, smiling face to appear, putting everyone's mind at rest. Instead, engine now turned off, the car remained still and dark.

Giggles just about under control, Vicky suddenly coughed loudly to get my attention. When I turned to see what she wanted, she ushered me back.

'What is it?' I hissed, already feeling like a bumbling amateur in front of the Bag Man. He was probably laughing his head off in there, watching the two of us all stressed and jittery – if we dallied around much longer we might get reported for suspicious behaviour ourselves.

Vicky coughed again. 'Um, just thinking, that if you *don't* end up being a drug's mule and it really *is* knock-off bags, can you get me anything by Celine, please? Or, failing that, a small monogrammed Saint Laurent?' She thrust some screwed-up notes into my jacket pocket. 'There should be enough here.' I hurriedly brushed her hand away, rolling my eyes and turning back towards the car, as she hollered, 'In grey!'

When I reached the side of the car, the door suddenly popped open and a female voice ordered, 'Get in,' in a crisp American accent. The fact that it was a woman inside immediately threw me.

I lowered myself into the passenger seat, painfully aware that I was carrying a large amount of cash, and didn't have a clue what was going to happen next.

I stole a glance at the driver – a blonde, glossy lady with long, straight hair and legs in shiny black leggings. She looked like a model herself. Although I couldn't see her feet, I was pretty certain she was wearing heels – designer ones at that. The double bluff that the Bag Drop Man was actually female wasn't what I was expecting at all.

'I'm going to drive around the block,' she began, speaking slowly, not taking her eyes off the road. 'There's a bag on the back seat – pull it onto your lap. Inside that bag is another bag – the three-point-one Phillip Lim Pashli, as requested. Take out that bag and replace it with your envelope of cash. It's three hundred and fifty dollars for the Lim. Zip it up and replace the bag on the back seat. We'll be back where we started when you've done it and you can get out. Don't speak of this again. Got it?'

'Got it,' I replied, my heart beating double time. I was so busy trying to focus on what I was meant to do, I barely had the energy to feel relieved that she wasn't dealing in drugs after all. But with her not being the friendliest of shop assistants, I wasn't about to start adding to our order, although I wouldn't have minded a small Saint Laurent or a Mulberry myself. As I turned and reached behind my chair onto the back seat, I couldn't see any more designer handbags hanging around waiting to be snapped up anyway. I wondered where she kept them all.

Quickly, I did as I was told, depositing the right amount of cash into the now-empty black holdall on the back seat.

As we turned the final corner back to where we had begun, I felt my shoulders relax a little. I inhaled the beautiful scent of genuine leather from the Phillip Lim sitting on my lap. I was dying to look at the Bag Lady properly, but was too scared to stare, so all I got were a few stolen glances. Just a few minutes later, I spotted Vicky pacing around under the lamppost, speaking into her phone.

'Who's she talking to?' the lady asked.

'Um... I'm... not sure. Sorry,' I stuttered, 'but I'm sure it's nothing to... be concerned about though.'

She grunted before replying: 'I hope not. And tell your friend not to talk of this either. If anything happens, I'll find you both.'

The car drew to a halt. 'Of course,' I said. 'Have a good evening!'

And I bolted out of the car to join Vicky, before anything else could happen, thinking that Pinky owed me, big time.

When we got back home it was nearly four in the morning. Rob had left a sleeping bag and a spare pillow folded up on the sofa, so he couldn't have been too annoyed that Vicky was staying the night. He stirred as I quietly got into bed and snuggled up behind his warm, naked body. I inhaled his back; I'd never been happier to be safely back home and in bed with him.

'What time is it?' he asked sleepily.

'Don't ask,' I whispered. 'But it's so good to see Vicky. Thanks for letting her stay.'

He babbled something in response, but I didn't take it in because I was already drifting off to sleep.

'I had a really vivid dream about Pinky last night,' Rob muttered, shortly after his alarm abruptly woke us up just before eight o'clock. 'It's ridiculous, but I miss that little creature. I hope he's okay.'

As I roused myself and realised what he was saying, I wondered whether to tell him that Poppy was actually right here in New York, not at home with his beloved pet. But although I hated the fact she had succeeded in making me lie to my boyfriend, my raging hangover couldn't deal with the fallout that would follow.

'Me too,' I replied quietly.

Rob looked utterly bereft for a little while, staring off into the middle distance, lost in the belief that a miniature pig was scuttling around Poppy's London flat, hundreds of miles away from us – only he had no idea that Pinky was actually scuttling around at some stranger called Charlie's home.

'I hope he doesn't know he's been left behind,' Rob said eventually.

'I'm sure Poppy's got things under control.' I tried to push aside the memory of last night. On top of the fact that she'd palmed off Pinky without asking us, Rob would be livid to know about the bag drop. I'd done something that could have cost me my job; it could have even got me deported. *Jeez, I feel nauseous.*

Keen to change the subject, I reached over to grab my phone and began my usual scroll through social media, going from Instagram to Snapchat to Facebook to Twitter and back, a few times in rotation, my heart picking up each time I clocked my total followers. I looked at Liv's Instagram page and sat up as I admired the photos of her taking Coachella by storm in a series of sexy burlesque outfits. Then I opened *vogue.com* and an even greater feeling of excitement washed over me. The fashion reports from Coachella were amazing and Liv appeared in the Top Ten Best Dressed list for the first time in years.

They even had a quote from her, as she praised her stylist for putting together her festival looks. 'My stylist, Amber Green, has saved me from myself,' she told the *Vogue* reporter, and it had been picked up and quoted everywhere from *elle. com* to *Women's Wear Daily*. I smiled to myself. *Your stylist saved the world from seeing your naked body, more like.* There was even a small photo of Liv in *The Times* newspaper back home as a notable fashion columnist discussed the rise of a new trend, epitomised by Liv, which they christened 'Burlesque Boho'. I was glowing with pride.

'I've got to call Maurice,' I said, showing the reports to Rob, adrenalin pumping. There was nothing like this to blast away a hangover.

'Marianne will be doing the cancan in the sky!' Maurice exclaimed when I told him the news. 'Amber, I can't thank you enough for this opportunity. "Burlesque Boho." *C'est magnifique!* Who'd have thought we could create a whole new trend while we were at it?'

I beamed. 'I know – Liv has texted me this morning. Mickey will drop off Marianne's items tonight and she's keen to keep riding this fashion wave when she gets home. What do you say to me introducing you? I'm sure there's so much more we could all do together.'

He paused.

'You are so kind, *ma chérie*, but let me think about it. To launch myself back into the fashion world is a big decision for me. Timing is everything and I'm not sure I'm ready for it.'

'Oh, but surely the time is now?' I reasoned. 'You and Liv – you're so similar in many ways, both staging a comeback, both keen to reinvent your image. I'm sure we could manage this brilliantly, if we plan it carefully. Will you think about it? I could get my agent involved to help us, if you like?'

'No – no agents,' he said forcefully. 'Like I said, *je vais y réfléchir*.'

And the conversation was closed, for now.

No sooner had I hung up than Dana rang, sounding stressed.

'Amber, I've been trying to get through for ages. Sorry for the early call, but I've been dropped in it by a stylist. She's sick and has had to pull out of a shoot and they desperately need someone at short notice. Are you free today?'

'Um.' I sat up straight and scratched my ear. 'Well, I had a bit of a—'

'Fantastic, I told them you'd be happy to help. It's baby wear. Don't panic, the client's providing all the looks, all you've got to do is turn up and make a few gorgeous little people look even cuter. They're all from an agency so they know what they're doing. Easy.'

Easy? From my limited experience of babysitting Nora, babies and small children do not equal 'easy'. And they definitely don't 'know what they're doing'.

'The good news is, I can pay you for this one,' Dana added, sweetening things. 'I spoke with our lawyer and your visa application is looking good so we can call this an advance.'

Rob was looking at me quizzically.

'Can you give me two minutes to think about it?' I asked.

'Sorry, I don't have two minutes, sugar. What are you worrying about?'

'Well, I've got a friend who's just arrived in town,' I stuttered, desperate not to have to let on that lack of sleep and a monster hangover were my main motivations not to work today.

'Great – bring her too,' Dana pushed me.

'You're not taking "No" for an answer, are you?'

'No, sweet cheeks. I'll email you the call sheet – you're needed from midday.'

I looked at my phone. There was still enough time to get a bit of extra sleep so I didn't give the babies nightmares.

'Okay, I'll do it.'

'Thank you! Mwah mwah!' And she was gone before I could change my mind.

'Sounds like someone just got their first paid work as a Manhattan stylist,' Rob said, going to high five me. 'Nice one, Am.'

Before I had time to really appreciate what this meant for my future, Vicky popped her head around our door. It startled us both – I'd almost forgotten she was here.

'Excellent, you're awake!' she announced, looking far too eager on not more than four hours' sleep. 'I've been awake for ages – jet lag – so I've booked us into SoulCycle.'

'You what?'

'SoulCycle. You can't live in New York and not know about SoulCycle.'

'She can,' Rob mumbled under his breath, unamused.

'I wasn't asking you,' Vicky responded, flashing him a smile. 'Class starts at nine thirty. I booked online and we're lucky to get a place. So you'd better get your butt out of bed, Miss Green... before I do it for you!'

'There's no time, I'm working today,' I protested.

'When?'

'Midday.'

'Great, plenty of time then. SoulCycle will get your creative juices flowing.' *Damn, should have lied.*

'I'm so dehydrated this morning I doubt I've got any juice to flow.'

Vicky smirked and said in a matter-of-fact tone, 'Put on your best Lycra, we leave in ten minutes.'

SoulCycle. Sounds inoffensive enough.

'Just as bossy as ever, I see.' Rob moodily threw back the duvet and clambered out of our warm bed.

'Heard that,' Vicky remarked as she disappeared behind the door.

After squeezing myself into some tighter-than-I-remembered active wear – unworn so far in New York – Vicky and I were rushing to the subway, ready to head across the water to the SoulCycle studio at Union Square. Once again there were some breakdancers on our train carriage. Vicky frantically found her phone and began videoing them, but I barely glanced at them – by now this was normal for me. I even knew the route to Union Square without having to look at a subway map. It made me realise how much had changed since I arrived here just a few weeks ago. New York finally felt as though it could become my home – maybe even long term. There was something about the city that was endlessly exciting – and there was still so much to explore – we had barely had time to take in any of the main tourist sights and I was still desperate to visit the Statue of Liberty and see the view from the top of the Empire State Building.

When we entered the SoulCycle studio it looked harmless – a room full of static exercise bikes, with the SoulCycle etiquette written across one wall. Number three was headed 'Laundry': 'We ride close together so we can feel each other's energy. That being said, your neighbour does not want to feed off your odour.' I shuddered. The bikes couldn't be packed in more closely and no one, not even Vicky, deserved to feel the dubious energy, never mind alcohol fumes that I was no doubt emitting after last night.

As the room began filling up, I realised that my classmates were not your average aerobics aficionados – most had model looks and were dressed as though they'd just stepped out of a sportswear shoot. Hair knotted on heads, neon trainers, T-shirts emblazoned with right-on slogans like CUP OF CHIA? and SOUL MAMA. I realised that they were all clutching litre bottles of mineral water, whereas Vicky and I didn't have any. *Ah, well, how dehydrating can something forty-five minutes long possibly be?*

It turned out that SoulCycle involved hard-core spinning plus positive affirmations.

'Experience the ritual!' the teacher called out as the lights were dimmed. Her bike was surrounded by candles, and she had abs that looked painted on, they were so good. 'Dedicate this moment to being the best you can be!' Then the music was turned up and we all had to get out of our saddles to begin a hard-core series of handlebar push-ups and chest presses in time to the pumping beat.

Where is the gentle cruising the name conjures up? And why are we standing on our bikes when there's a perfectly comfy padded seat?

Initially, I wanted to laugh, and I looked around the room at my fellow cyclists for assurance that this was totally barmy. But they were staring dead ahead, buttocks like iron, forearms solid, eyes focused on the instructor, as though she'd just told them the first past the post could have a free venti eggnog latte with cream and the calories wouldn't count. *Except this bunch probably only drink kale juice. And I've got a whole forty-five minutes of this torture!*

I soon found myself adopting the cheat's position of not turning up the resistance on my bike when we were instructed to. Feeling I was fooling the instructor at least gave me some power back in this masochistic 'ritual'. I *really* needed a swig of water. I kept staring at people happily taking a moment to glug back some mineral water in the unlikely hope that they might kindly offer their bottle to me; and when I wasn't doing that, I was daydreaming of waterfalls. After twenty minutes of manic pedalling, I was sweating profusely. I then became paranoid about body odour – being encouraged to fling my arms up and down the whole time was doing nothing to help – nor was the fact that the woman on the bike next to me bore more than a passing resemblance to

Victoria Beckham. I tried to mouth her name to Vicky when she stole a glance at me in between pumps, presumably to check I was still alive.

'VB!' I mouthed, indicating to my right.

'Eh?' She shrugged. Vicky seemed annoyingly good at this pretend cycling lark; her daily Pilates sessions in LA had clearly paid off.

'*VB! Look right*,' I whispered more loudly, wagging my head vigorously to my right.

And then, in a flash, my sweaty palms lost their grip of the handlebars. I felt my slippery, sweaty body slide from the saddle and pulled sideways and downwards until I landed in an ungainly heap on the floor sandwiched between Victoria Beckham's bike and my own. To finish things off, I somehow managed to knock her water bottle out of its holder on my descent and it bounced off my head before landing next to me.

'Oh, my God, are you okay?' Victoria Beckham was now off her bike and staring down at me, concerned. She didn't seem to have a single bead of sweat on her forehead, whereas I looked like I'd just got out of the shower. Even my eyelashes were sweating. And it got worse. The whole class had now stopped and were staring at me. Vicky had disembarked too and came round to help lift me out of this awkward space. I felt like a clumsy elephant.

'It's fine! I'm fine!' I yelled, my already puce face turning a very deep purple colour. 'I'm getting back on! No problem!'

I pulled myself up and back onto my bike quickly, trying to ignore a shooting pain at the top of my thigh, where I had scraped myself on my pedal on the way down. *Thank God, it hasn't actually ripped my leggings or drawn blood. Oh, it has.* It was as if everyone in the class noticed the gash on my knee at the same time. Blood was running down my leggings.

'Doesn't hurt. Just a graze!' I exclaimed, dabbing at it with my finger.

The teacher was off her bike now, too, heading my way. *Oh, God, oh, God, please don't come and humiliate me.* I wanted my bike to break free from its shackles and cycle right through the glass walls and out of here, *E.T.*-style. *And where's Bradley Wiggins when I need a backie?*

'Keep going with your personal affirmations,' she encouraged the rest of the class. 'Feel the strength.'

I lifted myself off my saddle again and began pedalling as fast as I could, willing the teacher to go back to her bike and do the same.

'Hey, slow down,' she said, placing a cool hand on my arm. *How the hell is she so cool? Does she actually have a pulse?* 'What's your name? I've not seen you in this class before.'

I slowed my pace slightly to steady my breathing so that I might actually be able to speak.

'Thanks, it's Amber. And, yes, um, this is my first time,' I admitted, praying that Victoria Beckham couldn't hear. 'Honestly, I'm fine, it's only a scratch.'

A trickle of blood was working its way down my calf.

'Listen, Amber, I think you should call it a day for this session,' she said gently.

Vicky was looking at me, concerned, too. 'Why don't you

take a moment on the couch just out there?' she indicated a sofa in the reception area, visible beyond the glass wall.

'I-I'm fine now, honestly,' I protested, smiling as best I could and picking up the pace again. I even twiddled with my resistance, to prove the point.

'I'm sure you are, but I'd really like you to just take some time out, please,' she said again, more forcefully, turning down my resistance as she did.

'I think it's a good idea, Am,' Vicky chimed in. *Whose side is she on?*

Victoria Beckham was thoughtfully not looking at me.

Not wanting to cause more of a scene by getting forcibly ejected from my saddle, I very carefully got off the bike again. My thigh was killing me and my knee had started stinging, plus from nowhere I was hit by a raging headache.

'Yeah, a bit of time out – I think you're right, good idea,' I muttered as I left the room, desperate to win some dignity back. 'I've been crazy busy recently. It, er, probably caught up with me. But I'll be back soon! Loved it! Thanks for the class.'

I smiled pathetically at the instructor and at Victoria as I left.

Vicky mouthed, 'Go to the bathroom – I'll meet you by the sofa afterwards.'

Go to the fricking bathroom? Is she trying to suggest I've wet myself too now? This can't be happening. As I exited the studio, the teacher must have given some kind of signal to the pretty girl on reception, because she came rushing straight over to me with a pile of tissues, a glass of water, and an ice pack.

'Poor you,' she tutted. 'Anyone would think you'd been on an actual ride. The Ladies' is just that way.'

All I could do was hobble off in the general direction she indicated.

CHAPTER FIFTEEN

I sat fiddling with my phone on the SoulCycle sofa with a plaster on my knee and the ice pack held on my forehead as I endured the final humiliation of having the whole class file out of the studio and past me. Some made little 'Ouchy!' expressions as they took in my obvious injuries. All this and it wasn't even eleven o'clock. I felt sure a sip of water could have saved me from falling off the bike and somehow blamed Vicky for not thinking that we might need to bring a bottle each; water might well have stopped me ending up with a giant egg on my forehead, an egg that would certainly scare the children at the photo-shoot. Some water might have enabled me to smash the class and become a SoulCycle regular, in fact water might have made Victoria Beckham my cycling buddy. *Why did she not tell me I needed water?*

I only looked up once, and that was when Victoria passed – only, now we were in daylight, away from the ambient studio lighting, I could see she wasn't the real Victoria Beckham, just a loosely passable lookalike. *Great, so I was hallucinating a Beckham in there as well.* On balance, I supposed this was a good thing, although 'Just bumped into

Victoria Beckham at SoulCycle!' was a fantastic line to put out on social media – no one need know the actual context. In the end, however, I decided to keep this little incident private; it didn't really work pictorially, however hard I might try to filter my bruised head.

During the class I'd been sent the call sheet for the shoot plus a text from Mickey asking him to call me urgently about Liv. The egg on my head was throbbing, and I was hideously aware that this look was a far from ideal for my first paid shoot. *As if my hangover isn't enough to deal with today.* The last thing I needed was Mickey wanting to see me, too; surely the great press Liv had received from Coachella was enough to buoy his mood today.

'That could only happen to you,' Rob chortled when I told him what had happened. Vicky and I had cabbed it back to the apartment to change ready for the shoot and Rob was on his laptop working from home.

Only happen to me. Why do I attract moments of sheer idiocy so easily? Why? 'Seriously, I've never seen a water bottle bounce off someone's head that hard before,' Vicky told him, reliving every painful moment at my expense and clearly finding it sidesplittingly funny.

'Shame it wasn't the real Victoria,' Rob said. 'You might have an argument for a claim there. An insecure water bottle on a spinning bike?' He sucked in his cheeks. 'I'm sure someone somewhere in America has sued over an incident like that.'

'Hmm, maybe…' I said, yawning, still resistant to accepting

there was a funny side to my accident. All I wanted to do was lie down.

Vicky had been fidgety since we got back, and, as she offered to make us a quick strong coffee, I asked what was wrong.

'I'm just wondering if I should pack my case now?' she stuttered, eyes glistening. 'Sorry, it's just I suddenly feel *really* hungover and I'm wondering if Rob's brother is coming soon?'

I looked at Rob.

'Oh, sorry, forgot to mention, Dan hasn't actually booked a flight yet,' he said.

'Which means you can sofa surf at ours for the rest of the week!' I added, relieved we could give her time to work out when she would go back to Trey and LA, or whether she really was gearing up to leave him for good.

I glanced at Rob, wondering whether I should have checked he was fine about Vicky staying too, but it was too late. 'Thank you! Thank you both so much!' She threw her arms around us. 'I'll make you dinner this evening.' *Fortunately, Rob doesn't yet know what a terrible cook my best friend is.*

'Meanwhile, some of us have to go to work,' Rob announced, standing up. 'We're filming auditions for the new stylist for the show today – should be interesting. Lola Jones is coming in for an audition, among others. It's going to go on into the evening, so don't cook for me.'

'Let me know if Lola makes any reference to wanting me skinned live,' I joked.

'Yeah, don't know why, but I think I'll omit to mention the fact her Instagram nemesis is my girlfriend,' he said sarcastically, winking at me as he headed for the door.

I smiled at the space where he had stood as the door closed and the sound of his footsteps disappeared down the corridor.

'You've got a good one there, Amber,' Vicky said, catching me. 'Tell me he's not that perfect *all* the time. He loves you to bits, you know.'

'Really? How do you know?' I asked.

'Just the way he looks at you. Plus, he's good-looking, successful, dependable – he's husband material all right.'

I blushed. It had to be said I did feel pretty smug that somehow I'd managed to bag myself a boyfriend as fantastic as Rob. For a few seconds, I allowed myself the daydream that one day I might actually become Mrs Amber Walker. I would certainly welcome losing the Amber Green moniker I'd had to put up with for twenty-eight years, with all the unfunny traffic-light puns that came with it.

'He's not bad,' I replied, modestly. 'I think I'll keep him, for now.'

'Don't mess it up, like I always seem to do,' Vicky warned me. 'I know I'm hardly the best person to be dishing out relationship advice, but there aren't many genuine good guys out there, believe me.'

'I know. I was single for two billion years before this – remember?'

'Ha. You just hadn't found your One.' She smiled. 'Well, I think you have now. You're lucky – I wish I had that.'

'We'll see,' I said, slightly embarrassed. I wasn't used to my love life being something someone might envy.

My eyelids felt heavy, but there was to be no duvet day, we had a shoot to get to, and it felt good to have my bestie by my side as my unofficial assistant.

We arrived at a smart house in a plum spot in the heart of Greenwich Village, and were greeted at the door by a woman who introduced herself as Irene, marketing manager at Kute Kids – one of America's biggest children's wear retailers. She looked irate.

'Tell me you're the stylist?' she said, her hair falling out of what probably started the day as a neat bun on top of her head.

'That's right, Amber Green,' I held out a hand. She blanked it.

'Thank God, I don't think we're going to keep their attention for much longer – we need to get this shoot started.'

She took in the egg on my forehead. My attempt to camouflage it with make-up had clearly failed. It felt as though it was pulsating like the lights on a police car.

'What happened?'

'I took a fall for an old lady, long story,' I said. Vicky gave me a sideways look, which I ignored.

I clocked a large damp patch on Irene's silk shirt.

'Puke.' She winced. 'Covered in the stuff on a daily basis. I don't know why I do this job. Or ever bother to wear silk.'

'Well, that makes me feel better about my head,' I said, smiling, egg-head nullified. 'Shall we come in?'

From nowhere a little person appeared between her legs.

'Jamie go out now!' the boy said excitedly; he couldn't have been much more than two years old, with a perfect blond bowl haircut, blue eyes and a seriously cheeky face.

'No, no, Jamie stay here!' Irene yanked him back. 'There are six more of these little dictators inside. You sure you want to come in?'

We all laughed nervously.

It was instantly apparent that the owners of the house didn't have young children – it was far too tastefully decorated and the walls were far too white. Vicky and I peered into a plush sitting room on our right, where a large, pale grey corner sofa loaded with a huge number of white and silver cushions took up most of the room, behind a large glass coffee table on which eight little cream vases containing green grass trimmed to a uniform length were positioned. Stunning abstract oil paintings hung on the walls, and a gallery of framed black and white photographs provided a feature on one side.

'The owner's an artist – his works are all over the house,' Irene informed us.

Next, off the hallway, was a grand drawing room with whitewashed wooden floors and pieces of contemporary furniture, which opened up into a dining room, where a plain white colorama had been set up against one wall by the photographer, who was introduced as Natalie. Her assistant, a small girl with short peroxide hair, was embroiled in a battle to prevent six pairs of sticky hands from ruining it.

Why they had bothered to hire a location as opulent as this when they wanted to shoot in front of a white colorama was baffling.

'Sugar rush. The bloody assistant was handing out candy when they arrived. I mean, how stupid can you be? I could have strangled her,' said Irene.

'Well, she's paying for it now.' I smiled wryly as the girl tried to remove a toddler brandishing a large red crayon.

'Do either of you have kids?' she asked.

'No,' Vicky and I replied in unison.

'Sensible.' She deadpanned. 'And you haven't met the babies yet.' She indicated an adjoining room, from which a chorus of cries was emanating.

'Aw, I love babies, let me at them!' Vicky proclaimed, tearing off towards the door, while I tried to locate the clothing.

'Great, your job is to keep tabs on this rabble!' Irene yelled at Vicky's back. 'Ensure all the doors, windows and other exits are locked – I've had a toddler escape through a cat flap before, you can't be too careful. The owner of this property is very particular, some would say he's got OCD. God knows why it was chosen as the location for this shoot. Someone's going to get fired over this. Nothing must get broken, moved or manhandled. And we absolutely must not let anyone on to the top floor. It's completely out of bounds, not that they can easily climb four flights of stairs. That said, they're scheming little tykes. Do regular head counts.'

'Roger that!' Vicky cried over her shoulder at Irene, whom I had decided to christen 'Irate'. *Why she works for*

*a children's wear company when she clearly hates kids is
beyond me.*

I was in the middle of hurriedly unpacking a heap of bags
and boxes full of Kute Kids clothes when a woman with dyed
red hair and dressed in a bright green jumpsuit, complete
with green knee and elbow pads, appeared in the hallway.
She began making loud croaking noises and leapfrogging
around. The toddlers, not to mention all the adults nearby
– some of whom I had identified as parents, others part of
the grooming team – immediately stopped what they were
doing and stared.

In a broad Australian accent her voice boomed: 'Can you
see what I am?' She crouched down on bent legs and then
sprung up, before repeating the action again and again.

'A froggie!' one of the brighter toddlers exclaimed.

'That's right!' she yelled. 'And where do froggies live?'

'In a pond!' the same little girl screeched, running towards
her, overcome with excitement that the world's biggest
antipodean toad was in our presence.

'Cuddle the frog!' shouted little Jamie, and ran towards
the bizarrely dressed woman.

I looked at Irate, who seemed to be cracking her first
vaguely happy expression of the day.

'That's Nicole,' she explained, 'the baby wrangler. She's
famous in kiddie-shoot circles.'

I snapped a quick shot of her on my phone and uploaded
it to Instagram. Clarendon filter; caption: The baby wrangler.
Can you guess what she is? #behindthescenes #photoshoot
#stylist #NYC #fashion #babywear #babiesofinstagram

Vicky poked her head out of the baby room.

'Hey, Amber and Irene, do you need the babies made up yet, someone's asking?'

Made up? Since when have babies been expected to wear lipstick?

My heart rate was beginning to pick up and a sweat last seen in SoulCycle had returned, as I realised I didn't have a clue where to begin with a styling job of this kind.

'Yeah, er, go ahead!' I called back, trying to sound more authoritative than I felt.

I'd laid out the clothes in colour schemes, as instructed on the shot list Dana had emailed me, thinking we had better get the all-white looks out of the way first, but getting ten babies into a selection of white babygros, top and bottom combos, jackets, booties, hats, coats and cashmere cardigans was much easier said than done.

And just when we thought they were all ready for their close up, a loud squelch and yellow, cottage-cheesy poo ruined one outfit. No sooner was that being changed than another little angel decided to cry hysterically for seemingly no reason, went bright red in the face and had to be ejected; meanwhile, another was quietly puking up milky sick all down its cashmere front.

'At least it's white,' I offered, smiling weakly as Irate appeared with a muslin and looked like she was going to lose it.

'We'll deal with it in Photoshop,' the photographer reasoned. I liked her, she was practical.

As she clicked away and various babies began doing

exactly what we didn't want them to do for the camera, Vicky was chuckling, finding it all hysterical. Within five minutes, I'd used up the whole of the one and only packet of Vanish wipes in my kit, dabbing various bodily fluids off ivory babygros. For such tiny things, babies could be insanely messy. Thank God for the baby wrangler, who pulled endless squeaky toys out of a duffle bag and made an impressive array of animal noises to encourage them to open their eyes wide and coo for the camera. It certainly was a skill.

Once we got going and Irate had accepted that we weren't going to achieve more than a handful of usable shots from the whole afternoon, we started to speed through the looks.

'Witching hour is approaching – we need to get all the shots!' she kept reminding us every time any of the team dared sit down for a second or stopped to make a coffee.

Witching hour. I've seen Nora at witching hour and it's every bit as scary as Irate is.

At long last, five o'clock rolled around and the shoot had dissolved into one big toddler meltdown; parents had started arriving at the front door to collect their little cherubs. I busied myself reuniting sippy cups and comforters with their rightful owners when I wasn't reattaching labels to tiny clothes, and neatly putting them back into bags and boxes. My head was really throbbing now and I couldn't wait to get back home.

Jamie's mother entered the house clutching his big, blue, expensive-looking parka and, when her precious son failed to bolt for his mummy as the other toddlers had, a few of us started looking around nervously.

'Jamie! Jamie, darling!' the well-groomed woman called, her eyes darting around from one blond-haired child to another. But none of them were Jamie.

'Jamie! Jamie! Mummy's here!' Irate yelled, to no one in particular.

But Jamie, who had been rushing around getting tangled up in all of us for most of the afternoon, was suddenly nowhere to be seen.

Irate looked sternly at Vicky. 'We're all present and correct, right?'

'I think so,' Vicky replied uncertainly.

'You *think*?'

Poor Vicky, she wasn't even meant to be here today.

'He's probably playing hide and seek,' Vicky tried to reassure everyone.

With still no sign of him, Jamie's mother was going from room to room and starting to look panicked as she parted curtains, looked under furniture and behind doors in an effort to locate him. Vicky and I joined in the search.

'There aren't exactly many places he could be,' Vicky correctly observed when we had scoured the minimalist interior several times over, even looking in drawers and cupboards too small for a toddler, on the off-chance that he was a secret contortionist. Nothing.

The photographer and her assistant had dispatched themselves out into the street to check he hadn't run out into the road when all of our backs were turned – a thought that none of us, least of all Jamie's mum, who had turned a shade of grey, wanted to contemplate.

'There's the out-of-bounds top floor…' I remembered just when the adrenalin began to kick in.

Irate began flying up seemingly endless flights of stairs, galloping upwards taking them two at a time towards the banished floor.

'The owners said it was all locked up – it's his studio, you see,' she puffed.

When we reached the top landing a door opposite was ajar, giving us a glimmer of hope. The room was dark and Irate fumbled for a few long seconds trying to locate a light switch. As soon as the room was bathed in colour we were able to call off the search, because there was little Jamie, clean alabaster skin no more, covered in a rainbow of oil paints. Thick, greasy paint was in his hair, on his probably expensive clothes, and smeared on any available bit of flesh, including his face, which now bore an uncanny resemblance to a Picasso portrait. Plus, there were tiny fingerprints and random splodges plastered all over a large canvas of a landscape leaning against the wall.

'Well, at least he's safe,' Vicky said meekly.

We watched Jamie sit there slipping and squirming in paint for a few moments, before he added a few extra dabs to the canvas. None of us was quite sure how to tackle him, he was so wet and slimy. I certainly didn't want to risk my oatmeal Marlene Birger dress near that mess.

'I think we'll let his mother get him,' Irate said.

'Good thinking,' I agreed, as we heard Jamie's mum ascending the staircase.

'But what the hell am I going to tell the owner about this mess? We'll lose our deposit on the location, for sure. My boss is going to go insane!' Irate turned and looked at me as if I was somehow responsible for what had happened.

'Well, it can't be the first time on a photo-shoot with a hoard of crazy toddlers that one of them has done something they shouldn't?' I offered.

'But *they* didn't sign the bloody contract with the location!' she snapped. 'If only you'd done your job and kept a closer eye,' she said, staring at Vicky now, giving her a scary headmistressy look.

She picked the wrong person.

'Now, hold on a minute!' Vicky was having none of it. 'I don't actually have an official job on this shoot, remember. And I certainly don't answer to you, Irene. As I see it, had it not been for my presence today, perhaps we would have found five toddlers up here ruining priceless pieces of art, while you were flapping about a collar being turned up on a starchy white babygro. I think we got off lightly.'

And she turned on her heel and headed downstairs, just as Jamie's mum led her crestfallen son past us, a smudgy trail of footprints on the landing carpet behind him.

'Starchy? I'll have you know these babygros are made of the finest quality materials!' Irate ranted.

'Um, we've got to dash,' I told Irate. 'The clothes are packed up ready for collection. See you again.' I said the last words in a tiny voice. *I hope I never see any of them ever again.*

Vicky and I spent the rest of the day back at the apartment, sprawled on the sofa, finally able to see the funny side.

'Please remind me,' I chuckled, 'never to work with exercise bikes or babies ever again. What a day.'

Vicky smiled, her eyes partially closed she was so jet lagged, as well as hungover. 'It was hectic, but seriously comical. I still can't get over your egg – it's a beautiful shade of emerald and purple right now, very this season.'

'I wonder if we'll see eggheads on the catwalks of Paris next,' I said.

'Or maybe the real Victoria Beckham will take inspiration from you for her new collection?' Vicky teased. 'I've heard of stranger things.'

We were sitting on the sofa trying to find some reruns of *Friends* on TV, when Dana called. Her tone was different to the persuasive, encouraging Dana of earlier in the day.

'I'm afraid I've got bad news,' she said, skipping any pleasantries. 'From what I've heard from the client, today was a major disaster. The location company have gone berserk following some vandalism of the owner's artwork, and Kool Kids are trying to pin the blame on your assistant.'

'They *what*?' I shrieked, standing up in horror. 'My assistant? You mean my best friend, who you said I could take along, and who stepped into the breach because no one else there seemed to be able to control the rabble? Those were the worst-behaved "agency" children ever.' I was seeing red.

Dana continued: 'They're threatening a law suit, Amber, and they will probably win. You were working without a visa, remember. I can't risk having to shoulder this. I'm sorry, but I'm going to have to strike you off my books.' She paused.

I said nothing. Hot air was building up in my lungs. '*Fine!*' I stormed, and cut her off.

Pretty soon after, reeling from the aftermath of the shoot, Vicky and I could only think of topping up our alcohol levels and finished the only bottle of wine in the apartment. And then we both dozed off, because the next thing I knew Rob had come home from work. It was close to ten and he looked stressed.

'Auditions didn't go well then?' I asked.

'You can say that again.' He headed straight for the kitchen and looked pissed off when he realised there was no more wine and supper wasn't on the menu. 'Ron was in a terrible mood. Hated everyone we brought in. They're casting the net wider now.' He paused. 'And he keeps mentioning Mona Armstrong.'

I shuddered. It was incredible how just the mention of her name could still make me go cold.

Vicky tittered. 'Mona, my God. What is the mad bitch up to these days?'

The last we'd seen of my old boss, self-styled 'stylist to the stars' Mona Armstrong, was when she disappeared off into a car in Hawaii with an eloping couple after the showbiz wedding she was supposed to be styling had gone horrifically wrong. It was an exit and a half – and an experience that I wasn't keen to relive. Not now, not ever.

'No idea,' I said, honestly. 'I don't want to know, either.'

'Your name came up again,' Rob said, leaning towards me, looking me in the eye, like he was about to say something very important. 'I showed Ron some of the press you got for Liv at Coachella, and he's asked if you would like to go for the job, Amber. You've got bags of experience and with your recent success you could make a name for yourself in the underwear world. Burlesque Boho, Angel Wear lingerie, they're not a million miles apart?'

'But I thought Ron wants a big name?' I replied. 'I'm hardly that. I've only got seven and a half thousand Instagram followers, compared to Lola's five hundred thousand.'

'After today, I'm not sure he does,' Rob said. 'Everyone we saw was more interested in putting their own stamp on things than working collaboratively with his in-house team. And I can't see Mona being a breeze, can you? You're so down to earth; plus, you know your stuff – honestly, you're just what we're looking for.'

I sat still, saying nothing because I really wasn't sure what to say. Although I didn't see this coming at all, my stomach was beginning to fizz with excitement about the possibility – the dream – that I might have a second stab at this job of styling jobs.

Vicky's eyes were shining. 'Honey, you've got to go for it, this could be the gig of a lifetime!' she enthused. 'People eBay bags of *air* from the Angel Wear show – it doesn't get any bigger! When I was at *Glamour*, we'd hold open the issue to get the show pictures in the mag. And a shoot with one of the Icons? Well, that was "hold the front cover". Amber, you'd be officially classified as insane – in fact, I'll take you to an asylum myself – if you didn't go for this. And think how gutted Dana will be when you nab the biggest styling job in the whole of New York City. In the whole of America! The bloody *world*, probably. You've *got* to go for it!'

Rob was nodding his head in agreement. 'She's right, baby, you've got to take this opportunity. Ron seemed genuinely keen today. You won't need an agent to broker the deal so we can shave off any commission by sorting it out directly. They're desperate.'

I chuckled. '*Desperate?* Well, at least you're being honest.'

'Don't take it the wrong way, baby. I just mean, this is the right moment – *Your* moment. Besides, what have you got to lose?'

'He's right, Am, you said yourself you're not satisfied styling snotty babies or Park Avenue princesses like Liv every week,' Vicky said. 'This is a once-in-a-lifetime opportunity.'

'Hang on, Liv's not a Park Avenue princess! And I'm enjoying styling her – I just wish she'd wear a few more clothes. You can have the babies though.' I set down my wine glass and tried to process what they were suggesting. 'It's not exactly an opportunity yet, though, is it?' I said. 'I mean, he rejected me before and if Ron didn't want Lola Jones, it doesn't necessarily mean he'll want me.'

'Aside from being too strong-minded, Lola's image wasn't right for Angel Wear, either,' Rob said. 'The shaved head, the piercings and tattoos – it was too harsh for Ron. Now that the preparation for the show is going to be televised it all has to fit with the brand image. She's not right – anyway, it wasn't just Ron, it was obvious to all of us once she auditioned. And he hasn't met you yet, so how do you know?'

I was silenced. *Poor Lola, her shaved head was partly my fault anyway.*

'One pretty mediocre glass shoe changed Cinderella's life forever, didn't it?' Vicky suddenly piped up. We both looked at her, unsure where she was going with this analogy. 'And you've got the opportunity for some pieces of underwear to change yours. You're streaks ahead of Cinders at the starting block. C'mon Amber, seriously, if you don't do this then I'm going to do it for you.'

I shuffled to the back of the sofa and hugged my knees into my chest. I wasn't quite sure if the Cinderella analogy was meant to be a compliment, but it resonated somehow. Everything about my styling career so far felt a bit Cinders; from landing my job as Mona Armstrong's assistant by accidentally putting odd shoes on a shop window dummy, to styling the stars during awards season because Mona was ill or hungover. And now here I was in New York – by virtue of my boyfriend – trying to ignite my career thanks to some social media blunders. *I've always felt like an opportunist – the ordinary girl accidentally dropped into a fairy tale. Maybe this is my opportunity to break the mould and take my career to the next level.*

'I'll sleep on it, okay?' It was the best I could offer this evening.

Rob then suggested we go to bed immediately, before I had time to think about anything else.

'Well, if you two love birds are having an early night, I may as well go out,' Vicky announced, having found some energy at the bottom of her wine glass. 'Amy mentioned some of the guys from the pool party have invited us out. I may as well enjoy the freedom while I can...'

CHAPTER SIXTEEN

Rob was already awake when I opened my eyes the next morning. His face was close to mine on the pillow and he was looking right at me. It was as if he'd been staring at me throughout the night, willing me to wake up and give him the answer he wanted.

'I love watching you come round,' he said, as I wiped away a bit of partially dried up dribble from the side of my chin. 'You're all woozy and cute.'

'Creep,' I said, embarrassed. 'Cute' was not a word that had ever been used to describe my morning face. I scared myself sometimes. I ran a finger under my eyes in an effort to remove any stray eye make-up and traced my eyebrows with my index finger, to straighten them out.

He smiled. 'Seriously, you're a natural beauty, Amber. You shouldn't feel embarrassed.'

'You didn't see the dribble then?'

'Actually, I did,' he said, smiling, licking his thumb and dabbing other areas of my face. 'Plus a bit of crust. That's better.'

'Hey, Mr Snores-so-loudly-he-wakes-me-up-most-nights!

You're not exactly a sleeping beauty yourself, you know.' Instinctively, I reached across for my phone.

'Hang on.' He clasped me around the waist, pulling me back. 'Leave the phone a minute. Anyway, I don't remember saying I *was* a sleeping beauty. I was trying to pay you a compliment. Maybe I like your crusty bits – I find them endearing.'

'Endearing? You patronising old...'

He put a hand over my mouth. 'Sexy! I mean I find them sexy!' He was chuckling now. As I tried to squirm free, he held me tightly and pushed his body against mine.

'Hmmm, you clearly want something,' I said, itching to check my Instagram account.

'Only if you want it too,' he teased, lightly running his fingers down the side of my naked flesh. Last night's conversation about the Angel Wear job came flooding back.

'Oh, is *that* what you want? I thought you had something else on your mind. Something we were discussing last night?'

'That can wait,' he said, as the caressing became more firm and he began planting little kisses on my lips to silence me. 'I was thinking we could maybe enjoy ourselves for at least an hour, before we get on to business talk...' He paused. 'Provided you're in such a state of orgasmic euphoria you then give me the answer I'm looking for, Miss Green.' And he rolled himself on top of me.

'You do, do you, Mr Walker?' I said, feeling a warm, tingling sensation shoot down my body and stop around the groin. 'But what if I don't give you the answer you want?'

'Then I'll have to punish you...' He smiled wickedly.

We were interrupted abruptly by a loud crash from the living room, followed by Vicky screaming, 'Fuck!' and then bursting into giggles a moment later. If it wasn't for the immediate giggling, I might have thought we were being burgled.

When a muffled, deeper voice began laughing mischievously with her, it became apparent that she was not alone. *And I'll bet it isn't a burglar.*

'What the...? Who's in there with Vicky?' Rob whispered. 'I don't remember her mentioning a friend would be staying over.'

'Hmm, me neither,' I said. 'Sounds like it's a bloke.'

'Yeah, obviously. And I strongly doubt it's Trey.'

There were more clunks from just beyond the door and then it went silent.

'Oh, man, don't say she's making out on our sofa...' Rob shuddered.

'No, she wouldn't... would she?' *Yes, she bloody would.*

'It's not on, I'm going out,' Rob said, pulling on a T-shirt and sitting on the edge of the bed. *There's our morning of passion gone.*

'Leave it,' I ordered. 'Please, just for a moment at least.' He stopped and looked across at me. 'I want to talk to you about what you were suggesting last night – about me going for the Angel Wear job.' I paused.

'And?'

'And, well, I can't do it, babe.' I hung my head. 'I just don't think I'm experienced enough. Plus, I'm really enjoying what I've got going here, with building up my followers and seeing where things go with Maurice. I feel like I'm getting somewhere, and I don't want to throw all that away.'

Another clunk and a loud giggle from the other side of the door.

'For God's sake!' And he walked towards the door.

I slithered back under my side of the duvet and pulled it up around my shoulders. It dawned on me that we might once have found the noises funny; perhaps we might even have tried to outdo them on the noise front. At least someone was getting some action. It had been a while since Rob and I had actually had sex; we'd both been so busy with work, we'd been like ships in the night, and now this. He seemed irrationally pissed off about it.

'Well, at least *she's* having some fun,' I mumbled, on behalf of us both.

Rob turned back but didn't laugh at my joke. It wasn't the first time he hadn't in the last few days. *He can be so uptight sometimes.*

'I don't imagine that Dan thought it was fun when he found out Florence was shagging another guy either,' he muttered as he opened the door and confronted the scene before him. I hoped his mood wasn't a sign that something was rumbling away beneath the bedrock of our relationship.

The door had slammed shut as Rob stormed out to confront Vicky and whoever she was making out with in our living room, so I was only able to hear the gist of their exchange. I made out the words 'fucking cheek' and 'cheap' from Rob, swiftly followed by 'Saturday night' and 'loosen up' from Vicky. I'd rarely heard Rob so angry and couldn't help feeling he was overreacting – it wasn't fair to compare Vicky to cheating Florence. I could only imagine the pressure Rob was under at work was taking its toll and Vicky was unfortunately in his firing line at just the right moment. If you asked me, Vicky was showing pretty stereotypical Vicky behaviour, having crossed a continent to escape a failing relationship. I reminded myself that Rob didn't know my best friend as well as I did.

Before the point where I would need to brace myself for the sound of smashing crockery, I got out of bed and joined them both. Whoever the man was, he had fled the scene and Vicky was sitting on the sofa, sobbing, a sleeping bag pulled around her naked shoulders, while Rob had his back to her in the kitchenette. Seeing my best friend in tears, my natural reaction was, of course, to run to her.

'Honey, don't cry, please,' I said, sitting down, putting an arm around her.

'Saturday night, what a joke,' Rob muttered scathingly from the kitchen. Our place was so small he hardly had to say it very loudly to have a big effect.

'Jesus! Give me a fucking break!' Vicky sobbed. 'You'd think I'd bumped off his bloody piglet.'

'Pinky's not a piglet, he's a micro-pig,' I said, trying to lighten the atmosphere.

'For God's sake, Amber.' Vicky was unamused.

'And do you think you'd still be in *my* apartment if you had?' Rob retaliated, not even turning around to face her. The way he had stressed the '*my*', made me twitch. *Isn't this my apartment too?*

For the next thirty minutes, he and Vicky put on a big show of ignoring each other and it started to really annoy me. You'd think we were in an episode of *Keeping Up with the Kardashians*, as Rob pottered around making himself coffee and toast and muttering little digs under his breath, like, 'Don't mind me, I only pay the rent,' and, 'Marvellous, someone's finished my peanut butter and not bothered to replace it.'

I didn't like to admit that it was actually me who had finished off the peanut butter.

His words were like little daggers flying around Vicky, as if she was a magician's practice doll that narrowly missed being hit with each throwaway remark.

But she was getting ready to retaliate, I could sense it.

Her smile was icy as she finally squared up to him, just after he swiped her damp bath towel from its position hanging over our bedroom door and had made yet another comment about her putting a dirty mug in the sink and not washing it up instantly.

'Rob, if I'm pissing you off, you may as well tell me to my face,' she said, stonily.

'Okay – you're pissing me off!' he shouted. 'When are you planning to leave?' I'd rarely seen Rob speak to anyone so bluntly.

Vicky narrowed her eyes, as if she were practising her aim. Before it could get out of hand, I stepped in. I smiled at him. 'I'll handle this, Rob.'

He huffed, 'I mean it,' in response and disappeared into our bedroom.

Not more than ten minutes later, Rob had showered and left the building, requesting that Vicky and I have a think about her plans.

'I think we can safely say I've overstayed my welcome,' she said, as soon as he was out of ear shot. 'He was crazy angry just then.' She shuddered.

'I'm sorry,' I said, immediately feeling traitorous towards my boyfriend. *I'm really not sure how to mediate this one.* 'He's stressed at work right now. Anyway – who the hell was the guy?'

'White-T-shirt man from Le Bain,' Vicky said, avoiding eye contact. She didn't seem very happy about it.

'Do you like him?' I asked.

'No, he had a fat bum, bad jeans and was boring as hell – to be honest I was wondering how to get him out, but Rob did the job very well for me. Thanks, Rob.'

Her face finally cracked a smile. 'He didn't seem too happy that I broke a mug though.'

I registered some pieces of broken black ceramic on the coffee table.

'Oh, dear, his Darth Vader goblet,' I uttered, suddenly understanding why he had sounded so venomous this morning. 'It is – *was* – pretty much his prized possession.'

'So I'll get him a new one.'

'They're out of production, he watched it for ages on eBay.'

She hung her head. 'Well, I'm sure Trey's credit card can afford another.'

'Vic, you're a nightmare. A certified nightmare.'

'Listen, I'm not staying where I'm not wanted,' she said,

with a serious tone now. 'Rob just made it crystal-clear he wants me out of here – he never really wanted me here in the first place, let's face it – so how about I check out some Airbnb's and you two go out for dinner this evening. The last thing I want is to come between the pair of you. When you get home the place will be spotless. Just one more night, I promise.'

'But…'

She raised a hand. 'Don't. Please do as I say, Amber. I'll be fine. Aren't I always?'

I had to concede she was.

I called Rob, leaving him a message that Vicky would be gone the following day and that we should go out for dinner that evening. Throughout the day I checked my phone endlessly but heard not one word back. Nothing. Not even a text message. Earlier, I had posted a photo of the broken Darth Vader cup on Instagram. Filter: X-Pro II; caption: May the force be with me #darthvader #starwars #heartbreak #stylist #NYC

I wondered if perhaps it had annoyed him. Rob could be hard to read sometimes.

Eventually, at nearly three o'clock, he replied 'Great', and in the early evening he and I headed over to Manhattan, to Soho House. A friend of his at work had offered to put our names down, so we could check out one of the city's coolest members' bars while spending some quality time together; something we'd been lacking of late. The building was very close to Dana's office and I considered taking a quick detour and popping in – she always worked late and I wondered if I could talk her around. Without an agent, I was washed up before I'd started my styling career out here. But I bypassed the idea, because Rob had been cool all day – he clearly still needed softening over the Vicky incident. We took the lift up to the bar. It was dimly lit and roomy with a smattering of people sitting at tables. We were led to a table for two by the windows. I looked around hoping to spot a celebrity as we strolled over. Suddenly, a sight I hadn't expected made me stop in my tracks. A mop of curly hair, a sky-high heel and a cocktail ring the size of a golf ball.

I tugged on Rob's jumper.

'Stop!' I whispered. 'We can't go over there!' He turned around to look at me, a confused expression on his face.

'Sorry, what are you talking about?' he said, as the waitress spun around to see why we had stopped.

I spoke through gritted teeth. 'We have to leave – now!'

'Amber, what is going on?' he asked again.

'Don't make it obvious, but over there,' I whispered into his ear, indicating another table by the windows, just next to the one we were about to be seated at. 'Look who's sitting there.'

He took in the couple on the table, locked in conversation, their arms entwined, the woman talking so close to the man's lips, it looked as though she was seconds away from chewing his face off. Then she threw her head back, laughing, as he ran a gentle finger up and down her bare forearm.

'Oh fuck.' Rob turned away again quickly. 'Let's get out of here.'

'Everything all right, sir, ma'am?' asked the waitress, as we quickly and quietly retreated to the entrance.

'Fine,' I told her through the back of my head.

When we reached the lobby, I stopped to catch my breath.

'Change of plan, I'm sorry,' Rob told the confused hostess. And we left the building as fast as we could.

'I can't believe Ron Angel is involved with Mona Armstrong!' Rob exclaimed, shaking his head in disbelief when we were safely outside.

'You can't?' I laughed throatily. 'I bloody well can. Didn't you mention there's currently a vacancy for New York's top styling job?'

'Hmmm. You think she's trying to get her claws into Ron so she can style the show?'

'Of course, Rob, don't you remember? She's a schemer. I wouldn't put it past Mona to try to sleep her way into that job.'

'But Ron wouldn't be so stupid,' he said.

'She's dangerous,' I reminded him.

Just the sight of Mona had brought memories flooding back – and they weren't any less painful. It had been in Soho House in London that Mona had virtually broken down on me, sobbing into her champagne flute as she confessed she was bankrupt. I had been her shoulder to cry on that evening and came up with a plan to help her, only to end up being used and abused, just like her many assistants before me, so I wasn't feeling much warmth towards her today.

We decided to head to Balthazar in SoHo, on Amy's recommendation.

'There's no way I'm going for the stylist job now,' I said to Rob as we walked east. 'I can't bear to give Mona the satisfaction of winning it over me. Besides, it's not as if I'd be given a fair audition now. And I bet she had a hand in him not wanting to see me in the first place.'

Rob paused for a moment before replying. 'Sorry, I disagree. I brought you up again today, as it happens, and Ron is really keen to meet you. I couldn't have set you up any better.'

'But wasn't that before we knew he was shagging Mona?' I said, finding it bizarre that Rob was even entertaining the thought that I was in with a serious chance of getting the gig.

He didn't reply.

'Rob? Surely you can see it's pointless me going for it now?'

He seemed to be thinking hard about what to say.

'Rob?'

'I heard you,' he snapped at last. 'I'm just trying to find a way to word what I want to say.'

'Come on – this is me,' I urged.

Another lengthy pause, until: 'What I want to ask is this: since when have you let someone like Mona defeat you, Amber? I thought you were a fighter – it's one of the things that first attracted me to you – you weren't a pushover. And now you're willing to walk away and hand her this amazing opportunity on a plate?' I felt my cheeks redden. 'Besides, Ron's no mug,' he continued. 'I don't think he's the type to mix business with pleasure, so Mona's an even greater fool if she thinks she can forward her career by getting him in the sack. Ron's not short of offers either, believe me.' He smirked. 'I strongly doubt he'd just hand Mona such an important position even if there was something romantic going on – which I find very unlikely, by the way.'

Now it was my turn to remain quiet as we completed the journey to Balthazar, his words, 'I thought you were a fighter,' ringing in my ears. *But I just don't know if I can face the battle again.*

Rob could be very persuasive when he wanted but, once at the restaurant, we made a pact to stop talking about Mona before she ruined our entire evening. When our food arrived, I noticed he was taking forever to break into his fries; he then proceeded to prod his steak for at least fifteen minutes, as if to check whether it was still alive. Normally, he'd be guzzling down his favourite meal while making appreciative 'mmm' sounds, but I was over halfway through mine before he'd even had a mouthful, *and* I'd been doing nearly all the talking since we got here – updating him on my growing social media presence. Just this evening I'd been direct-messaged by a huge Miami-based fashion blogger who was interested in meeting me next time she was in New York. Plus, a cool handbag brand wanted to gift me a clutch personalised with my initials, in the hope that I'd Instagram it; *and* a hip online fashion site wanted to interview me about how I sourced my Queen outfit for a piece on 'cool costume-party looks'.

'I think I'm really taking off, babe,' I bragged. 'All these people want to know me!'

I then updated Rob on the stats for each of my accounts, individually, before telling him about a locked Pinterest board I was going to set up for Liv, so we could discuss her looks for upcoming events quickly and easily in private. It reminded me that I hadn't got round to calling Mickey back and he'd left another message on my phone while we were hurrying out of Soho House. 'Dana said I was the most resourceful newcomer she'd seen in years... before she sacked me.' I told him.

As I paused for breath, Rob set down his fork, looked at his watch, then at me.

'Before she sacked you,' he repeated, slowly, not smiling.

I stopped in my tracks, literally biting my tongue because I was dying to tell him that I'd Instagrammed a photo of my dinner in Balthazar (filter: Lo-fi, because it's the best for food; caption: Dinner of champions #steak #frites #BalthazarNYC #foodporn #datenight) and the official Balthazar Instagram account had reposted it, resulting in fifty more followers within seconds!

'What is it, babe?' I wondered if he'd cracked a tooth he'd been so slow to eat anything.

He sighed, as if he could barely be bothered to reply. Then he took a deep breath. 'If you must know, the way you're talking, you're becoming a real protégé of Mona Armstrong,' he said. 'Look at yourself – all you talk about is your growing fan base. But you don't even know any of these followers on Instagram that you're so obsessed with impressing. Meanwhile, you're neglecting the people who do know you and care about you the most. You're not living in the moment, Amber. Do you even realise you've checked your iPhone every ten seconds since we've been out? This evening is meant to be about you and me hanging out and chatting like we used to. You have a better relationship with your notifications centre than me.' He stopped for a moment and nudged his steak again. 'You don't seem bothered that we haven't spent any decent quality time together for ages.'

I felt as though a golf ball was lodged in my throat. Then he looked straight at me with those green eyes of his – the ones I found so bewitching the first time we met – as he said, 'You're not the Amber I fell in love with in London right now. And I'm not sure I know who this new person is.'

I sat back in my seat, totally floored. And then the golf ball plunged deep down inside my body, like it was made of lead, and stopped with a thud in the pit of my stomach. I was unable to swallow or speak; my food was instantly unappealing. *Wasn't this the same guy who was trying to have sex with me only this morning?* I tried to pull myself together, but I couldn't think straight. At last, all I could muster was a feeble, 'What?'

Suddenly, nothing in the world mattered but him. I half expected – hoped – that his face would break into a smile, revealing that this was just a joke to test my reaction, to see if I loved him as much as he loved me. But his expression remained stony.

'I don't understand,' I said, 'of course I'm the same person.' He averted his eyes. 'Baby, what's happening?' I continued, feeling panicky now. 'Is this to do with the Angel Wear job, or Vicky? Are you *really* that pissed about the Darth Vader cup?'

'Do me a favour,' he scoffed. 'It was before Vicky.'

Before Vicky? How far before? There was a tension between us that I had never felt before.

Inwardly, I tried to process what could be going through his mind and how I could respond. *I'm only trying to earn my keep out here. I'm trying to build my career, and having a social media presence is a part of that. I haven't gone on about it that much, have I?* And then I began to feel angry. *Jesus, if he's hanging out with gorgeous models all day, what am I meant to do, laze around at home eating Hershey's Kisses in a onesie? I'm only telling him about my followers because he's my boyfriend and I want him to be proud of me. Is that such a crime?*

I'd been metaphorically talking to myself for a couple of minutes before I managed to vocalise: 'Well, you're hanging out with models all day.'

He tutted in response. It was a cheap retaliation and we both knew it. I deeply suspected my Instagram account wasn't at the heart of this horrible conversation. And then an ugly thought crossed my mind that perhaps he *had* fallen for one of the Icons and was trying to find a reason to break up with me so they could be together. For a while, sitting opposite, we looked at each other with new eyes. Looking into his soul, I knew there wasn't anyone else. And I knew I wanted him more than anything in the world.

Rob clearly wanted something else though, because he ordered another bottle of red wine. And, at some point after that, it all became a bit of a blur.

CHAPTER SEVENTEEN

When I woke up, my mobile phone told me it was four in the morning. A siren blared outside and the streetlight, so inconveniently positioned directly outside our bedroom window, cast its orange glow into the room. For a moment, the shadows on the wall looked as though a man was standing there, watching me; my heart flipped as I thought it might be Rob. But, as the orange light blinked on again, there was nothing there. A shiver ran down my spine and I pulled the duvet tightly around me. My head was pounding and my mouth was dry. I had a vague memory of slurping, slurring and slapping the table as I shouted important things at Rob and he shouted things back – things I couldn't remember now. I knew it was bad, even my bones knew it was bad. And judging by the fact that he was currently sleeping on the floor with just a thin blanket partially covering him, Rob's bones knew it too. Suddenly the building felt very cold and dark. Rob was within an arm's reach of me, but he felt a million miles away. The feather tattoo on his upper arm was visible each time the light blinked on. *Please don't fly off and leave me, Rob. Please don't.* I closed my eyes, repeating the words over and over, like a prayer. Even though my eyelids were pressed tightly shut, a tear still broke free. I wished for a moment that I had never left London.

About an hour later, I peered over the side of the bed again. Half of me had been confident he'd have a change of heart in the middle of the night and come and join me up here. I sat up on my elbows and studied him, expecting him to wake up and wonder what on earth he was doing down there. Rob was deeply asleep, his breathing slow and even. He looked beautiful. *Probably too beautiful for me.*

'I love you,' I whispered to his sleeping body before shutting my eyes, tears building up again. To stop myself from crying, while he couldn't see me, I quickly, guiltily, checked my phone. There was the regular stream of Instagram likes, retweets, and a large number of +1s. Bizarrely, it seemed that an image of a broken Darth Vader goblet was good for followers. *At least it's good for something.*

It was seven o'clock when I next found myself gazing at Rob on the floor again. More than anything I wanted him to wake up and wrap his arms around me, like he used to do so readily. *So readily that I took it for granted?* Right now there was nothing I needed more than a big Rob bear hug. I ached for his touch. But he just lay there, sleeping, like he didn't have a care in the world. My mind started racing, trying to piece together the rest of the evening. I had a nagging feeling that somewhere along the way I'd agreed to interview for the Angel Wear stylist job. Rob would definitely hold me to it. Every time he stirred, I fluctuated between worrying what he was going to say when he woke up – and being terrified that if I opened my mouth I'd say something so wrong, he would leave me. *Maybe it won't be so bad to go for the interview, even if I fail it miserably, Rob can't then accuse me of not trying.* I just lay there, thoughts circling, staring at the ceiling, waiting for him to rouse and break the icy shield around us. Only he didn't; he carried on sleeping peacefully for the next two hours.

I heard Vicky stirring in the room next door and when I joined her I found an immaculately clean and tidy apartment. There were even fresh-cut flowers in a vase on the coffee table and the scent of furniture polish filled the air. She'd been working hard to make amends, but she only had to take a look at my face to know our date night hadn't gone well.

'Jesus, Amber, I'm so sorry,' she said, once I'd told her in a hushed voice what I could remember about the evening. 'I feel partly responsible.'

I still felt shocked by it all. The last thing I had expected was an argument with Rob. *My Rob. Perfect Rob. How could I have not seen this coming?*

'By the way,' she added, sensing correctly that I was on the verge of tears, 'some guy called Mickey tried to get hold of you last night. He came to the door.'

'Damn, I'll call him back now,' I said, glad of the distraction. The fact that I couldn't remember half of what was said between Rob and me last night wasn't helping my state of hangover-induced anxiety.

'Amber, what took you so long?' Mickey snapped when he answered his cell phone minutes later. I didn't bother filling him in on the truth, not that he gave me time. 'I've been desperate to reach you to tell you some fantastic news – Liv's been invited to the Met Gala! The invitation came from Anna Wintour herself. She's a late addition and we need to get her paired up with a fashion designer quick smart. They want to know who will be dressing her. I wondered about the burlesque guy – do you think he'd do it?'

Even my scrambled brain knew this was huge for Liv – the Met Gala was the biggest, most prestigious night in the fashion calendar, when New York's Metropolitan Museum of Art's red carpet becomes awash with A-list stars dressed in incredible one-off creations by the world's top designers. Colourful, daring, and glamorous are the buzz words of the evening as celebrities try to outdo each other with their eye-catching attire. Plus, you have to be personally invited by American *Vogue* editor Anna Wintour to attend – it simply doesn't get any bigger.

'Oh, my God, amazing!' I shrieked, causing Vicky to jump up and stare at me agog.

'We need to get together to talk about it as soon as possible,' Mickey continued. 'Dana has said she's not repping you any more, so I'm keen to deal direct. But Liv's schedule is insane. She's co-hosting a charity auction tonight and I wondered if you could sort her a dress for that? And I've got a spare couple of tickets, so you can catch up with her there.'

'Well, yes, I'm sure I can make that work,' I replied, my mind already racing. 'I'll have some gowns sent over. What time does the auction start?'

'Seven o'clock. Great, I'll have the tickets biked over and we'll see you there. Later.'

And he was gone.

'Wow,' I muttered, placing my phone on the coffee table and sinking into the sofa as I took in the news and resisted the urge to immediately post something about it on Twitter. I had a haunting feeling that I'd promised Rob I would try to be less obsessed with impressing a host of strangers with my every thought. *It's going to take some weaning-off.*

'What is it?' Vicky joined me, brandishing two steaming mugs of tea. 'Dare I offer one to Rob?' She glanced in the direction of our bedroom door.

'Still asleep,' I replied, not particularly keen for Vicky to see him snoozing next to our bed rather than in it.

'Anna Wintour has only invited Liv to the Met Gala – and Mickey wants me to style her for it. The Gala is just a week away though and designers will have been working up their costumes for months. She can't afford to mess this up. Anyway, he's invited me to a charity auction Liv's hosting tonight to talk about it. I'm going to have a selection of gowns from Rose's sent over for her to choose what to wear for that.'

Vicky's eyes widened. 'The Met? That's incred! Go, Amber – that means Anna Wintour herself was taking note of her Coachella outfits, as styled by you! If Liv's invited to the Met Gala, she could turn up in a black bin bag and it would be lauded around the globe – she's won fashion immunity, and it's all down to you.'

'And Maurice Chan,' I corrected her. 'He lent her all the clothes. In fact, you've hit the nail on the head – I'll ask him to design her something for the event.'

'I'm sure he'd cut some holes in a bin bag with his typical *je ne sais quoi*,' she said, giggling.

I rolled my eyes. 'I can't believe I don't already know what the theme is for this year's Gala.' I grabbed my iPad and began furiously googling to find the answer. 'Ancient Civilisations,' I uttered. 'Hmm, this is going to take some planning.'

When he surfaced, Rob was in a surprisingly good mood. I played along with it, wondering if perhaps the evening hadn't ended as badly as I imagined. He even offered to make Vicky and I another cup of tea.

'What's going on?' Vicky mouthed, as soon as his back was turned.

I shrugged. Unnerving as it was, this was a big improvement on the moody Rob of the previous morning.

'Do you fancy coming to an auction with me tonight, babe?' I ventured when he joined us on the sofa. 'Liv's been invited to the Met Gala and she needs to discuss outfits with me, she's going to be hosting this charity event.' I hoped we might be able to have a more successful date night if we went out again and this time stayed off booze.

'Can't, I'm afraid, we've got a late shoot today,' he said brightly. 'Plus, you might not want to be out too late this evening because Ron has agreed to see you for an interview tomorrow at noon. I called him as soon as I woke up. He's really looking forward to meeting you. How cool is that?'

'Whoop!' Vicky jumped up.

They both watched me spit out a large sip of tea.

'That's fast work,' I said, flummoxed.

'Ron doesn't waste his time,' Rob continued blithely.

'Did he mention Mona?' I asked.

'Not a thing.' He smiled. 'Maybe you'll have some *real* news to post on social media before the week is out.'

A little dig there, but I was willing to let it go – I couldn't actually believe I might be in with a chance.

'And if you're looking for a partner in crime for the auction tonight, I'm up for it,' Vicky offered. 'Keeps me out of your hair,' she said, winking at Rob.

'I guess it's a deal – on both fronts.' I smiled, cautiously – mostly just relieved that peace had returned to the sardine tin.

In our bedroom, as we both hurriedly got ourselves ready for the day ahead, Rob squared up to me.

'I heard you in the middle of the night,' he said contemplatively.

'I thought you were asleep,' I said, laying down the pile of clothes I'd been about to transport to the laundrette. 'I meant what I said, you know. I do love you – so much.'

He smiled. 'I know, and I wanted to get back into bed with you, so badly. But I whacked my knee on some iron railings giving you a piggyback, last night. Remember?'

A vague recollection of the incident came into my mind.

'Come here,' he said, pulling me into the warmest embrace. I relaxed and the aching to feel his lips on mine subsided. 'Promise you won't Instagram this moment?' he said when we came apart.

'Promise,' I simpered.

*

Suddenly, my day had gone from quiet to insanely busy. First up I busied myself calling Maurice to explain the situation. When I suggested he design Liv's outfit for the Met Gala, thankfully – I actually kissed my phone – he said he was up for the job.

'You know, dear Anna did actually ring me about a celebrity pairing for the Met last year,' he revealed, 'but the timing wasn't right, I was still in the grip of depression. In Liv, I see a kindred spirit though. If she's happy, I'm up for it.'

Shortly afterwards, the doorbell rang and a courier dropped off our tickets for that evening. It was a charity auction in connection with the Armoury Show – New York's annual international art fair, held in the ballroom of the grand Waldorf Astoria Hotel. Liv would be on stage presenting some of the artworks to be auctioned off. It was a black tie event, which called for a suitable floor-length gown. Vicky had a red Ralph Lauren dress bought the other day on Trey's credit card, but I needed something to wear.

'Darling, your new best friend is one of the biggest names in fashion – surely, Maurice can lend you something?' Vicky suggested.

I shrugged. 'I don't like to ask him.'

Vicky held up a hand. 'Oh, per-lease, Amber, this is America. Everyone asks for everything. Call him back immediately.'

I was glad I did, because Maurice was only too excited to tell me about the new collection of dresses he had been working on in secret. 'I've been using Cleopatra as my muse,' he whispered into the phone, though there was no real need to keep his voice down. 'The Egyptian queens were so powerful yet so sexy, elegant and feminine – I'm going to put Ancient Egypt back on the map. And I've been thinking about what to call my new label. I'm thinking "De Retour", meaning "Comeback", symbolised by an image of a phoenix. I think it represents all of us – you, me, Liv – we are *les trois amis*, arising from the ashes to seize the day once again.' I could feel a wide smile in his voice.

'I love it, Maurice, it's perfect!' I said, smiling. 'And you do know the theme for the Met is ancient civilisations?'

'Of course!' he said. 'And wouldn't Liv make the ultimate Cleopatra? I'm thinking statement gold choker, snake cuffs, bejewelled bra and elegant skirt. I'm so inspired by this, I can't wait to design for her. Everyone will be talking about it!'

'Yes! I can see her as Cleopatra!' I shrieked, thinking how making a spectacle of herself being partially clothed was exactly Liv's thing. 'I love it!' It was so great to hear his voice full of enthusiasm – I had a sense the old Maurice was coming back. And I liked this Maurice, a lot. 'I'll tell her all about it this evening. Also, I was wondering whether you – whether De Retour – had anything I could borrow for the event tonight?'

'Of course, *ma chérie*! Why, I have an exquisite flowing ivory gown. I've been using my old seamstress and she's just finished it. It's beautiful in its simplicity – low cut at the front, with just a hint of Egypt about it, if you pair with a thick gold cuff. I'll send it over in a cab.'

As I put down the phone I turned to Vicky, who had been listening in. 'I think you could say a plan is coming together.'

Instinctively – *well, we are in America* – we high-fived.

When the ivory gown arrived, swathed in reams of tissue paper, we were both floored by its beauty.

'You can tell in the detail that it's been made by a top designer,' Vicky gushed, running her fingers over the cool, silky fabric and admiring the delicate gold detailing around the deep neckline. Although undeniably a thing of beauty, there was something immediately jarring about me, Amber Green, in an insanely delicate ivory gown, that would cling to every love handle and show up every sweat spot, but I felt duty bound to try it on.

'Va-va-voom!' shrieked Vicky as I came back out of my bedroom.

'Va-va-doom!' I winced. I'd been holding in my stomach so intensely I was feeling light-headed. 'I feel like The Snowman,' I said, grimacing. 'Tell me, honestly?'

'Honestly – it looks stunning.' She took in my expression. 'But if you're going to be afraid of every glass of red wine and terrified of even looking at a bread roll in it, maybe it's not going to work.'

I sighed. 'In other words, I look fat.'

'I never said that!' she screeched.

'You didn't need to…' I was already itching to take it off.

Dana rang just as I was on my way to the bedroom to peel myself out of the dress.

'What's this I hear – you're going to the Armoury Auction

tonight?' she said, sounding a big annoyed. She was clearly outside, I could hear the clip-clop of her heels on the pavement and traffic noise in the background. A siren blasted, so I shouted into the receiver: 'Yes, Dana, Mickey—'

'I know,' she quipped, equally loudly, 'I just bumped into him in Soho House. He also said Liv's been invited to the Met. Were you going to tell me, or were you going to poach my client? It's not right, Amber.'

Her confrontational attitude startled me. 'Well, yes, of course,' I lied. To be honest, it hadn't even crossed my mind to ring her before we went out tonight.

She read my mind: 'Honey, I'm your former agent – you can't steal clients without letting me know. What are you planning for the Met for her?'

I feel faintly ridiculous being told off while wearing a red-carpet gown. Even hugging my love handles, it managed to upstage everything in the entire apartment – including Vicky's red Ralph Lauren dress. She knew it too.

'Liv's going as an Egyptian Queen in an outfit designed by Maurice Chan – for his new label.'

'Maurice Chan's new label?' Dana sounded shocked. 'He's got a new label? That's big news. Are you up to this?'

I could see my reflection in one of the windows. *Let's face it, this gown is stunning; Maurice is indeed big news. Of course I'm wearing the dress.*

Later that evening, the area outside the ballroom entrance of the Waldorf Astoria Hotel was buzzing. Women in long flowing dresses with fur stoles and men in penguin suits littered the pavement as they bustled to get out of the cool evening and into the grand hotel. A stream of limos and taxis was rhythmically depositing even more gowns and suits onto the pavement, as we tottered down the street to join the queue to get in.

The ballroom was stunning to behold, a huge space, lit by twinkling chandeliers. There were elaborate floral displays in the centre of at least sixty big round tables and the air was thick with the smell of perfume, champagne and excited conjecture.

Mickey had organised our table of ten, and he appeared briefly to introduce us all. To my left was an ageing art collector and his blonde-bombshell girlfriend who claimed to be an 'actress' but was really his 'arm candy' – a quick Google revealed she didn't even have a *Wikipedia* entry. Next to them was the owner of one of Manhattan's top art galleries and a man who was presumably his boyfriend and, to our right, a young heiress and her dashing boyfriend, neither of whom could have been over the age of thirty, but Mickey had quietly informed us that they were probably worth all the money in the room put together. And there were two empty seats to our right, for Mickey and Liv to return to once she had fulfilled her presenting duty.

The conversation between the eight of us was strained, so Vicky and I took it upon ourselves to crack open the two bottles of champagne for the table. Thankfully, most of them were teetotallers, which meant more for Vicky and me. Despite all this, I was still the only person to eat every bit of my wilted beetroot salad, masses of chicken in an indistinguishable gravy, and no less than three dry dinner rolls, with an entire portion of butter. White dress or no white dress, this spread was too good to waste. As the evening wore on I kicked my heels off under the table.

Vicky had been in a fidgety mood; there was no phone reception in the ballroom so she kept popping out to check her messages.

'What's going on?' I asked, when she returned to her seat for about the fourth time since the meal had begun. I'd been left bluffing my way through a conversation about David Hockney with the art collector and was now hopelessly out of my depth.

'It's Trey,' she said, 'he's been messaging me non-stop today. I think he's finally realised I may not be coming back. It's only taken him the best part of a week.' She rolled her eyes.

'Is it too little, too late?' I asked.

'Too right!' she fumed. 'He's had the cheek to ask me to FedEx my credit card back. I mean, what does he think I am? I'm no gold-digger.' She looked across at the heavily Botoxed woman sitting next to the old man. 'He said he's been working non-stop, blah, blah, blah, the same old crap. I've had enough of it. He couldn't even tell me he loves me.'

'And is that what you really want to hear?' I asked, sensing that she was feeling more angry than heartbroken. 'I mean, do you still love him?'

She sighed. 'I don't know.'

As the lights were dimmed and the auction was about to start, I noticed her turn and coyly smile at a very handsome man at an adjacent table. He looked vaguely familiar. And he seemed to recognise Vicky, giving her an appreciative smile back. I observed him continue watching her with a mixture of amusement and fascination even after she had turned away.

I nudged Vicky's knee. 'Do you know him?'

'No, but he's Noah West – he models for loads of the top brands.'

'He seems very familiar with you,' I replied.

'We met in the foyer, just now,' she said, eyes shining mischievously,

'Vicky...?'

She was saved any explanation by the lights dimming as the evening's host – a brash male auctioneer, took to the stage and began hawking round-trip holidays to Europe, ten-day cruises, customised Louboutins and epicurean experiences with New York's top chefs, alongside some one-of-a-kind pieces of art from New York's hottest artists. Liv kept appearing on the stage to illustrate the detail in the pieces. She looked ethereal in a sheer pale-green gown – it was the kind of dress that wore a person, rather than the other way around, and it couldn't have been more perfect for the occasion.

Just as we had all become accustomed to works of art fetching staggering amounts of money – including one that I swear was just a blank white canvas – Liv came onstage alongside a painting that looked familiar. A simple beach landscape that appeared to be covered in the multicoloured hand and fingerprints of a young child.

'And next up we have this unique landscape by the famed Greenwich Village-based artist, Boris Cosgrove,' announced our host. 'It was completed in his home studio only last week – the paint is just dry. You can see the tenderness of every brushstroke in this stunning canvas,' he continued, as Liv, pointed out a few of the brushstrokes to illustrate his point, 'where Cosgrove conveys the playful nature of childhood against the backdrop of a spirited young tide.'

The discerning art collectors in the room nodded their heads sagely.

'Er, "spirited young tide"?' I mocked. 'What the hell is that supposed to mean?'

'And, "playful nature of childhood"?' Vicky replied, nudging me in the ribs. 'Isn't that the painting from the artist's house on the baby shoot? The one that got you the sack?'

'Oh, my God, it is!' I sniggered. 'Those are the prints and splodges of Jamie, the toddler, all over it. The artist is blatantly trying to pass it off as a masterpiece!'

Neither of us could believe it when the collector on our table entered the bidding at twenty-five thousand for the 'masterpiece', only to be outbid, and as it finally fetched sixty-two thousand dollars.

'Jesus Christ! We are in the wrong business,' I muttered to Vicky, as the winner of the painting celebrated with a very public, passionate kiss with his elated partner.

About halfway through the long list of lots, suddenly a spotlight shone brightly onto the male model's table, illuminating him for the entire ballroom's appreciation. The auctioneer then announced they were auctioning off a kiss with Noah West, to be delivered during a dinner date with him in a fashionable restaurant.

The auctioneer invited Noah onstage, before sharing his story of being born to a single mum in a poor area of Los

Angeles and working his way to the top of the fashion world. 'Today, he's one of the top philanthropists in the US – as well as one of the world's most eligible bachelors,' he said, Noah's story capturing the attention of every woman in the room. I had never seen such a beautiful man in the flesh – he looked like he'd just stepped out of a Burberry campaign. The auction for this lot began apace – the price feverishly escalating from ten thousand to fifteen thousand to twenty thousand dollars within moments. The top collector's girl-friend at our table enthusiastically raised her hand a couple of times, bidding against a platinum-blonde woman with gigantic sparkling earrings sitting a couple of tables away. As the auction reached a crescendo at a staggering thirty-eight thousand, all for just one dinner date and a peck on the cheek from this man – who I supposed was as dull as ditch water to actually hold a conversation with – the person sitting right next to me flung themselves into the air. It was Vicky, her arm raised skyward, heart pounding, making no mistake that she was placing a bid – for forty thousand dollars!

'Wow, thank you, ma'am!' shouted the auctioneer, who had descended from the stage and was approaching our table rapidly. 'I now have forty thousand dollars on the table from this beautiful lady in red, for a dinner date with Noah. And what a lucky lady you are, unless you are to be outbid!' He turned back to survey the tables spread before him, diamond accessories twinkling from each one. It felt as though all the eyes in the room were trained on Vicky and me. A spotlight shone directly onto us, warming my cheeks.

Vicky was smiling wildly, her eyes locked on Noah, and he was staring seductively right back at her.

'Do I have an advance on forty thousand dollars?' the auctioneer asked again. 'For this once-in-a-lifetime opportunity to be wined and dined by the world's most handsome man?' Heads began swivelling like lollies on sticks, as we all searched the room for signs of another hand in the air. *Come on, someone bid, please. Anyone?* 'And not only is he the most good-looking single man the globe has to offer, he is also one of the most generous!' the host continued. 'Who knows where this could lead! I'm thinking marriage, babies, pets!' He laughed, throwing his arms up, making a heart-shape with his hands, as Noah jokingly blew him a kiss from the stage.

Still no counter-bids from the room.

I looked at Vicky, panic in my eyes.

'Forty grand, babe, forty grand! What the hell are you doing?' I gently tugged on her dress, willing for her to sit down and stop.

Through gritted teeth, she turned slightly, and replied, 'Amber, I know what I'm doing. Trey's paying. He bloody deserves to.'

Vicky wasn't going to take no for an answer, and, as the spotlight shone brightly on her, she basked in the attention smiling a mega-watt smile – admittedly, she did look really hot this evening – as her audience wondered who on earth this lady was, to fritter away enough money for a down payment on a small apartment, on just one night with a model.

And then it was over: the auctioneer's hammer fell and Vicky won the kiss, which would be delivered during a dinner date to be scheduled for following week at a top New York venue.

'That was the most fun I've had in ages!' Vicky exclaimed, as people began turning back around and the auctioneer got the bidding going for the next lot – an all-expenses-paid weekend for two at the Monaco Grand Prix.

I found myself speechless, my mouth visibly hanging open.

'Oh, come on,' she said, nudging me, as if she was surprised by my reaction.

'You just—'

'Yes, I know what I just did,' she continued. 'And I don't regret it at all. Trey will barely notice the money gone from his account. Besides, it's going to a fantastic cause – I've always wanted to do more for charity.' She winked at me. *Nothing is going to rain on Vicky's parade this evening.*

'How come you didn't bid on the lot that was to build an entire school in a remote part of Uganda then?' I asked.

Vicky paused, but was saved from replying when a girl from the auction house approached our table, brandishing an iPad to take down her credit-card details, presumably before this mysterious winner could do a runner. The girl was wearing an expression to suggest she'd seen it all before. I suppose in her world it was common practice to see a young woman spend forty thousand dollars on something so inane.

'I swear that Noah guy was making eyes at me all evening,' Vicky said, once the girl had gone. 'Come on, Amber, just be happy for me. If anything, it will be a great night out – one to tell my grandkids about. You and Rob could come and join us after the dinner if you like?'

I admired Vicky's confidence; she was already certain the dinner would be a success. Joining them would probably be Rob's idea of a nightmare though.

'Yeah, maybe,' I said diplomatically.

'Hey, Amber!' We were interrupted by Liv, throwing her arms around my neck from behind and pulling my head into her chest for a hug. I felt the eyes of the room on us as she took her seat next to me.

'Man, that was fun!' she gushed. 'We must have made close to a million dollars this evening. It's unbelievable how much money is in this room – you can smell it. Did you see some crazy bitch shelled out forty thousand for a date with Noah West?'

'Yes,' Vicky piped up. 'That crazy bitch happens to be me. Champagne?' She poured a glass for Liv.

Liv wasn't one to be embarrassed easily. 'Honey, you nearly killed me,' she giggled. 'You do know he's gay, don't you?'

I could see Vicky struggling to keep her face in a neutral expression, and I wanted to laugh out loud – as surely she would, had the tables been turned. Instead, I let out a grunt. *Forty grand, on a kiss with a guy who prefers to date men. This is the funniest thing I've heard in ages.*

'Yeah… course I-I do,' Vicky eventually stuttered. 'Just doing my bit for charity.' And she promptly excused herself for the loo.

'That's some mate you've got there,' Mickey commented as we all watched her disappear.

'Yes, one of London's greatest philanthropic exports, bless

her,' I muttered, before swiftly moving the conversation on to the reason we were here in the first place – Maurice and the Met Gala.

CHAPTER EIGHTEEN

The next morning, I arrived for my interview at the Angel Wear offices in mid-town Manhattan fifteen minutes early. Tightly clutching my iPad, I hovered by the entrance wondering whether to go in or not. The bright spring sunshine was making my all-black ensemble feel even hotter. Suddenly, I really wanted this job. Meeting Liv was fun, but choosing clothes for a naturist? Surely, a dead-end job for a stylist. Rob and Vicky had successfully convinced me there could be nothing bigger on a New York stylist's CV than being the lead stylist for the Angel Wear show. I had been too nervous to eat breakfast, so now my stomach was audibly gurgling. It was hard to believe I'd been considering not even going for an interview. After wasting a few minutes debating whether I had enough time to neck a double espresso from the nearby Starbucks to help focus my brain and quell my tummy rumbles – I didn't dare risk it – I leaned against the wall and decided to call Rob. A good-luck snog would definitely help. He appeared in the street minutes later.

'Baby! You look stunning!'

I smiled; his compliments still made me feel like the only girl in the world.

'Ron's in a great mood today,' he continued, 'but he's running a bit late for the interviews. Why don't you wait inside?' He squinted in the sunshine. 'It's boiling out here.'

'Interviews *plural*?' I said, slightly surprised. I didn't want to come across as presumptuous, but... 'I thought I was the only person he was seeing today?'

'There's someone else, too,' he revealed, looking shifty.

'Well, tell me who, won't you?'

He pulled an expression that suggested I probably didn't want to hear the answer. And he was right. 'He's seeing Mona for her official interview too.'

'But—' He stopped me from blowing up by placing both hands on my shoulders.

'Look, he's got to go through the motions, and it's all good for filming. She won't get the job.'

Filming?

'Rob. First Mona, and now you casually mention my interview is going to be filmed? You know how much I hate surprises – and surprises on film is probably my biggest nightmare. I would have spent longer on my make-up. Jesus, I was fifteen minutes early, I could have gone to Sephora for a free five-minute makeover – and now I barely have time to powder my forehead.'

He calmly cupped my head in his hands and smiled, as though I was amusing him. 'Amber, you look absolutely gorgeous, believe me, and you're an amazing stylist. You don't need heavy make-up to prove anything. This will be a walk in the park, I promise.'

I looked at him with exasperation. 'I wasn't talking about heavy make-up, just *some* make-up. And Mona? Jesus, Rob.'

'I told you before, Mona's not going to get the job – I've told them how impossible she was when we were filming last year. It's purely a formality, to keep her quiet and make life easier for Ron.'

'Quiet?' It wasn't a word generally used to describe Mona. 'When's her interview then?' I squirmed, feeling incredibly exposed standing right outside the entrance to the building. Mona was probably watching us right now, through Louis Vuitton binoculars.

'It's after yours, so she won't be here yet. Anyway, let's head in.' He put his arm around me protectively and we entered the building.

Inside, a security guard gave Rob a familiar smile, and two women, who looked remarkably like Angel Wear models themselves, looked after reception behind a slick white-marble desk. The taller one, with a sharp, jet-black, elfin hairstyle and immaculately applied make-up, lowered her headset as we approached. I studied her face enviously.

'This is Amber Green, she's here for an interview.' Rob spoke for me.

The woman looked me up and down.

Not, er, for modelling, obviously, I felt the need to add.

'Go through,' she ordered. 'Rob will show you where.' I was slightly perturbed by the affectionate smile she gave him. *Hey, giraffe features – that's my boyfriend.*

I noticed my palms were sweaty as I entered Ron Angel's

penthouse office. It was a large room with white furnishings, a gigantic zebra-patterned rug on the floor. Taking up almost the whole of one wall was a huge photograph of the five Icons dressed in sexy lingerie and linking arms on the catwalk; they looked even more intimidating in double height and with seriously big glamorous hair being blown off their faces by what must have been an industrial wind machine. On the opposite wall hung another large image, this time of Ron's face, created from what appeared to be a collage of images of the models' body parts barely covered in skimpy underwear. Inevitably, Ron was a man who appreciated a pert, tanned bottom. Ron's desk stood in front of a big window, and there was a clear glass conference table to one side, around which the camera crew were set up. A light was already trained on Ron, sitting at the head of the table and engrossed in his laptop. Another light was set up by an empty swivel chair to his right, presumably reserved for me.

Rob had to cough a few times to announce our arrival and, at last, Ron stood to greet me. He was a tall man with a puffed-out chest, long slim legs and a Brillo Pad of salt-and-pepper hair. He wore a black suit with a white T-shirt underneath; the suit looked expensive and I'd bet the T-shirt wasn't from GAP. He was reasonably good-looking, in a classically American kind of way, and when he smiled his eyes closed to slits. *He probably thinks he looks like Pierce Brosnan, but in actual fact he's more Phillip Schofield crossed with Simon Cowell.*

There were two other people sitting opposite the empty chair around the table. One was an effeminate-looking man introduced as Dimitri, the lead Angel Wear in-house designer, and another a face I recognised as Caroline Bourne, a leading celebrity make-up artist, who I had met during awards season in LA last year. Thankfully, we had parted on good terms. She smiled warmly in recognition. It was reassuring to see a friendly face as I took my seat with not enough caffeine inside me, in front of the boss of one of America's biggest fashion retailers, about to be interrogated – on camera.

Rob whispered 'good luck', as he attached a small microphone to the inside of my blouse. I remembered the first time he had done this when I met him last year, how I had squirmed and prayed I didn't smell of BO or that he hadn't caught a glimpse of my greying M&S bra. How things had changed. *Except for my menagerie of old M&S bras!*

Rob then announced: 'Three... two... one... Action!'

And Ron began speaking: 'So, Amber, tell us – why is fashion such a powerful medium for you?' He took me aback with such a philosophical line of questioning. *Why is fashion such a powerful medium?* I hadn't really thought of it like that before. I paused for a few seconds. I thought about Maurice and how his words in the coffee shop had resonated with me – how there could be no mistaking that fashion was in his blood. *What was it he said again?*

'I suppose I like telling stories with clothes,' I replied, eventually. 'I guess I think of my life in outfits – I can remember what I was wearing when I had my first kiss, on my first date with my boyfriend,' (I avoided looking at Rob) 'and on my first day in New York.' I stopped, wondering if this was the kind of answer he was looking for. His expression gave nothing away. 'But most of all, I like the idea of turning someone into the woman they always dreamt they could be.' I had Jas very much in mind when I said that – my former boss at Smiths boutique in London said such things all the time and I had learned so much from her. I spared a moment to imagine being back there, safely ensconced in the stock room, away from the rolling camera.

'Great. Good answer,' Ron said, leaning forward and rolling up his sleeves. He wasn't as cold as I'd imagined. 'So how will you apply this to Angel Wear?'

'Clothes define moments,' I replied, buoyed by his reaction, and Caroline's encouraging nodding. 'Though the audience may not remember every single item they see on the catwalk, I want them to leave the Angel Wear show remembering the feeling it gave them. I want to empower the audience – make them proud to be a woman.'

'There certainly won't be many clothes to remember!' Dimitri interjected, smirking. 'We're talking about a lingerie show, after all.'

'Of course, and that's even better,' I said, undeterred. 'I want each woman there to feel proud to be female.'

The room tittered in response. I became aware that I was clasping my hands inordinately tightly, so I took a moment to relax a little, to unfurl my fingers and take a sip of water. I was shaking slightly as I lifted the glass to my lips.

'I always think, with styling, that less is more, anyway,' I quipped.

Another ripple of laughter. 'You can say that again.'

'What I mean is that we don't need to show the entire

collection to make an impact. It's about the theatre of the moment and a few choice pieces on the Icons' incredible bodies – the spectacle of the hair, make-up, visual effects and music will do the rest.'

'Great vision,' Ron said, without giving away whether he really meant it, or whether he was trying to bring the interview to a close. 'Thanks for your time, Amber Green. We'll be in touch. Great name by the way.'

Dimitri was disarmingly quiet as the interview finished and, although Caroline gave me a wink as I got up to leave, I wasn't sure if she was just offering me moral support. I thought I'd given it my best, but had no idea which way this was this was going to go – Ron hadn't even asked to look through my portfolio.

Rob led me out of the room and back towards the lifts.

'You were brilliant!' he gushed. 'Seriously, that comment about wanting each woman to feel proud to be female – it was inspired! Honestly, *no one* could give better answers. I think Ron was impressed.'

'Really?' I quivered. 'But what about that Dimitri guy? He was a cold fish – he barely said a word.'

'He's always like that,' Rob assured me. 'A tortured-designer-type. Plus, I think he's had so much work done to his face, he can't actually show what he's thinking any more. Caroline would love to work with you again – I heard her telling everyone so as you left, and Ron listens to her.'

He saw me off by the lifts with a lingering kiss on the lips and a promise to come home early. I was rushing to leave the building, to get to Maurice's house to discuss the Met, when I nearly bumped straight into Mona Armstrong in the foyer. She was camera ready, dressed up in her big round shades, skintight leather jeggings, billowing cream silk shirt, Christian Louboutin ankle boots, oversized tomato-red tote, and a bizarre matte-black whistle hanging on a chain around her neck. Probably Chanel, but kind of odd. The thought crossed my mind that it could be her latest way of keeping her current assistant in check – blow one for a macchiato, two for Nurofen. The poor person. *Thank God, she's not my problem any more*.

Before I could back off in the direction from which I came, Mona spotted me.

'Satisfied?' she spat.

I risked a glance over my shoulder, just to check she was in fact talking to me. Mistake. She was striding towards me now, looking menacing, desperate to engage with me.

'Hey, Amber? Haven't you even got the decency to say *anything* to me?' she was shouting.

I had two options: keep walking backwards and end up reversing into the lift, or answer back and try to make her stop. I thought about Rob's comment the other night, about not being a pushover, and I took a deep breath.

'What do you mean?' I said, hedging, in case she didn't know why I was here.

'Why would you make such an effort with your outfit? You never used to.' *Cheap punch*. 'You fucking planned it all,' she barked. 'You used me to climb your way to the top.'

A couple of people turned to see who the dressed up woman was shouting at.

'I'm sorry, Mona, but I don't know what you're talking about. I was asked to come to an interview today – just as you were. Now, if you don't mind, I've got somewhere to—'

'*Was*,' she seethed, sticking her arm out to stop me passing. 'I *was* going to be interviewed today – and *before* you, you conniving little bitch – but you got in there first and told them not to bother seeing me.'

'Told them what?' I said, feeling my cheeks redden. We were causing a scene and I felt uncomfortable, but I couldn't let Mona walk all over me. 'I said no such thing!' I replied, raising my voice.

Well, why has Ron just called to tell me not to bother coming up then? she screamed.

'I have no idea!' I said, truthfully. 'I certainly didn't say anything to him.'

She stopped for a second and stared at me, as though she was trying to work out if I was telling the truth or not, her eyes like icy blades.

My mind was galloping. *If Ron doesn't want to see Mona, could this mean I've got the job?*

'Yeah, right!' she fumed.

'Maybe my rates were cheaper,' I replied, faint-heartedly, feeling immediately annoyed with myself for being apologetic. I really wasn't in the mood for this today. A few more people had noticed the raised voices and stopped walking to wherever they were going to stand and gawp. I swear a few were sniggering behind their hands. I hated Mona for making us both look ridiculous.

'Yeah right, stupid cow,' she said. 'And after I gave your big legs a hoik up the ladder. You were just a shop girl when I met you. You seem to have forgotten that fact.'

Big legs. I turned away, looking towards the water machine. I needed a minute to work out how to get out of this horrible situation. *Just a shop girl*. My cheeks were burning and the women on reception were anxiously looking around, trying to locate the security guard.

'I think you need to wash your mouth out, Mona,' I said, finding inspiration from the water cooler and turning back to face her, slightly thrilled to have thought of a half-decent comeback in time.

'Really? Well, you can pour yourself a great big glass of "shut the fuck up", Amber,' she said; before muttering, 'What kind of fool do they take me for?' as she called for the lift. Luckily for her, the doors opened before I had a chance to consider throwing a full glass of cold filter water over her silk shirt.

'Hey, ma'am – you haven't been signed in!' shouted one of the women on reception, just as the security guard skidded on to the scene and asked me if everything was all right.

But the lift doors had shut and Mona was heading to the penthouse floor to give Ron a piece of her mind too. *Poor guy*.

As I raced out of the building I felt a mixture of emotions – disbelief at how rude some people could be and exhilaration that perhaps Ron did want me for the job. One thing I knew for sure: *I hope I never have to see that pathetic excuse for a woman again.*

When I reached Maurice's apartment to give him the news that we might not be able to style Liv after all, there was no reply on the intercom and, looking up at the windows, his floor was bathed in darkness. I loitered around outside for ten minutes, just in case he was taking a while to come to the door. It was odd, considering (a) he knew I was coming over and (b) he is a self-confessed recluse.

I kept thinking he'd appear at any second, but after ten minutes my toes and fingers were beginning to freeze. Just as I was about to give up, Vicky phoned, so I sat on the steps leading up to Maurice's front door and spoke to her while I waited.

'You're not going to believe it,' she said, bursting with excitement. 'The auction house called about that date – you know, the one with the hot model?'

'Yes, I am aware of your expensive date with a gay guy.'

'Well, it's happening *tonight*! Apparently, Noah's got to leave town on Thursday so we're meeting right away. How cool is that?' She seemed to be blanking the fact he might be more interested in guys.

'Great, hon, I hope you have a fantastic time.' I couldn't help feeling flat about this 'date', which had cost more than my wages in the last year; it seemed such a grotesque waste of money, especially when she was dossing at ours, causing tension between Rob and me.

'What time will you be home this afternoon?' she asked. 'I'd love to get your opinion on what I should wear.'

'I'll be a couple of hours,' I replied, not feeling particularly enthusiastic.

'I'll get some wine in,' she offered, giving me some kind of incentive to get back.

Just before she hung up, a cab containing Maurice pulled up.

'*Chérie! Je suis désolé!*' he gushed. 'I would have called but my battery died. I had to pick something up – for the costume.' He grinned wickedly. 'Hurry, let's get inside, I can't wait to show you.'

He patted a black satchel worn across his slim body. His Cuban heels looked as though they'd had a bit of a polish; even his trademark bun hairstyle looked a little neater today. Maurice was on the up.

I followed him into the apartment building, feeling just as wowed by its splendour as the first time I set foot in there, just over a week before.

'So what's in the bag? The suspense is killing me,' I begged as the little lift rattled it's way upwards.

'Not here, wait until we get inside,' he whispered, his hand hovering over the clasp of his satchel, as it had been since he exited the cab.

We entered the apartment and headed straight for his lounge. The birds in the bird cage seemed to spring to life as soon as they saw him.

'*Bonjour mes douces filles!*' he exclaimed. 'No time to let you out today, I'm afraid, my friend and I have work to do.'

I walked along beside him, absorbing more about the grand room as I went. On every table were framed photographs and little trinkets, porcelain pill boxes, statuettes of dancers, and pretty vases of flowers. Maurice clearly took great pride in maintaining his ancestor's former home.

He pulled aside a chair and ushered me to sit down. And then he opened the satchel and took out another bag – a fairly large black-velvet drawstring pouch, clearly filled with something reasonably heavy. He set it down on a side table positioned between us.

'I had an idea,' he began. 'That photo of Marianne, you remember – the one that struck you, in the hallway, where she looks sad and is wearing the bejewelled ruby bra?'

I smiled. 'Of course, it's a beautiful photo.'

He pulled it out of the bag now too. I hadn't noticed it was missing from the wall when we came in.

'Clark Claybourne – that's the name of the multi-millionaire boyfriend who gave it to her.'

I nodded as he continued. 'Well, it turns out he's still alive. He's in a nursing home in Long Island.'

He got up and moved across the room to an ornate French walnut desk with inlaid brass embellishments and three deep drawers. He opened the middle drawer and I could see from the other side of the room that it was full of letters. He ran his hand through them, lifting up a pile to show me that it was full to overflowing – there must have been hundreds in there.

'These are all letters from Clark,' he said, eyes shining. 'He has been writing to Marianne every week for years now. I opened the letters at first, but then I gave up. They all say the same thing – that he thinks of her every single day and his one big regret in life is ending their relationship, that he would give anything for another moment in her company.'

My mouth fell open; it was such a sad story.

'But what are you going to do with the letters, Maurice?' I asked, wondering what this had to do with what was in the pouch.

'Clark always leaves his phone number, and so, as part of my journey to move on with life, I thought it was about time I put him straight.' He sighed. 'So I called him, and he immediately invited me to Long Island. He said he had something he wanted me to have. So that's where I've been. I went yesterday and stayed the night in a nearby motel. I met Clark for dinner – I took him a picnic of French foods and we ate it together, with me sitting by his bed. It was quite magical, as we told stories of Marianne into the evening. He really did love her. But he was never formally divorced from his first wife, so it was impossible for them to be together, he said. He eventually felt duty-bound to return to his wife because she was terminally ill. But he never forgot Marianne. He said she was the one who got away.'

Now my eyes were beginning to fill with tears too. He continued. 'Anyway, as I was about to leave, he handed me this.' He held up the velvet pouch.

'What's in it?' I asked.

Gently, he teased it open and a pulled out a string of the most stunning, shimmering red rubies. As more and more rubies cut into the shape of petals appeared from the bag, I could see that it was heavy – much heavier than a necklace or another piece of jewellery. Other than the Crown Jewels exhibition at the Tower of London, I had never seen so many glittery precious stones on one item. I looked back at the black and white photo of Marianne.

'The ruby-encrusted bra...' I sighed.

'*Mais, oui.* Clark insisted I take it. He had given it to Marianne when they were dating, but she returned it in the post when he called things off. Miraculously, it reached him without his wife ever getting wind of it, and he kept it hidden for seventy years, in case he ever saw Marianne again. I guess I turned out to be his only link to her and when I told him about my career in fashion, he knew I would put it to good use. He didn't want to just leave it to a grandchild who wouldn't fully appreciate its beauty or understand the significance of it. He wanted it to be close to Marianne again – and the closest thing to her, is me.'

'That's so romantic.' I sighed. 'What an incredible piece. How much do you think it's worth?'

'Clark told me to insure it for one million dollars,' he whispered, and looked over his shoulder towards the birdcage, as if he didn't even want his feathery friends to be privy to such information.

'One. Million. Dollars.' I repeated, awestruck. I put my fingers out to touch the cool, smooth stones; there must have been at least a hundred of them covering a very delicate boned bra. It was in immaculate condition. Maurice offered the bra to me and I held it. It was much heavier than I imagined – it would be quite a thing to wear. I realised I had never held something so valuable before in my life – the closest I had come was a limited-edition crocodile Birkin bag in Smiths, a snip at sixty-two thousand pounds. Holding something so valuable and rare had a strange, kind of hypnotic, effect on me. As the gemstones twinkled in the light, I marvelled at its uniqueness and beauty. 'That's incredible Maurice, it's absolutely out of this world.'

'My darling, I too nearly fainted when he told me. But this guy is a multi-millionaire, remember. One million dollars is a drop in the ocean for *un homme* with that kind of bank account.'

'So what will you do with it?' I asked, imagining ways that I could burn through a million dollars: property around the globe, vintage Chanel handbags, exotic holidays for all the family, a bathroom cabinet full of Crème de la Mer, a classic cream Porsche...

'Why, I would never sell it,' he stated.

I batted my eyelids and muttered, 'Of course not.'

'But I know what I'll do with it,' he continued. 'The timing of all this, it is quite *incroyable*. I can't think of a better, more eye-catching centrepiece for Liv's Egyptian Queen outfit for the Met – can you? The ruby has long been associated with love, beauty and balance – in fact the Ancient Egyptians honoured the gemstone for these qualities. It is perfect for Liv, in so many ways. And I would bet that she is a very similar size to Marianne when she was in her twenties. It would be an honour to see it take centre stage once more and there is no bigger event – I'm sure Marianne would be deeply moved and it will entertain Clark, for sure.'

'I think that's a brilliant idea!' I said. 'It's just so sad that Clark was never able to give it back to Marianne, under happier circumstances, himself.' I exhaled deeply, and looked back at the lovelorn image of Marianne in the photo.

'I know, it is tragic,' he murmured, consumed by it all once more.

'And what will you do with the letters?'

'He asked me to burn them,' Maurice replied, glancing at the overflowing drawer. 'And I intend to fulfil his wish, they have no use now. This bra is the only legacy of a love story that was never consummated.'

We both took a few moments to ponder this beautiful, bittersweet tale.

'Anyway, come this way,' he said, pulling himself together and placing the bra back in the pouch. 'We have work to do.'

It was dark outside and well into the evening by the time I looked at my phone and realised how late it had got. For hours, Maurice and I worked side by side in his makeshift studio in Marianne's room in the apartment.

'I'm finally ready to put this room to use,' he had said, when he led me there. It already looked different from the shrine to Marianne I had found when I was last here. 'You have had such a profound effect on me, Amber. I'm finally ready to move on.'

And without even knowing it, Maurice was helping me to move on, too. The whole time I was with him, I didn't once think about posting on social media. It would seem so crass to trivialise this wonderful story – the seventy-year journey of a one-of-a-kind red-ruby bra – by condensing it into 140 characters for a tweet or a filtered photo. Plus, any sneaky behind-the-scenes Instagram photos of our project would be a terrible faux pas. No, our Egyptian Queen creation for Liv was back on – I would convince Dana to let me do this job and prove to her that I was better than a disastrous baby shoot. And the rubies would remain strictly between Liv, Mickey, Maurice and me, plus these four walls and a flock of songbirds, until Liv appeared on the Metropolitan Museum of Art's red carpet in just one week's time, I swore it.

CHAPTER NINETEEN

I treated myself to a cab home that evening, wondering whether anyone was actually going to be in our apartment when I got there. I'd had five missed calls from Tina and three texts from Vicky – the final one telling me she was off out. She was clearly annoyed because there was no kiss at the end. But I didn't care. *For once, it isn't all about Vicky.* There was also a text from Rob saying he was working late again, and presumably Tina wondered if I wanted to pop by for a drink. I considered ringing her back, but decided a long soak in a hot bath was probably a more sensible option for me this evening, and it was nearly ten o'clock. But that idea went swiftly went out of the window – because when I pulled up outside our apartment building it was lit up like a film set. A big red fire engine was parked right outside, its ladder extended as it reached into – *Oh, Jesus, our bedroom window!*

Before I had even paid my taxi fare, I saw Rob striding towards me. 'Your bloody best friend, Amber!' he was yelling.

My heart began to thud. *What the hell has Vicky done now?*

'That's it – she is never setting foot in this building again,' he fumed.

'What's happened? Is everyone okay? I thought she was going out?' I uttered, my eyes no doubt big and round, my mouth hanging open, aghast, as I took in the scene.

All the tenants in our building were congregated in the street. There were at least ten people – including Max and Tina, who were huddled together, chatting to another couple on the doorsteps; they were nursing mugs, which, knowing them, probably contained red wine.

'Everyone's fine, our stuff is fine. But it might very well not have been if Tina and Max hadn't been home. We could have lost everything,' Rob said. 'Luckily, Tina noticed a strange smell and called the fire brigade, at the same time as calling me. She couldn't get hold of you.' He said the last sentence with exasperation.

'Sorry, I was in the middle of everything with Maurice,' I mumbled.

'Yeah, and I was in the middle of an important shoot,' he hit back.

A couple of fireman strode past me – I recognised one of them as one of the guys who'd helped us when we got locked out, the day after we moved in. He gave me a look that screamed, 'You again!', but not in a good way. It was nothing short of a miracle that we had chosen to move into an apartment opposite a fire station.

'How did she do this?' I muttered, grinding my teeth together.

'She left your hair straighteners turned on, on our bed,' Rob said. 'One of the guys said he's seen a whole building go up in minutes thanks to faulty straighteners. We're bloody lucky it seems to have only ruined our bed covers.'

Vicky, you idiot.

I looked up at our wide-open bedroom window; a curtain was blowing through and the light was on inside. A hose pipe had been fed into the apartment and a fireman's helmet could be see bobbing around inside. I assumed he was pouring water over the ashes on our bed. There wasn't any sign of smoke billowing out, so it looked like we were lucky. *I never really liked that bedspread anyway.* But by association, because they were *my* hair straighteners and she was *my* friend, in Rob's eyes, this was my fault as much as Vicky's. Everyone in the block seemed to be looking at me as if it was my fault too. At this moment, I felt embarrassed by my ineptitude for picking friends. *How could she do this to me; to us?*

I dialled Vicky's number, but of course it went straight to voicemail. She was probably downing her umpteenth cocktail on her forty grand date night with Noah West. The thought of her giggling with him, without a care in the world, made my blood boil. I texted her:

Call me ASAP

No kiss. No friendly emoji.

God knows, there wasn't a hashtag to cover this situation.

Rob had joined Max and Tina on the steps; he didn't seem to want to speak to me. For a moment I just stood there, staring up at our window and then back at Rob. I didn't know what to do with myself.

Minutes later a fireman appeared at the main doorway and told everyone they could return to their apartments. Head bowed, I followed Rob inside. I was sure everyone was itching to see the damage to our bedroom, but we went into our apartment alone. Tina hung back to speak to me as we went in. 'One of the benefits of the early stages of pregnancy,' she whispered, winking, 'a strong sense of smell.'

I turned to give her a hug. 'Oh, Tina, that's amazing news! I'm so happy for you.'

'Shhh,' she said, patting her belly, 'it's only very early days, but I've got a good feeling.'

'It's not so bad,' Rob said, as he pushed open our bedroom door to survey the damage. We both took in a pile of wet bedding on the floor. Thankfully, the mattress and bed itself were unharmed, just a bit damp on one side.

'Thank goodness,' I said, breathing out deeply. 'Honestly, I'm going to kill Vicky for this. She's pushed us too far this time.'

'Let's see if I get to her first,' Rob said, sitting on the edge of the dry part of the bed. 'But, let's face it, things haven't exactly been amazing between us recently anyway.'

He looked at his shoes as I stared at the side of his head, searching it for clues. A nasty feeling began to creep up on me again. *He's not in love with me any more. He's going to end it. This is it.* Daring to think these horrible thoughts made me feel bereft. I was aching to feel his lips on mine, because I already knew how good that kiss would be. But instead of turning towards me, he stood up and went to leave the room.

'It's nearly eleven, there's no point in me going back now, they'll have wrapped,' he said, without looking at me. His tone was flat and tired. 'I'll sleep on the sofa tonight, seeing as the mattress is only half habitable. You take the bed.'

That sofa's seen more action than our bed this last fort-night.

'But I want you to stay with me,' I said abruptly, thinking how being forced to snuggle up on one side would have been sexy and fun, once upon a time.

'Well, maybe you can't always have what you want,' he snapped.

I tried and failed not to look completely desperate.

'Please,' I said, shutting my eyes, tears building up behind my eyelids. He went quiet. 'Otherwise, what are we doing out here together? What's the point of it?'

'That's exactly what I'm wondering,' he said, before getting up and leaving the room.

It was some time in the middle of the night and I couldn't sleep. I was chilly, with only one sheet and a blanket wrapped around me on half of our bed. I decided to check on Rob, in case he was lying awake in the darkness feeling cold too. I reached for my big house cardigan from the chair and slipped my feet into the slippers Lucy had sent over to keep me warm. Slowly, I teased open the bedroom door. It was much darker in the open plan room, and I had to open the door a little wider to let some of the light from the bedroom help my eyes focus and make out the shape on the sofa. As I crept forwards and my pupils adjusted, I realised that the lumpy shape on the sofa was just cushions. No Rob. No Vicky, for that matter, though I hadn't imagined she would come home last night. *Where the hell is everyone?*

I switched on the free-standing lamp, the distressed

copper one we had bought together from the Brooklyn flea market only three weeks ago, so full of excitement about our own little love nest and the adventure ahead; back when I discovered new things about Rob every day; back when we couldn't get enough of each other; back when we had sex. Right now I'd do anything to get those days back. I even missed his slightly annoying habits like going to the loo with the door open and leaving his pants drying on the radiator in the front room. It had been so long since I'd had a proper boyfriend. *How could I have let this one go? It's the feather – the bloody feather tattoo, it's told him to fly away from our nest.*

I sat down on the empty sofa and wondered what to do. Vicky, I was fairly sure, would be holed up with Noah – whatever his sexuality – trying to sleep off a hangover, in some hip Manhattan hotel. But Rob? Who would he turn to when he didn't want to sleep under the same roof as his girlfriend?

He must be really mad.

Still clinging onto the hope that maybe he was having a sleepless night too, wherever he was, I retrieved my phone from the bedroom and texted him:

Miss you. Are you coming back? Ax

At seven o'clock, I was woken by a call from Vicky, but I let it ring out. I was too angry and I wanted to gather my thoughts before we spoke. Plus, I was desperate to hear from Rob first. My heart physically ached when I saw there had been no response to my text. After flitting around Instagram for a full hour and obsessing over the accounts belonging to the Angel Wear models, feeling like the saddest frump in the world, I pulled on my cardigan again and decided to bite the bullet and call Vicky. Before she had a chance to speak, it all came spilling out.

'"Don't mess it up with Rob," you told me. "He's a keeper," you said. Well, I didn't need to mess it up, did I, because you're doing a bloody good job for me.' I needed to be standing up to have this conversation, so I strode from the bedroom into the living room, slamming the door behind me for added effect. I'd still not heard a thing from Rob and I blamed Vicky. *How dare she just turn up and cause this strain between us.* 'Just because your relationship is on the rocks doesn't mean you can come here and ruin things for me and Rob,' I yelled. 'We were getting on brilliantly, until you arrived and messed everything up.'

'Amber, Amber, calm down will you,' she was saying. 'I don't know what you're on about. Everything seemed great again?'

'I thought so too – until you nearly set our apartment on fire.'

'On fire?' She sounded genuinely bemused.

'Didn't Rob leave you a message? You left my bloody straighteners on, on our bed last night and it caught alight. The fire brigade were here.'

'Oh, shit, honey, are you being serious?'

'Er, do I sound like I'm joking?'

'Is everything okay? I mean, they put it out and nothing was harmed, right?'

'Only our bedding. But that's not the point. Rob went nuts and understandably so.'

Silence on the other end, while she took it in. I could hear chinking china in the background; she was having breakfast somewhere.

'But thank God you weren't in.'

'Vicky, if I'd been in, it probably wouldn't have caught fire, because I'd have turned them off.'

'Okay, fair point. Where's Rob now?'

'Good question. I don't know. He wouldn't sleep in the same room as me last night and now he's gone AWOL. He's mad, Vicky, thanks to you. I really think he's had enough of both of us and I'm bloody furious about it.'

'You're so angry; try to calm down.'

'Calm down? Are you having a fucking laugh?'

'Anger isn't good for you.'

'Pah!'

'What's happened to you, Amber? You're not the girl I left in London.'

'The girl you left behind? No, Vicky, I'm not. I'm the girl you tracked down in New York, remember? The girl who was happily loved up and living in a cosy apartment on an adventure with her boyfriend. And now this girl seems to have lost her boyfriend and, as a result, is really pissed off. I'll leave your stuff in the hallway.'

I slammed the phone down. *That's it. If I have to choose between her or Rob, I choose Rob.*

It took me a good ten minutes and a strong cup of tea to calm down after that. When I had remembered that it was

Saturday and I didn't actually have to be anywhere urgently, I decided to run myself a very full steaming-hot bath. I poured in a hefty glug of Rob's muscle soak and allowed myself to sink down into the water. It felt like heaven. The stream rose all around me and beads of sweat soon began dropping down my face. I lay back further, until my hair and half of my face was submerged too. Just the tip of my nose remained above water. I closed my eyes and let the water tickle my cheeks. For a moment, I lay very still, holding my breath and thinking dark thoughts: *I could just disappear under, get rid of myself. Maybe it would make life easier for Rob if I did.*

Then I felt a sudden rush of heat to my cheeks and sat bolt upright. My phone, which I'd carefully positioned on top of a towel on the lid of the toilet next to me was lit up.

Text from Rob:

Hi, I'm at Amy's. Back soon. Rx

He's at Amy's. Great, he's probably sat there with her discussing how to dump me. And then he'll probably start going out with her flatmate, Kate, after having a night of rebound passion with an Angel Wear Icon.

Suddenly, the bath didn't feel so warm and comforting any more. I got out and put on my dressing gown and slippers before rough-drying my hair and padding back out to the kitchenette to make coffee. Caffeine was the only thing to make any sense this morning. My eyes wandered to the fridge door and four photo booth images of Rob and I, held up there by a magnet. I had brought them with us from London and put them there to make the place feel more homely the day we moved in. We were laughing wildly at the wedding of an old uni friend of his last summer, soon after we got together. His arm was wrapped around my neck pulling me close in one, my fascinator sitting at a wonky angle as I jokingly pushed him away in another, and finally there were two kiss shots, the last a full snog, with Rob's hand dramatically reaching out to cover the lens, as though he was a hounded celebrity lashing out at a paparazzo. I had wondered at the time whether we might be the next couple in his circle to take the plunge. It had only been a few weeks, but I already knew without a doubt that I'd say 'yes', if he asked. *Still would*. More than a few times I've wished it under my breath, at opportune moments like blowing out candles or putting an eyelash on the back of my hand. But we were yet to have the marriage chat, and today the photos looked like somebody else's life. It felt as though something amazing was rushing past me at breakneck speed, but my arms were clamped to my sides and I couldn't make it stop. It felt as though he was passing me by.

You should have seen this coming Amber… you idiot… he was never going to marry you. And then I began the heart-wrenching process of sitting down and methodically scrolling through all of the hundreds of photos of the two of us on my iPhone, going right back to when we first got together after he tracked me down at Selfridges. There were hundreds of them: messing about in his old flat with Pinky; lazy Sundays eating our way around farmers' markets in various parts of London; the mini-break to Venice; the time he won over my entire family at Mum's sixtieth party; the time we went glamping in Cornwall and it rained non-stop;

a selfie that night at the pub, when we nicked the bugle horn, just before he told me he loved me for the first time. Of course it was easy to look back with rose-tinted glasses, but we really seemed the perfect couple. I wondered whether a host of iPhone photos, not even backed-up to the cloud, would be the sum of our relationship. *How could it have gone so wrong?*

I hadn't even managed to get dressed when the key turned in the lock and Rob walked back through the door. I cursed myself for looking like a slob. *Should have at least made a bit of an effort, like brushed my hair.*

'Hey,' he said, head bowed, giving nothing away. 'Did you sleep okay?'

'Not really. It was pretty cold,' I replied, searching his face for a clue about what he might say next. 'Did you?'

'Same,' he said, peeling off his coat and hanging it on the overly full coat hooks by the door. 'I think Amy's sofa is even more uncomfortable than ours. Have you spoken to Vicky?'

'Yes, I gave her a piece of my mind. Said we'd leave her stuff in the corridor.'

He didn't respond. 'I'm as angry with her as you are, Rob,' I continued. 'She had no right to come here and be such a nightmare.'

'I've calmed down a bit now, but I'm glad she's going,' he replied, heading towards the kitchen area. 'At least nothing was damaged. I never really liked that bedspread anyway.'

'Neither did I.' We exchanged a small, uncertain smile.

'Anyway, Dan's decided not to come over; he's going to try

to make it work with Florence,' Rob continued. 'Personally, I think he's insane; but what can I say? It's his life.'

'What happened to the guy she was having the affair with?'

'Obviously, it didn't work out. She came crawling back a couple of days ago, saying it was all a huge mistake – blaming "last-minute wedding nerves". It's such a cliché. But he loves her and, I'm afraid, for some reason my mother loves her too, even she is encouraging Dan to work through it. They might get some counselling.'

'Jeez, they're not even married and already having to work at things. It doesn't sound promising.'

'No,' he muttered.

This time neither of us smiled. We both paused, processing what this meant and if it was relevant to us, too; were we going to have to work at things? I'd walked right into that one. *Speaking before I've had a chance to think. Aargh.* Here we were in a state of unhappiness, looking at each other with new eyes, wondering whether a bunch of photos and fading memories were worth saving.

'Tea?' he said at last and turned to flick the kettle on. I caught myself scowling at the kettle – *our* kettle – the one we jointly decided to buy in that tasteless shade of green, the bright lime kettle that had seemed so quirky, cool and, well, fun, when we bought it from Crate&Barrel not more than three weeks ago. The idea of a kettle being 'fun' seemed ridiculous right now. *I'll let him have it if it comes to dividing our jointly owned belongings.* Everything around me seemed kind of different.

Before the whole conversation died a death right there, we were saved by a knock at the door. It was Tina.

'Hey!' she said, all bright and breezy – the polar opposite to the atmosphere in our apartment. She took in our glum expressions. 'Everything all right?'

'Yep,' we both said in unison, suggesting that everything really wasn't all right.

'Tea? Or something stronger?' Rob said jovially.

'I wish,' she smiled coyly. 'I'm, er, not drinking at the moment.'

'Not like you, Tina.' He smirked.

She smiled. 'I'm taking care of myself.'

'Fair enough.' He failed to pick up the hint. *Typical man*.

She turned and winked at me, and I got the impression I wasn't to mention the 'pregnancy' aloud, even in front of Rob.

'I was wondering if I could borrow you for a sec, Amber,' she said. 'I want to show you something at mine.'

I shrugged my shoulders. 'Sure. Do you need me dressed, or shall I scare Max with my slobby Saturday get-up?'

She smiled again, before opening the door. 'Come slobby, Max's out anyway. I'll only steal her for five minutes, Rob. Keep the kettle on.'

I was relieved to escape for a moment.

Tina and Max's apartment, although almost the exact mirror image of ours, somehow looked twice as big. Perhaps it was because their kitchen units were a much better design than ours, giving an illusion of more space, or maybe they'd had a spring clean and didn't have an uninvited lodger cluttering up their lounge with her bits and pieces.

Tina seemed to register what I was thinking. 'Nesting kicking in already. I was up at the crack of dawn this morning cleaning. Can't get enough of the smell of Pledge. Weird, I know.'

'Want to come and get another fix at ours? You're welcome any time. Where's Max?'

'He's gone for a run. This baby thing, it's had a crazy effect on him already – he's gone fitness mad, bless him.'

I chuckled. 'Go, Max.' Seeing as I'd rarely seen him without a cigarette or some kind of alcoholic drink in his hand, Max didn't strike me as the type of guy who was predisposed to a morning run.

'I'm so happy for you,' I said, reaching out to give her a hug.

'All natural, too,' she replied, letting me envelop her in a big bear hug. 'We were ready to start in vitro next month, but I guess someone was looking down on us.

'Anyway, I wanted to get your opinion on this dress, being a stylist and all. I'm already busting out of some of my old faithfuls. It's my boobs more than anything.' She jiggled her bosom for effect. She did have an ample cleavage. 'I'm going to look like a house before this pregnancy is out, I know it, but I don't give a monkey's. Bring on the Ben & Jerry's.'

'Too right. If ever you need a Ben & Jerry's cohort, you know who to call. Where are you off to anyway?'

'A wrap party for Max's latest TV show. A few actor types

and the production team. It won't be nearly so much fun pretending to drink. What are you guys up to?'

'Nothing much.' *I don't even know if we'll still be together by this evening.*

'Why don't you come too? I'm sure Max would love that, he was just saying he'd like to hang out with Rob more – they can talk cameras and we can talk babies. What do you say?'

'I'll ask him.' It possibly wasn't the wisest decision to become broody when on the brink of breaking up with your boyfriend, but perhaps a night out, at least under the same roof, would do us good. Gladly, I helped Tina style her outfit, before being consumed by a feeling of impending doom as I went back into my own home.

Rob was hunched over the cooker making breakfast. On the outside, it looked like a normal Saturday scene of domestic bliss, but the nervous energy around us told a different story.

'Do you fancy going out later?' I offered, by means of an olive branch. 'Tina and Max are wondering if we want to join them at a party.'

'Yeah, maybe,' he said, monosyllabic. 'Tea or coffee?'

'Tea, please.' *He knows I can't drink coffee before eleven in the morning.* 'I'll get Vicky's bits together.'

'Already done it,' he replied, nodding in the direction of one corner of the room, where Vicky's suitcase lay flat on the floor; on top he had piled her laptop, toiletries bag, and three pairs of shoes and a coat.

'Okay, well, I'll put it all in her case,' I said helpfully, and began stuffing it all in.

When I was finished I hauled it out into the corridor. It felt cruel to be literally turfing my best friend out of my home, but I had no option. I was doing it to save my relationship.

The rest of the day felt strained. Rob clearly wasn't in the mood to discuss 'us'; I gathered this by the fact that he was wearing his headphones to watch *Game of Thrones* on his laptop. So I pottered around, vaguely home-making; fluffing up cushions and arranging mugs in cupboards, until Mickey called me to catch up on Liv's outfit for the Met.

'She's got a few ideas of her own,' he said, before I had a chance to tell him I wasn't sure I could do the job unless Dana agreed. Thankfully, I had decided to keep the ruby bra a secret, to be revealed at her fitting. 'You know Liv – she has very definite ideas about her style.'

'Yes, I'm aware,' I said, feeling a little sad. I was convinced that whatever Liv had in mind, it couldn't possibly beat what Maurice had in store; it ticked all her fashion boxes, including the main prerequisite – that she was only partially clothed. Before I could back out, I found myself agreeing to do a fitting on Monday at Maurice's home-cum-studio. *I'll worry about Dana after that.*

I made an extra effort with my appearance that evening, getting ready long before Rob got around to changing his T-shirt, and spending almost an hour doing my hair and make-up. I layered my eye make-up into a near-perfect smoky, come-hither flutter, and managed to successfully create some beachy curls in my shoulder-length hair. I hadn't bothered to wear my hair down much these last weeks because I always seemed to be rushing to get out of the door, so it instantly made me look and feel a bit different. I slid into a dainty little red and black Marc by Marc Jacobs minidress, a recent 'I'll pay it off once the paycheques come in' credit-card purchase, that I was now unsure I could justify.

'Nice dress,' Rob said, when I presented myself to him in a slightly pissed off, you-could-have-noticed-the-effort-I-made-earlier fashion, just as I was putting my coat on.

We got a cab across the Hudson with Max and Tina. No matter how many times I had taken this route, I always found it thrilling to travel over the Brooklyn Bridge and see the spectacular skyline view of Manhattan before me.

We were dropped off outside a trendy little cocktail bar called Mother's Ruin in Nolita, and the party was in full swing when we entered. Max was instantly whisked off to the back of the bar by a colleague and the three of us perched beside a table of pre-made cocktails. Rob and I immediately dug in.

The atmosphere suddenly became excitable as a couple of actors from the show walked into the bar. Necks craned to see what they were wearing and who they were with. I recognised one guy from a TV detective series.

Tina whispered in my ear: 'Oliver Chester. Such a player, Max says he had a different woman in each hotel during the shoot.'

'Hmm, not surprising,' I replied. 'Totally would.'

She sniggered. 'She must be the latest,' Tina continued, as the top of a mop of curly blonde hair came into view just behind Oliver, in the midst of his entourage. If you looked closely, you could see they were lightly touching fingers as he led her through the parting crowds. I noticed a black Philip Lim bag come into view. *How funny, that's the same bag that— oh, shit, it's Poppy.*

'No way, Amber!' she trilled, before I had time to consider the fact that I really didn't want Rob to know I knew Poppy was in New York. 'We must stop bumping into each other like this!'

'Yeah, I mean, how come you're over here?' I stuttered, trying to fudge it so Rob might not click. *Surely she'll get it, she's the one who didn't want Rob to know she wasn't Pinky-sitting any more.*

'What are you on about? I told you the other night. I got the part! Hey, how gorge does the bag look?' She stroked her soft leather three point one tote; the bag that could easily have cost me my visa and my career. And then she clocked Rob, standing next to me, looking confused. 'Oh, Rob!' she exclaimed, like she'd seen a ghost.

'Poppy,' he said, unamused. 'I thought you were in London?'

'Er, obviously not,' she replied, eyes doing anything but look directly into his, because she knew what was coming next.

'So where's Pinky?' he continued, looking properly moody.

'Um…' she glanced towards me for help.

I stayed silent.

'I trusted you with one of my most precious possessions, Poppy.'

'You shouldn't talk about a wild animal as a possession,' she quipped.

'Pinky's hardly wild,' I jumped in, 'and Rob has a right to know.'

'Well, why didn't you tell him then, Amber?' she said, before turning to face Rob. 'Look, he's with a friend of mine in London, he's fine. I'm going back next week anyway. You can FaceTime him then if you like.'

'Are you getting hassled here?' Oliver had turned to see why Poppy had stopped. He puffed up his chest and fronted up to Rob like he was willing to give him a kick where it hurt.

'No, babe, it's cool, just some old mates from London. Shall we get a drink?' Poppy purred. She laced her arm into his and he led them off to be seated in a nearby reserved booth.

'"We must stop bumping into each other?"' Rob repeated to the space they left as they disappeared into the crowd. I knew full well that he was aiming the comment at me – and he was within his rights to be cross.

'I'm sorry,' I said, and looked at the floor. There wasn't much I could say to get out of this one. 'I hadn't had a chance to tell you.'

'Didn't you think I'd want to know that Pinky had been re-homed?' I looked up but didn't say anything. I didn't know what I could possibly say. 'I'm over this party,' he continued, turning on his heel. 'I'll see you at home later.' And he went to leave.

Tina grabbed my arm. 'What's got his goat this evening?'

'Me,' I replied.

'Well – don't just watch him leave,' she said, giving me a gentle shove. 'Go after him!' She didn't need to say it again. I hung back as I watched Rob collect his coat from the cloakroom and then I followed him out of the bar. A cacophony of tooting horns greeted us in the street – the perennial soundtrack of Manhattan – a noise that I found almost comforting now; it helped take the edge off the fact that I felt as though I barely knew the person I was striding behind. Rob was walking fast, heading for the subway at Prince Street. Despite the people all around us, I'd recognise his walk anywhere, slightly right leaning, with a lightness of step. I could almost smell him too – warm washing powder and a light aftershave, the scent that had drawn me to him from one of the first moments we met. Right now, my love for him felt all-consuming. I didn't take my eyes off the back of his head as we pounded up Spring Street. A couple of times I opened my mouth to shout out his name, but each time something stopped me. *I can't let us break up. I can't.*

When Rob approached the top of the subway steps, I could almost have reached out to touch him, but again I stopped myself. I was beginning to feel like his stalker now and worried that it would seem strange for him to know I had trailed him all the way from the bar without calling out. He went to glance behind only once, but I ducked out of sight. He jogged down the steps into the subway and instinctively I followed him, passing my ticket through the gates and expecting him to walk down towards the N line, heading downtown, on our route back to Bedford Street. But instead he took the R line heading uptown.

My heart began to pound in my chest as I questioned why

he wasn't taking the quickest route back to Brooklyn. What was it he had said in the bar? 'I'll see you at home later.' By that I assumed he meant he was on his way there. *Where would he be going if not home?* My mind was in overdrive. '*You can keep an eye on me,' he had said, when he was encouraging me to go for the Angel Wear job. Well, maybe he didn't say it in jest, maybe he is seeing an Icon after all and she's got some posh Upper East Side apartment.* Adrenalin was rushing through me now, as I made a decision to keep following him. I felt as though I was in a film as I ducked and dived out of sight any time I thought he might turn around. Skilfully, I managed to board the same train, in an adjoining carriage. Luckily, it was busy on the subway on a Saturday night, so there were enough bodies to keep me hidden, but still able to keep sight of the back of Rob's jacket and the top of his sandy hair.

He got off the train at Fifty-ninth Street. I followed suit and, despite one moment when I thought I'd lost him as I hung back to let him leave the station barriers ahead of me, I was just a few people behind as he came up to street level.

I hadn't yet had the time to explore this far uptown and it instantly felt very different to our cosy neighbourhood in Williamsburg. The buildings were bigger and grander, there were huge high-street chain stores on either side of the road, and impressive looking hotels. Rob continued to head northwards until he reached the entrance to Central Park at Fifty-ninth and Fifth Avenue. Here he slowed his pace. It was nearly ten at night, and dark, but the path ahead was lit up and joggers, couples, and tourists were still going about their business, making the pathways barely less busy than during the day.

I let him walk for a minute or so down the path. And then it happened – he did turn around and, before I had a chance to do anything but stop dead in my tracks, he had clapped eyes on me, immediately in his wake. He stared at me, clearly puzzled, but saying nothing; he didn't need to, he was trying to fathom what it meant that I was here, standing right in front of him, just inside the entrance to Central Park.

'Amber, what are you doing here?' he said at last.

I was almost breathless, a mixture of walking so fast to keep up with him and nerves. My heart was beating hard and despite the cold I felt hot and clammy.

'I followed you,' I said, equally unsure about what on earth I was doing here. It didn't seem such a good idea any more. It sounded creepy. 'I was going to catch you up to go home… and then I saw you weren't going home.'

'And you wondered where I was going?'

'Well, yes, I did wonder,' I said, almost defiantly, waiting to catch him out. When he said nothing my eyes grew bigger and my hands more sweaty. 'Well?'

'Well, I needed a bit of space,' he replied after what seemed like a never-ending pause. 'I didn't want to go back to an empty flat, so I decided to come to Central Park for a walk, to clear my head.'

'On your own?'

'On my own, Amber. Why, who would I be walking with?'

'I don't know,' I said, now feeling a little silly for being jealous. 'But why turn around?'

We both stopped again, momentarily lost in our own thoughts, but this time we didn't take our eyes off each other. He looked as though he was searching for a way to phrase something. After a few seconds his expression seemed to soften.

'If you must know, I had just changed my mind about a cold walk through the park, on my own, among all these loved-up couples.' Just to illustrate the point, at that moment a romantic couple holding hands and giggling walked past. 'So I was actually about to head back home, hoping you might be there too.' He paused. 'But, as you're here now, would you like to walk with me?'

I could tell from his face that he was telling the truth.

'I'd love that,' I said quietly. He put his left hand in his pocket and held out his arm for me to interlock mine with his. Quietly, I sighed with relief. An arm lock had to be a good sign.

We started walking down the pathway, saying nothing at first as we took in our surroundings. Pretty maple trees partially covered the path and the street lamps on either side gave off a warm, orangey glow.

'I'm sorry I didn't tell you I saw Poppy,' I said, feeling the need to start things off and address what had happened earlier.

'Why didn't you?' he asked. 'It's bad enough that she didn't let me know about Pinky, but you knowing too and saying nothing... When did you see her?'

'That night I went out with Vicky, when we ended up in Le Bain with Amy and Kate. Poppy turned up and she asked me to do something. I'm not proud of it, hence it was easier to blank it all out and not tell you, rather than have you be ashamed of me too.'

'Ashamed of you? What on earth did you do?'

'She asked me to pick up a fake designer handbag for her.'

'She what?' The corners of Rob's mouth had turned up. Something I said obviously tickled him.

'There's this thing called a "bag drop", and Poppy somehow talked me into meeting some dodgy woman in a blacked-out car, and handing over some cash for a fake designer bag. In a nutshell,' I explained.

'You're being serious?' he said, really trying not to laugh.

'Afraid so. I guess it does sound pretty stupid now.'

'You know, you never have to keep secrets from me,' he said, 'I'll never judge you. I mean, I already know you're nuts.' His eyes lit up.

'I don't have to take that, you know,' I said, pretending to look away, offended.

'It's lucky I like nutters then,' he qualified himself, squeezing my arm in his.

'But it's not just about Poppy – what's happened to us, Rob?' I asked, warily.

'I know I've not exactly been fun to live with,' he said. 'Work's been stressful – much worse than I imagined, and then the Dan thing, and Vicky turning up – I guess I ended up taking it out on you. And I'm sorry for that. None of it was your fault really.'

'I should have discussed Vicky moving in with you,' I said. 'But I felt I had no option. She's a very old friend and she just turned up out of the blue. I'm still furious she nearly set our place on fire, though.'

'She didn't do it on purpose, I suppose,' he conceded.

We both eyed another amorous couple heading straight for us, kissing as they walked.

'I'm glad you're not here meeting up with some Angel Wear giraffe,' I said.

'You what?' He stopped again and took both my hands. 'You didn't seriously think I was meeting up with another woman?'

'Maybe slightly,' I conceded, though it seemed absurd. 'You made a comment about me keeping an eye on you, if I went for the job.'

He laughed. 'It was meant to be a joke. I'm sorry if it wasn't funny. I genuinely think the job would be great for us – we work well together. Remember?'

And he turned my face towards his with his hand. *His lovely hands*.

'I love you, you know,' he said. 'There's only ever been you on my mind.' And he kissed me. He kissed me like he used to – soft and gentle at first, building up in urgency, until he was lost in my lips, my mouth, and I was equally lost in him. And then he was lightly kissing my neck and gently holding both my hands. Every now and again he stopped and stared deeply into my eyes and smiled. He still had the ability to make my knees go wobbly. And he was back. *My Rob is back*.

Pretty soon after that we caught a taxi back downtown and were kissing for most of the way, my leg over his, his arms around me. We were so consumed with lust that it was all he could do to thrust a fistful of cash into the driver's hand as we got out. On the pavement we instinctively pulled apart for a moment and looked up at our bedroom window, half expecting the fire brigade to be at it again. As we each caught the other doing the same, we cracked up.

'Window's still intact tonight then,' he said. 'I think that fireman was starting to think you had a crush on him.'

I laughed. 'Can we forget all that and start again please?'

He gently brushed my cheek with his thumb. 'Oh, yes...' He beamed.

Neither of us commented when we noticed Vicky's suitcase had been removed from the landing outside our front door. Instead he led me inside and straight to our bed; tonight it didn't matter that there were sheets on only one side.

CHAPTER TWENTY

When Liv and Mickey arrived at Maurice's apartment at eleven o'clock the following morning, we couldn't have been better prepared. Maurice had enlisted the help of an Italian seamstress called Bella – 'the very best couturier' from his atelier back in the day – and they had been working hard all weekend to create Liv's Met Gala outfit. There were images of Elizabeth Taylor as Cleopatra and other references from Ancient Egyptian mythology pinned to the walls. A mannequin stood tall in the middle of the room, covered with a white sheet, ready for the big reveal.

The five of us stood in a line, eyes trained on the sheet. When the moment came, Maurice theatrically lifted it up and I gasped. The red rubies caught the light in the most beautiful way, sending beams of red sunlight around the room like a disco ball; it was such a magnetic piece. Maurice had teamed the bra with a long, flowing white skirt made of fine silk. There were thick gold cuff bracelets on each arm of the dummy, and a dramatic falcon gold headpiece on top of a black wig.

'A replica of the one worn by Elizabeth Taylor,' Maurice explained, looking pleased as punch with his design. 'And, *la touche finale*,' he continued, pausing for dramatic effect, 'I have arranged for Liv to arrive with a real live leopard on a lead, to walk her up the red carpet.' He noticed a look of horror on our faces. 'Tame, of course,' he qualified, turning to retrieve a large hardbacked book from a nearby table, and leafing through the pages until he came to a colour print of a painting. 'It's called "Egyptian Queen of the Leopards",' he announced. 'Liv, *mon chérie*, you are to be our beautiful, smouldering Egyptian Leopard Queen.' He replaced the book and smiled proudly. 'What could garner more attention at the Met then that?'

My jaw hit the floor. 'Where will you get the leopard from?' I asked.

'I have my sources…' He winked. 'It's about time my little black address book was dusted off.' While I found it hard to contain my excitement, Mickey and Liv stayed expressionless – well, it was rather a lot to take in. Undeterred, Maurice continued. 'Your make-up is key to this ensemble, Mademoiselle Liv – kohl eyeliner and defined cheekbones. If you want to go the whole way, I suggest the black braided wig to really pull off the Elizabeth Taylor look.' He indicated another image of the legendary celluloid icon. 'But you could leave your hair *au naturel* for an original take on it. Your red hair will look *incroyable* with the rubies.'

We all turned to gauge Liv's face for a reaction. *Surely she'll say something?*

'Oh,' she muttered at last.

'*C'est bon?*' Maurice asked, hopefully, the suspense clearly torturing him.

'Oh, no, I mean, *non*, it's not what I was expecting,' she replied awkwardly, looking to Mickey for help.

'You see,' Mickey began, 'Liv's a little unsure that it's attention grabby enough. You know?'

Maurice and I exchanged a look. *What is more attention grabbing than a priceless red ruby bra and a leopard on a lead, for heaven's sakes?*

'We've come up with an idea for Liv that is based on the original ancient civilisation – you know, before all the other ones,' he continued shiftily, obviously hoping no one here was a History graduate. 'Liv is going to be Eve, fresh from the Garden of Eden.' He smiled, looking more slimy than the snake from said garden.

Silence from Maurice, Bella, and me, while we took this in and realised the same thing at the exact same time: That means no clothes.

'*D'accord*,' Maurice said after a while, scratching his head and trying desperately not to look as crestfallen as he must have felt.

'We brought her outfit,' Mickey replied, while Liv looked listlessly out of the window.

And from his inside coat pocket, he presented the tiniest nude G-string with a few fig leaves made from material attached to the front. He pulled the elastic around the knickers wide and let it ping back into shape. *He's so sleazy*. I winced.

'Sexy, hey Amber?' he asked, as if to antagonise me. I looked at Liv. *Surely she isn't happy about this.*

'If you say so,' I replied.

Bella had sucked in her cheeks and was shaking her head. She muttered something in Italian under her breath and I'd bet it was to do with going to hell.

I was trying to summon up enough confidence to tell them where to stick the fig leaves and convince Liv that she would be insane not to take up Maurice's incredible offer, when my phone vibrated in my pocket. It was a text from Rob:

'Hey sexy, can't stop thinking about you xx

I smiled, before quickly replying:

What time will you be home? x

Quickly as possible – 5?

Meet you there. I'll pick up new bedding. xx

Great, we'll be celebrating x

What – the new linen?! x

You'll see xx

Shortly after that, my phone buzzed again, this time a text from a number I didn't recognise:

Amber, you've got the job. Can you come in tomorrow morning to discuss the details? Best regards, Ron Angel.

I read the message ten times in a row. Then I muttered 'Holy crap,' under my breath, before texting Rob:

OMG! xxx

'Everything okay?' Maurice asked, sensing correctly that I was distracted.

I smiled. 'Yes, great, just Rob.'

'*C'est de l'amour.*' He shrugged.

I looked over to the mannequin again. Maurice and Bella had worked so hard to create a truly original costume, stitched to Liv's exact dimensions, that would be bound to attract attention at the Met, even without the leopard. If Mickey and Liv were too stupid to see it, then it was their loss. Armed with this news about my job, I found my confidence and an idea began to develop in my mind.

'So, I guess we're done here,' Mickey said after a few more awkward seconds of nobody saying anything. He had put the G-string back into his pocket and was zipping up his leather jacket, evidently keen to get out of the apartment in case the actual leopard has been summoned to turn up.

'I guess we are,' I said, brightly. 'Never mind. Besides, I'm not sure if Dana has spoken to you yet, but she's not representing me any more – I'm branching out on my own. And as for the Met, Liv should wear what she feels comfortable in.' I grinned a big fake, cheesy grin. Maurice shot me a puzzled look; even Mickey looked a little miffed that I had taken their snub so well.

'But—' Maurice began.

'But-ter wouldn't melt!' I interjected. 'I mean, Liv will look so pure on the red carpet when she becomes Eve. I, for one, can't wait to see it.' And I began walking towards the doorway, ready to usher them out.

'We'll show ourselves,' Mickey said, as keen to leave as I was to see the back of them.

'I guess I'll see you around then?' Liv offered me a faint smile.

'Yep, probably,' I replied, the door half closed. 'Good luck. Au revoir for now!'

When their footsteps had disappeared down the hallway and the main front door had banged shut behind them, I collected myself, ready to begin my next big pitch to Maurice.

*

'Well, you are a woman full of surprises,' Maurice said when I told him about my new job and the Dana situation. 'Seriously, congratulations, *chérie* Amber, that has to be the most prestigious styling job in Manhattan.'

'I can't quite believe it myself.' I blushed. 'I'm sure it's got something to do with the fact my boyfriend is directing the documentary about the show, but I'll happily take your congratulations. And I've had an idea. I'm going in for my first meeting tomorrow and Maurice, I would love to suggest that you work with me on some show-stoppers for the finale of the Angel Wear catwalk event. The ruby bra – it couldn't be a more perfect addition to a lingerie show. Thinking about it, it's far more suitable for this kind of project than the Met Gala – it was clearly wasted on Liv. It's right up Ron Angel's street though – it will blow this mind! What do you say? Are you up for it?'

Maurice thought for a moment.

'Well, Amber, of course I'm flattered that you would think of me in this way, but surely they already have an in-house design team at Angel Wear?'

'The lead designer didn't seem to take much of a shine to me at my interview,' I replied, thinking of Dimitri, and how unfriendly he was when we met. 'Anyway, hold the thought, I'll let you know after my meeting tomorrow. But just don't pack up the rubies yet.'

When I arrived back at our apartment, Rob was already home. I could smell cooking from the hallway and almost as soon as I entered, I noticed a new addition to the kitchen area – a champagne bucket with a bottle poking out of it.

'Come here, you,' he said, walking towards me with his arms open. When he reached me, he wrapped his arms around my waist and lowered his head so his lips were hovering just above mine. 'I'm so proud of you, you're going to be amazing,' he said.

Instead of replying, I lifted my lips to meet his and we kissed. It felt like the first kiss we had shared, on the pavement in London. Although under a year ago, that moment had felt so distant recently, but now the feelings were back with a vengeance, rushing over me, warming me up – like slipping on an old, well-loved winter coat for the first time after the summer.

'So this is how it feels to be in love,' I whispered as we eventually pulled apart. I hadn't meant to actually say the words aloud.

'You what?' he said, as lost in that kiss as me.

'I love you,' I replied.

'I love you more, Amber Green,' he said. And although he couldn't possibly have been right, my heart was filled to the brim.

Dinner was cold when we eventually ate it, on our laps, covered in blankets on the sofa. We hadn't even made it to the bedroom before our limbs were entwined and we were lost in sex as good and lusty as the early days. Soon afterwards I spotted something on my lower neck in the bathroom.

'You've given me a love bite!' I exclaimed, charging back

into the living room. 'I've got my first love bite, on the evening before I start the most important new job I've ever had.' I shook my head, slightly disgusted with myself.

'Polo necks are very this season, aren't they?' he grinned. I frowned.

'Think of it as a good luck talisman,' he said, winking.

It was late in the evening and I was in bed when I checked my phone and noticed a text from Vicky:

Found my stuff. Are you seriously cutting me off? Vx

I sighed and read it to Rob. We had decided that if things were going to work between us, we needed to share everything.

'She's been my closest friend for ten years,' I said, feeling slightly sick about the fall out.

'She needs to start treating you better then,' he muttered sleepily, before rolling over, suggesting the conversation was closed. He was soon snoring loudly next to me; champagne had never agreed with his sinuses. Even a sharp dig in the ribs wasn't enough to stop him.

It was two in the morning the next time I looked at my phone. I'd been lying awake for ages, replaying our sex, thinking about Vicky, and fretting about my new job – there was so much on my mind, it wasn't surprising I couldn't sleep. I'd been staring for ages at the shaft of light on the ceiling from the streetlamp outside. After replacing my phone on the bedside table, I noticed the shadow from my hand move across the ceiling and into the light. I spread out my fingers, watching the shadow fan out, creating a gigantic version of my hand. Then I squeezed my forefinger and thumb together in a pincer movement and held up my next two fingers. The shadow now resembled a rabbit. For a second, I was transported back to my bedroom at home and making shadow puppets on the wall with my sister when we shared a room. We couldn't have been older than twelve and eight. I could almost smell my childhood bed sheets and hear the sound of the ancient bedside lamp wobbling on the little table between us. A pang of home sickness shot through me. It would be coming up to eight in the morning in London now. Little Nora would probably be sitting in her high chair at Lucy's house throwing blueberries at whoever was nearby; and Mum and Dad would be eating toast with marmalade and sharing a pot of tea in their kitchen. Everything so comfortingly normal.

I reached for my phone again and scrolled back through my photos to the ones I had taken at Christmas-time, when we were all at my parents' house. I felt embarrassed for my moody behaviour, how I hadn't really wanted to be there because I was thinking about Rob every thirty seconds, texting him instead of engaging with my parents – wishing away the time because I couldn't wait for it to be Boxing Day when he and I would be reunited. I didn't know why but I was driven to zoom in on a photo of my mum at the Christmas table. I'd primarily taken the photo to show Rob the size of the turkey, but there was Mum, looking at the lens with such warmth in her eyes: a mother's love. I could suddenly see myself in her face, especially the shape of her hazel eyes, and, when I stared into them, through the screen I could almost feel our connectedness. Our DNA, the distillation of who we are as humans, linking both of us to our family – it was so reassuring to see. Perhaps I could only see it because I was so far away. I made a silent promise to call Mum for a long chat in the morning. I'd been terrible about replying to her messages recently. *What a selfish, thoughtless daughter.*

While I stared at the ceiling unable to sleep, my thoughts then turned to Vicky, and how pleased I was to see her familiar face when she first arrived on our doorstep. We had been best friends for so long. I knew her face as well as I knew my mother's; her brown eyes, my blue eyes. She was like family to me. *I can't let all of that go. I'll call her tomorrow and sort things out between us. If she has somewhere else to stay, what can possibly go wrong?*

I could only have had about five hours sleep by the time the room was full of daylight and I was woken by Rob singing in the shower.

'Why are you in such a jovial mood?' I asked, when he had got out and finished singing 'Man in the Mirror' at the top of his voice.

'Eh?' he said, through a mouth full of whirring electric toothbrush, bare chested, bath towel tied around his waist.

'What's going on?' I asked suspiciously.

'It's your first day in your new job, in case you'd forgotten,' he said, holding the brush down, his mouth still full of toothpaste.

'Yes, I am aware. It's probably the reason why I only had a few hours' sleep last night.' I yawned for added effect.

'I thought I'd make you breakfast, to set you up.' He looked his sexiest when he'd just got out of the shower.

'Or we could…' I smiled, attempting the best 'come-hither' expression I could muster.

'Yes, we could,' he returned, coming over to sit on the end of the bed. 'But then I'd be having filthy thoughts about you all day, and it would be impossible to get any work done.'

'Won't you be having those anyway, after last night?' I teased.

'I've just about got those under control,' he retorted, 'I'm *trying* to be professional.'

'Yes, and so was I, before I had a giant hickie on my neck!'

'Sorry about that.' He pretended to look sorry for himself. 'Tea or coffee?'

'You know I—'

'Tea it is then! Jeez, we've not set foot in the same office yet and you're already acting the diva. I'm going to have to keep an eye on you…'

When I had discovered that the one polo-neck jumper I had brought to New York was in the wash, and tried on all other vaguely high-necked tops in my wardrobe, I finally settled on a sheer black blouse from Whistles with a ruffled collar that almost entirely covered the love bite if I remembered not to crane my neck. Not easy when I was going to be spending the next few weeks working with a herd of giraffes. *Note to self: stop calling my new aesthetically blessed colleagues giraffes.*

Ron Angel smiled generously as I entered his room for the second time in a week – this time as a bona fide employee. There was a whole crowd of people waiting to greet me.

Caroline came over straight away and gave me a hug – a very media one that didn't involve much skin contact, but nonetheless was warmer than the reception I received from Dimitri who sort of flinched in the corner of the room as Caroline gushed: 'I'm *sooo* happy we're working together again!'

'I'd like you to meet my Icons.' Ron smiled, placing a large hand on my back and leading me towards the line-up of extraordinarily tall and beautiful women. There were all five Icons in the flesh, and they were all looking at me, smiling with their perfect, wide mouths.

Astrid gave me a wink.

'You know each other?' Ron asked. I got the impression very little escaped his attention when it came to his models.

'We've met once before,' I admitted.

'If you know Astrid, let me introduce Krystal, Jessica, Roxy and Leonie,' he said, moving down the row and touching each around the waist as he passed. Though I might have objected to my boss touching me in that way, the Icons didn't seem to mind. I suppose when you're a professional clothes horse, you get used to your body becoming public property to an extent. Each one greeted me with a dewy, rosy lipped peck on the cheek.

'Hey, let's do a selfie!' Jessica exclaimed, one of two brunettes; she had an exotic look with enviable olive skin. Before I could protest that I needed to apply more make-up, she was pulling me by the arm into the bosom of their ridiculously good-looking gang.

And there it was, my return to Instagram for the first time

in what felt like a lifetime. I looked like a prissy librarian in my high-necked blouse, next to the tanned skin and glossy faced Icons. Rise filter, caption: The sixth Angel Wear Icon? #firstday #newjob #AngelWear #stylist.

After I had spent a couple of minutes exchanging pleasantries with the models and listening to their excited gushing about how we were going to have 'so much fun' creating the show – *the show that I hadn't yet decided what I was going to do with. Crap!* – at the end of the line was head designer Dimitri.

He was dressed head to toe in black, save for a small polka-dotted handkerchief poking out from the top pocket of his long trench coat, which ended just above his black boots. His clothes were almost certainly all designer – McQueen, probably. He had heavy dark eyebrows, crease-free tanned skin, black hair in a crew cut and, like Maurice, he was slightly elevated from his natural five foot six-ish height by a Cuban heel. Perhaps he too was feeling a little insecure, hanging around statuesque models every day. *If there is a day to start wearing heels to work, it's today.* His face showed an expression of faint disappointment as he shook my hand, like a child being forced to make friends at school.

'I hope you like working hard,' he said. He had a slight Italian accent.

'Show the girl a little warmth, Dimitri,' Ron chastised, vocalising what we were all thinking.

'He can't, it's not in his blood. Don't take it personally, he's like this with everyone,' Caroline quipped.

Ron shook his head with an air of amused frustration,

and swiftly moved past Dimitri to introduce me to a tall man who had entered the room late. He had ginger hair in a gelled quiff and his arms were covered in tattoos.

'Sorry, Ron, I was held up stocktaking – we've got some rad new spray – even Krystal's hair won't move a millimetre in gale force winds.'

'This is Sonny, our hair maestro,' Ron said. 'He can turn a hay bale into a soft wave.'

Krystal tutted and fluffed up her long, wavy, raven hair, pushing it over both shoulders. *She sure has a lot of hair.* 'What are you trying to say, Ronnie?' she drawled.

'Nothing, baby girl!' He winked. 'Now, as you know, the show is in a week's time. We've got the collection ready for you in the studio, but we still need to work on the finale. I'll need you to present your vision to me and the board tomorrow at three o'clock. Dimitri and Caroline will show you the ropes. Let's get to work.' He clapped his hands and everyone scurried out of the room – except Dimitri, who hung back.

'Let's grab a coffee en route,' Caroline said, putting an arm around my shoulders. *Thank God. I thought no one was ever going to mention caffeine.* It was nice to have at least one ally in this strange environment, because I was feeling hopelessly out of my depth.

A brief stop at the in-house canteen, which had miso soup, kale juice, and cucumber wraps on the specials menu – presumably the diet of the Icons – and we were heading to the tenth floor and the Angel Wear Studio, a level so exclusive it required its own entry pass to gain access. Caroline paused before we went through the glass doors.

'A word of warning,' she whispered. 'Watch Dimitri.'

'He doesn't strike me as the friendliest,' I admitted.

'For some reason, he didn't want you to get this job – he was rooting for Lola Jones,' she said. 'I thought you needed to know. Watch your back.'

'Watch *your* backs, I'm coming through!' a voice behind us said. 'Gossiping already, ladies – glad to see it!' Caroline and I both jumped and turned round immediately. Thankfully, it was just Sonny. 'Amber, darling, I'm dying to discuss the hair with you. I've got some huge ideas.'

An image on his forearm caught my eye – a large pair of scissors with a caricature of a naked woman with an abundance of red curly hair lying provocatively between the blades. I was dying to have a guided tour of his artwork.

'I'm just going to check out the collection and I'm all yours,' I said.

The main studio was an expansive white space with a colorama roll at one end. Caroline led me over to a room off the main studio filled with rails of clothing – it was an Aladdin's Cave of lingerie.

'Welcome to your new home!' she declared. 'All the prototypes are on this side.' She indicated two rails heaving with all kinds of underwear from rhine-stone encrusted matching bra and knicker sets in a rainbow of colours, to delicate peach negligées and super-sexy black and red lacy items, some of which I couldn't immediately tell how you might go about wearing.

'And the entire back catalogue is over on this wall,' she explained, pointing to more rails of clothing reaching the entire length of the studio. 'I'll leave you to get acquainted. If you need me, I'll be next door in the make-up area. Catch you later.'

I had just begun studying the mood boards on the walls when Rob appeared at the door. 'Lunch?'

'Is it that time already?' I pulled out my phone to check the time: 1.30. The day was flying. I tried not to seem distracted by the fact that my home screen was filled with Instagram notifications, plus four unread text messages.

'I've got so much to do,' I mumbled.

'Honey, you need to eat. Plus, I need to talk to you about something. It's pretty urgent.'

'Give me five minutes,' I said. 'Shall I meet you in the canteen?'

'See you there,' he replied, smiling widely. 'Isn't this cool? Lunch date on the job.'

I flicked through the unread messages. It seemed news of my new job had travelled fast. My heart wrenched as I saw one from my mum. I hadn't called her yesterday as I'd promised myself:

Karen from next door's daughter says you've got a big job. Love you darling. Call me. x

There was also a message from Shauna at Selfridges:

Hey babe, congrats on the Angel Wear gig – love it! Can me and Joseph come to the show?? xx

Another text from Vicky:

So you got the job. Miss you x

And finally, one from Mona:

Good luck. You'll need it.

I immediately deleted her from my phone. I didn't have time for bad karma today.

When I joined Rob in the canteen, he was sitting with Astrid, and she was flanked by the two reserve Icons she'd been with when we partied at Le Bain.

'So, Amber, what have you got for us?' she asked. 'Everyone's buzzing about having you on board. We can't wait to hear your thoughts on the finale.'

'Well,' I began, wondering whether it might be an idea to nip out and get the words 'Winging it' tattooed onto my forehead. 'I've got an idea for something pretty spectacular. I'd like to get it worked up a bit more first though. Ron's asked me to present to him and the board tomorrow.'

'Ooh, mysterious!' she cooed, nudging Rob. 'Is your girl always this secretive?'

'She can be,' he replied diplomatically.

Thankfully, as well as miso and kale, the canteen served real food, too, and after Astrid had left, as I devoured a chicken wrap and a blueberry muffin, I divulged my plans to Rob. He listened patiently and looked enthusiastic in all the right places.

'I knew you'd be perfect for this job, my super stylist girl,' he said, leaning across and touching my cheek when I had finished. 'I've got a bit of news too,' he continued, fiddling with the empty wrapper for his sandwich on the table. 'Ron's asked me and the team to fly back to London to film a bit

about the excitement for the show building there. He's keen
the brand feels transatlantic, doesn't want it to be too New
York-centric, you know?'

I gulped. 'For how long?'

'Only a few days. It will give me an opportunity to catch
up with Dan and Mum too. But—' He looked up, pulling
a mild grimace expression, as if he was afraid to tell me
something.

'What?'

'He wants me on the plane this evening.'

'*Tonight?*'

'Afraid so. We're on the red eye.' He read my face. 'I know.
But what can I do? What Ron wants, Ron gets.' Now that
we shared the same employer, I couldn't deny that I knew
exactly what he meant. 'So I'm going to finish up here then
pop home to pack. If you leave bang on six, we can grab
something to eat together before I go.'

'Oh, baby, I'll miss you!' I squeezed his hand under the
table. What I really wanted to do was envelop him in a big
bear hug, but I wasn't sure how many people in this company
knew we were together – and whether displaying affection
in the staff canteen was cool.

'I'll be back by the end of the week. Surely you can't get
into too much trouble before then?'

'I'll try,' I said, despite the fact that my stomach was
already feeling tight with nerves. *I'll be alone in New York.*
Suddenly, I really wanted to call Vicky.

CHAPTER TWENTY-ONE

The rest of the afternoon went in a flash. I was like a child in a toy factory as I combed my way through the lingerie, familiarising myself with the whole collection and dreaming up some formidable outfits for the show. Caroline had left me sketches of the costumes Ron had approved from the former stylist, as these were already underway, being crafted by Dimitri and his team behind locked doors in his design studio on the opposite side of the floor to mine, so, thankfully, I wasn't starting completely from scratch. I also spent some time on the phone with Maurice, telling him my vision and winning his support for the finale. We agreed to meet the following afternoon, assuming my pitch to Ron was successful.

Rob had already left the office to go home and pack by the time I was ready to head back too. Taking the subway, I felt exhilarated when I was stopped by a tourist asking the best way to Times Square and was able tell her off the top of my head, as if I had lived in this city all my life – only my accent could have possibly given me away. In my head I had developed a new persona: Amber Green, New York native, but educated at a fabulously expensive English school on the

Upper East Side. Yet knowing Rob was about to be out of town for a few days had suddenly given me the feeling of being the tiniest cog in the Coney Island ferris wheel. I felt envious that he was going to be back in our home city – that he would be able to sniff the steely London air and feel the warmth of a hug from his mum. I was craving the familiarity of home so badly that my finger hovered over Vicky's cell number in my address book. I knew meeting up with her wouldn't be a good idea, though. I had a few precious days to focus on the Angel Wear show and get my plans off the ground, and I needed to take advantage of it. The more Dimitri seemed to want me to fail, the more I wanted to prove him and any other doubters wrong. Instead, on the subway, I wrote a note on the back of an Angel Wear promotional postcard for Rob to post to my parents. It helped to annul a little of the guilt I felt for not being in proper contact with them.

'Dear Mum and Dad,' I wrote.

'Firstly, let me apologise. I'm sorry for being a rubbish daughter this past month. New York has felt like a whirlwind and I've been caught up in trying to get some work to pay my way out here. Anyway, it's going well. I did a few jobs through an agency, including one styling babies (never again). But now I'm freelance and Karen from next door's daughter is right, I'm the lead stylist for a big fashion show out here! It's happening in a week's time so I'm crazy busy getting all the costumes together, but it will be amazing for my CV.

'Rob and I have a cosy apartment in a place called Williamsburg in Brooklyn. Yes, we have contents insurance, before you ask. We've not had much time to check out the big sights yet, but we plan to, when he gets back from London. He's popped back for a couple of days for filming. I wish I could go in his suitcase, so I could come round for a roast dinner, but I'll be back before you know it, I promise.

'Please squeeze Nora for me and tell Lucy I love the slippers. I'll bring them back a ton of Reese's Pieces when I return.

'Love you,

'Amber

'xx'

When I got back to the apartment, Rob was packed and getting ready to leave.

'I'm sorry, the flight was earlier than I thought,' he said. 'Don't get into trouble. And remember, you're the hottest thing since Vicky left your straighteners on.' I went to swipe him, and he ducked.

He smiled cheekily. 'I love you.'

'I love you too,' I replied.

'Now come here,' he said, pulling my waist to meet his and then taking my face in his hands. 'I wish we had longer,' he whispered.

'Me too,' I gasped, moving my hand down to his belt and gripping it. 'Miss your flight?'

'Oh, baby, you know I'd love to, but can you imagine? I'd be sacked on the spot.'

After one final lingering kiss, he pulled away and picked up the handle to his case. I closed the door behind him and New York suddenly felt a whole lot bigger.

About an hour later, after I'd put some washing on, nibbled some cheese and spent a while stalking old friends back home on Facebook, I picked up my phone.

'Hello, Victoria speaking,' answered a very polite Vicky.

'I know,' I replied. 'I called you.'

'Oh, sorry mate, wasn't sure who this was,' she replied.

'You deleted me from your phone already?'

'Well, you did chuck me out of your flat! It wasn't exactly what friends are meant to do to one another. Remember?'

I bit my lip.

'I know. I'm sorry. We didn't know what else to do.'

'Is that why you're phoning – to apologise?'

'Apologise? You nearly set our apartment on fire! I'm not sure we're the ones who need to—'

'It's all "we" and "our" now, is it? You and Rob. Rob and Amber. Love's young dream. What happened to "we" being you and me, Amber? What happened to not being one of those people who gets a boyfriend and ditches their girlfriends?' I could picture her face frowning. I frowned back. 'Anyway, the fire was an accident. Haven't you left your straighteners on before?'

I mentally pictured the hundreds of times on my way to work in London that I had sprinted back from the end of our road, or got to the tube and called Vicky to check my straighteners weren't still on. Roughly half the time they were. 'This isn't about straighteners, anyway, is it?' Vicky continued.

'Listen,' I reasoned, despite the fact that her comment about ditching my girlfriends was stinging. 'I just wanted to tell you that Rob's in London for a couple of nights, so, if you're homeless, you're welcome back here.' I hadn't yet mentioned this idea to Rob, but I would, if she said yes.

'That's sweet of you,' she said, coldly.

'If you're sorted, it's no worries,' I added breezily, despite the fact that inside this frostiness between us was hurting me deeply.

'Don't worry, I've not been sleeping on the sidewalk,' she said, 'I've been staying with Noah, in an amazing hotel suite. So...'

'But I thought he was gay?' I asked.

'He is, so it's perfect,' she trilled. 'We top and tail. It's like I've known him forever. He is *so* much fun. He needed a beard to be his plus-one at events, and I needed a roof over my head, so what's not to love?'

'Sounds perfect,' I muttered, berating myself for bothering to make the call.

'Anyway, I've got to go because we've been invited to a screening of his latest commercial. It's for Tom Ford.' Her voice moved away from the handset. 'Yes, babe! Two secs! That's Noah. Got to dash. Bye, Amber.'

And she hung up. I sat on the sofa, dumbfounded. *I've lost my best friend. I really have. How could this have happened?*

Instead of drowning my sorrows in a litre of wine with Tina from next door, which would have been my natural reaction to this horrible situation – her pregnancy saved me from this option – I decided to put my energy into creating a brilliant presentation for Ron and the board for the following day. I spent over two hours Skyping with Maurice, marvelling at how he had already managed to turn my vision into some beautiful fashion sketches, a talent from his decades in the industry. As he held them up to the screen the aesthetic blew me away and we could hardly contain our excitement about bringing it to life on the runway.

It was eleven o'clock by the time I realised I was starving and, as I pulled back the cellophane on a microwavable meal for one, there was a knock on the door. I imagined it was Tina in need of Gaviscon, or Max checking whether Rob fancied an impromptu bottle of Jack Daniel's. Max seemed to have ditched his health kick and was now displaying signs that he was having issues dealing with his wife's decision to quit alcohol, from what I could glean from Tina.

My heart rate quickened when I opened the door and saw Vicky.

'How did you get through the main door?' I asked, surprised.

'Max was outside having a fag, he let me in.' She held out her hand, formally. 'Hi.'

I took her hand and we shook. 'Hi,' I said, warily. *Has she really come round to have a go at me in person?*

She apologised: 'I'm sorry for being a bitch earlier. I was hurt and you caught me by surprise.' She was dressed up in a beautiful long grey coat, presumably cashmere, which was open at the front revealing her extraordinarily long legs in a short black dress and some towering silver sandals.

I looked into her brown eyes with my blue ones. The same eyes that had looked into one another's for so many years, through so many life stages.

'I couldn't be in the area without popping by,' she said, and looked down at her amazing shoes and polished toes. 'Especially knowing you'd be home alone. Rob going to London – is everything okay with you two?'

'With *us*?' I almost choked on the words. 'God, yes! Of course – we're great, never been better!' I sounded way too cheery, defensive almost. 'Why *wouldn't* we be okay?'

'Well, you know, just how things were last week.' She was clutching the door frame as if she might topple over if she let go. I was sure she'd been drinking – I recognised that wobbly, slightly pissed Vicky instantly.

'But are *you* okay?' I asked warily, turning the tables. 'I mean, do you want to stay? Is that what this is about?' There had to be another motive behind her sudden appearance on my doorstep this late on a Monday night.

'No, God, no, I'm great! Never been better! I'm off out!' she said. It tickled me that we were as stubborn as each other and now we were in an 'everything's great!' stand-off. We stood there looking at each other for a moment, fake smiles across our faces.

'Vick, shall we go now?' a male voice called from downstairs.

'Who's that?' I asked.

'There's someone who wants to meet you,' she said, grabbing my hand. I flicked the latch on the door. *Two run-ins with the fire brigade in a fortnight is more than enough – I'm not falling for that one again.* And I followed her downstairs.

Noah West was standing on the doorstep, smoking a Marlboro Light with Max.

'Hey, you didn't tell me you had celebrity friends, Am?' Max said, his eyes sparkling with excitement. 'Tina's gonna be so pissed she went to bed early.'

I looked at Noah. He was ridiculously handsome: piercing blue eyes, groomed wavy dark-brown hair with subtle chestnut streaks, stubble that surely had a stylist of its own, and a jaw more perfectly chiselled than something by Henry Moore.

'Noah,' he said, holding out a hand. Even his hands were good-looking. He definitely went in for manicures. *What a waste for womankind.* 'I've heard so much about you from Vic. Great to meet you.' Then he turned his attention back to Vicky. 'Listen, babe, we're meant to be at the after-party and Tom won't be impressed if I don't make an appearance.' He sucked deeply on his cigarette and took a swig from the large silver hip flask Max had passed back to him. *Max didn't know it but the Tom he was referring to was the one and only Tom Ford. Squee!*

'I know, babe. Come too?' Vicky turned to me. 'We can get Amber in, can't we, babe?' *They call each other babe?*

'Sure, babe.'

It wasn't necessary for his camera-ready eyes to look me up and down, I knew.

'Give me thirty seconds to sling on a dress.' There wasn't enough time to consider whether this was A Good Idea the night before a big presentation. I was more disturbed by the fact that I never seemed to have more than two minutes to get glammed up for a night out.

*

The location was the rooftop of the Natural History Museum. Above the Halls of Dinosaurs, Birds and Amphibians, the terrace had been boxed in matt black and filled with sleek cube seating, in keeping with the current slick and minimalist Tom Ford aesthetic. We were immediately ushered through and led to a roped-off area. The place was heaving.

'These are for you,' Noah said pushing two miniature glasses in my direction, no sooner had a waiter deposited them on our table. 'You're playing catch up.'

I sniffed one of them and recoiled. *Tequila. Lots of.*

Before I could make an excuse about having a big presentation tomorrow morning, Noah was whisked off by a woman introducing herself as 'Mr Ford's PR' – *presumably, she doesn't need an actual name* – to schmooze the glitterati at the party.

I stared at the shots and wished Rob was here to down one of them for me; he was good with tequila. I was less so.

'Well, go on,' Vicky mouthed.

'Okay, okay,' I mouthed back, thinking, *I really shouldn't but I'm out now, I may as well enjoy myself.* I shuddered as I lifted the first to my lips, swallowed and sucked on the wedge of lemon she thrust into my palm immediately after. The second went down better. And then a glass of champagne sailed down, followed by a whiskey-based cocktail that was supposed to 'embody the flavour of the new collection'. *Only in fashion.*

While Noah was busy mingling, the drinks kept arriving at our table and with each one, the ice thawed between Vicky and I. She informed me that Trey had been back in touch.

'He's traced me to New York,' she said, not looking particularly happy about it.

'Isn't that great?' I replied. 'Must mean he's missing you.'

'Doubt it,' she quipped. 'He's left a couple of voicemails.'

'Well, what did he say?'

'Nothing really,' she continued. 'Just that he knows I'm here and he arrives tomorrow. I haven't replied.'

'Well, if he's flown all the way here, he must want to make things up to you.' I looked at her expectantly. 'So, are you going to meet up with him?'

'Not sure yet,' she muttered. 'Anyway, it's not like he flew in to make it up with me – he's in town for a junket. Of course, he had to mention that.' She rolled her eyes. 'Putting work first. Again. I'll see. He's here all week, so there's no hurry. Besides, I'm starting to feel that I don't need him any more, anyway.' She looked across the room to where Noah was bathed in the glow of five photographers' flashes, as he posed with Tom Ford and supermodel Dara Kashova.

'Of course you don't – you're best bloody mates with Noah West, babe! It isn't exactly a bad position to be in, let's face it.'

She laughed. 'Yeah, and I figure if I hang out in the gayest venues in the whole of Manhattan, I'm unlikely to run into Trey.'

'Sounds like a plan,' I said, and we chinked cocktail glasses.

By the time Noah had rejoined us, Vicky and I were back to BFF status, just like before the awkwardness of 'Sardine Tin-gate' – as we had christened the episode. It felt so good to have cleared the air, and having Noah around didn't feel like a crowd at all – the three of us had a great time together, gossiping about all his fashion industry friends. It turned out Maurice had given Noah his first big break, inviting him to walk the catwalk for him, when he was starting out in modelling as a teenager. As the evening progressed and the music became louder and louder, we hit the dance floor. At one point, the actual Tom Ford came and danced next to us – Vicky nearly went flying over her heels when she noticed it was him and we spent an entire Lady Gaga medley trying to avoid eye contact whilst dancing self-consciously alongside Tom. It wasn't easy, especially when my arm brushed against his and I got a whiff of an extraordinarily sexy scent. At some point I remembered my promise to Joseph back at Selfridges, but it didn't feel opportune to slip a phone number into his slick suit top pocket. I'd probably get escorted out of the building if I were to attempt it. *Sorry, Joseph.*

By one in the morning my head was beginning to spin. I could have danced all night, but the effect of the cocktails was starting to wear off and I remembered, with shocking urgency, that I had a very big presentation to make in just a few hours' time. I was in the cloakroom queue, rummaging around in my clutch for my ticket when— *Oh, shit! I don't believe it. Where are my door keys?*

Five more minutes of frantic groping of items in the small bag and then tipping the contents onto the floor to make absolutely certain the keys weren't in there and I was running back into the main party to track down Vicky and Noah. I found them taking selfies in the smoking area.

'I'm frigging locked out!' I stormed. 'And Rob's away.' *Infuriatingly, I couldn't even blame Vicky this time.*

'Are the keys in the apartment?' Vicky asked. 'You know what that means: "Hello again, Mr Fire Officer!"' She put her hand to her forehead before erupting into giggles.

'*Not helpful,*' I wailed.

She leaned over and whispered loudly into Noah's ear. 'Amber's got a bit of a *thing* for the NYFD.'

A panicky sensation suddenly made me feel a lot more sober than the pair of them. I badly wanted to call Rob, but he would be mid-air and anyway, he'd be furious.

'When did you last have them?' Vicky asked, correctly surmising that I wasn't amused.

I paused to think. 'Well, Rob let me in before he left today, and I had the door on the latch when you were over... so that must mean I last had them at work,' I recalled. 'I was in a hurry to leave and get back to him. I must have taken them out of my bag at some point. Oh, God, yes, of course, I put the key to the studio safe on the same ring and I was using that today – that means they've got to be at work.'

'Well then,' she grabbed my hand, stood up and straightened her skirt against her thighs like she meant business. 'To the Angel Wear offices it is. I'll come and make sure you get them okay. Where are they based?'

'Seriously, it's fine,' I replied, feeling a lot more together now I was pretty certain I knew where they were and luckily the building was manned twenty-four hours. 'I'll keep the Uber waiting while I run in.'

Noah interjected: 'No way, Amber, we're not going to

leave you. What will you do if they're not there? I'm over this party anyway – and Tom's gone.' He looked around the room, at exactly the same time that most of the partygoers lowered their phones and pretended to be doing anything but look like they were taking unsolicited photos of him – which they had been doing for most of the party. *So this is what it's like to be one of the most aesthetically blessed men in the world.* 'Let's *all* go,' he said now. 'I know where the office is, and it's not far from our hotel anyway.'

'Ooh, yeah, we could come in with you!' Vicky squealed. 'I'd love to see where all the Angel Wear action happens! And you have a *safe*? Does this mean there are actual diamonds on the bras? This, I've got to see.'

Before long we were all in my Uber, heading across town.

We were standing in the revolving doors at the Angel Wear offices for a few seconds before we realised they weren't actually moving, which prompted a huge giggling fit from both Vicky and Noah. Although it was late at night, there were still lights in the high-rise building and the street out-side was buzzing with people – there was only marginally less traffic on the roads than at any other time of day in Manhattan. Being in the centre of the city at this time of night was buzzy. The same security guard who witnessed my unfortunate run-in with Mona last week was on duty, and I had since discovered he was called Larry. This, I felt, was bad. Hopefully, I smiled at him through the glass door and saw his face change from an expression of neutral boredom, to dutiful concern, as he recognised me. But, as he didn't seem to be reaching for an alarm, I made my move.

'I know what you're thinking, Larry!' I shouted through the glass between us, trying to sound as sensible and sober as I could. 'But I come in peace!' I held up my hands. *I'm funny, right?*

He didn't seem to think so. 'Lady, it's nearly two a.m.'

'Is it really?' I said. 'I'd barely noticed. I'm working late, you see.' I hoped he couldn't see the party wear under our coats.

'Any access late at night has to be approved in advance.' He scowled.

'Sorry,' I mouthed. 'It's just I'm fairly new.'

'I know.' He was unimpressed.

'I'm *really* trying to impress Ron with my designs for the catwalk show. I wanted to put in some extra hours – show him how committed I am. But I need to pick up some prototypes from my studio to take home, so I can continue working there.' I looked up at him with my best 'trust me, I'm a doctor' expression. Vicky and Noah lowered their heads to disguise yet another giggling episode behind me. He eyed them suspiciously.

'How long will you be?' Larry eventually replied, sensing that we weren't budging.

'Not long – ten minutes max?'

Vicky dug her index finger into my back. *Ouch.* 'And us too?' she whispered.

I know I shouldn't do this. I should just go in myself, get the keys and leave.

Vicky could read my mind: 'Come on, don't be square. Where's the old, fun Amber gone?' *The old, fun Amber. The Amber who could be the life and soul of the party. The one who put her girlfriends before any man.*

'And, um, I need my two friends here to give me a hand with bringing some of the items down,' I continued.

His eyes narrowed and he fiddled with the large bunch of keys on his belt. I could tell he was weighing up this unlikely trio of me, a shockingly good-looking male model and a pretty girl in a short dress, all beaming hopefully. We didn't exactly look threatening.

'Yeah, go on, Amber – you're the lead stylist, surely it's up to you anyway,' Vicky whispered, her breath hot on my ear.

'I'm the lead stylist, you see, sir,' I continued.

'Oh, I know who you are. I don't forget a face.' He half smiled. He seemed to be softening.

'Are you a whiskey man?' Noah piped up. He pulled his hip flask out of his coat pocket and dangled it over my shoulder in the direction of the security guard. Larry paused, he was tempted. 'Have a drop of fire water,' Noah said.

Suddenly, we all jumped as the revolving doors jolted into life.

'Single malt?' Larry muttered, taking the flask from Noah and lifting it to his lips. We were finally inside the building. He swallowed back a hefty glug. 'It's good stuff.'

'I won't forget this, Larry, sir.' I said. 'I'll tell Ron how helpful you've been, when I have my meeting with him tomorrow.'

'Make it quick,' he said. 'I'll give you this back on your way out.' He winked at Noah.

'Do I need to turn off any alarms up there?' I asked, warily.

'I'll do it from here,' he replied. 'Anyway, the CCTV isn't activated until everyone's left the building. I'll be here to let you out. Be quick.'

'I will. And, thank you,' I said, looking serious.

'Thank you, sir,' said Noah.

'Yes, thank you very much!' said Vicky, smiling her sunshine smile. One by one we filed across the lobby towards the lifts.

When we were safely zooming our way up to the twentieth floor, Vicky let out an exhilarated shriek. 'Wah! The actual Angel Wear offices!'

'Shhh! Seriously, hun, you never know, Ron could be working late, too,' I hissed. 'Jeez, I'm sure this is a sackable offence.'

'Oh, Amber, honestly, of course it's not, you're just doing a bit of extra work and picking up your keys – chill the hell out.'

'Now, now, you two,' Noah interjected. 'We'll be out again before you know it – after a quick tour of the studio. I didn't give up my whiskey flask for nothing.'

CHAPTER TWENTY-TWO

The next morning, a quick scan of the room revealed I was in my own bed and a wiggle of my fingers and toes suggested I was still in my own body. My hands were shaking slightly as I lifted my head off the pillow and checked the time on my phone: 7 a.m. So I hadn't overslept. *Thank God for impending dehydration – nature's way of stopping me oversleep, despite a banging hangover.*

Suddenly a calendar reminder popped up: 10 A.M. PRESENTATION

I shut it down. *Why is my phone so spritely this morning?* I wasn't stupid enough not to remember that it was the day of the presentation. I replaced my head on the pillow and winced as some mortifying flashbacks from last night played out in my mind.

A text-message alert made me jump. I didn't recognise the sender's number. Instead of a message, there was a video clip attached. I clicked on the link, immediately regretting it, assuming it was a virus about to eat up my phone. *Stupid idiot!* But instead, a slightly blurry image began playing out. At first I couldn't make out what it was but, after a few moments, the camera lens focused and – *Oh, God, no! Please, this can't be happening*. It was lucky I was still lying down, because my legs went to jelly.

There in front of me was the Angel Wear Studio. The camera then panned out to reveal Noah, wearing nothing more than some tiny pale-pink rhinestone-encrusted briefs and a huge pink feather boa and, behind him, hands around his waist in a conga formation, was Vicky, in a sheer-red negligée, complete with nipple tassels, which were spinning wildly as her hips swayed left and right and she kicked her legs out sideways. And last but not least, taking up the rear, hands around Vicky's waist, clumsily following them around the main studio area, was me, wearing an eye-catching pair of over-the-knee leopard-print heeled boots, a matching pair of big briefs and a black-satin corset-style top, some giant fluffy white angel wings precariously attached to my back. We were all laughing our heads off, as we shrieked, 'Work it girlfriend!' in OTT American accents. *And to think I thought I was quite sober by the time we reached the office. Mortified doesn't cover it.*

I couldn't watch it to the end; there was a sick feeling in my stomach and a lump in my throat so big I could barely breathe properly, so I switched off, turned over my phone and buried it under my pillow. Perhaps putting it out of sight might make it all disappear. To make matters worse, there was an open bottle of champagne clearly visible in the studio foreground. Encouraged by Vicky, I had pilfered it from a fridge in Caroline's make-up area and we had been merrily swigging from it while we held our own little fancy-dress party. In my work place.

I looked so drunk. Even worse, the video gave the impression that we were mocking the catwalk show and poking fun at the brand. It gave completely the wrong impression of me. *I wouldn't dream of doing such a thing, sober.*

There was a muffled ping from my phone, indicating another text had arrived. I looked at the pillow for several seconds, praying this was just a bad dream and my phone and I could start the day again, just as soon as I woke up. But after blinking a few times, the pillow was still there and the ping hung in the air even though the sound had melted away. Tentatively, I pulled it out and my face collapsed as I saw another message from the same number. This time there were words. I closed one eye as I read them:

Ron was very interested in this little film from last night. He'll see you at 10am. Don't be late

I covered my face with my hands. When I plucked up the courage to part my fingers and look at the message again, it was still there, staring at me in a pale-grey bubble.

Oh. My. God. I'm getting fired. I've had my dream job for twenty-four hours and now I'm getting the sack. I knew it was too good to be true.

Seconds later, another ping. It seemed to echo in the air like a death knell. This time I closed one eye to look at my phone. *Surely there can't be worse?*

It was a message from Rob:

Morning baby! Just about to have lunch with Mum, trying to stay awake. How's it going, you ready for today? Sock it to them! Love you xx

I threw my phone on the bed and got into the shower.

The hot water washed over me, rinsing the actions of the night before off my skin and down the plug hole; and, in a bizarre turn of events, instead of a worsening sick feeling in my stomach, I emerged with a feeling of strength. I was pretty certain I knew who had taken the video – it had to be Dimitri – and although shaking with anger, I sure as hell wasn't going to let him defeat me; not even over my own stupid mistake. As I stood on the bath mat, dripping with water, naked as the day I was born, I put my hands on my hips and struck the Wonder Woman pose in front of the mirror. *If he wants a war – he's got it.*

'Do you want to tell me what the hell happened last night?' Ron asked sharply, as I stood nervously just inside his office, bang on ten o'clock. There were no pleasantries today but, thankfully, there was no camera crew either – *my only saving grace*.

Dimitri was flanking him on the right, wearing the same trench coat and polka-dot hanky ensemble as he'd had on the day before. His eyes were aggressive, yet there was a slight smirk across his face, like a perverse army drill sergeant about to order me to hit the deck and give him a hundred press-ups.

I took a moment to compose myself, my heart thumping hard in my chest and my cheeks radiating heat.

'Well? What have you got to say?' Ron snapped.

'I was working late when I heard a clatter in the design studio. Fearing a breach of security, I—'

'No, not you, Dimitri,' said Ron, cutting him off. 'I know all that. Amber – explain yourself. How could you think it was a good idea?' His voice was raised and it seemed that he was struggling to keep his temper under control. Although I had so far avoided any eye contact with Dimitri, I could feel his gaze drilling into my flushed face.

There was nothing I could do but tell Ron the true version of events – about how I'd returned to collect my forgotten keys and, in a moment of weak stupidity, given in to Vicky and Noah's suggestion that they come with me, too. I embellished the part about how dazzled they were by the latest Angel Wear designs – thinking some flattery might claw me back a teeny bit of goodwill – '…and somehow we found ourselves putting on a catwalk show – a rehearsal of sorts.' It sounded infantile, but there was no point in trying to pretend it hadn't happened, when the CCTV footage clearly told the story.

When I had finished, I stared foolishly at them. This felt like being at school. In fact, I *wished* I was at school, because then there'd be a good chance I'd get suspended. It might only be ten in the morning but what I really fancied was a day off and maybe a cigarette and a can of Strongbow behind a bike shed.

'So where do you suggest we go from here?' Ron asked. *The pub?*

'We fire her, of course!' Dimitri snarled. 'She abused her position, Ron, there's no other option!'

'I didn't ask you,' he retorted, giving me a glimmer of hope that perhaps there was some room for manoeuvre.

'Well…' I began, a little unsure of exactly how I was going to talk my way out of this one, but determined to give it a shot; there was nothing like fear to get the juices flowing. 'It was wrong on every level, and for that I can only apologise.' I held up my hands, like I'd seen them do in American dramas when the accused is about to be carted off by the cops. 'But, let me assure you, it was a stupid mistake and completely out of character for me. Please, Ron, if you'll give me a second chance, I'd like my work to be judged here, not my behaviour, and I'd like to use the rest of this meeting to present my ideas for the show's finale to you, as we originally planned.'

Then, as Ron took a seat behind his desk in his big, Dr Evil-style rotating chair, and Dimitri paced around in front of the large windows behind him, I told them how I was keen to bring the controversial designer Maurice Chan on board to create some hype for the runway show. I told them about the ruby bra, even showing a photo of it on my iPhone. 'It will make the perfect centrepiece to the finale,' I explained, 'completing my theme for the show.' The two men looked at me expectantly. 'Ron, I'd like to present to you the theme for this years' runway extravaganza – Wonder Woman. This ruby bra is going to be worn by the last Icon to walk the runway, bringing the show to a spectacular close.'

As I pitched my idea, I could visualise it clearly – *Krystal coming out of a cloud of dry ice, hips gyrating, tanned limbs strong and beautiful, big blue hot pants with white stars, paired with the ruby bra, spinning shafts of light around the room, thanks to a giant disco ball suspended way above. Her hair big and loose, save for a shiny gold headband, a red cape flowing behind her buoyed by some strong wind machines, and red and white platform boots completing the look. She is framed by a background projection of gigantic shooting stars as she strikes the iconic, powerful, hands-on-hips Wonder Woman pose, in all its trail-blazing glory, to thunderous applause.*

'The fashion press will go mad for the kitsch coolness of resurrecting one of the greatest female icons of all time,' I enthused, on a roll. 'Feminists, who might otherwise have protested about the objectification of women in their underwear, will applaud you for using powerful imagery. And young people? They'll have a strong role model to aspire to.' As the words flowed, I realised just how much I cared about this project – it was not only about seeing Maurice finally get justice, but about doing something good; it was about making women not only look amazing, but feel empowered, too, silencing Angel Wear's critics at the same time.

Dimitri scoffed. '*Wonder Woman?* For God's sake, we're not in the nineteen eighties!'

I chose to ignore him. 'This theme will perfectly communicate the fact that Angel Wear is a heritage brand, finding inspiration in the past, while creating cutting-edge fashion for today's woman. The Wonder Woman pose is a feminist phenomenon and, by giving it a platform on the Angel Wear stage, we can show that using your body is a powerful tool. You don't have to be provocative to gain power – do the pose at home in your Angel Wear underwear before you go out, or in the loos before a big interview. Do it in the shower.' I pictured myself this morning. 'It doesn't matter, what *does* matter is how it makes you *feel*.' I paused to give them a moment to take this in. 'You're worldly men – surely you can see how it will perfectly complement the lingerie collection and win you fans from all walks of life?'

While I was talking, Ron was listening – he nodded his head a few times; he even made some notes on his desk jotter, which encouraged me. If he was going to fire me, why would he be making notes?

'I love the Wonder Woman idea... but Maurice Chan?' he said at last. 'He bothers me. Wasn't he the guy who put Hitler moustaches on the catwalk?'

'He certainly was,' sneered Dimitri. 'He was forced into hiding, and for good reason. Quite frankly, to be honest with you, Ron, I don't think you should be the guy to put him back into the limelight. It's far too dangerous for you *and* the brand.'

'Amber, what's your thinking behind Chan?' Ron asked, cracking his knuckles.

'There's a different side to every story,' I replied, finally confident enough to raise my voice. 'As it happens, Maurice was wrongly vilified. He was set up and ended up taking the fall. He's paid the price – a whole decade away from the profession he loves. Fashion design is in his blood and, Ron, I believe a talent like that shouldn't be allowed to go to waste. Maurice is ready to relaunch himself into the design world. He's not after huge accolades – Wonder Woman will take all the praise – he just wants to do what he loves best again, and that is design clothing – however skimpy that clothing might be,' I qualified.

Ron was rubbing his chin. With the show only six days

away, he really didn't have much time to sit around deliberating it for long.

'I think you're on to something, Amber,' he said.

I breathed a sigh of relief and almost immediately my whole body felt more comfortable.

'I can't listen to this crap any more,' Dimitri said, pulling up the collars on his trench coat and getting ready to storm out of the room. 'This is a guy who used Hitler for fashion inspiration – who held his show in a former Nazi bunker under the Paris Metro. The guy's been living in some dead great-aunt's flat for the past few years. He's a lunatic. He's washed up. For God's sake, Ron, how can we have this association?'

I looked at Dimitri. I *really* looked at him, suddenly able to see through his moody persona. Caroline was right, he wasn't just unfriendly, he was malicious – and he seemed to know a lot more about Maurice Chan than your average lingerie designer would know.

'So,' I concluded, deciding to blank Dimitri for now, 'I just think *everyone* deserves a second chance. Maurice paid the ultimate price for mistakes that were not even his own. And he is one of the greatest fashion designers of our time. I think we could make this a huge success – in fact, I *know* we could. He can make lingerie cool again and the unholy trinity of Maurice, Wonder Woman and the ruby bra will have *everyone* talking.' Ron's face seemed to soften as he took this in. 'Look,' I said passionately, ready to give it my final shot, 'you gave me this incredible opportunity and I'm not going to let you down. I'm afraid the show is not an option for me without Maurice.'

And then I stopped and just stood there in front of him, hands on my hips, strong, defiant, a Wonder Woman of sorts, with my stinking hangover and big ideas, unsure whether I could pull this off, but with a fire in my belly and the determination to give it a bloody good shot.

'The two clowns who were with you last night will be barred from the premises,' Ron declared.

I nodded earnestly. 'Goes without saying.'

'And last night's little "dress rehearsal" will be kept between us.'

'Of course,' I replied.

'So bring Maurice to me,' Ron said.

Seconds later, without a word, Dimitri stormed out of the room, slamming the door so hard we both turned to check the glass hadn't shattered.

I'm sure Ron had already decided he was going to put his faith in me and get Maurice on board, even before I introduced them later that same afternoon. Dimitri stayed ensconced in his studio, refusing to come out like a petulant child, which didn't surprise me considering his behaviour so far.

As Maurice recounted to Ron the very same story that had won me over in the coffee shop just a few weeks ago, Ron was rubbing his hands together knowing, as we all knew, that having such a big name on board was going to attract a huge amount of media attention.

As the meeting drew to a close, he asked his head of PR and marketing to join us – a friendly, busy woman called Melissa, and instructed her to draw up a press release to go out to the media immediately, telling of his controversial appointment and building hype for next week's show.

In an effort to retain relations with Dimitri, Ron carefully carved up our roles, leaving Dimitri in charge of the introductory runway show, and making Maurice and me responsible for producing five show-stopping costumes for the Icons to wear for the finale, which would culminate with the appearance of Wonder Woman. At Melissa's instruction, we finished the meeting by sending a selfie of Ron, Maurice and I, standing with the huge image of the Icons behind us, to all of Angel Wear's social media channels.

Minutes later, news of Maurice's return to the fashion world was ricocheting around the virtual landscape. It became the top news item on all major fashion sites – including *vogue.com* –

FABLED DESIGNER MAURICE CHAN MAKES HIS COMEBACK WITH ANGEL WEAR one excited headline, among many, ran.

My phone was alight with messages and social media alerts, as my thousands of followers reposted the news, complete with my re-grammed photo. Caption: Meet my new design partner, Maurice Chan #AngelWear #runwayshow #comingsoon #NYC #watchthisspace

It was impossible not to feel exhilarated by it all.

CHAPTER TWENTY-THREE

With Rob away, Maurice and I spent the next three days and late into the nights behind closed doors at the Angel Wear offices, burning the midnight oil discussing seams, fabrics and shapes as we created costumes alongside his seamstress Maria. We stopped only to take delivery of pizza dinners, to fetch coffees from the canteen, and for Maurice's cigarette breaks – which became increasingly frequent. By a stroke of good luck, Maria turned out to be as skilled at making tiramisu as she was at turning up hems, so we happily worked into the small hours in a haze of coffee, cream and couture. We were in our element tearing up plans when a concept wasn't working, and adding adornments until the costumes sparkled to perfection, always with Maurice's motto 'You can never have too many sequins' clearly in mind. We vowed not to stop until each one of the five finale costumes was as headline-grabbing as its wearer. Alongside fittings with the models themselves, there were also endless meetings with lighting directors, sound engineers, pyrotechnics experts, choreographers, not to mention lengthy discussions with Caroline and Sonny about the hair and make-up for each look.

*

I was in our little kitchen, about to make myself a studenty dinner from a tin of tuna, some cheese and a potato that was past its best, when Rob came through the door.

'You're early!' I exclaimed, furious with myself for not having embarked on my planned beauty regime earlier.

'Yes, surprise!' he said, taking in the look of horror across my face. 'Don't look too happy.'

'Sorry, baby. Of course I'm happy you're back,' I said, walking towards him, my arms open, ready to be enveloped by his. *I need a cuddle so badly.*

He set his suitcase down and planted a long kiss on my lips, and then I noticed another person standing behind him.

'Look who I brought back with me.' He ushered the person forwards.

'Dan!' I threw my arms around him, probably with too much enthusiasm, but I wanted him to know in one big bear hug that I was sorry for what had happened with Florence, without having to actually say it. Not right away, anyway.

'It's great to see you, Amber. Thanks for the welcome. I got a bigger hug than you did, Bro!' He winked at Rob.

I blushed. I had forgotten how classically good-looking Dan was. Whereas Rob had the more pretty-boy features of the two brothers, Dan was definitely the more chiselled. A couple of inches taller than Rob, with his neat, dark-brown hair to Rob's slightly messy mousy, his piercing blue eyes to Rob's green, he was the thoroughbred of the two. I was dying to find out what the latest with Florence was.

'How are you getting on?' I asked.

'Oh, you know,' he said with a small smile.

'I bet,' I replied, skirting around the issue.

'So how are the costumes coming together?' Rob changed the subject.

After I rustled up a pretty revolting tuna hash for us all for dinner, Rob and Dan decided to watch reruns of *Game of Thrones* on the sofa, so I retired to the bedroom to look over the photos I'd taken of the costumes so far, and make plans for the following day. I hadn't had much of a chance to look on Instagram during the last few days, and was quickly distracted by the amount of activity there had been surrounding the announcement that Maurice Chan was now part of the Angel Wear team. There was even a hashtag for my name with over a thousand posts. *I guess this means I'm becoming a sort of celebrity*. The thought was exhilarating and terrifying at the same time. But although my To Do list was endless, I felt energised by the adrenalin of the build-up to the greatest styling gig of my life.

My scrolling was brought to a halt by my phone ringing. Vicky. I hadn't had a chance to fill her in on the details about how I was nearly fired. One thing was for sure, I wasn't going to let her anywhere near Angel Wear, ever again.

'Hey, babe, before you say, "No"…' she began. *This is never a good start to a conversation with Vicky*.

'Hi, Vicky,' I replied. 'Why do I sense that I *want* to say, "No"?'

'I've got a massive favour to ask,' she continued, breathlessly. 'Noah's been invited to the Met Gala on Tuesday and he wants to take me as his plus-one.'

'That's amazing, hon, I'm happy for you,' I said, knowing

there was more to come. I'd been so busy with the costumes, I'd completely forgotten it was fashion's *other* big night out in two days' time.

Ron had specifically planned for the Angel Wear show to piggyback the Met Gala the following night, because all the biggest stars and designers would already be in town and on the party circuit, so the runway was guaranteed to attract an A-list front row. I had learned that you always find big fashion and celebrity events clustered together, because the fash pack like partying in convoy.

Vicky barely drew breath: 'I was hoping that you might be able to source me something to wear, or if I could borrow something from Maurice? I was thinking the Egyptian Queen idea you were going to do with Liv – if she's still going naked, that is. It's just that Noah's really up for being a Pharaoh. His agent's already got Tom Ford knocking him something up. But me? Well, I don't think a ten-dollar-ninety-nine Egyptian Queen outfit from the local costume store is really going to cut it for the Met – do you?'

My mind turned to Liv. She was no doubt on a treadmill at some over-priced gym at this very moment, honing her body ready for her 'Eve' moment. I shuddered at the thought.

'Fortunately, I've still got the white dress,' I replied. 'I've not had time to dry-clean it since the auction but, if you can express-clean it tomorrow, it's yours for the borrowing. I'm sure Maurice will lend you the falcon headdress too, if you pick it up from his apartment.'

'Amazing! I knew I could count on you!' she hooted. 'I'll jump in a cab now – see you in thirty.'

And there wasn't any time to complain that I hadn't seen my boyfriend for the past three nights and was planning an early night. *Vicky*.

'So great to meet you, Dan. I've heard so much about you,' Vicky said, admiringly, no sooner had I introduced them. Her eyes were sparkling and she couldn't stop smiling. They shook hands, and at the exact same moment there was a crackle above our heads and all the lights went out.

As was our natural reaction when something went unexpectedly wrong, Vicky and I burst into giggles.

'Um, I know I'm electric, but seriously,' she guffawed.

'Must be a power cut,' Rob said, jumping up and fumbling around, looking for a box of matches or a lighter on our untidy bookshelves.

'I have this effect on women,' Dan whispered in my ear. He smelt nice, too, even for someone straight off a flight. *I mustn't fancy my boyfriend's brother. I mustn't fancy my boyfriend's brother*.

Rob lit the large candle on our wooden coffee table. In the soft glow of candlelight, I found myself looking in to Dan's steely blue eyes and blushing.

'Nice candle,' Vicky commented.

The Jo Malone candle had been a present to myself in Duty Free on the way out here. It was to remind me of home, and the freebie Jo Malone candles that regularly decorated our flat when Vicky worked at *Glamour* magazine.

A few hours later, with no sign of the lights coming back on, Rob was so jet-lagged he'd begun to stare into space, and

I was feeling exhausted from the long hours I'd been pulling. Rob gently touched my hand.

'Excuse us,' he said to the other two, 'but I need to take this one to bed. We're glazing over and we've both got a few big days ahead.'

Dan and Vicky stood up, politely.

'Sit down, will you,' I commanded. They looked a bit too cosy there, together on the sofa. In fact, with their good looks, they made a cute couple. *But, euch! No, that's practically incest.*

'There's a sleeping bag in that cupboard,' Rob said to Dan, pointing to the side of the room.

'I'll show him,' Vicky cooed, flashing a look at Rob, which successfully reminded us both of the fact that we had evicted her from that very sleeping bag not so long ago.

Something told me Vicky was in no hurry for the evening to end.

The following morning, as I crept out of the apartment, I was relieved to find Dan asleep alone on the sofa. The sleeping bag had half slipped down, revealing the top of a pair of paisley boxer shorts. *Bad taste in underwear. Crush averted. Phew!*

Shuttling over the Hudson and across Manhattan on the subway had become second nature to me now and I spent most of the journey head down, scribbling a list of things to discuss with Maurice as soon as I reached the office.

As I walked from Forty-second Street to the Angel Wear building, I called Vicky.

'Well? What happened with Dan then?'

'Dan?' she sounded surprised. 'Nothing. Why?'

'I saw the way you were looking at him,' I teased her. 'He's fit. Don't tell me you didn't notice.'

'The way *you* were looking at him, more like,' she retaliated. 'Anyway, he's not my type – too much of a city boy.'

'Hasn't stopped you before,' I said. 'Remember that time I found a patent slip-on shoe in the hallway?'

She laughed. 'They were Gucci – a classic design. How else is a rich banker meant to spend his bonuses?'

'Anyway – Dan?'

'He's damaged goods, way too heartbroken. He was in tears on me at one point. I kept trying to leave and he kept talking. I had to cancel three Ubers – my bill's going to be huge.'

I sighed. 'Poor Dan.'

'Poor Dan?' she scoffed. 'He's his own worst enemy.'

'So you're sure nothing happened?'

'You've got to be joking. For some reason, he still loves his frisky fiancée – he seems to be seriously thinking about forgiving her. He's got no spine, if you ask me.'

'He's still getting back with Florence?' I was annoyed with myself for not having grilled Rob for the gossip.

'Seems so, from what I could gather; he was bawling so much. Yep, sorry, Am, but you can call off the double wedding, he's not enough of a bastard for me.' There was a hint of sarcasm to her tone. 'Anyway, I've got to dash. Noah wants me to go to his Pharaoh fitting.'

'Of course.' *Thank God she didn't kiss Dan.*

*

At work, slowly but surely, the close of the catwalk show was coming together. With each outfit nearing completion, Maurice and I held a fitting with the supermodels. We chose Krystal for our Wonder Woman on account of her long, raven hair and had created a preppy, secretary outfit for her 'before' appearance, then she was to spin on stage, disappearing momentarily in a blaze of indoor fireworks and into a trap door in the stage floor. Under the stage, Maurice and I would work fast to pull away the secretary outfit, revealing her Wonder Woman costume underneath, and then she would be elevated back through the floor to finish spinning and emerge as the superhero, in a burst of glitter from two cannons on the ceiling and yet more pyrotechnics. Seeing Krystal stand there for the first time in the Wonder Woman pose, all strong, long and tanned in the hot pants and sparkling ruby bra, we both got goosebumps; she was so convincing as the embodiment of Woman Power.

'You know, Amber, I never would have believed I'd see this moment,' Maurice said after her fitting, as we dug into yet another portion of tiramisu. 'Seriously, *chérie*, I can't thank you enough for this opportunity. You really are my guardian angels – you and Wonder Woman here.' He looked across at the dummy, on which stood our *pièce de résistance*. 'You make me feel invincible.'

'I'd never have believed I'd be in this position either, Maurice,' I said, putting down my dessert bowl as I spied a frayed edge that needed snipping from Wonder Woman's cape. 'I'm still pinching myself and, in all honestly, it has been a privilege and an absolute pleasure working with you. But it's not over yet.'

We grinned nervously at each other.

'*Mais, non, mon amie*, the fun is just about to begin,' Maurice said.

Late in the evening, I quietly unlocked the door to our apartment, crept past Dan asleep on the sofa and into bed with Rob, snuggling up against his warm naked body, spooning him woozily until I fell asleep. I woke up several times in the night, feverish with new thoughts to do with the detailing on a costume, or in a panic that I'd forgotten to let the lighting guy know about a new idea we'd had. And then I would drift back off, ready to rise before the guys and leave for the studio ahead of most commuters.

'I love you,' Rob whispered groggily as I dressed as quietly as I could.

'I love you too,' I whispered back.

We were so used to saying those three little words now. The next time I saw Rob was when the filming crew popped by for an update during the day. Seeing him come through our studio door was always the highlight of my day – less so, the actual filming part – but he was always so encouraging telling me I was 'a natural on camera'.

The day before the show, Ron came to the studio to survey the final looks.

Maurice and I had barely slept the night before. My hair

was full of white streaks of dry shampoo and I was paranoid I was beginning to stink. Maurice was clearly feeling the same, because he kept edging backwards whenever Ron got a bit too close. And Ron liked to get close. He put a big hand in the centre of my back, over my bra strap, making me bristle.

'I couldn't quite envisage it when I first heard your idea,' he said. He had been walking around the mannequins in unnerving silence for ten minutes. 'You're the biggest gamble I ever made.' I toyed with a safety pin in my hand. *Heck, where is this going? What will we do if he sacks us?* Ron continued, pausing for dramatic effect. 'But…' He was laying a hand on Maurice's back too, like a puppeteer with his two new toys. 'The girls are going to look sexy as hell in these costumes. I love it! Move over Dolce and Gabbana, you're the greatest double act fashion has seen in a long time.'

Feeling happily relieved, I headed to the canteen to get yet another coffee for Maurice and I. Despite Ron's positive appraisal, there was no time for celebrating – it was straight back to work; we still had final tweaks to make today before we could relax in the knowledge that the costumes were going to be finished on time.

As I exited the lift on my return journey, my head was so full of work, I didn't notice Dimitri heading straight towards me. As we passed, he purposefully jolted my arm sending hot coffee spilling onto my sleeve.

'Oh, just sod off!' I muttered, feeling the liquid burn through my top.

'Just – *what*?' he said. He was looking for a fight.

'You heard,' I said, turning to face him, my heart racing

inside my chest. I didn't have time for faking niceties today. 'Why do you have such a problem with me? What have I done?'

'You're a joke,' he replied with a snarl, fiddling with his polka-dot handkerchief. 'This is fashion, dear little English girl, and you're not cut out for it.' He looked me up and down. 'Anyone can see that.'

'Shame Ron doesn't agree with you then,' I quipped.

'What does he know?' he said, half laughing. 'He's just the pervy head of a lingerie company; he loves the girls more than the garments. Are you blind too?'

I drained the remaining mouthful of coffee in my paper cup, wishing I was less tired and could think of a brilliant comeback. 'Well, let's see what happens tomorrow night, shall we?'

'I can't wait,' he said, looking creepier than an ivy-covered wall.

And he turned on his Cuban heel and flounced through the double doors.

When I got back to the studio, I didn't manage to complain about Dimitri to Maurice because all five of the Icons had arrived for their final fitting before we all transferred to the venue, the famous Broadway theatre, the Winter Garden, ready for show night. As I crawled around with my coffee-stained sleeve rolled up and a pin cushion between my teeth, I was too busy tweaking angel wings, shortening hems on negligées, and adding or removing strategically placed sequins and feathers over certain body parts, to think about Dimitri again. Maurice stood back, scrutinising each look, to ensure everything hung together as a collection. It wasn't just about Angel Wear now – it was about his return to the fashion world as well. It was thrilling to see all the costumes together – they were opulent, sexy and cool – and there was a collective 'Wow!' when Krystal emerged from behind our changing-room curtain in the full Wonder Woman regalia, larger than life in custom-made platform boots, her killer body shown off in bright-blue hot pants, a dramatic cape hanging off a golden choker necklace, and her ample breasts encased in the ruby bra, which had been meticulously cleaned up by Maurice and sparkled brightly. Her abs were so perfectly formed, you could practically play the Wonder Woman theme tune on them!

'Man, I *love* this costume. It's the best I've ever worn – no question!' Krystal beamed. 'I honestly feel I could take on the world!'

'In that outfit – you could.' I smiled back.

'Anything's possible when you're Wonder Woman, ain't that right, Krystal?' said Astrid, popping her head around the door right on time. She was followed by Jessica, Leonie and Roxy.

'Come in, girls,' Krystal called out.

The four other girls all struck the pose. They were a formidable sight – a cast of heroines – with their hands firmly on their hips and gutsy expressions, before they all fell about laughing.

Maurice and I stayed late to carefully pack up the clothes and fill cases with all the shoes and accessories ready for the production crew to transfer the whole lot to our backstage area at the Winter Garden. The last item to leave the Angel Wear building was the ruby bra, which Maurice insisted on transporting himself and locking away in the theatre safe – to which he had now added a pin-coded padlock, as my reputation with misplacing keys had been playing on his mind.

'*Chérie*, I love you to the end of the world, but if you accidentally lost the safe key, I don't think I could ever forgive you,' he had teased, dangling the new lock under my nose earlier. 'I'll take care of the code.'

Although deliriously tired, I barely slept a wink the night before the show; nerves crackled through my veins. Trying to take the edge off it, I took to social media to watch the action unfold at the Met Gala, across the city at the Metropolitan Museum of Art.

Photos flooded Instagram, and Snapchat heaved with clips of the great and the good of the fashion world sporting a fantasia of fabulously outlandish creations. Anna Wintour held court as dresses the size of small houses paraded up the wide, red-carpeted staircase at the entrance to the museum. One famous pop star arrived in an elaborate gown with a corset so tight she fainted halfway up the steps and had to be speedily stretchered into the venue by her bodyguards. Her stylist was later forced to give a statement to the media, stating that the star had been corset-trained for the past fortnight in preparation but, unfortunately, had sipped from a can of Coca-Cola on the way to the event, which must have made her gassy and so the corset was way too tight. *You can bet she won't be working for a while.*

Noah and Vicky made a handsome couple in their Egyptian Pharaoh and Queen outfits and even made it on to *People* magazine's photo gallery of the Met Best Dressed, with Vicky referred to as Noah's 'unidentified plus-one'. I couldn't help but smirk at gossip blogger Perez Hilton's quip that Noah should have been the one dressed as the queen.

Finally, arriving fashionably late and peeling herself out of a limo slowly enough to ensure the entire bank of paparazzi got an exclusive photo, was Liv. Her hair was teased into a cascade of *Flashdance* curls, but that couldn't detract from the fact that she was wearing just the tiniest silk fig leaf covering her waxed nether region, the rest of her assets clearly on display under a fine nude body stocking. Anna Wintour was visibly unimpressed, so much so that she snubbed Liv at the entrance. I cringed as I spotted Mickey in the background, looking as sleazy as ever, while images of Liv's bare body were sent around the world. Her ten seconds of fame ended abruptly when Lady Gaga arrived atop a golden chariot pulled by male models who she was gleefully whipping. As the spectacle she created was bathed in the glow of the evening's largest frenzy of flashes, Liv was forced to creep up the steps and into the venue almost unnoticed by the line of fans along the red carpet.

When I peeled myself away from the frocky horror show at the Met – feeling mighty glad that I'd had nothing to do with Liv's lack of clothing – a series of stress-related dreams kept me awake. At one point, I woke with real tears running down my cheeks after dreaming Rob had been electrocuted by a rogue live wire during the show. I decided against telling him about this premonition, but I had an overbearing sense that something was going to go wrong.

It was only six o'clock but Rob was already up, presumably feeling as hyped as I was about the day ahead. Before I could call out to check whether he was still in our apartment, he was coming through the door, bearing a plate of toast and a mug of tea.

'Today's the big day!' he said. *Thanks for the reminder. Not a trace of nerves from him then.*

'I wish it wasn't,' I murmured, sinking back under the covers, pulling the duvet up around my shoulders, so only my nose and eyes poked out over the top. 'I don't feel ready.'

'Well, it's happening,' he said. 'Anyway, you couldn't be more prepared. It's going to be amazing. Come on, rise and shine, breakfast will help.'

As I sat up, a wave of nausea ran through me. I sipped the hot tea and began scrolling through social media. Bad idea. While, the Met Gala was still trending, fashion-industry insiders had moved on and were busy building hype for the Angel Wear show:

'It's the sexiest day of the year!' said one well-known fashion blogger with a cool three million followers.

'The Icons are ready to rock Manhattan!' said *Fashion News Daily*.

'Angel Wear Forever!'; 'So excited about today!' said hundreds and thousands more as #AngelWear gathered momentum on Twitter, Instagram and Snapchat.

Even swallowing a mouthful of toast was making me feel sick. I had zero appetite for anything other than more sleep.

A stream of text messages came through – wishes of luck from family and friends. I switched my phone to silent. They were just making my nerves even more frayed.

When I had hastily showered and dressed and was just about to leave, I turned to Rob. 'Double-check your cabling, will you?'

'You what?'

'Nothing. I love you, babe.'

'I love you too – and I'm so proud of you already. See you behind the camera. I'll be there at eight-ish.'

I was just about to descend the steps into the subway at Bedford Street, while mentally berating myself for forgetting to wear my lucky tights – the proper full-scale suck-it-all-in ones I was wearing on my first date with Rob – when my phone rang. It was Maurice. I almost didn't pick up, wondering if it would be better to just get to the venue quickly and see him there – he was bound to be on his fifth coffee and umpteenth cigarette of the day and getting jumpy; *I'm already nervous enough*.

'Amber, thank God. I've been trying to reach you. Where are you?' He spoke with a panicked tone.

'About to get on the subway. What's up? You sound as jittery as I feel.'

'Darling, if I was nervous I'm petrified now. Our worst nightmare has happened.'

I stopped dead in my tracks. 'Don't tell me someone has been electrocuted?'

He replied sharply. 'What? No, but it's almost as bad.' I sighed. *If no one is dead, what could be worse?* He breathed deeply into the phone. 'The ruby bra is gone.'

'Gone? What do you mean? You took it to the Winter Garden last night.'

'I know, I locked it away myself but, when I arrived this morning, the safe was open and the bra was not inside. I've made a few discreet calls – not wanting to raise the alarm, or risk Ron getting wind of it – and no one has seen it.'

'But wasn't Larry meant to be there, guarding the valuables all night?' My heart was racing.

'Larry and his hip flask?' he said mockingly. 'The empty one I found by his chair this morning when I woke him up?'

'Jesus Christ.'

'We need a miracle all right,' he said.

'But the code?'

'No one knew the code except me, and there doesn't seem to have been any forced entry. I'm baffled, Amber. Just get here as fast as you can.'

Now it was my turn to panic.

'Oh shit, Maurice, what are we going to do? The bra is the focal point for the finale.'

'Don't you think I know that?'

'Okay, don't get snappy with me. It's not my fault. Who could have done this?'

'I fear it's a professional job.' Maurice sighed. He was probably right – news of the bra and its value had been spreading between the models these past days; it seemed to be the worst-kept secret in the entire show. 'The sale of those rubies could set someone up for life. We've got to be dealing with an organised gem thief.'

'Well, then, we need to get the police involved!' I exclaimed, adrenalin rushing through me. I was attracting a few strange looks from people passing me on the staircase now. I was glued to the spot, hands shaking as I spoke into the phone. If they guessed I looked like a woman who had just been floored by some horrific news, then they were right.

'*Non*, no police!' Maurice wailed.

'Why?'

'It will ruin everything. Can you imagine, Amber, darling? This will be the talk of New York! Never mind the show, it will be all about the robbery. There will be police crawling around the building – the show may even have to be cancelled. Ron will go *insane*.'

'Are we insured?' I asked.

'*Zut alors*, Amber! Do you really want to get Ron involved, on the day of the show? We're going to have to come up with a Plan B. Just get here will you? *Rapide!*'

When I reached the theatre it was already busy. The entire Angel Wear workforce was involved with the show in some capacity and many had already arrived. There was a flurry of activity around the entrance to the theatre, which was being turned the signature 'Angel Wear pink' by members of the production crew, easily identifiable in their all-black clothing; a pink carpet, still rolled up in its cellophane wrapping, stood to attention by the door, guarded by other members of the crew. It was only seven in the morning and there were already a couple of fans standing behind a metal railing by the entrance; there was even a lone paparazzo loitering, hoping, presumably, to catch a glimpse of one of the Icons arriving for her rehearsal. My stomach did a flip.

Inside the theatre, the dress circle was in the middle of its transformation. A team of workers had clearly been busy through the night, taking out the theatre's main seating area and erecting the U-shaped catwalk. An intricate web of scaffolding was still partially visible underneath as at least ten people worked on stapling reams of pink fabric drape to cover the drop. Two giant glitter cannons were being hoisted into position on either side of the domed roof. Every now and again music blasted into the auditorium as sound technicians tested the level of the speakers, nodding at each other when it reached a level I would have described as 'deafeningly loud'. The scale of the whole production hit me all at once. I only just managed to stop myself being sick by shoving a chewing gum into my mouth.

I used a side entrance to go backstage and down a small dark corridor into the belly of the theatre and our dressing area. Here, the atmosphere was completely different – it was eerily silent. The dressing tables with their chairs, mirrors and lights laid out in neat rows were all empty, waiting in anticipation for pert bottoms to fill them. Caroline and Sonny would be here soon with their team of twenty hair and make-up artists ready to lay out every shape and size of brush needed to transform the thirty models taking part in the show.

Maurice appeared from behind our screened-off area, where the rails of clothes were hung in readiness, clearly labelled for each of the Icons. I took in his woeful face. His right eye was twitching, a sure sign of nerves. I'd witnessed his twitch a few times during the course of our friendship, but today the tremble was worse than ever. There was a film of sweat over his forehead, with little beads breaking on its deep ridges. Nothing about him looked good, which only made my nausea stronger.

In silence, he took my hand and led me into a tiny side room, where the safe door was wide open and the small space inside spookily dark and empty. I had hoped this might be some kind of sick, late April Fool's joke and the bra would be there, glinting away as usual, safely within its pouch.

'I was here at six and it was gone then,' Maurice said in a hushed voice, as he ushered me closer. 'But there is no sign the door was forced. It's bizarre.'

I looked at him in awful silence. 'You did put the lock on, didn't you?' I had to ask, I needed to know.

'Amber, of course I fucking did! I'm not that *stupide*!' he fumed.

'I'm sorry,' I muttered, dropping my eyes back to the safe. I put my hand inside and fumbled around in the darkness, just to be absolutely certain it hadn't somehow attached itself to the lining of the safe. Of course it hadn't.

'But it gets worse,' he continued. *I want him to say something positive; I can't handle any more bad news.*

'What now? Don't tell me Krystal's decided to pull a sickie?' *I'm really not in the mood for more nasty surprises this morning*.

'Ron wants a full dress rehearsal at midday. Stan, the production manager, came round this morning to let us know. So how are we going to explain the absence of his centrepiece? *Mon Dieu*, this is the worst day of my life.'

He staggered backwards and sat down on a chair, looking as though his legs might have crumbled had it not happened to be there to support him.

'Right, well, we need to come up with a plan – fast,' I said, thinking out loud. 'Someone clearly wants us to fail. And I have a few ideas who. But that's not going to happen. We've worked so hard for this, Maurice, and we have an amazing concept with or without the ruby bra. At the end of the day, only Ron and the Icons have actually seen it – to the rest, its very existence is just a rumour – so we're going to have to carry on with a stand-in item, as if everything is fine. We tell Ron and Krystal we don't want to use the real bra in the rehearsal, for security reasons. And then, during the actual finale, we cause a distraction at the moment the bra is meant to appear, so Ron doesn't see it's missing.'

Maurice sneered. 'What, we wave, shout, "Over here, this way, Ronnie!" just when the finale is taking place? As if he'd miss it, Amber – he's entertaining a load of executives in a box. He'll be expecting to blow their tiny minds when Krystal appears as Wonder Woman. He's hardly going to miss the big reveal.'

'I'm not suggesting that, Maurice, but what if a little *accident* happens and he *can't* actually see the bra?'

'We blind the boss?' He laughed manically. 'You've really gone insane.'

'No, no, listen, I've got an idea,' I said, thinking about the production crew I'd seen setting up just now. 'There is someone we need to let in on this, though. I need Rob involved. We can't do it without him.'

CHAPTER TWENTY-FOUR

'Tell me you're not serious?' Rob said gravely, when I'd finished telling him my idea. *Okay, so it did sound a bit barmy when I said it out loud. But what option do we have?*

'Well, can you think of anything better?' I asked urgently.

'Someone's going to get fired for it,' he reasoned.

'Yes – me, if we don't do it,' I replied, taking his hands in mine. 'Please, Rob, I'll never ask you to do anything like this ever again, but I *really* need your help. I'm hours away from a full-scale disaster if you don't.'

Rob was shaking his head, but he didn't say anything, giving me a sense that he might relent.

'You can do it during the dress rehearsal,' I continued. 'We're not using any of the actual special effects in it, so you'll be clear.'

'Okay. But no one can ever know it was me, all right?'

'Of course. I love you.' And I flung my arms around him.

'You're quiet today,' Sonny commented, joining me at the catering table after the rehearsal, as I helped myself to another can of full-fat Coke and a raspberry cheesecake brownie. *All this amazing food from Magnolia Bakery, and it's not as if any of the models are going to touch it. What a waste.* 'Feeling nervous? Or just bulimic?'

'Nerves,' I simpered. 'Cheesecake brownie is helping though.' Maurice and I had used a stand-in red-rhinestone bra from last season's collection during the rehearsal and eagle-eyed Ron hadn't missed a trick, coming backstage to comment on it afterwards.

'Clever idea saving the actual ruby bra for the show, Amber,' he had said, nudging me in the ribs conspiratorially.

Dimitri had been keeping a low profile backstage; I'd only seen him briefly during the rehearsal and now, just a few hours before curtain up, he was nowhere to be seen.

I couldn't help but wonder if he had had something to do with the ruby bra's disappearance. If there was someone who wanted to see me fail, on the biggest night of my career so far, it seemed to be him. *But would he really go as far as theft and ruining the show for everyone?*

Rob joined us at the table; he looked as tense as me. I picked up another brownie and took a bite before handing him the rest.

'Mission accomplished,' he whispered, lifting it towards his lips.

I didn't even feel relieved. It didn't feel real. None of this did any more. It felt as though it was all happening to someone else.

Amy came past to let Rob know that Ron was ready to do his piece to camera ahead of the show.

'Good luck, Amber!' she said excitedly. 'I've heard the finale is going to rock. Can't wait to see it!'

'Thanks,' I said faintly, and scuttled off to find Maurice and tell him the plan was in place.

By mid-afternoon the backstage area was awash with waxed, tanned flesh, big hair and shining sequins, and the smell of make-up and hairspray was heavy in the air.

You could barely move for people and no one seemed to know who most of them were. The ten theatrical hair and make-up stations were lit up with bright lightbulbs around the mirrors, and Angel Wear models, each wearing the signature pink-silk dressing gown, with 'Heavenly Body' embroidered on the back, sat in front of them having their make-up artfully applied by members of Caroline's team; some were being tended to by a manicurist or pedicurist at the same time. *It must be quite a skill to sit that still with all the hubbub going on around them.*

Journalists, TV film crews and photographers from all around the world buzzed about between the models, desperately trying to speak to one of the five Icons – the biggest draws – who each had their own dressing room, plus a personal bodyguard to whisk away over-zealous reporters at the bat of a fake eyelash. At one point, Astrid and Krystal, the most well-known of the Icons, thanks to their love of the party scene, were surrounded by a crowd some five people deep, as they snapped selfies with fans and chatted into Dictaphones being held in front of them from all angles.

An hour before show time, we watched on screens as a host of invited celebrities and the fashion press entered the theatre, having walked the length of the pink carpet that stretched for half a block, stopping for a picture at the Angel Wear step and repeat boards in the theatre's entrance, before making their way inside, taking their seats on the front row. Girls wearing black shorts and satin bomber jackets with 'Angel Girl' embroidered between their shoulders wandered around handing out G-strings neatly packaged in imitation cigarette boxes to the delight of guests. The VVIPs were led to named seats in the front row by Angel Wear ushers, all of whom looked like male models. I noticed Lola Jones, her crew cut now dyed-peroxide blonde, being led to a prime spot along with her permanent escort of two handsome young men. And then there was an eruption of flashbulbs to her right as Poppy Dunn took her seat, linking arms with another actress, who I recognised immediately as Lila Hawkes – a hip young thing, rumoured to be being lined up as the next Mrs Tom Cruise. They basked in the flashbulbs, enviable long legs crossed, giggling behind their iPhones as they snapped selfies.

A stream of recognisable music stars, actors and TV personalities filed to their seats, along with a host of people so beautiful that they had to be somebodies. And then the camera panned left and my eyes nearly popped out of my head as it zoomed in on Liv Ramone, making her entrance wearing a strange kimono ensemble, her skin alabaster white, lips red, hair in a tall ginger beehive and, under her open kimono, the skimpiest black bra and knickers. Like a psychedelic geisha. It was bizarre, but 'attention grabby', you couldn't deny that. Even more disturbing was the fact that right in front of this kaleidoscopic array of guests was the catwalk, standing there proudly – expectantly – waiting for the Icons to turn it all shades of fabulous, dressed to kill in costumes crafted by Maurice and I, with the most important costume currently incomplete.

Just after six p.m., Stan, the production manager announced over a Tannoy that the show would commence in thirty minutes' time. I glanced at Maurice, his complexion ashen with fear.

'So we're fucked,' he moaned, clutching some Gothic-black rosary beads. And we just stood there looking at each other, willing the floor to open and the earth to swallow us up.

The catwalk show got off to a glittering start in a shower of bubble-gum-pink, lemon and peach confetti, dropped from a huge transparent balloon as a stream of models wearing lingerie from the new Angel Wear collection were paraded on the runway. I had to concede that Dimitri had done a great job transporting the audience to a place that resembled Barbie's boudoir. But although the masses were entranced, I couldn't enjoy any of it. I was too busy pacing around backstage.

My phone buzzed a number of times in the pocket of my black GAP dress – everyone backstage was wearing black tonight – but didn't bother looking at it. I was sick of well-wishers sending me luck. It was probably Mum, anyway, saying she'd had a text from what's-her-name at number forty-two, saying their niece had seen my name associated with the show currently streaming live on Angel Wear's online video channel.

It was only when I popped to the Ladies' and managed to catch my phone before it landed in the toilet bowl that I saw some twenty missed calls and a text message from Vicky.

At first I felt slightly irked that she was bugging me on the biggest night of my career. But when I read the first line, I took it a little more seriously:

Babe, hate to tell you this but your ruby bra isn't a one-off. Good luck tonight. Love ya, V xxx

I read it three times in a row, and then I called her from the cubical. No answer. *Damn you, Vicky, answer!* I sent an urgent text:

Hey, just picked up your text – what do you mean the ruby bra isn't a one-off? Have you seen it? Call me urgently.

Then I stood staring at the ceiling for ten seconds before dialling again.

But someone began knocking on the cubicle door so I was forced to leave and, as I hurried back down the corridor to find Maurice, another text from Vicky came through:

Sorry babe, in a drag club, it's noisy. You ok? x

I texted back:

That ruby bra you've seen? I think it's the actual one. It's been stolen. Long story. Please, call me!

A minute later and a fuzzy picture message came through.

It was taken from below, but it was the ruby bra all right, *our* ruby bra. I'd recognise the shape of the stones anywhere. But someone seemed to be wearing it. My hands were shaking as I replied:

That's it! It's the bra! Who's wearing it???

Finally she called.

'Hey, what do you mean stolen?'

'Oh, Vicky, it's the worst night of my life! I don't have time to go into the details but the bra is gone and we've currently got no centrepiece to close the show. It's a disaster. On a humungous scale. Where are you? And can you get the bra? Maurice and I will do whatever it takes, just get it back, please!'

'Wow, I didn't realise we were dealing with theft. Is the NYPD involved?' She sounded slightly thrilled.

'Not yet – we'd rather avoid all that if we can.'

'Leave it with me,' she replied, and rang off.

Hurriedly, I filled Maurice in on my conversation with Vicky. For the first time all day I saw a glimmer of hope in his eyes. We threw ourselves into dressing the other Icons to ensure not a single sequin or piece of tit tape was out of place on the other four costumes.

It was as though time was moving at double speed, as, when came up for air, the halfway interval was nearly over. I'd heard nothing from Vicky since the initial phone conversation.

I called her to let her know that we had maybe twenty minutes maximum before it would be time for Krystal to take to the stage – no reply. My heart was pounding so hard in my chest as the five Icons had their hair and make-up touched up and popped a bottle of champagne, passing it around and swigging from it for good luck. Then they huddled together and performed a sort of high fashion haka to psyche themselves up for their turns on the catwalk.

A panicky feeling began to filter through me as the final

chords of the interval music played out and the opening strains of our music began. First up was Astrid, taking to the stage in a pneumatic silver ensemble. A strobe light flashed brightly as David Bowie's 'Let's Dance' boomed out across the theatre. The audience burst into applause and a chorus of wolf-whistles could be heard as she strode in time to the beat, hips swaying – our Ziggy Stardust in skimpy underwear.

I should have been feeling elated now. I should have been swigging from the champagne bottle too, as Maurice and I watched the fruits of our labour come to life, but all I could think was that it was now precisely fifteen minutes until Ron would be expecting to see Krystal emerge from a blast of indoor fireworks and glitter as Wonder Woman, ruby bra and all, to close the show. Krystal was getting nervous, too.

'Hey, Amber, don't you think it's time to get my final costume in position?' she kept saying, grabbing my elbow and trying to drag me to the dressing room.

'Just a minute. Just keep the secretary look on for now,' I kept replying, shaking her off and pretending to busy myself nicking a stray thread from another part of her costume, or stooping to give her shoes an extra polish. *Calm, calm, calm. Vicky will come good. She has to.* But every time I looked at my phone there was nothing from her.

'Where is she?' Maurice whispered into my ear at least twenty times in two minutes as we desperately busied our-selves.

'I don't know!' I snapped back.

Vicky, where the hell are you?

Then, just as Leonie was about to step onto the catwalk in her 'Rio Carnival' get-up, complete with a vibrant three-foot-fruit-bowl-inspired headdress and accompanied by a live samba school especially flown in from Brazil, there was a loud commotion at the far end of the corridor. Amid a tangle of flesh and feathers from the carnival dancers limbering up ready to join her on the runway, a few more faces could be seen bobbing above the fray. I stood on my tiptoes and was desperately relieved to make out Vicky and Noah, and not far behind them two security guards, one of whom was Larry, and he was shouting loudly.

'Hey, I know your faces! Unauthorised persons backstage! Stop them immediately!'

Larry was under strict instructions not to let anyone who wasn't on my list into the dressing area and, after the ticking off Maurice and I had given him this morning about the safe, he wasn't taking any risks – especially after recognising Vicky and Noah from our little late night trip to the studio just a week ago.

As the commotion grew louder, people began turning to see what was going on.

'Amber Green! The stylist! Where is Amber Green? I need to find her immediately!' Vicky was shouting at anyone who would listen.

I dropped my kit and began heading down the corridor towards the hubbub, swerving sequinned bodies.

'Vicky! Over here! Thank God!' I screamed before waving at Larry. 'It's okay, Larry, I know them. Let them through!'

And then a sight came into view that made even me stop in my tracks. The bewildered crowd of models, assistants and backstage hangers on parted and there in front of us, holding tightly on to Vicky's hand, behind Noah, who had been clearing the route for them, was the largest woman I had ever seen.

When Vicky finally reached me she was panting she was so out of breath.

'Did we make it in time?' she asked.

I looked at her companion, speechless for a few seconds while I took it in.

'Meet Wonder Winnie,' she continued, stepping back by way of introduction as the woman held out her very large hand.

'Great to meet you,' she said in a deep voice.

Krystal whirled around and did a double-take. A half-laugh, half-howl escaped from her mouth. 'Can someone tell me what the *hell* is going on?' she yelled.

The whole of the backstage area fell silent for the first time all day as we collectively absorbed the sight of 'Wonder Winnie' – a larger-than-life woman, who looked as though she had probably been a man at some point in her life, with jet-black hair cascading around her shoulders, and an ample cleavage, which was encased in – the real ruby bra. There was no mistaking it was the stolen original, Maurice and I would have recognised the intricate arrangement of those priceless stones anywhere. Sensing correctly that all eyes were on her cleavage, Winnie rearranged herself. She appeared to have no idea of the value of what she was wearing. Or, for that matter, what she was doing behind the scenes at the Angel Wear show.

'It's on the small side, so I had to add an extension to the back – and I can still barely breathe, but who doesn't suffer for their art?' She winced, as the entire corridor stared, open-mouthed, at her voluptuous chest crammed into the bra. 'Now, can someone tell me what I'm doing here?'

'There wasn't time to argue,' Vicky hurriedly explained to me, 'so we gave Winnie her biggest tip all year and bundled her in a cab. Well, we couldn't exactly take the bra off her back!' She took in the horrified look on my face. 'We found your bra, didn't we? I thought you'd be happy.' I wanted the bra back – more than anything – but I hadn't expected a towering drag queen to come with it.

'*Attention! Maintenant!*' Maurice yelled from behind me. He pushed his way to the front of the rubber-neckers and reached for Winnie's hand. 'You are a vision, *ma chérie*. But there's no time for gawping.' He looked around us. 'Wonder Woman is up next. Have you ever walked a catwalk?' he asked Winnie urgently.

'Ever walked a catwalk?' she drawled. 'Honey, is Caitlin Jenner a woman? Of course! I do it for a God damn living every night in the club!'

'*Alléluia!*' Maurice exclaimed. 'Then you're on next!'

'She... he... is *what*?' came a shrill call from the bottom of the staircase that led to the start of the catwalk, but nobody really heard Krystal, because, at that moment, Leonie appeared at the top of the stairs, back from her turn on the runway – amped and grinning from ear to perfect ear.

'That was *amazing*!' she shrieked. 'The crowd is electric! Everyone's hollering and whooping. I felt on fire out there!' She high-fived Roxy, who was standing next to her at the top, practising some deep breathing and stretching her arms skyward as she prepared to step under the bright lights next, in her ivory, feathered 'Swan Queen' look.

Noticing her wings were slightly off-centre, I sprinted up the stairs to make a quick adjustment and, as the opening strains of a special electronic arrangement of *Swan Lake*, performed by Taylor Swift's band, kicked in, a collective intake of breath could be heard, as Roxy – a classically trained ballerina – appeared *en pointe*, under a single white spotlight.

But while there was calm on one side of the catwalk, there was pandemonium on the other.

'*Amber, can you tell me what the fuck is going on here, please?*' stormed Krystal.

I looked to Maurice for help, but he was still clutching Wonder Winnie's hand as though his life depended on it, showing his feelings without having to open his mouth.

'Sorry if I'm talking out of turn,' Vicky chimed in, 'but it strikes me that there's very little time here and I think Winnie looks hot to trot as Wonder Woman so…' She shrugged at Krystal.

'Can the next model please come to the entrance!' came an urgent voice over the Tannoy. Stan didn't like being kept waiting. 'Two minutes until the next girl walks. I repeat, the final model to the top of the stairs. Now!'

'You're on!' I turned to Winnie, avoiding Krystal's line of

vision. If I had thought she was an intimidating sight in her four-inch platforms, it was nothing compared to Wonder Winnie, a statuesque six foot eight in her red-and-white-starred boots.

But Krystal wasn't about to give up the gig of her life without a fight.

'Where is she going?' she screeched, reaching for my arm but missing as I sidestepped out of the way.

I climbed on to a nearby chair to straighten Winnie's gold headband. There wasn't time to argue with Krystal. Then I called Caroline and Sonny and their teams, who had been hovering close by watching the spectacle.

'Give her the once-over!' I commanded, and Sonny sprang in to action with a can of Elnett, while Caroline whipped out her tool belt, which contained an array of make-up brushes, to touch up Winnie's hair and face. She enhanced her blue eyeshadow and added an industrial amount of gloss to her already cherry-red lips.

Maurice carefully polished up the stones on the bra as I fanned out Winnie's cape to ensure it hung just so and covered the bra extenders at the back. We both had to concede her ensemble was fantastically accurate to the original character and Winnie had an impressively waspish waist for such a tall frame. I added two gold cuffs from the Angel Wear accessories line.

Perfect as she looked, my mind was in a spin as I desperately tried to imagine whether Ron was going to go ballistic when he saw Winnie instead of Krystal emerge as our Wonder

Woman. She was hardly the traditional image of an Angel Wear Icon.

'Where is the final girl? I need Krystal in position! Amber, what the hell is going on down there?' Stan called over the Tannoy again, his tone more than a little agitated.

With seconds to spare, I herded Krystal upstairs and then Maurice carefully guided Winnie down a narrow set of steps leading under the stage, ready to pop through the door in the catwalk floor at the appropriate moment. I said a silent prayer that her broad shoulders would fit through the slim opening. By the time they were both in position, I gave a thumbs-up to Stan and the announcer informed the excited audience that the final Icon was about to appear.

'We've got no choice. Winnie has to be Wonder Woman,' I told Krystal in no uncertain terms. 'When you come through the trap door, she will replace you. Trust me, it has to be this way. You can re-join her for the encore.' *If there is one.*

And then the music blasted out and, after a gentle push, Krystal appeared to the audience. Excited cheers gave her the boost she needed and she was soon striding to the front of the catwalk in her sexy secretary get-up, a biro holding her hair in a loose bun. After a few moments, the lights in the theatre went out, plunging the space into darkness, then flashes of bright red lit it up again. The *Wonder Woman* theme tune blared out loudly and Krystal ran back up the runway towards the trap door. In a flash of pyrotechnics she then began the famous Wonder Woman spin, turning faster and faster, until she was barely visible, seemingly engulfed in flames as an impressive firework display crackled around her.

Finally, following a powerful blast of dry ice, an ear-splitting *bang!* rang out across the auditorium and the two glitter cannons shot out their loads at the exact same time.

'Shit!' I screamed loudly backstage, and I gripped Maurice's arm beside me. 'The glitter cannons! I completely forgot to tell Rob we no longer needed the plan for the glitter cannons!'

We peered out through a crack at the side of the stage and watched in horror as the two large cannons dumped their entire contents – at least half a ton of gold and silver glitter between them – into the premiere box, where Ron was supposed to be entertaining the execs. I froze in horror. The box was momentarily completely obscured there was so much glitter falling in and all around it.

Back on stage, the mist had cleared and there was Wonder Winnie in place of Krystal, her arms outstretched, spinning around, her loose hair big and bouncy, limbs large and strong, her costume in place and red rubies sparkling under the bright lights.

For a second there was a hush as the audience tried to make sense of Krystal's transformation from sexy secretary into larger than life superhero. Then, Winnie's facial expression turned into a broad smile as she put her hands on her hips, her legs apart, shoulders back, chest out and chin tilted upwards – strong, confident and proud. Instantaneously, the audience erupted into the loudest cheers of the evening.

Buoyed by their reaction, Wonder Winnie began sashaying down the runway, swinging her hips to the beat of the music as she let the stunned audience appreciate every inch of her womanly curves. When she reached the end, she stopped and adopted the power pose once more. She just stood there, looking around, breathing it all in, elated yet slightly bewildered; unsure what to do next, savouring every long second.

And then something quite magical happened. Slowly but surely, like a wave spreading through the theatre, the audience began rising to their feet and clapping in admiration; at Wonder Winnie – a vision of womanhood they certainly weren't expecting to see at an Angel Wear show, or at any fashion show for that matter, but so captivating and so powerful, you couldn't help but feel moved.

Lapping up the attention, Winnie turned and wolf-whistled in the direction of the entrance of the catwalk and out skipped Krystal, holding hands with Astrid, who was leading out Roxy, followed by Leonie and Jessica, still wearing their costumes, onto the stage. When they reached Winnie, Krystal and Astrid each took one of her hands and clasped it tightly. They all stood there, a row of six women, joined together in a show of unity, sending the message that women, however they look, whatever their size or shape, their colour or their history, make an unstoppable force when standing shoulder to shoulder together.

Spontaneously, because none of this was something any of us could possibly have scripted, the six raised their clasped hands skywards, whipping the audience into an even greater hysteria. The front row followed suit – women and men took the hand of the person on either side of them and gripped it tightly, and then every row behind them did the same. There was a domino effect, until everyone in the whole theatre was standing up and joined together.

Distracted from the sight of the glitter still settling in the box, Maurice, Vicky, Noah and I – all huddled together, watching from the side of the stage – reached for each other's hands too and, when I looked around, the rest of the backstage staff, glued to screens showing the action on the catwalk, were also holding each other's hands.

Tears sprung into my eyes. I squeezed Maurice's hand and noticed that he was crying.

'This is almost a *religieux* experience,' he wept, tears streaming down his cheeks. 'Look, even Ron is crying!'

I turned my gaze up to the balcony again. Inside it was a mountain of glitter. Thousands more tiny pieces were spilling over the edge, falling like a shimmering waterfall onto a section of the audience below. Whoever had been on that balcony was certainly not there any more; they would have been flattened by the sheer weight of all that glitter.

'Where? I can't see him,' I said, panicked. *I didn't mean to actually kill Ron and the execs.*

'Over there, at the front of the stage.' Maurice pointed in the opposite direction from the box to a group of about ten people standing together at the foot of the end of the catwalk. I spotted Ron in the middle, clutching the hand of a suited man and a polished woman on either side of him, their mouths smiling and eyes visibly glistening with emotion. *Thank God, Ron isn't in there.* He must have made a last-minute decision to take his guests to the heart of the action beside the catwalk.

For a little while it felt as though we had brought the whole of Manhattan to a standstill.

My phone vibrated in my pocket. I dropped Maurice's hand to check it.

Text from Rob:

Look at the box.

The cascade of glitter had stopped and the box now contained a huge pile of tiny pieces of gold and silver. Looking more closely, there seemed to be a waving piece of fabric in the middle of the mountain. I nudged Maurice, who confirmed what I was thinking.

'*Cieux!*' he exclaimed. 'There's someone up there – and they're signalling for help!'

Vicky and Noah were squinting in the direction of the box, too, and we all made out a polka-dot handkerchief held aloft by a disembodied hand, frantically waving to attract attention. *I recognise that handkerchief.* Instantly, I knew who it was – Dimitri.

'Someone from the production team will be on their way to help, I'm sure,' I said, before turning my attention back to the runway, where the girls had turned and were strutting back down the catwalk. When they reached backstage, we flung our arms around them, screaming with joy. But the audience wasn't going to let Wonder Winnie go just yet; the thunderous applause and drum of hundreds of feet stamping on the floor seemed to go on and on.

'*Encore!*' shouted Stan over the tannoy. 'You're wanted back out, girls! Quick!'

'Come with us,' Winnie commanded, reaching for me and Vicky, taking our palms into hers.

'Not without Maurice!' I yelled, grabbing hold of him with my other hand.

'Or Noah!' screamed Vicky, as Noah rushed forward.

This time the five of us took to the runway: A line of friends, unexpectedly thrown together this evening and celebrating something extraordinary.

Flash, flash, flash! Emerging on the other side of the partition wall, centre stage on the catwalk, was like coming up for air in a whole new world. We were greeted by a wall of white light – it felt as though a flare had been let off in my face, blinding me momentarily. There appeared to be a black abyss where the audience should be – I couldn't make out any faces as my eyes adjusted to the bright lights baring down, heating me up. Winnie confidently led us down the catwalk until we reached the end, where we stopped and were at last able to take in the excited faces of the audience, still on their feet all around us. Everyone, that was, except for Mona Armstrong, who remained seated, quietly seething at one end of the front row. For a second I caught her gaze, but nothing could wipe the smile off my face this evening.

The announcer called out my and Maurice's names, introducing us as 'the head stylist and designer behind the finale', and we took a bow to a fresh round of applause.

'And they are joined by some, er, friends,' he continued, on the hop, as caught off guard as the rest of us by this unplanned ending to the show. Vicky and Noah beamed and then stooped to bow, revelling in the fuss.

As Vicky came up and took a moment to breathe in the excited faces around us, both of us noticed a face in the crowd, waving to attract her attention, right at the foot of the stage beneath us.

'*Trey?*' she squealed, taken aback. 'What are you doing here?'

He cupped his hands around his mouth. 'I love you, Vicky!' he cried. Fresh tears sprung into all of our eyes.

Then we were skipping back down the catwalk, trying to keep up with Winnie as the five Icons re-emerged to join her for the first of what became several more encores.

Finally, when it seemed as though the audience members were wrung dry, with no more claps or whoop's within them and the theatre lights had been raised, I allowed myself to collapse into a seat in Krystal's dressing room, where we had all gathered.

Rob appeared at the door and flung his arms around me.

'Baby! That was incredible! Seriously, you're a dark horse sometimes. I had no idea you were planning something as awesome as that!' he exclaimed. And then his expression changed. 'But the glitter!'

I shot him a look that screamed: *Don't mention the glitter cannons!* Thankfully, he picked up the hint. Then Ron entered the room; with open arms he headed straight for Winnie. 'That was an Oscar-winning performance!' he gushed, shaking her sweaty hand. 'I have no idea who you are, but you can be an Angel Wear Icon any time.' Then he turned to me. 'Amber, you surpassed yourself this evening and I can't thank you enough. No one will forget this year's Angel Wear show, and it's all down to you.'

I looked across to Vicky, Maurice and Noah.

'With some help from my friends...' I beamed. 'I hope you don't mind, but I couldn't have done it without them.'

CHAPTER TWENTY-FIVE

As soon as I stepped outside the stage door, the gravity of what had happened in there hit me. I was immediately pounced on by an excited mob of photographers and journalists. Cameras, phones and Dictaphones were shoved in my face, as voices cried:

'Hey, you, the stylist – tell us about your choice of model for the finale!'

'Is Wonder Winnie the new transgender Icon?'

'What was it like working with Maurice Chan?'

Meanwhile #WonderWinnie zoomed around cyber space as endless photos of her closing the show were posted and re-grammed on every available platform.

For a few minutes, I was almost the most famous person in New York City – almost, because, as Winnie emerged from the theatre not long after me, the crowd broke into loud cheers. Larger than life, big brown eyes, plucked eyebrows, cushiony cherry-red lips, huge hair and ample chest still encased in the priceless ruby bra, she was glowing with happiness and basking in her new-found fame. Larry and another burly security guard gently guided her elbows through the throng. When she reached me, via stopping to sign autographs and give a few exclusive quotes to some of the assembled press, she put her hands around my still tense-with-nerves body and bent down to kiss me on both cheeks. I was overwhelmed by the smell of make-up and hairspray, mixed with a whiff of nicotine.

'Darling, you are absolutely fabulous,' she said, her deep voice loud enough for some journalists to hear. 'Thank you for doing this for us.'

'Us?' I asked.

'The transgender community,' she said, tears welling in her eyes. 'It wasn't just about me up there.'

I smiled. 'You're the "absolutely fabulous" one. You owned that catwalk, sister.'

Winnie held out her hand and we fist pumped. Photographers captured the moment.

'You're coming to the after-party, right?' she asked.

'After-party?'

'Get in the cab, we'll go together.'

And before I could decide, she was pushing me into a yellow taxi waiting with its door open right in front of us.

'Rob!' I yelled over my shoulder.

'I'm here!' he called back, and squashed into the back seat on the other side of Winnie.

She winked. 'Plenty of room for a hunk like you.'

'We'll see you there!' another voice called out. It was Vicky, with Trey and Noah. And behind them were Dan, Max and Tina, who had all been watching the show from the audience.

'We'll all follow you!' Dan called.

Finally, as the door was closed and the taxi horns began

chiming away together on the busy road, I allowed myself to breathe a small sigh of relief.

Rob leaned forward and reached across Winnie to squeeze my knee. He beamed. 'You did it, baby, you did it!'

'She didn't just do it, honey, she blew the God damn roof off that theatre – not to mention the minds of most of the audience! My heart nearly failed on that catwalk, it was so amazing. I've never seen a venue go so wild. Seriously, I'm going to party like it's the end of the world tonight, and I want *you* dancing on the bar with me.' She put her hand on top of Rob's and they both squeezed my knee cap.

'Try to stop me!' I grinned. 'But there is one thing I need to know – I need to know how you came to be wearing the bra, Winnie. I have my suspicions but I need to be sure. Who gave it to you?'

'I had no idea it was stolen goods, I assure you,' she said, turning serious for a moment. 'It was sold to me at the club last night. Come to the back room when we get there and I'll show you the CCTV footage.'

When we reached the Purple Rain drag club in Hell's Kitchen, a cabaret act was in full flow. A lively crowd was being entertained by a brassy blonde sitting on a swing at the end of a small makeshift catwalk singing '*Je ne Regrette Rien*'. Winnie wasn't lying when she said she walked a runway for a living, but it was miniature compared to the huge construction at the Winter Garden. Vicky, Trey and Noah joined us as Winnie led our party straight through the bustling club and into a dingy back room. There, she cleared the desk of empty beer cans with a swipe of her arm and we gathered around an ancient-looking computer to watch the CCTV footage. It didn't take long for Winnie to find the right place.

'I was on the door for most of last night, so I remember it well,' she informed us, freezing the screen at precisely twenty-two minutes past ten.

We all crowded around the screen, necks craned to get a better view of the slightly blurred black-and-white still of a man entering the nightclub.

'It was him,' Winnie said, pointing at the frozen image.

A shaved head and a long trench coat with a polka-dot handkerchief in the top pocket gave away all the clues I needed to confirm the man's identity. Then Winnie advanced the film a little further, so we got a clearer view of the side of his face.

'That guy in the trench sold me the bra for fifty bucks,' Winnie confirmed. 'And, by the way, so far no one's mentioned when I get my hard-earned fifty dollars back?'

We all peered at the image. I recognised the man instantly – Dimitri. Although shocked to have discovered the truth, at the same time it only confirmed what I already knew. No wonder Dimitri had relocated to the box in the theatre; he wanted to ensure he had the best seat in the house, to watch my downfall unfold when Krystal emerged as Wonder Woman without the priceless bra. But now there was something ironic about the fact he had been caught red-handed on CCTV, considering Dimitri had tried to have me fired, thanks to some other CCTV footage not so long ago.

I turned to Maurice. 'I told you he was trouble. But we got the last laugh.'

Maurice wasn't listening. He had pulled out his reading glasses and was so close to the screen his nose was almost touching it. His face had turned white and he looked like he was about to be sick. Vicky grabbed her Chanel handbag from the floor and urgently struggled to open the clasp. She held it open for Maurice and there was a retching sound as he leaned over the side of the desk and brought up a large amount of congealed coffee into the bag.

'Gross!' said Noah, holding his nose, as we all stared at Maurice, hunched over and heaving. Instinctively, I ran across and began rubbing his back sympathetically.

'*Mon Dieu*,' he winced.

'A Chanel as well.' I shook my head.

'It's okay, it's fake – the detailing is shit,' Vicky replied. She was sitting on Trey's knee; the pair had barely been able to keep their hands off each other since being reunited after the show. 'The Bag Drop woman isn't as good as Poppy might have led us to believe. I shouldn't have bothered going back.'

Rob glanced at me. The mention of Poppy's name and the bag-drop night still created a bit of tension between us.

'Anyway, we're going shopping for the real thing tomorrow.' Trey winked, squeezing Vicky around the waist. 'At the airport.'

But I couldn't take my eyes off Maurice, whose extreme physical reaction to seeing the image of Dimitri puzzled me.

'The guy was clearly trying to do his best to avoid the cameras,' Winnie explained as the image played out, showing

Dimitri raise his collar as high as it would go, before taking the pouch containing the bra out of his bag and handing it over. 'He told me he worked in fashion and had a sample he thought would look great on stage. It happens sometimes, when designers are having a clear-out of last season's collection, they know we'll provide a home for anything attention grabby. Obviously, I loved it immediately.' She glanced over to Maurice, who still looked pale and was sitting very quietly. 'It's an exquisite piece. But why the long face, sugar? Aren't you glad we've found the culprit? You look like you've seen a ghost.'

'A ghost,' Maurice repeated, his head down. '*Oui*, unfortunately, I feel like I have. I haven't seen him in years, but I'd recognise that face anywhere. What I need to know is what my ex-boyfriend was doing selling the ruby bra?'

'Wait a minute, I don't understand,' I said. 'Are you saying Dimitri is your ex-boyfriend?'

'Dimitri? That's Alexanda,' Maurice informed me, before lowering his voice to a whisper. 'Alexanda Dimitri Bellafonte, the assistant who set me up with the Hitler moustaches all those years ago. How could I not have put this together?'

Something clicked in my head.

'So Dimitri from Angel Wear, he was your assistant and ex-boyfriend too?' Maurice didn't need to confirm, his distraught face said it all. I realised that the pair had not actually come into direct contact the whole time I'd been working with Maurice; Dimitri must have made sure of it.

'And of course he would know the code to the safe – it was one-nine-three-seven, the year of Marianne's birth,'

Maurice continued. 'I used the same four digits for all my security codes back in the day. It didn't even cross my mind to change it. *Merde*, he must think I'm an *imbecile*.'

I shrugged. 'I never thought for one moment you might know Dimitri. I thought he was trying to ruin *me*.'

I sank down into my seat.

From the other side of the door, we could hear loud music and laughter from the club; no doubt the Icons were getting stuck into shots at the bar or tearing up the dance floor, but inside this dark stuffy backroom – which now smelt of puke – we were reeling from the evening's big revelation.

'I need to get out of here,' Maurice said, rising unsteadily. I stood up, ready to try to convince him to stay and talk it through, but Rob put out a hand to stop me.

'Let him go,' he whispered.

And he was gone.

CHAPTER TWENTY-SIX

Maurice Chan entered the bar. Thanks to the success of the Angel Wear show he was, at this moment, once again one of the world's most famous fashion designers. He was ushered straight in and offered his choice of table by the maître d'.

'Monsieur Chan, it's fantastic to see you again,' the host said, warmly shaking his hand.

His surprised tone implied Maurice hadn't been to the restaurant for a long time.

But Maurice had no appetite for food this evening. Instead, he headed straight for the last chair at the end of the bar. The chair was occupied – as he knew it would be.

'I thought I'd find you here,' he said to the man sitting there. 'A chameleon in many ways, but a leopard in so many others.'

The man didn't look up. The collar on his long trench coat was turned up and there was a shabby looking polka-dotted handkerchief shoved into the top pocket. He was hunched over a cut-crystal tumbler containing ice and a dark spirit. Maurice looked down to the man's feet – he was wearing almost identical Cuban heels to his own. The fact that glitter was spilling out from them confirmed he was indeed talking to the right person. Not that he was in any doubt.

'Alexandra,' he said. 'Or should I call you Dimitri, these days?'

The man grunted in response.

'You really thought you could ruin me for a second time? Well, how your plan spectacularly backfired.' He chuckled.

'Can I get you a drink?' asked the bar tender, slightly embarrassed to have interrupted what was clearly an awkward moment.

'I'll have what he's having,' Maurice replied. 'Another for you, Dimitri, or have you had enough?'

'Whatever,' Dimitri replied sarcastically, without moving his body.

'Cold-hearted until the end,' Maurice stated, addressing his remark to the waiter.

'Cold-hearted? How can *you* of all people, call *me* cold-hearted?' Dimitri fumed, suddenly enraged. His voice raised further. 'You dumped me for your career, remember? You seem to have conveniently forgotten that.'

Maurice was taken aback. He tried to cast his mind back, but Dimitri was hell bent on doing the job for him.

'You were so obsessed with your work you dumped me because I wasn't "a good fit for your career" – and those are your words, not mine, Maurice.' He paused and took a deep breath. It was taking every muscle in his body not to let ten years of built-up anguish come tumbling out all at once. 'I thought that if your career failed, there might be a chance it would work between us and you'd want me back.'

Maurice was floored by this news. 'You mean to tell me you did all this for love?'

'The first time around,' Dimitri said, wiping away a stray tear as it fell down his cheek. 'But this time I just needed you to go away. The minute Amber walked through the Angel Wear doors, I knew you wouldn't be far behind. You were all over her Instagram account – flaunting yourself and your "return". It wasn't hard to work out what the two of you were planning.'

'As it happens, I wasn't planning anything at all,' Maurice said honestly. 'One thing seemed to lead to another.'

And then the pair sat and drank in silence.

'I did love you very much, you know,' Maurice said sadly, as he swallowed the last drop of rum in his glass. The passage of time had made his anger soften. 'And you're right, I was married to my work. Hasn't the last decade been payback enough for you? Anyway, it's irrelevant now. I made a decision when I took to the runway with Amber this evening. This world isn't for me any more, it's time for new talent to shine. I've had my moment.'

'So, what will the great Maurice Chan do now?' Dimitri asked bitterly. He had turned to face him front on, even though his eyes were shining wet with tears.

'I'm thinking of the antiques business,' Maurice revealed, unfazed. 'Not only because I'm an old croc myself, but because I enjoyed bringing the ruby bra back to life – that was the greatest part of all this for me. I'm wondering about a business restoring old love tokens to their former glory.'

'Very romantic,' Dimitri commented, unable to resist a parting dig.

'Maybe I've changed.' Maurice smiled as he got up from his chair to leave the bar. 'Maybe you could change, too.'

CHAPTER TWENTY-SEVEN

At exactly the same moment, across town, 102 floors up on small private terrace on the Empire State Building, Rob produced a bottle of chilled champagne and two glasses from the rucksack I hadn't even noticed he was carrying.

He set it all down and we took a moment to breathe in the view before us. Manhattan had never looked so tranquil; millions of white and gold lights twinkled beneath us and tiny yellow matchbox taxis silently moved around the grid of high-rise buildings – but none higher than where we sat now.

'It's pretty awesome, isn't it?' he said at last.

'Just slightly,' I replied. 'How on Earth did you sort this out?'

I was referring to the limo that had picked us up from Purple Rain and brought us here, to a floor away from the rest of the tourists, so exclusive that you have to be a VVIP to book it, so Rob had informed me on the way up the narrow staircase.

'Ron might have had something to do with it,' he conceded. 'He's connected.'

'Lucky we didn't actually bury him alive in glitter then.' I chuckled. 'He might not have been so accommodating.'

'What a night,' Rob said, shaking his head.

'And it's still going on back at the club – I'm sure I saw Astrid giving Dan the eye at the bar. And as for Vicky and Trey – it wouldn't surprise me if they're on the first plane back to LA in the morning.'

Rob laughed. 'I think we're probably best out of there. But what about you?' He turned to look at me.

'Me?'

'Yes, how are you feeling this evening, Amber Green?'

'I think I'm starting to look forward to going home now,' I said. 'I don't think anything could top today. Has Ron told you when filming will end?'

'We had a rushed conversation after the show,' he revealed. 'He's already got plans for Wonder Winnie – he mentioned something about sponsoring her to develop a range of transgender lingerie, for all stages of the transformation process. If Winnie's up for it, he wants us to film her journey.'

'I wonder how the Icons will take it…?' I looked at him curiously, feeling slightly tickled by the prospect of them being overshadowed by a little-known drag queen.

'I'm sure they'll be thrilled for her,' he said, sarcastically. 'But none of them were particularly interesting on camera, to be honest – at least Winnie has a proper story to tell. Anyway, filming has been parked until he can get to Winnie.'

We both paused, contemplating what this might mean. He peered over the railings again.

'I used to have a thing about heights,' he revealed, changing the subject. 'I should be clinging to you, begging to go back in.' He jokingly grabbed my arm, making me jump. 'But instead I feel strangely calm up here. Do you?'

He turned to look me straight in the eye, and he didn't move his gaze for what felt like the longest time. It made me feel slightly embarrassed.

I looked back over the edge. 'I'm okay with it. I think it comes from climbing to the highest branches of the pear tree in my parents' garden and staying there for hours on end when I was little. If they couldn't find me in my room, they always knew where I would be.'

'So you're a secret tree hugger?' he teased.

I nudged his shoulder. 'Watch it, you're in a very vulnerable position right now, remember.'

But instead of flinching, he just kept staring. *Why is he looking at me so intensely?*

And then he delved into his rucksack again; he seemed to be looking for something. *Oh, God, he's not, is he? Oh. My. God. He's going to propose.*

'Are you going to propose?' I surprised myself by saying the words out loud. They hung in the air between us, as a panic swept over Rob's face. 'Oh, this is awkward.' I lowered my eyes, fixing on the tip of my shoe.

Right on cue a man holding a camera with a large flash popped his head around the door.

'Hey, official Empire State photographer – okay if I take a few snaps now?'

'Eh? I didn't… just give us a minute please.' Rob held him

back by raising his hand. Then he swallowed hard. 'W-would you like me to, Amber? Ask you, I mean?'

My legs had gone to jelly. I gripped the railing in front of me tighter.

'Honestly?' I began.

He nodded nervously in response.

'Um, I don't know if I could handle it after today,' I said softly.

He looked uncomfortable. 'So, you wouldn't be disappointed if I didn't?'

'Not at all, in fact, I'd really *rather* you didn't.' I looked him in the eye, trying to gauge his reaction. 'If that's okay?'

He breathed a sigh of relief almost as big as my own. 'Thank goodness for that.'

I smiled. 'So you weren't going to?'

'I was more thinking we'd just enjoy the view,' he continued.

'Oh, God, this is really embarrassing,' I said awkwardly.

'So, it's okay, me not proposing, I mean?'

I threw my arms around his shoulders. 'It's more than okay. It's perfect!'

'But I do love you very much, you know,' he said earnestly.

'I know,' I said, as he offered me a champagne flute. 'Seriously, I'm not ready for marriage – not yet anyway.' I meant every word.

'There is something I was wondering about though,' he said, eyes shining brightly. 'I was thinking that, when we get back to London in a few weeks, perhaps we could flat hunt together? I've loved waking up with you every morning and I don't want that to end.'

I beamed. 'Robert Walker, are you officially asking me to move in with you?'

'Yes, m'am, I am,' he said, looking at me in his adorable, slightly shy way. 'As long as we can find somewhere with space for Pinky. And a spare room in case of unexpected guests.' He winked.

'It's a deal.' I held out my hand. 'Somewhere bigger than a sardine tin.'

He smiled, popping the cork from the bottle. 'Then I would like to propose a toast, excuse the pun, to you, Amber Green.' He filled our glasses and gestured to the vista beneath us, which resembled a scene from a sci-fi film. 'You never cease to amaze me and I can't wait to get our own flat together in London.' He smiled tenderly. Then he raised his glass and we chinked. 'Oh, hang on a minute. Photographer!' he called over his shoulder and the man immediately reappeared. 'Now is great.'

The taste of cold champagne bubbles fizzing down my throat was delicious. 'Here's to us!'

We melted into each other's lips and began kissing passionately, eyes glazed. For a few seconds I was unsure where each of us ended and the other began. We didn't care that the photographer was merrily snapping away around us.

'Now surely you're not going to stop me from posting a photo of *this*?' I said when we finally broke apart.

'Would you mind?' I asked the photographer, holding out my phone.

He shook his head, and muttered, 'What's the point of the official…'

We put our heads together and posed. I immediately uploaded the photo to Instagram. Amara filter; caption: The stylist and her man take Manhattan.

ACKNOWLEDGEMENTS

Very soon after I had finished writing my debut novel, *The Stylist*, and waved Amber Green and Rob Walker off into the hazy sunshine of a boiling-hot July afternoon on Oxford Street, I just couldn't get them out of my head; I needed to know where their story would go next. And I already had some ideas bubbling away.

I wrote much of *The Stylist* on my first maternity leave, so this was the only way I knew how to write a novel – and, as luck would have it, I fell pregnant again! As well as a bonny boy named Rex, *Amber Green Takes Manhattan* was born.

Amber's experience of Manhattan and her home in Williamsburg came to life for me during a research trip there to visit some close friends. To my trusty Brooklyn contingent: thank you for your neighbourhood knowledge (Marc), brilliant stories about being a New York stylist (Nina) and cocktail drinking inspiration (Jane and Gemma).

Also, thanks to Zoe and Max for a hilarious anecdote to inspire the 'bag drop', and Michael for introducing me to dream boat 'Noah West'.

Many chapters were written in Belle Amie café in Earlsfield, London, during snatched hours away from my babies. Thanks to them for the great coffee, which powered me through the pages, and for letting me commandeer my regular table for hours on end.

Thank you, Jenny Savill, for encouraging me to keep going, and the brilliant team at HQ – Lisa Milton, Anna Baggaley and Alison Lindsay – for enabling me to share this story. Your belief in my books means so much.

Also thanks to Holly Nesbitt-Larking and Charlotte Seymour for your much-appreciated proofreading.

Warm hugs to my incredible family, especially Mum and Dad for being so supportive and loving, my darling husband Callum for his patience and generally putting up with me, and to Heath and Rex for bringing such joy to our lives. You have no idea what on earth I do at my laptop, but I'll enjoy showing you one day.

Finally, importantly, thanks to you, for reading. Without you, none of this would be possible.

Two boys, two books: my husband is a little concerned I seem to need a baby to write a novel…

HQ
One Place. Many Stories

The home of bold, innovative
and empowering publishing.

Follow us online

 @HQStories

 @HQStories

 HQStories

 HQ Stories

HQMusic